THE UNSEELIE PRINCE

MAZE OF SHADOWS: BOOK ONE

KATHRYN ANN KINGSLEY

Copyright © 2021 by Kathryn Ann Kingsley

Cover illustration by Grace Zhu.

ASIN: B09B7XVLJG

ISBN: 9798489004381

KATHRYN ANN KINGSLEY

All rights reserved.

No part of this book may be reproduced in any form or by any electronic or mechanical means, including information storage and retrieval systems, without written permission from the author, except for the use of brief quotations in a book review.

This is a work of fiction. Names, characters, places, and incidents either are the product of the author's imagination or are used fictitiously, and any resemblance to locales, events, business establishments, or actual persons—living or dead—is entirely coincidental.

CHAPTER ONE

Abigail brought the cleaver down onto the neck of the hen, digging the metal into the wood block and severing the chicken's spine with a *crunch*. The carcass kicked and thrashed, blood spurting from the stump that remained.

She cringed, same as she did every time. "Forgive me, Dee-Dee." She didn't know why she always apologized. She supposed it was simply to make herself feel better. The carcass was still twitching as she tied its feet together to hang it over the wooden bucket on the ground to drain the blood. She already had a pot of water to scald the bird to make the feather-plucking easier. That was a trick she'd learned from her aunt. She'd learned a great deal from her aunt.

With a sigh, she walked away from the bloody scene and went to clean her hands. She hated killing animals, but it was just a simple fact of life. Death was always the sad result of having lived. Dee-Dee had grown too old to lay eggs, and one extra mouth to feed who didn't contribute was one more than she could afford.

1

Not like it will matter for much longer, anyway.

Dunking her hands in the cold water she had fetched from the brook near her cottage, she watched the crimson liquid lift from her hand and tint the surface. Shutting her eyes, she fought back the sudden tears that rushed forward.

Pretty soon, her chickens would be the problem of someone else. As would be her goat. And her bed. And her furniture. And her land. And her home.

Everything.

Everything she owned would belong to someone else. *In truth, it already does. It's just out of the kindness of Roderick's heart that he's given me some time, even if we all know I have nowhere to go.*

Fetching the now-still body of the chicken, she picked up the bucket of blood from the ground and headed inside her home. The single room building was small, but it was all she needed. The hearth took up the majority of one wall, stacked stones and mud bricks reaching up nearly as high as she was tall. The pot of water she had placed in the hearth was far enough away from the coals that it wouldn't boil, but close enough to properly help in cleaning Dee-Dee for dinner.

Placing the animal in the water to sit for a few minutes, she took the blood over to her door. Dipping her finger into the already-cool liquid, Abigail reached up and drew a symbol on the exterior of the wooden planks of her door. As she drew the lines of the strange shape, she murmured two words to herself over and over again until the shape was completed. *"Come home."*

She knew it wouldn't work. It never did. But it didn't stop her from trying.

Heading back outside, she went to her garden. If life had to be spent, it should not be wasted. She dug a small hole by the roots of each of her plants, and one by one, poured some of the blood into the dirt.

Life fed death, and death fed life. Dee-Dee was gone, but she would always be part of the cycle.

Putting the rest of her chickens into the coop for the night, as she did not intend to feed the fox that lived in the woods nearby, she locked the wooden gate and finished her chores. Finally, she returned to her fire.

After adjusting the coals around the loaf of bread she was baking, she took the chicken from the water with a wooden spoon through the twine. Sitting down on a blanket on the ground, she began plucking the feathers.

As she did, she began to sing an old tune quietly to herself. She wasn't sure where she learned it—most likely her aunt, like everything else in her life. Regardless, the simple song calmed her nerves and distracted her from her plight all the same.

Halfway through cleaning what was left of poor Dee-Dee, she heard something outside—a heavy and thick *crunch!* It startled her so badly she dropped the carcass of the bird.

Frowning, she stood from the ground and lit a candle from the hearth. Setting it into her lantern, she took it to the door.

Had Marcus come home? Had her spell finally worked? Flicking the latch, she swung open the wood door and peered into the twilight. The sun had just set, and the sky was losing its ruddy colors into the blues and blacks of night. "Hello?"

No one answered. Furrowing her brow as she saw something—the bright white splinters of freshly broken wood against aged, old timbers—she stepped out of her house to investigate. One of the logs that ran between her fence posts had snapped in half, as if something heavy had landed on it.

But what?

Whatever had done it had been far too big for a fox, and she wouldn't even know why it would have landed there in the first place. An owl or a hawk were far too light to shatter the wood. The beam had been old and beginning to rot, but it had been sturdy enough for a fence panel.

Touching the bright white exposed wood of the inside of the beam, she shook her head. "Odd." Turning her attention back to the darkness around her that seemed to inch closer with every breath, she called out again. "Hello? Is someone there?"

Silence.

"If you are *not* my husband," she said to the shadows with a slight, self-effacing smirk, "then I have summoned you by mistake. I forgive you for the damage to my fence and will say that our inconveniences are now matched. If you come in kindness, I will have dinner on the table shortly. While I do not have much, I have enough to share."

Turning back to her home, she thought for a moment she heard something in the line of trees. A whisper, perhaps? She whirled, lifting her lantern, and tried her best to see into the encroaching night.

I'm just frightening myself. The log let go of its own accord. I suppose I should be grateful I do not have to fix it.

With a shake of her head, she headed back into her home. Latching the door, she blew out her candle and began to hum her old song once more. The fire of the hearth was enough to see by, and she didn't want to waste what she had.

Touching the necklace she wore, a carved owl made of wood that hung around her neck from a twine, she turned to look at the one candle that did still burn in the dim light of her home. One candle that never blew out or burned low. Since the moment it had sparked to life, it hadn't once flickered, nor had the wick grown shorter.

Casting it a baleful glance, she returned to her work of cleaning Dee-Dee and preparing the chicken meat for a stew. It was just as she finished slicing the meat and bones and putting them in her vegetable broth that she was once more startled so badly that she nearly upended the contents of the pot.

Wham, wham, wham!

It was a heavy knock on her door.

"If you are not my husband, then I have summoned you by mistake."

It took every ounce of Valroy's willpower not to howl in laughter at the irony.

He settled for grinning from within the darkness of the woods. He watched the silhouette of the young woman lift the lantern high to seek out whatever had made the noise and broken her fence. But no matter how she searched, she would not find him. Not unless he wished to be seen.

And for now, he was content simply to watch.

"I forgive you for the damage to my fence and will say that our inconveniences are now matched."

Hardly! The fact that the fence could not hold my weight is entirely your fault, silly thing. He had landed on it from a height, and it had snapped under him like a twig. She was the one to blame for that, not he.

"If you come in kindness, I will have dinner on the table shortly, and while I do not have much, I have enough to share."

That was intriguing enough that he shifted, unfurling one of his wings so that he might lean his arm on the tree he was standing beside. She was inviting in whatever it was she had summoned? Either she was a fool, or she was a fool who thought she could protect herself.

Which was it?

He watched as the young woman returned to her house,

shutting the door behind her. He could smell the scent of baking bread and simmering vegetables. Nothing interesting, and nothing terribly savory, but likely edible.

Walking out from the darkness, still hidden from view, he jumped over the fence as he made his way to the tiny hut that the woman called home. It was made poorly—as most mortal structures seemed to be—with little more than mud and muck and slabs of trees to keep out the weather. The roof was straw thatch and looked as though it had not been maintained in some time.

In fact, most of the house looked neglected. The windows were covered by thick leather curtains that looked fairly new, and everything looked tidy—but water was a destructive force, especially to human construction. It was beginning to rot and wear, much like the woman's fence.

He ran a hand along the outside of her little home as he circled it slowly, thoughtfully, peering into the few gaps in the leather curtains over the glassless windows as he passed. He saw her, kneeling by the fire next to a basket of feathers, slicing up a chicken and tossing pieces into a pot of water.

You do not have much, indeed. He huffed. *Mortals.*

It was when he passed around the front door—the only door—he paused. There, drawn on the wood, was a symbol. He touched the symbol, pressing his fingertips to the craggy, worn wooden surface.

Biting his tongue was the only thing keeping him from cackling. It was too perfect! Now he knew precisely what kind of fool she was.

The kind who thought herself a *witch*.

He wrapped his wings around himself like a cloak, effortlessly changing his form. Lifting a gnarled, bony hand, he grinned wide…and knocked on the door.

THE UNSEELIE PRINCE

Abigail paused, her hand hovering over the latch. Someone had knocked. Someone was there. Her heart had lodged into her throat, pounding loudly. Had Marcus truly returned? She swallowed down her heart and her hope. No. She wouldn't let herself believe it was her husband standing upon the other side of the door.

She would almost believe it to be a shade or a corpse of the man, some broken resemblance of the man she had married, if she had not known for certain that Marcus still lived. Her magic was not strong—she was not like Aunt Margery—but the candle that told her of Marcus' life still blazed upon the windowsill, bright and strong as ever.

He was alive. And he was not here.

Then who was it?

The knock came again, harder than before, making her nearly leap out of her own skin. It was rude to leave whoever it was standing on her stoop. With a breath, she clicked the latch and opened the door, not knowing what to expect.

Her heart, which seemed to not want to stay where it was supposed to, sank straight from her throat, past her ribs where it belonged, and right into the pit of her stomach. She had known it was not going to be Marcus standing there to greet her.

But she had childishly hoped all the same.

No, instead it was…one of the tallest men she had ever seen. Even hunched over, his back curved with age and the weight of years, she had to look up to greet him. She was not particularly short by any means, but he was nearly two handspans higher, and at least twice as broad.

Long, white hair hung down by his face, unkempt and unwashed. A ragged gray cloak was slung around him, looking as though it had once been dyed a great rich blue. He had a wood cane in his hand, as crooked and wrinkled as the hand that gripped it.

"I—hello."

"You summoned your husband, didn't you?" He grinned. His features revealed a man who, when younger, must have been beautiful. His eyes were like dull sapphires, grown over with a haze of age like the rest of him. "Here I am." He held out an arm at his side.

She couldn't help it. She chuckled at his bad joke. "Good evening, sir." The man was a vagrant, living off the dirt and in the wilds, judging by his condition. "Do you come in kindness, or cruelty?"

"Hmmm…" He scratched the gray and dirty beard that adorned his face in teasing thoughtfulness. "Tonight, kindness, I think."

"Then come in. Dinner is nearly ready. I apologize for having *summoned* you." She shook her head with a smile and took a step back to let him in. "My magic must have misfired."

"Perhaps it did. Perhaps it didn't. But I see I am in the presence of a dangerous witch and should take great care." The teasing tone to his voice made it clear he didn't take her seriously.

She played along. "Oh, yes. I am a powerful sorceress and could turn you into a chicken quite easily if angered."

"Goodness. At least I would make a tasty stew." He stepped into her home, moving far easier than she would have expected for someone of his age. His cane clicked on the wood slats of the floor as he swiveled his head this way and that, taking in everything around him. "In truth, I was merely passing by and heard you. I'm not one to pass up an invitation for dinner."

"No, it doesn't seem that you are." She shut the door behind him and went back to the hearth. "Make yourself at home."

"Oh, I very much plan to."

There was a darkness in those words that gave her pause. But when she turned to him, he was poking at several of her dried bunches of herbs on the wall, a harmless smile on his face. He was just a doddery old vagrant. If he attacked her, even with his added height and weight, she was certain she could stick a knife in his neck before he got very far. Just in case, she pocketed the one she was using to clean the chicken after wiping it clean on a rag. "What is your name, good sir? I'm Abigail Moore."

"Abraham. I have no family name. I have no family."

"Neither do I, I suppose." She paused. She wasn't sure why she had the impulse to say it, but she hadn't stopped herself in time. She did not know this man. But she had said it all the same. Grabbing some rags, she pulled the bread from the pot over the coals and brought it to her table. Abraham was standing by a window, staring at the candle that burned upon the sill.

He reached out to touch it.

"No!"

He jerked in surprise at her outburst, turning his head to her with such sharpness and such a look of anger that she recoiled, worried he might strike her. But like it was only a dream, the moment was gone as fast as it had come. His expression was confused and soft, not violent. "Forgive me," he said with a lopsided smile.

"It's…" She didn't know how to explain it.

"A candle of life." He walked away from it, cane clicking on the wood floor. He walked up to her, dull sapphire eyes seeming to look straight through her. "For a man who lives but is not here, by my estimation."

"My husband—"

"Ah, ah—" He chuckled. "Your husband is right here, remember?" He pressed a hand to his chest, twisted fingers splayed wide.

She shouldn't be surprised that a vagrant who lived in the woods would be odd in the head. But her aunt had taught her to be kind to all, regardless of her concerns, and she would stay true to the wise woman's words. "Yes. Right. Forgive me, I forgot."

"Forgetting your own husband! Tsk, tsk." He walked to the table and sat down at it, the wood chair creaking beneath his weight. He picked up a pitcher of water and poured them both a mug, and then began to slice the bread into pieces. "The stew smells ready, don't you think?"

Abigail stood there, stunned for a moment, watching the strange man as he truly did make himself right at home. But that was not what concerned her. That was not what made fear crawl up her spine.

It was that the wooden goblet he lifted to his lips should have been filled with water. Water was what was in the pitcher. Water was what he poured out.

But what stained his lips was wine.

I have made a terrible mistake.

CHAPTER TWO

As Abigail brandished the knife from her sleeve—one he watched her put there but moments prior—Valroy grinned broadly. Good. She wasn't a *complete* idiot. He lifted his goblet of wine to her in a salute and took a sip.

"Who are you?" She kept the sharp little blade pointed at him.

"Abraham. Nothing more, nothing less." This was such a wonderful game. Reaching out a hand, ensuring that he made it tremble with his apparent age, he touched the lip of the pitcher, and turned the contents to wine. *It really isn't so hard. Silly Christians.*

She watched him, wary and unsure. "A warlock."

"Simply someone who can use magic, same as you. Don't throw stones, as the saying goes. It's hard to survive in the woods without the help of the unseen world. Hard enough life with it." He sat back and lifted his goblet to his lips again. "Now, dear, that stew? You *did* promise your husband a meal, after all. Terrible form to break a promise."

She wavered, then with a heavy exhale, tucked the knife back into her pocket and went to the hearth, careful not to turn her back on him. Likely, the young thing was telling herself that it was best to quickly feed him and be rid of him.

Unfortunately for her, he had no intentions to leave so fast.

Or perhaps not alone, at any rate. But that was still up for debate in his mind, as he turned the topic over and over. He watched Abigail keenly, studying her. She was beautiful. Young. Perhaps not even twenty-five years of age. She had wonderful curves that he knew he could sink his claws into. He wanted to feel them give way beneath him, supple and soft. Her hair was long, and the color of the setting sun—a pale orangey red that fell in waves down her back. She kept it lashed with a single leather tie at the base of her skull, but unbraided. She must prefer it down. Her eyes, when he had seen them, matched her hair. They were such a light brown that they bordered on amber.

And he found himself wanting to count her freckles.

She was a suitably attractive young human. Physically, she would do just fine. He would enjoy breaking her in. But what about the rest of her? He had to tolerate her for a little while, and he wanted to make sure he didn't end up ripping her apart in frustration before he had what he needed.

She was naïve. A little foolish. And an absolutely *miserable* excuse for a witch. The candle of life on the windowsill was a tricky thing for a human to make, but not impossible. And the symbol she had drawn on the door buzzed with no more power than a passing bee on a summer day.

But there was potential in her. Some of the talismans he noticed on the walls were decently made…if she were a Seelie child. But humans were tiny and strange, and their magic was the same. It barely scratched the surface of a frozen lake that would drown them if they knew what lay beneath.

She was a capable housekeeper, and a decent cook. The

smell of the stew revealed it was seasoned properly, and as she ladled it into bowls, he found himself surprisingly interested in eating it. Even if it did look like it was more liquid than not.

"Tell me, Abigail, whose candle did you make?" He knew. He had already guessed. But he wanted to hear her say it.

"My—" She paused, stopping short of saying *husband*, remembering his odd and insistent game. He couldn't wipe the grin from his face. She learned quickly. Good. "The man who married me."

Very good! "And thou shalt have no other husbands before me. Yet here we are. Ah, well. All's forgiven." He laughed. "Where is he, this man who thinks he is your husband?"

"Gone."

That one word was delivered with the weight of a war hammer. He could almost hear the ribcage of the victim crush beneath the blow. And in this instance, he knew the victim was her.

Such sorrow.

He found himself frowning briefly, before shaking it off as she turned to him with two bowls of stew. She placed one in front of him, followed by a wooden spoon and crude metal fork.

Silence. She gave him nothing more as she sat across from him, her amber eyes a burnt umber in the dim, flickering firelight.

"Aaaaaand?" He drew out the word, reaching out with his crude fork to poke her in the arm.

At his action, she jolted in surprise. Those eyes turned up to him, so full of pain and loss that he tilted his head to the side in curiosity. What could she have possibly lost that had hurt her so very much? She was nothing but a peasant girl. She had nothing worth losing.

With a shake of her head, she began eating her own stew. "I do not know you, Abraham. This is a personal matter."

"We break bread together, do we not? You invited me to your home. I am a very powerful wizard. Perhaps I can help you." He hummed. "Mayhap I am Merlin. You never know."

"Are you?"

He snorted.

She rolled her eyes. Taking up a piece of bread, she ripped it in half and dunked the piece in the liquid, soaking up what was mostly water. After considering her thoughts for a long time, she finally began to talk. "His name is Marcus. He left me to go to the Americas. He…said he would send for me as soon as he arrived."

"He did not send for you?"

"A letter did come."

"Oh?"

She paused. She debated telling him the truth once more. With a shrug, she seemed to decide there was no harm in it. "The letter was a signed contract, selling this home and all our property to Mr. Roderick Taylor, a man who lives in the village down the road." She ate the piece of bread, her tone matter-of-fact and cold after she finished chewing. "It made no mention of me."

He laughed.

At her glare, he swallowed the sound and did his best to smile sheepishly.

"It is not funny." Oh, now she was mad. Her eyes lit up like embers—not literally, although perhaps they should have for all the energy in them—and she glowered at him like an annoyed housecat.

Keeping his smile to himself, he decided…he very much liked her when she was angry. "No, no. Forgive me. It isn't. I was merely laughing at how those of us who can tap into the unseen world tend to find ourselves homeless, despite all our power and knowledge."

"What power? What knowledge?" She gestured at the room around her. "My Aunt Margery could work wonders. I'm nothing compared to her."

"She taught you?"

Her hand went to a necklace she wore, touching the crudely carved thing absentmindedly. "She raised me."

"Why not go be with her?"

"While it's tempting to commit myself to the grave, I'm not quite ready yet." She stabbed at a piece of chicken in her stew. A little more violently than was warranted. She was still angry, and he wanted to poke the embers and turn that little spitfire into an inferno.

Smiling, he went back to his dinner as well. "This… Roderick. He owns your home, your lands, this house. Yet you are here. Why?"

"He gave me a month to gather my things and be gone. That was a week ago."

"I see." He hummed. "You could curse him, perhaps. Blight him with a pox."

Abigail laughed sadly. "No. He isn't a bad man. This isn't his fault."

"When does that ever factor into anything?" He waggled his fork at her. "If you have the gifts to be rid of him and your predicament, do it. Curse him with all that you can. Demand the Tuatha Dé Danann themselves come to rip him apart, if you must. Eat"—he stabbed a hunk of potato in his stew—"or be eaten."

Abigail studied him thoughtfully for a moment then let out a breath. "I am not powerful enough to hurt him."

"Have you tried?"

"Well, no."

"Then you aren't sure." He ate the piece of potato. "And you're making excuses."

The look on her face was unreadable. The enchantment he placed on the wine was working. Now she was conversing with him freely and without hesitation. It wasn't enough to compel her to do his bidding, just enough that she might ignore how peculiar the situation was.

"Fine. I do not wish to hurt him," she finally replied, having clearly reasoned out the truth in her own mind. "Mr. Taylor has a family. A wife and three children. He could use this land. I…I am by myself."

Interesting. "You have no family, then?"

"None."

Good.

"And you are about to lose everything?"

"Yes."

Good.

"And why did this little man abandon you? You are pleasing enough on the eye,"—he smiled as she chuckled in the way a woman did when complimented by an old man—"you're a decent cook, and your house is in fine shape for someone living by herself. Was he alarmed that you are a witch?"

She hesitated, her rage flaring for a moment, and then he saw her anger crack. It shattered at the edges, and like a wineglass against stone, the emotion within couldn't withstand the damage. Her anger gave way to grief, and she turned her attention back to her meager dinner.

Perhaps she wouldn't tell him. The power of the wine could only go so far. But she took in a breath, held it, let it out in a long rush, and admitted to him what it was that she had been abandoned over.

"I am barren."

He took a bite out of his bread to keep from cackling.

Barren! The human girl couldn't bear children? *Mother Morrigan, you have given me a gift this night.* Well, that eliminated a wonderful possible complication he had no interest in bringing on himself.

After a long pause, realizing that the mortal was staring at him, he coughed and swallowed the piece of bread he was chewing. Yes, yes. He supposed he was expected to *say* something about that. "I'm very sorry he didn't understand how convenient it is to have a woman who cannot spawn."

That seemed to have been the wrong thing to say. Her anger was back again. "Excuse me?"

"Well..." He waved his fork in the air idly. "It can be such an annoying aftermath to making love, don't you think? Having that removed, you could live your life free to f—"

"Stop. Stop." She rubbed her temple as though she might have a headache. "I understand your statement. I disagree. But I understand."

"Why do you disagree?"

"Do you—" She stammered then sighed. "Never mind. I take it you have no children."

"Not that I know of." And that was true. Magic was wonderfully convenient, but sometimes unpredictable. "And you want some of your own?"

"I want..." She looked out at her home, growing darker by the moment. With a grunt, she stood and went to the fire to put a few more logs on the flame. When it was burning well enough to her liking, she stood there gazing at the fire thoughtfully. "I wish..."

"What do you wish for, Abigail Moore?" He stood from the table as well, slowly, careful not to make a sound as he moved closer to her.

This was a very important moment.

Wishes were nothing to be trifled with.

She shook her head. "Childish dreams. Nothing more."

She turned to him and jolted in surprise, finding him not where she left him. He enjoyed her angry, and he also enjoyed her afraid. *How tasty.*

He let his voice drop low. "Tell me what you wish."

"I—" Fear crossed her face again, a kind of recognition, perhaps. Her dead aunt had likely told her stories, warning her of muttering wishes to strangers. *Damn.* "Nothing. It's all right. Thank you. It's dangerous to tell your wishes to strangers."

Damn, damn.

"Even if they are your husband?" he teased, taking another step toward her. He towered over her. He towered over everyone. He enjoyed it greatly.

"Especially strange husbands."

That made him genuinely laugh. She was a mortal, and she was a fool, but she was at least a *fun* mortal fool. "I'll strive to no longer be a stranger, then. For tonight, however, I should be on my way." He looked out the window at the darkness beyond. "Thank you for the hospitality." Scooping up her hand, he kissed her fingers, knowing his lips would feel far dryer and more cracked than they were beneath his glamor.

He headed to the door of the cottage and opened it. A cold wind blew in, flickering the fire in the hearth. She was standing there, watching him, expression a mix of confusion and relief. He smiled.

"I will see you again soon, *wife.*"

He laughed to himself as he left.

CHAPTER THREE

Abigail stared down at the farthings in the woman's palm. "He is worth twice that." She gripped the rope that kept James, her goat, leashed to her. Not like it took much encouragement to get him to follow. She had raised him since the day he was born, and oftentimes she had to pen him in or leash him to keep the animal from shadowing her. Several times he had managed to sneak into the cottage, and she found him sleeping next to her.

"Times are hard." Mary sighed and leaned against the post of her fence. "And I'll be truthful with you, Miss Moore—"

"Mrs."

Mary shook her head, the deep lines of her forehead creasing as she frowned. "I know you've not got a lot in the way of choices. You're out in three weeks, by my count, and those hard pressed to sell can't haggle. Besides, how do I know that goat don't come…weird?"

Abigail dug her nails into the twists of the coarse rope in her palm, digging the fibers into her skin hard enough that it stung. "Weird."

"Bad luck follows you. Not sure I want to take the risk if it comes with the animal."

"He's just a—" She took a moment to swallow down her anger. It wouldn't do any good to shout at the old woman. "He's just a *goat*."

"Aye, and aren't they with the devil? You'd know, wouldn't you?" Mary held the farthings out toward her again. "Take it or leave it, Miss Moore. Might soon be what keeps you from starving."

In her mind, she fantasized about leaping at Mary and punching her square in the jaw. Maybe she would make her eat the miserable excuse for payment for James out of spite— force her to swallow her damn farthings whole.

Or perhaps she would work a terrible curse upon her. Blight her home and all within it.

But she didn't do any of that. She just stared, sighed, turned, and walked away, James happily trotting along beside her. "No."

"Suit yourself."

The beautiful morning was completely at odds with her mood as she walked from the village of Haltwhistle and headed back toward her cottage. The birds were chirping, the sun was shining, and the early summer air was still cool as the sun worked to make it less so. It was perfect.

And she was *miserable*.

No one else in Haltwhistle had entertained the idea of buying anything from her. Most times, Mary was the only one willing to talk to her. Everyone else just looked the other way or avoided her. With a long sigh, she straightened her back and cracked her shoulders. "I hate to say it, James. I think I'd rather you feed the wolves than her. 'Aren't they with the devil? You'd know, wouldn't you?'" She mocked Mary's tone and accent.

James let out a quiet bleat.

Her Aunt Margery had broken Abigail of her accent, teaching her instead to speak "properly," whatever that meant. She had also taught Abigail to read and write, which made for rare skills this close to Hadrian's Wall and the moors.

Unfortunately, none of it had done her a lick of good, and probably wouldn't anytime soon.

She looked down at her goat and reached out to scratch him on the head between the ears. "I don't think you're evil."

With every ounce of her, she had wanted to scream at Mary that she was a witch, not a devil worshipper, and that the two were *very* different. None of the dark magic she knew had anything to do with demons. Her magic came from the Earth. From life and death.

But there was no point in arguing about that with Mary. Mary didn't see the difference, and never would. *"Arguing with ignorance is like putting out the flames of Hell with a single bucket."* Gods, she missed her aunt so terribly.

The walk home from the village was a peaceful one, which was both good and bad. It left her alone with her thoughts, and by the time she put James back in his fenced-in pen, she was ready to break down in tears.

But she had work to do. She wasn't certain why she bothered pulling up weeds from her garden and tending her animals. She had enough dry storage to last her the three weeks until she was evicted from her home. The activity kept her mind off her impending homelessness, she supposed.

There was one last thing she had to do before the end of the day. One last precaution.

The stranger.

Taking the whittling knife that Marcus had left upon his departure, she carved symbols into the posts of her home. They were simple sigils of protection, meant to ward against spirits of any kind.

Just in case Abraham returned.

By the time the sun began to set, she was exhausted. Unwrapping some bread and cheese from where they sat in baskets on the wall, she began to make herself a meager dinner.

And once more, nearly jumped out of her skin as there was a heavy knock on her door. *Wham, wham, wham!* Glancing out the window, the sky was still a faint bluish purple. The sun had fully set.

She had no doubts about who had come to call. Her new "husband."

Fear shivered up her spine. *Perhaps he's just a stray dog, once fed, now returning for more.* Perhaps. Or perhaps he was something else entirely. He had wanted to hear her wish... and the warnings of her aunt had rung out loudly in her head.

Wishes held power—wishes held strength—and they were not to be uttered lightly.

A second knock stirred her to action, and she put down the half loaf of bread to answer it. Opening the door, she looked up into the grizzled, wizened face of her new vagrant guest. Dangling from his hand were two skinned, dead rabbits, recently killed by the looks of them.

He smiled, both vicious and warm. "Good evening, wife. May I come in?" The way he said it was both teasing and dangerous, like a cat rolling over and inviting a belly scratch. It could go wrong at any point.

Something about him made her hair stand on end. She glanced at the symbol she had carved on her doorjamb. He followed her gaze and chuckled. "I see." And with that, he... stepped inside. Right past her wards. Which meant he was either not a spirit, or her magic was useless against him.

Either way, his point was made. Her invitation to come in was for her benefit, not his. Chewing on her lip, she stood aside as he walked to the fire, his worn robe rasping on the wood floor. "I mean no offense, but…"

"A fellow wielder of magic comes to call, and you took precautions in case I am not of the *human* variety. I understand." He hooked the rabbits onto the fireplace crane and, with the end of his walking stick, pushed it over the flame. "'Tis prudent. Never know when a fae might come lurking about, ready to snatch you away to the Otherworld beneath the hills."

She laughed at the notion.

That seemed to catch his attention. He turned to her, gray and overly long eyebrow raised at her. "Why do you scoff? Do you not believe the legends?"

"I believe them, and I know better than to scoff at them. That's not why I laughed." Pulling the cork from a glass bottle, she poured some of the wine he had made last night into a pair of goblets. It had seemed wrong to waste it. Wine was not something she had frequently. She began to break up the cheese and bread onto two plates for them while they waited for the rabbits to cook.

It was nice of him to bring meat for the table. *He has already provided for me more than Marcus really did.* Her husband had been a terrible hunter. She was always the one who had set the traps and fetched the kills, although she had left it to him to butcher the animals. She hated taking life.

The realization that Abraham had brought her a hunt when Marcus so rarely did almost made her laugh again. How ludicrous.

"Then why laugh at the fae?" He sat down at her table, grunting with the movement of old bones, and settled into the chair that creaked beneath him. He didn't seem *that* heavy, and her chair was built strong. The curve of his shoulders and his back suggested a frail form, but her struggling furniture told her otherwise.

"What could the fae possibly want with me?"

"Do they need a reason to steal mortals away?" He sipped the wine first before going for the cheese and bread. "They take what they want, when they want, for their own amusement if nothing else. A pretty little creature like you would make a wonderful plaything."

She smirked. "I would not last very long. Besides, I do not think I wish to be dragged away. I will have to be more careful."

He sat back in the chair, which once more squeaked in protest, and pondered her, amusement flickering in his faded blue eyes. "What is it you want, then?"

"You seem awfully keen on prying my wishes from me, Abraham. It's suspicious."

"Suspicious! What could possibly be suspicious about me?" He laughed again, pressing his hand to his chest. "A poor old man."

"Who can turn water to wine."

"A poor old man with carefully honed skills." He waved a gnarled finger at her. "You would be wise not to mock someone with my experience. I have lived off the Earth and soil for decades. And, so it seems, you're about to join me."

The reminder of her pending homelessness soured her mood immediately, and she found herself once more furious to the point of tears.

Abraham frowned. "What is it, wife? What troubles you?"

Shaking her head, she picked up the wine and drank its contents in one gulp and poured herself a second. "Nothing that can be fixed."

He eyed the wine, then looked back to her. "Do you wish to keep this home?"

She opened her mouth to answer, and then stopped. One, it seemed he was now trying to trick her into admitting what it was she wanted. And two…she quite honestly didn't know the answer. She took in her surroundings for a moment. Marcus's father had built the home with his bare hands. Every inch of the small dwelling belonged to her husband. Each brick of the fireplace, each post…this place was *his*.

And it was his to sell out from underneath the wife he abandoned. She clenched her fists. It had once been her home, but now it was simply where she lived. "No. I merely have nowhere else to go."

"Surely someone in the village will take you in. I passed a tavern the other day—do they not have need for serving girls?" He broke off a chunk of cheese from the serving she had given him. He made a face upon eating it. It was not great, but it was what she had. "You would make a wonderful wench."

She rolled her eyes. "They think me cursed. That I am strange and odd, and that my dabbling in the arts has brought darkness and bad luck upon me. Marcus had no problem telling them of his woes over the bar in that very tavern. They avoid me at all costs." She took another gulp of the wine and sat back. Her appetite for solid food was gone, but her desire for alcohol remained. "Perhaps they are right. Perhaps I am cursed. No, when I am gone from here, I'll go to Carlisle. Someone there might have need of a woman who can read and write."

"And decently tend a hearth." He eyed his plate. "Your bread is good, but your cheese…"

"It isn't mine."

"Oh, thank the Morrigan." He pushed the plate away from him. "I've eaten bark with better flavor."

She laughed, shaking her head. "A hermit with discerning taste. How charming."

"Why do you think I learned to make wine from water?" He huffed.

She took another sip of the red liquid. "It is good."

Without realizing it, she had finished her second glass. He pushed the bottle toward her, encouraging her to refill her goblet. She shook her head, but he insisted.

"Drink. What does it matter?" He smirked beneath his thick mustache and beard.

"I do not know you, Abraham."

"Are we not married? Are we not friends now?" In mock offense, he waggled his cane at the fire. "Have I not brought you gifts of wine and food?"

Oh! The rabbits! She flew from her chair, nearly knocking it over, and ran to the fire to tend to them. Luckily, they weren't burned, but she flipped them over on the fireplace crane. Placing another log on the pile, she pushed the coals around with the fire poker to even out the heat.

Muttering swears under her breath, she wiped her hands on her apron and returned to the table.

Abraham was chuckling quietly, clearly entertained by the whole scene before him. "You are a silly thing."

"Tease me if you like."

"Good. I like it very much."

Rolling her eyes, she sank back into her chair. "It has been a trying day. A trying week." *A trying life.*

"So it seems. A villager wronged you, I take it? They slighted the powerful Abigail, threatening the wrath of a witch." He gestured at her collection of rocks and trinkets on her hearth. "Use your magic. Show them what it means to be cursed."

With a weary shake of her head, she sighed. "What would be the point?"

"Revenge."

"And what else?"

"Do you need a second reason?" He sneered. "Those who wrong you should be wronged in return."

"It's not out of spite that they turn away from me, Abraham. It isn't out of cruelty. It's out of ignorance that they think I am cursed. It's out of greed that they covet what little I have. They seek to tend to their own lives and care nothing of mine. If I sought revenge for that, I'd have all of the human race as my enemy."

He muttered something into the lip of his goblet that she didn't hear. When he put the goblet down, he refilled it. And then reaching over the table, poured more wine into hers. "Drink, Abigail. This bottle shall not run dry. Enjoy yourself."

She hesitated. The wine left her feeling strange. Not drunk, perhaps. But something else she discovered was far more dangerous, as it was far more pleasant. "Have you enchanted the wine, Abraham?"

"I have used magic in its making. Of course, it is enchanted wine." He shook his head. "Truly silly."

"No, I'm asking if you have placed a spell upon it, in addition to that which made it." She peered down at the glass. "It does not feel like normal wine."

"Is it distasteful to you, somehow? Discomforting or disquieting? Have I turned you into a frog? Do you not wish to drink more?"

The answer came from her without hesitation. "No." She should have lied. But she found herself without the stomach for the deed. Odd.

"Then what does it matter? I am just an old man, seeking to bring comfort to my wife."

"You do know how to adhere to a game, I will give you that." She chuckled and, with a long, tired exhale, sipped the wine. It might be part of whatever ploy he was furthering, but it eased the tension in her shoulders and the sense of impending doom that seemed to follow her wherever she went.

Perhaps whatever enchantment he was placing over her was worth it.

"There you go." He patted her hand. When a log rolled over in the fireplace, nearly spilling onto the floor, she moved to stand. He tutted and motioned for her to stay. "Sit. Drink." He stood instead and went to tend the fire and the rabbits that she could smell were nearly done.

She shut her eyes. The wine had already gone to her head. It worked quickly, whatever it was. But it didn't stop her from having another sip. She felt as though she were floating —warm and cozy. It didn't feel like any of the other times Marcus would bring home a wineskin and they would have too much. "I just wish…" She trailed off.

The memory of laughter stung her like bees. Betrayal only hurt when there was something to betray. "We weren't together long. A few years, at best. We met only a few days after Aunt Margery died. I was on my own. Perhaps I was naïve, but when a gentleman came calling, I—I found myself swept off my feet. He was kind and sweet at first. He wished to have a family, and so did I. But when it seemed that I was unable to bear his child, he soured toward me. I was not shocked when he said he wished to seek fortune in the Americas. I was not surprised when he left. And yet I still found myself somehow agog when he sold all this for his own ends." She opened her eyes to turn her attention to the candle of life that burned on the windowsill. "I dream of him. I see him in his home in Virginia. He has a wife…and a baby boy. He's happy. He has everything he has ever wanted."

"Do you wish him harm?"

"Sometimes it makes me furious, thinking about how he left me here, and then—and then this. But no." She sighed. "Who am I to wish harm on anyone, Abraham? What do I matter?"

"Fah!" He pulled the rabbits from the fire and half-threw them onto the table. She jolted in surprise at his outburst. "I see your anger burning in you. But you tamp it down! Who

THE UNSEELIE PRINCE

taught you to swallow your wrath, eh? This dead aunt of yours?" Storming to the window with a speed that she did not know the old man owned, he plucked the candle of life from the sill and held it in his hand, glowering at it in disgust. "You've mixed his hair into the wax. Good. I'll use it to poison him. He'll rot slowly and die painfully, even far away across the water as he is. And I'll make sure it starts with his cock. Would that make you happy, Abigail?"

She flew up from her chair, nearly toppling it again. "Wait —don't—"

"Why? Do you love him?"

The word came from her without thought. "No." She blinked, stunned. Never once had she admitted it, even to herself, that she hadn't loved Marcus. She hadn't hated him, not by any means. She had even cared for him. But that was where it stopped.

Abraham stormed toward her, and before she could react, he had backed her into the wall. He held the candle between them. "Tell me why I should not curse him, knowing that as his manhood turns black and falls from his body, he'll think it was you who did it. He would die knowing that he had wronged you and been wronged in return. Tell me why I should spare him."

Everything about the old man had changed in an instant. His shoulders were no longer stooped. There was no tremor in his limbs. His cane lay on the floor where it had been abandoned. And there was little of the haze left in those eyes of his.

Reaching out her hand, she took his empty one in hers. He let her, his expression flickering to one of curiosity. An amused curl of his lip followed as she lifted his palm toward her cheek. Perhaps he thought she was going to embrace him, grateful for his use of dark magic to her benefit.

Instead, she planted his palm against the wood beam of her home.

Right atop the symbol she had carved that afternoon.

Abraham hissed in pain, revealing cyeteeth that were a little too long. A little too long…and a little too sharp.

He was not human.

My life is over.

CHAPTER FOUR

Abraham staggered away from her, his face a mask of rage. But all at once, like a candle being snuffed, the rage vanished. He laughed, hard and loud, as if what she had done had truly amused him. "Little hellcat!"

His voice had changed.

It was no longer old, haggard and worn with time. It was like lush fabric sliding over a deadly blade. Both sharp and low, cutting and rumbling, he straightened. His back cracked loudly, and he snapped his head from one side to the other, causing the bones to pop. "Little hellcat, indeed."

Terror like ice ran through her veins. She kept her back pressed to the wall, terrified, watching the creature who had entered her home. Her head spun. *Damn the wine!*

He lifted his hand, eyeing the candle that still burned within it. "Die."

"No!" She ran forward to stop him.

But it was too late.

With one word, the wax turned to sand in his hand and fell to the floor at his feet. He dropped what remained. She dove for it, landing hard on her knees at his feet, but could only watch as he crushed the smoldering flame beneath his foot.

His bare foot.

He had been wearing boots before. She had heard them thumping on the wood floor.

"I do think I rather like you down there."

Abigail looked up. She screamed.

The creature laughed.

She flew back away from him as fast as she could, the broken candle of life forgotten as she scrambled to her feet. Toppling a stool in her haste, she slammed her back against the wooden wall of her home.

Standing before her was a man—or something similar—that she didn't know how to comprehend through her shock. He was tall, barely fitting inside the structure. He would have to duck beneath the doorway. Bright sapphire eyes that faintly glowed were fixed on her. They watched her from features that she could only think of as the most beautiful she had ever seen.

But there was unwavering malice in his eyes, marring his expression and turning it into something more akin to the way a wolf might look at his meal. No. It was worse than that. Where a wolf might kill for food, this creature before her clearly took great pleasure in her fear. There was fiendish delight etched in the smile that split his features, revealing once more those too-sharp eyeteeth of his.

A cape, that looked as though it were made of some strange form of leather, draped from his shoulders and hung behind him. It was clasped to his bare shoulders by large, claw-like things. He wore no shirt, revealing a frame built of pure muscle. A bizarre circular marking that resembled a labyrinth decorated his left pectoral. It connected to more strange lines and ink that ran over his chest and down his left arm. Large triskelion spirals tangled with what looked like vines, though they were all too jagged, vicious, and pointed to be like any she recognized. They were inked on him in dark, sapphire blue.

The color matched his long hair that cascaded in midnight waves down to his thighs. Silver rings, half a dozen each, decorated pointed ears. His fingers shone with matching silver adornments. A necklace hung around his throat, and a large blue crystal or tinted glass vial hung at the end of it. A pair of dark leather pants was the only article of clothing that he wore.

He held his arms out wide at his sides, presenting himself to her. She didn't know how long she had stood there, gaping in horror and shock. Perhaps it had been a solid minute. "Do you enjoy what you see, *wife?*"

"No—no! You—you killed him—Marcus—"

"Is dead. Faster than I would have liked, but you spurred me to action." He nudged the cindered wick with his toe and shrugged dismissively. "Your childish wards ruined my plans…you should have left well enough alone, Abigail."

"Plans?" She pressed her palms to the wood wall, as if she might will herself through it. The creature was blocking her path to the only door out of her tiny home.

"Oh, you know." He gestured idly as he stepped toward her, his movements smooth and predatory. "Woo you with gifts, win your trust, trick you into telling me your deepest wish…and then tear you away from this pathetic life of yours." He grinned. "Nothing out of the ordinary."

"Don't come near me!" She dove for a knife on the nearby table. But in one swift movement that left her stunned and confused, she found herself face-first on the wood surface instead. The wooden plates clattered to the floor, scattering their contents. Her arm was bent behind her back, and she felt a heavy weight press against her thighs.

"Hm…well, this is unexpectedly nice." The weight against

her increased. "Very nice, indeed." A hand, tipped in sharpened nails that were painted—she hoped they were painted—a dark blue-black, slammed against the wood beside her head. "I might have to invest in a taller table. You are just a *little* short for this to work right."

"Get—get off me!" She struggled, but it was useless. He was three times her size, if not more, and far stronger. It was like being trapped beneath a fallen tree. "Get *off* me!"

"So many demands…" He laughed. His hips pressed against her. She could feel his hot breath wash against her ear as he lowered his head close to hers. His voice was a low growl, barely audible despite his nearness. "For a human who finds herself the prey of an Unseelie."

When his tongue ran along her cheek, slow and hot, right beside her ear, she froze. Every muscle in her body went rigid. The only thing she dared to do was shiver in terror.

Unseelie. A creature of the dark and cruel court of the fae. She should have known—she shouldn't have been so foolish! She hadn't believed that a fae would knock on her door, let alone the one who now had her pinned.

All fair folk were to be feared. They were all to be respected. The Seelie who claimed the daylight hours were tricksters. Those who walked the night…were monsters.

Oh, no. Oh, no, no, no…

"Please—" The word left her in a choked whisper.

"Oh, now she says 'please,' does she?" He chuckled into her ear. When he nuzzled into her hair, a low rumble leaving his chest like that of an animal, she let out a terrified whine. It only made him laugh louder as he hovered his lips once more near her ear. "Silly, pretty thing…"

Her world was in movement again, whirling around her without warning as he straightened her up and nearly threw her from him. It sent her staggering away, catching onto one of the wood posts of her cottage to keep her from toppling to the ground.

He licked his lower lip slowly, his gaze sliding down her body and back up. If she had the purchase to be anything less than terrified, she might have been offended. As it was, she was debating if she could make it out her front door before he could catch her. She highly doubted it. She also highly doubted that she had a choice but to try.

The Unseelie took a slow step toward her. As he did, he passed one of the wards she had carved on the posts of her home. Lifting a hand, he dug his sharp nails into the wood and raked across it, carving trenches in the surface deep and wide enough to have been put there by a knife. "You have insulted my hospitality, Abigail…"

Numbly, she shook her head. "Please, I—I meant no offense. I didn't know what you were."

"Oh, but you did. Or else you wouldn't have carved these foolish wards. You may not have known what kind of soul I was—be I boggart or gremlin, elf or pixie—but you sought to protect yourself against me. Me!" He snarled, taking another step toward her. She took one back. "I brought you gifts. You invited me in. I was kind to you."

"I—I'm sorry, I—" She didn't realize he had been prowling toward her, forcing her to back away from him, until her shoulders once more hit the wall of her home. Squeaking in surprise, she tried to turn to escape, but it was too late.

"Oh? Now you're even sorry. How quickly your attitude has changed." He stepped into her, his hand against the wall beside her, caging her in. "No. You insulted me. I demand satisfaction, pretty thing." When she turned her head away from him, he caught her jaw in his hand, forcing her to look up at him. He was massive, and she felt so very small in his wake. "What will you give me? Hm? I, who have done you no wrong?"

"The wine—you tricked me. You—"

"It dulled your worries and let your tongue run free, the same as any wine." He smirked. "My wine is simply more effective than most." A clawed thumb pressed against the valley beneath her lower lip. His sapphire eyes were heavy and lidded as he spoke again, his gaze fixed on the point where his nail just barely dug into her skin. "What will you give me, Abigail?"

"I don't know what you want," she whispered. Oh, she did. But she prayed to all the old gods that she was wrong.

"You shall tell me your deepest wish. You know what will follow when you do."

Yes, she did. She knew what became of all souls foolish enough to whisper their wishes to the fair folk. It would spell her undoing. He would grant her wish, but he would take everything from her in return.

There was no doubt in her mind about what he would do to her. He would kill her, if she was lucky. Torture her, if she was not. Either way, she would be his slave. "No, please. Give me another way to correct this insult."

"Hm? You ask for me to be even more magnanimous than I already am? You want me to be kinder to you than I already have been?" He grinned, slow and cruel. "Very well. Here is your other option. I will forgive you the slight you have paid me if you go to the village, strip naked, and get on your hands and knees. I will take the shape of a wild boar, and I will show you what it means to mate. You and I will have a night you will *never* forget, and only when the dawn breaks will I stop rutting you like the animal I am. Used and dirty, you'll limp back to a home you no longer own."

Her stomach rolled at the mental image he painted, and she squeezed her eyes shut.

Snarling, he shook her once. "Look at me, Abigail!"

Startled and shocked at his outburst, she had no other

choice. She found herself staring into those bright sapphire eyes of his.

He smiled, an expression that would have been dazzling if not for its cruelty. "Here are your choices. I will *fuck you raw*, little witch, right in front of all the villagers who hate you. I will do so as a big, slobbering, disgusting, stinking pig. I'll break you into a mare who can't even breed. I'll even make you beg for more before we're done." He tilted her head back as he zeroed the distance between them. His body pressed to hers, and she gasped at the warmth of him.

He smelled like winter, crisp and sharp. Or like the breeze that drifted in from ocean cliffs. No, he carried the scent of the night itself. Of grass, and trees, and *darkness*.

"Or…" A twist to his lips told her precisely which was the option he preferred the most. "You tell me your deepest wish."

One night of embarrassment. One night of pain, and torment, and being used in the street like a whore by a wild beast. One night of horror, compared to a lifetime of the same. She knew what dangers were promised to come with a wish made to a fae.

Let alone the one who towered over her.

But the idea of being broken like that…

It was sparing a single lash with the whip now for an eternity of them to come. "And if I tell you my wish?"

She felt a surge of excitement wash through him as he shifted his weight to press harder against her. He laughed, quiet and harsh. "Well, I did tell you that you would make an excellent plaything, did I not?"

When tears stung her eyes, he tutted and shifted his hand to wipe them away. "No, no. None of that, little witch. You insulted an Unseelie, and now you are paying the price."

"You killed my husband."

"I killed a man who left you and disavowed all knowledge

or care for you. One who you would have never seen again." He scoffed. "I did *nothing* to harm you."

"And my wards did nothing to harm you. No more than a fly might annoy a cow."

"I do not care. You turned your nose up at my kindness. That is enough, even to Seelie scum. Which will it be, pretty thing? *Choose.* Will it be the boar? Hm?"

She just simply could not do it. "I—I will tell you my wish." With a wavering breath, she signed the contract of her own doom.

His smile revealed those wolfish teeth once more. "Good…" The words that left him were a purr. "Speak it, and we shall be on our way. Speak it, and you are mine." He sneered. "Make your wish, little witch."

After a long pause, she made the most foolish decision of her life. She spoke her wish to a fae. "I wish for a home."

"Done."

Perfect, perfect, perfect!

Valroy fisted Abigail's hair in his hand and dragged her from the wall. She shrieked, swatting at his hand, but he cared not. She was a waif, a little imp of a thing, and he had fought the most powerful warriors that the Isle had to offer.

But she was *perfect.*

Witty enough to keep him entertained, stupid enough to challenge him, fiery enough to fight back, but smart enough to know when to cower in fear. For his needs—of which he now had a few more upon meeting her—she would do quite nicely.

And her wish? It could not have been better. It fit perfectly into his plans like he'd soon fit into her body. Tight and like it was meant to be. He was almost disappointed that she hadn't chosen to let him rut her as a wild boar. *Perhaps that'll still be in the cards later.* He had chosen the most vile option, knowing it would send her into his hands. And it had.

But he had expected her to desire wealth, or a babe, or her husband to return. All of those he was prepared to grant, if not in the way she could have possibly imagined. He was already prepared to deposit a screaming, wailing goblin spawn into her arms and announce her its mother.

But this was better.

A home?

Oh, little witch.

You make this too easy.

"No—no! Please!" She kicked and swatted at him as he marched her out onto her lawn.

He pulled her around to face him, gripping her tightly by the hair at the base of her skull. "Your wish is being granted. What are you fussing about?"

"Where—where are you taking me?"

"Home, of course." This was altogether far too much fun. Yanking her around in front of him, he pressed her back to his chest. She went rigid, but with one arm banded around her waist, there was nothing she could do. "You never did specify *where*."

He lifted a hand toward her cottage and turned his palm up to the night air. Slowly closing his fingers, he forced the fire in the hearth to flare up. Soon, it was an inferno, and the flickering orange inside the house belied it was not just the hearth that burned.

Valroy lowered his head to her ear, stooping to reach her, and whispered to her as she stared ahead, wide-eyed and agog. "This place is now a funeral pyre to the life you no longer have."

Tears rolled down her cheeks, but there was more than

just grief in her eyes. There was anger. *Yes, yes, yes!* Oh, she was far too much fun. He snaked his tongue from his mouth to lick up one of her tears, causing her to jerk her head away from him in revulsion.

"Now that is done, let us be done with this place. It's time to grant your wish. Where is this new home of yours, you ask? You'll be happy to know I already have the answer."

He whirled her back to face him, jarring her in the sudden movement. He wanted her to see him, though. He wanted to watch her face as he unfurled his wings in the flickering light of the burning house.

She stared at him in horror as he stretched out his large, leathery, bat-like wings behind him. He flexed the talons that topped the peak of them, glad to move them after being cramped in that miserable little box for so long.

Amber eyes turned white as they rolled into her head. She went limp in his arms.

Laughter filled the night sky as he flew home with his new prize.

CHAPTER FIVE

"What in the stars are you doing, Valroy?"

Valroy put Abigail down in the grass next to a pond. He was gentle. Mostly. "What does it look like, Anfar?"

"You said you were going stag hunting."

"And so, I was. And lo,"—he gestured dramatically down at the unconscious woman at his feet—"I present to thee… my hind."

The heavy sigh from behind him was all he needed to hear to know precisely how disapproving Anfar was of his actions. "Hardly a stag."

"Pah. You haven't met her. She has horns, believe you me." He turned his head to the side slightly as he studied the woman who now lay sprawled in the dark grass. "Tiny ones, perhaps. But they're there. Maybe I can get them to grow."

"You still haven't told me what it is you're doing."

He turned to his friend as he curled his wings around his shoulders, letting them drape around his chest like a cape. Anfar was leaning against a nearby tree, his uneven, unkempt sea-green hair soaking wet as it always was. Valroy grinned. "I am finding a loophole, my dear friend."

"A loophole...?" Eyebrows furrowed, and then he groaned in dismay and placed a thin-boned hand over his eyes. "Valroy. Tell me you jest."

"No, no, this is brilliant. You know it is." He strolled from Abigail over to his friend and leaned against the tree next to the sullen and soggy creature. "And the best part is, it is so wonderfully simple. Why bother myself with some insipid court member, when I might simply steal what I need?"

"You stole her." He shook his head. "When was the last time you've taken a mortal?"

"A few nights ago."

"No, not one you haven't killed or turned into a groble—" He blinked. "You could not seriously be planning on—" Anfar looked at him, suddenly startled at the idea. "You would not sink so low."

Valroy barked out a laugh, grinning wide. The sudden sound made Abigail stir. She turned her head to the side and let out a small, unhappy sound. It made him smile. "No. I don't plan on making her part of the horde." *Yet.* "Ease your fears, brother."

"I have learned to never ease my fears when you are involved." Anfar stepped toward Abigail, moving from the shadows of the trees to stand in the light of the moon overhead. He crouched beside her, studying Valroy's latest catch. Reaching down, he plucked up a strand of her ginger hair and wound it around his finger before releasing it. "She is a pretty thing."

"Mine. Not yours."

"Merely admiring." He stood, his thin frame cutting a silhouette against the glowing waters of the pond. "You know she is not my normal fare, regardless."

"Mmhm. She is not a boat full of sailors for you to consume." Valroy yawned, covering his mouth with a talon. "I tire. It has been an eventful evening, and the dawn is rising. I flew through the night to get here. Let us leave my little witch to her own rest, and—"

"Wait." Anfar whirled to face him. "You took a *witch?*"

He shrugged. "And?"

"A—" Anfar groaned and covered his face with his hands. "You enormous fool."

"She merely dabbles at magic. She collects sticks and rocks and ties them together to make her crops grow." He waved a hand in the air dismissively as he talked. "Hardly a sorceress of import."

"And you have dropped her in the Maze. What do you think shall become of her power, if she tries to harness it here?"

"I'm not sure." He cackled. "But it will be great fun to watch!"

"You enormous, excessive, *exhausting* fool." Anfar threw his hands up in frustration. "It is too late now. Once the organ between your legs is set on something, there is no deterring it, even if it means our destruction."

"I'm so glad we are friends. I would hate to think of what you'd say to me if we weren't." Valroy smirked. "Well, stand there and stare at her if you're so threatened by a little witch. I am going to bed." He turned to head into the shadows, intending on folding through space to go home. Inside the Maze, all things were under his command. There was no reason to be concerned for her safety. But it would be fun to watch her struggle.

A great deal of fun.

"Good morn, Anfar. Sleep well, if you choose to." And with that, he departed.

Anfar stood over the sleeping body of the young woman. He let out another long, dreary sigh. It was not that he cared for the mortal's plight—he didn't. He had devoured more than his own share of foolish humans who thought it wise to idle too close to the dark water's edge or played at mastering the ocean.

No, he sighed because he knew precisely how much trouble this young thing was going to cause. And she was a witch, no less. What disaster would come of that? *Of course, he could not make this simple. Of course, he could not take a normal, harmless mortal.* Therein lay the issue, however. To Valroy, she *was* harmless.

Perhaps she was.

Perhaps she was not.

Anfar was not one to play games of chance. Valroy very much was the opposite. But soon, the Crowned Prince and High Lord of the Court of Stars would take the throne, and Anfar's woes would exponentially increase.

It was an ascension that was long overdue, to be fair. But it was one that even he, as Valroy's friend, was happy to delay for as long as possible. The only thing that stood between Valroy and his goal was the law passed down by the Morrigan herself.

A law that was now threatened by this "little witch" he had fetched.

I should kill her now. He pulled his sword from the air around him. It was a short blade, but no less vicious for its size. He could hear the prince mocking him about how "the weapon suited his stature." He turned it over in his hand, noting the rust that had grown along the pommel. Saltwater did tend to do that.

He debated driving the blade through the throat of the girl or gutting her like the hind Valroy teased her to be. The bloody prince would be livid, but the rest of the court would be relieved. He would be lauded behind Valroy's back.

But it would only delay the inevitable.

The prince had found a "loophole."

A loophole in the shape of a mortal girl. And where there was one, there was bound to be another. Killing this one would only spur his friend to find a second in half the time. And he would be certain to seek out one more dangerous simply out of spite.

There was one hope, however fleeting. He crouched again by her side. "You must not agree to marry him, little witch." Reaching out, he stroked a hand over her hair. "No matter what he does." He did not know if the mortal could hear him. He did not particularly care. "Accept any fate other than to stand at his side."

Straightening, he dropped his sword into the grass beside her. If this folly were to play out, let it play out in full before she died at the hands of a hungry groble or torn to shreds by a broog. "Refuse him everything he asks of you. Lest you kill us all."

ABIGAIL AWOKE WITH A GROAN. Rolling onto her side, she pressed a hand to her head. It pounded angrily, as if she had drunk too much wine and—

Wine.

The fae.

Marcus' candle.

Her home.

My home!

Every single thought slammed through her head at once, and she bolted up to her feet, only to collapse again as her stomach revolted at the sudden movement. She doubled over with another long groan and pressed her head to the cool grass she had been lying in when she awoke.

Where *was* she?

Her memories were all a jumbled mess. Abraham had arrived with two rabbits and urged her to drink more of his summoned wine. Foolishly, she had, having been lured in by its taste and the easing of her rattled nerves. He had touched a ward…

Marcus was dead. His candle cursed and destroyed. It hadn't been meant to be used like that—it should not have been able to harm him—but what did she know of the power of the Unseelie? Nothing.

Her home had been set ablaze. She could still smell the smoke.

Wings. A glimpse of stars through translucent skin that stretched wide. Great, and terrible, and the color of the sky at the end of twilight before it disappears into the night.

He had not been wearing a cape at all.

When they unfurled around him, talons flexing like three-fingered hands that ended in viciously long, pointed claws, she knew the devil himself had come for her. Then, she remembered nothing. Perhaps flashes of the sensation of wind. Of the sound of those wings, beating against the air.

And then…this.

She bit back a sob. No. She would *not* cry. It would do her no good. Bursting into hysterics would do nothing to solve her predicament. Lifting her head, she was happy that the world did not spin as much.

The question still remained—where in the seven hells *was* she? There was still a sun overhead, blazing away, illuminating the trees, and rocks, and grass, and pond with its bubbling brook. That was not the problem.

She should not be able to stare directly at it. Yet there she was, doing precisely that. It was brighter than the moon, yes, but only barely. A great, dark haze covered the bright blue sky.

"Shite." She put her head in her hand for a moment, squeezing her eyes shut in hopes that when she opened them again, the world would be put right. Attempt one didn't work. "Shite." Attempt two had the same results as attempt one. *"Shite!"*

The sound of laughter came from behind her. She whirled but saw no one and nothing. Just dense forest. The trees towered high overhead, pressed close together, the underbrush making it look nigh impossible to stray from the single path that broke through it into the clearing where she was sitting.

But she had definitely heard laughter. A lot of it. Like there had been a crowd of *somethings* giggling at her expletives. "Hello?"

Silence.

Standing, she wavered, but managed to get her footing. The ground was soft and mossy beneath her. The pond next to her was startlingly clear—she could see straight to the rock-covered bottom. The shapes of fish darted back and forth, nibbling on plants and roots. When she moved to inspect it closer, her toe nudged something lying in the grass at her feet.

It was a sword. Blinking, she crouched to pick it up. It was rusted and damp, dripping water from the edges. Had it just been wrenched from the ocean? It smelled of saltwater. But the blade, despite the rust, looked vicious and sharp.

Had the fae given this to her?

Why?

But a gift horse was not to be examined, and she was utterly defenseless. *The sword will do me no good, either. What am I to do with it? I know nothing of battle.* But it was something to clutch to in her fear. Which she did. Eagerly.

All around her was the sound of the forest. Birds and insects, rustling leaves in the wind, and all that she would expect to hear. But all of it seemed just a little bit *off.* She didn't recognize any of the calls of the birds. The shrill sounds of the insects made the hair on her arms stand on end.

An Unseelie fae had taken her away. And though she had no proof save the dark veil of the sky overhead, she knew where she was. This was the Otherworld. He had brought her to here and now she was likely trapped here until she died.

Or worse.

But for the moment, there were two options before her—sit on the mossy stones of the pond and weep until a monster came from the shadows to devour her…or walk.

Walking it was. Besides, she didn't enjoy the sight of the fish in the pond. They looked normal—they looked harmless—but nothing here was to be trusted. Taking the path from the clearing, she headed off into the woods. She knew not where she was headed, but it did not matter.

When something shifted loudly behind her, she whirled, gripping the rusty short sword in both hands and holding it aloft. She expected to see a monster, lurching forward, ready to devour her. And perhaps it was. But greeting her was no slobbering maw of sharpened teeth, or even an Unseelie fae with a wicked smile.

It was a wall of trees and boulders.

The path she was on had led to a pond—she knew it had. She had just been there! But now…it was an impassable wall of growth. The forest itself had *moved.* And it had blocked her path.

When she let out a dismayed whine, she heard that giggling again from behind her. Whirling once more, there was no one there. Turning back to the forest wall, she yelped in shock. It was now only an arm's reach away from her!

Staggering back, she fought the urge to turn and run. The forest was alive, and it seemed set on herding her down the path toward where, she did not know. And the living forest was filled with creatures that cackled at her but hid when she turned to see them.

Suddenly, all her problems with Roderick Taylor and her impending homelessness seemed so trite and small.

I should have chosen the boar.

I really should have chosen the damn boar.

CHAPTER SIX

Abigail walked. And walked.
And walked.
And reached precisely nowhere.

It might have been for hours, if she could trust the odd sun overhead. Her feet ached by the time it dipped below the level of the trees. And all the while, no matter where she turned, she felt as though she were being watched. It kept her nerves on edge as she treaded the path through the eerie, strange forest.

There were only so many times she could glance behind her before her neck began to get stiff.

But she couldn't help it.

The forest felt wrong.

The strange, smoky haze over the sky never cleared. The shapes cast by the sunlight that came down through the trees left fuzzy and indistinct shadows. It should be a blazingly hot day, even in the shelter of the forest, but instead the air felt cold.

With nothing else to contemplate, she found herself studying the trees themselves. Great and ancient trees towered over her. Oaks and lindens, elms and beeches, all crowded in close. She knew them all, and they seemed normal enough, but something about them made her skin crawl.

Their branches were neither jagged nor sharp, their leaves looked green and lush—even in the dark haze that covered the sunny sky, they seemed to thrive. But after a while, it began to dawn on her what precisely it was about them that unnerved her so.

It was not the laughing creatures that she could never catch sight of that were the source of her nervousness.

It was the trees.

They were the ones who were watching her.

When the sky began to darken as the sun slipped lower on the horizon, she grew even more worried. What was she to do, lost in the woods of the Otherworld, unable to find her way home? She had not come across a single clearing or opening. She could make a camp in the center of the path, but she had the distinct sensation that the trees would *not* appreciate her starting a fire in their midst.

But to be lost in the darkness seemed far, far worse.

And far more dangerous.

Unfortunately—or fortunately—she didn't have to debate her problem for long. Just as twilight took over the hazy sky, darkening it further, the path finally opened to a clearing.

To a small pond with mossy shores, crystal-clear water, and the darting shapes of fish beneath the surface.

It was right where she had begun her day.

The choked noise of frustration she made was half a whine and half a growl. Pushing her hand through her tangled hair, she took a deep breath, held it, and let it out. "You cannot say you're surprised. You cannot. Look where you are. Look what has happened to you." But it didn't stop her from stepping closer to the pond and collapsing into the grass. Placing the rusted sword beside her, she began to unlace her shoes. Her feet were killing her. The fact that it was pointless suffering, as she had achieved nothing, just added salt to the wound.

She had walked, and walked, and walked, and gone precisely *nowhere.*

Putting her shoes aside, she groaned as she kneaded the soles of her feet, trying to lessen the ache. Desperately, she wanted to stick her feet in the pond. She didn't dare. There was no telling what lurked, invisible and terrible, in its deceivingly clear water.

When the clearing grew too dark to see, she sighed. She wanted to start a fire—the night would likely be cold, and she had no shelter. But she had nothing with which to start a flame. She had no flint or match.

But it didn't mean she had to spend the night in the dark. Cupping her hands together in front of her face, she blew into her palms as if she were warming them on a winter night. Shutting her eyes, she closed the gap between her thumbs, and focused.

When she was done, she opened her hands. Smiling, she watched three small, glowing orbs fly from her hands. Pale green in color, they darted around the clearing, swirling lazily as they illuminated the world around her.

They would last for the night. Although they were dimmer than she would like, their glow seemingly unable to penetrate the darkness of the woods around her, she wouldn't be sitting there unable to see.

"At least this way, I can see what terrible monsters are about to eat me." Sighing, she picked up a stick from the ground beside her and began nudging a pebble around in the grass. What was she to do? Walking did her no good. She could hack away at a tree with her rusty sword in an attempt to do…something…or she could sit here in a clearing and wait to be eaten.

I should have chosen the damn boar.

The stars began to peek out in the sky, strangely visible through the haze she assumed was still there. But perhaps it only came out during the daylight? The stars were brighter than they were at home, shining like beacons in the sky. Studying them, she didn't recognize their arrangements.

The stars she knew were gone, replaced with strangers. *I have no north star to guide me. Not like it would do me much good, I suppose.*

She was still glad for her little summoned orbs of light, but she discovered her concern about being left in the dark was unfounded. She barely needed them, even though the moon had not yet risen—if the Otherworld had a moon. The stars themselves were bright enough to see by.

Yet, even with the comfort of light…she wanted to cry. Her feet felt as though they were still attempting to fall off. She was tired, she was starving, and she was terrified.

And she was alone.

But tears were useless. She held them back. In some strange way, they would give that terrible fae some kind of power over her, as if crying would be admitting that he had won. *But he has won. I'm lost. I have nothing but this strange sword that somehow always seems to be damp. And I—*

"Well, I see we're already off to a great start."

She screamed. Whirling to her feet, the moss damp beneath them as she still was without her shoes, she held the rusty sword aloft toward whoever had spoken.

There, leaning against the tree, was the towering Unseelie who had taken her. His skin was pale in the starlight, and she could see now that his sapphire eyes did indeed glow, if dimly, on their own.

He stepped toward her, and she watched in rapt horror as

he unfolded his wings from where they were draped around him like a cape.

They were both beautiful and grotesque. Monstrous and graceful. They looked almost like an extra set of arms save for that they had an extra hinge that made them all the more uncanny. The peaks of his wings were three-taloned claws—two fingers and a thumb—that ended in viciously sharp points.

She stared. No, she gaped. He was…beautiful. There was no way else to describe him. But he was twisted all the same, with those morbid and graceful wings.

He smirked at her, a sharp twist to full lips. Holding out his arms at his sides, he bowed slightly at the waist, his wings widening. "Do you like what you see, little witch?"

There was no doubt he was gorgeous. There was no doubt in her mind that he was achingly perfect. She would stare at him for that reason alone, but there was another reason he arrested her full attention. He was also a predator. The Unseelie fae before her was a vicious, venomous snake. Gorgeous to behold…and no less deadly.

Shaking her head dumbly, she took a step away, still holding the rusted sword between them, even though she knew it was useless.

"Oh? You don't? A shame I don't believe you." He chuckled. Those glowing sapphire eyes glanced to the sword and then back up. "Anfar left you a gift. How charming."

"Anfar?"

"Hm. You'll meet, I'm sure." He shrugged dismissively. "The serpent can't help but meddle." He took another step toward her, bare feet sinking into the blue-green grass, and she took a matching one back. That seemed to amuse him. "You're insulting me again, little witch."

"I do not want you near me." She raised the sword again,

though she gripped it in shaking hands. She knew she might as well be holding up a butter knife. "And you know why."

That made him laugh. "That is but half the grievous wound you pay me this evening! The other half is how blatantly you refuse my hospitality."

"Excuse me?" That time, it was her turn to laugh. "What hospitality?"

"I leave you here by a pool, where you might rest, and drink, and eat the fish and mushrooms, and"—he wrinkled his nose—"most importantly, *bathe*. By the stars, you stink, do you know that?"

"How dare you—"

He kept talking as if she weren't. "And instead, I find that you've spent the entire day walking in circles! Instead of resting safely here, where none of my boggarts, grobles, or klen'hale might come too close." He shook his head with a long sigh, *tsk*ing. "Instead, I learn you spent the whole day wandering about in circles like an idiot. Foolish little thing, you are. Next, you'll tell me you'll refuse to sit at my table and eat dinner with me."

"I—I have no intention of eating anything here. Or with you."

"Oh?" He arched a thin eyebrow. "You intend to starve, then?" He laughed. "The stubbornness of your race never ceases to amaze me."

"If I eat or drink anything here, I will never be able to leave. I will not be tricked into—"

"Leave?" Cutting her off seemed to not bother him in the slightest. He barked a laugh and took another step toward her. She took another one back in return. Retreating from a predator was a good way to get chased, but she had no interest in being anywhere near the creature before her. "I hate to tell this to you, little witch…but you are never going back to that pissant little village, no matter if you partake of my world or not."

"I'll find a way out!"

"Mmhm." He folded his arms behind his back and took another slow, pointed step forward. She took another, far less confident one back. It only widened his smile. "You will, will you? You will succeed—you, a little, helpless, weak, starving witch—where everyone else has failed in escaping Tir n'Aill?"

Tir n'Aill? She had never heard that name. But she figured a great deal of the legends she had heard of the Otherworld were false. "Y—yes. I will."

"Hm. While I think I will love watching you try, I fear I must tell you that your situation is far worse than you think. You are not simply in Tir n'Aill. You are in the Maze. *My* Maze."

At her confused, stunned, overwhelmed silence, he spread his wings wide, snapping them open. They almost touched the trees on either side of the clearing! She squeaked and fell back, staggering and nearly falling to the ground.

"We have not properly been introduced, have we?" He grinned, revealing those sharp eyeteeth. Holding his arms out wide once more, he tilted his head back slightly, the starlight shining off his blue hair that was nearly black. "I am Master of the Maze. I am the Champion of the Blood Ring. I am the Commander of the Horde. I am the Duke of Darkness. I am the High Lord of the Moonlit Court. He who stands before you is no mere Unseelie fae, little witch…for I am Valroy, son of the Morrigan, and Crown Prince to the Silvered Throne."

She stared at him in silence.

His eyebrows raised.

There was only one thing she could think of to say.

"Shite."

Valroy blinked.

Then began to howl in laughter.

The little thing looked so mortified! The color had drained out of her already pale, freckled face. Her hands that gripped the rusted sword nearly went slack, almost dropping the blade to the ground at her feet.

Her fear was delicious. He couldn't wait until she was truly lost in his Maze, wandering in circles, so that he might hunt her down. And what wonderful prey she would make. The hunger surged in him, but he let it simmer.

The best hunts were slow.

The doe must be tired before she was taken. She should tremble and know that the wolf led her right where he wanted her to be before he sank his teeth into her throat. Victory in battle was a savory treat, but surrender was the true delicacy.

And surrender, she would.

In more ways than one.

But for now, his hunger would go unfed, and that was all right by him. Toying with his new plaything was fine enough for him.

Relaxing his wings from their full span, he took another step toward his frightened doe. But very much like the metaphoric comparison, it seemed she couldn't take any more of his grandstanding—and it *was* grandstanding. He knew it was. But what was the point of having so many titles, if he couldn't rattle them off dramatically from time to time?

Abigail turned on her heel, meaning to flee into the darkness of the woods. Seeing his opening, he pounced. Leaping forward, he snatched her by the back of her clothes with one of the talons of his wings. His claws tore through the fabric, ripping huge gashes through her bodice and her slip. It ruined her clothes, but he didn't care in the slightest.

She screamed in terror, kicking and flailing uselessly, as her feet left the ground. The rusted sword finally fell to the grass with a quiet thump.

"And where do you think you're going?" He huffed. "You are so very rude! I offer you hospitality, and you refuse it. I offer you dinner, and you refuse it. And when I tell you the truth of my nature, you don't even *kneel*. Pah! Peasants, these days."

"Let me go! Put me down!" She flailed, unable to reach him where he held her from his outstretched wing.

"Hm? Very well. As you wish." He grinned.

And promptly hurled her into the pond.

CHAPTER SEVEN

Abigail sputtered as the cold water hit her like a wall. She sank quickly, the water filling her mouth as it caught her mid-scream. Desperately swimming to the surface, she gasped for air as she reached it. Coughing, she swam closer to shore, her feet finally touching the slick rocks that lined the bottom.

Valroy—*prince of the Unseelie*—sat on the shore, leaning back on his hands, a single foot dangling in the water. He was laughing at her. *Hard.*

Pushing her hair out of her eyes, she glared at him.

"Oh, do not give me that look. You deserved that."

"Yes, for all these imaginary insults you think I've paid you!" She coughed and looked down at herself. She was soaked through to the bone, and she could feel the chill air on her back where his claws had ripped through her clothing, leaving what must be huge holes.

"And mighty insults they have been. A prince has made offers to you that you have refused with no explanation or grace." He flicked his hand, and a rectangle of soap appeared in his hand. He tossed it to her. It splashed in the water beside her, bobbing on the surface. "While you are in there, clean yourself. You look pathetic. And disgusting."

"I am not going to bathe in this pond."

"Oh, yes. Yes, you are. Or I will hold you down and do it for you." He grinned viciously. "On second thought…keep protesting. That sounds like fun."

"I'll amend my previous statement." She narrowed her eyes at him. "I'm not going to bathe in this pond with you watching."

He leaned farther back, propping himself up his elbows now, the foot he had in the water kicking idly, creating small waves. His toes were painted the same color as his fingernails. Or perhaps that was just how they grew. "Why not?"

He seemed honestly confused.

For a moment, she was confused as to how to explain it to him. "You are not going to watch me strip and bathe. It is lewd and inappropriate."

"How so?" He tilted his head to the side slightly. "Your body is your body. Clothes are merely decoration. If I want to see you naked—and believe me, I do—then what is the harm? I have no plans on molesting you." Another flash of sharp teeth. "Yet."

Her cheeks went warm, and she looked away, not wanting to see the expression on his face as he looked at her. It was hungry, it was lascivious, and it…

No.

She shook her head. "Go away. I will bathe as you command, but not with you here."

"Suit yourself."

Turning back to him, she blinked. He was gone. He had vanished into thin air. Frowning, she looked around for him, not believing it. "Hello?"

Silence.

There was no way the fae had just left. She had only just

met him, but there was no doubt in her mind that this was a game. Reaching down between her feet, she picked up a small rock that lay on the ledge she was standing on. Standing back up, she turned it over in her fingers thoughtfully for a second.

And then she threw it at the spot where Valroy had been sitting.

Smack. "Ow!"

He reappeared in a shimmer, glaring at her, rubbing a spot on his chest where she had hit him. "Violent, stinky little witch." He smirked, leaning back on his elbows again. "Good shot. I approve. Well, of the violence. Not of the smell. Now, bathe, human. Then we will eat dinner, and we can discuss the terms of our arrangement."

"What arrangement?"

"You made a wish. And this"—he gestured to the world around him—"is the price you are paying for my having granted it."

"You have not granted my wish."

"Oh, but I have. You wished for a home." He smirked. With a hand, he waved at the world about him. "Welcome to it."

"This is—no—this is not what I meant!"

"You were not specific." He sneered. "Your wish is granted. You have a contract to fulfill, and a debt to repay."

"N—no, that isn't—this—" She sputtered. "This is not fair!"

He simply laughed as she sputtered, a confident and knowing smile on his face.

"My wish was…" She was arguing with a fae. She knew better. She knew it would get her nowhere. With a whine, she pushed her wet hair away from her face. With a wavering breath, she shook her head. "You tricked me."

"I am fae." He let out a huff. "And I am a fae with no plans to sit and talk with a stinky, dirty peasant, wearing tattered clothes." He wrinkled his nose again. "It just will not do."

"Then *go away*, and I will bathe. As for the clothes, they were quite fine until you ripped them up."

"They were terrible before I put holes in them."

"No, they—" Growling in frustration, she rubbed her hand over her face. "I have nothing else to wear, and I will not strut about naked."

"A shame. Well, you could ask me for something new, if you insisted."

Clenching her fists, she glared at him. "I will not owe you favors."

"You already owe me many, by my count." He shrugged. "What's one more?"

"I—I—" She stammered for a moment, trying to find some way to argue with the smirking, smug, dangerous fae. But what could she do? There was nothing she could say. Nothing she could leverage against him. If he wanted to jump into the pond, rip her clothes off, and do whatever he wanted to her…he could.

Her cheeks went warm again, and she swore under her breath, turning away to hide her blush. She prayed to the old gods that he didn't intuit why.

"So bashful, you humans. So hung up on *nudity*." He scoffed. It was a relief that he assumed she was blushing because of the idea of being naked, not at the thought of what he could do to her.

She didn't want the image that played through in her mind.

She very much didn't want that at all.

No, not in the slightest.

What is wrong with me?

He kept talking, thankfully dragging her out of her thoughts. "You mortals paint shame upon the only physical thing you are born with. How does that make any sense?" He shook his head. "If it makes you more comfortable, I'll join you."

"No!" Taking a step back, she slipped off the rock she was on. She squeaked as she was suddenly submerged back up to her shoulders as she fell down onto a lower ledge.

Valroy cackled and lay back onto the grass, stretching his arms out. "Adorable, silly, violent, angry, foolish, stinky little witch. Bathe, and we can eat. I'm starving, and my patience is running thin."

The threat was clear.

With a wavering breath, she began to undo her bodice, unlacing it from the front. It took her a little while before she rolled up the sopping cotton fabric and tossed it to the shore. It landed on the grass with a wet slap. Her petticoat was next, laced in the back. The wool was heavy and hard to move, and it took a great deal of effort to step out of it without landing back in the water. When all she had left were her chemise and bloomers, she stepped back until she was in the water up to her shoulders.

Why she bothered, she did not know.

The water was crystal clear, even in the moonlight.

Valroy was watching her again, an unreadable expression on his face, sapphire eyes glinting under half-closed lids. For once, the seemingly ever-present cocky smile was gone. He just stared at her. Silently. Waiting.

I am about to disrobe in front of the Unseelie prince. He is doing this to demean me and mock me. This is a show of power. Nothing more.

But there was no humor on his features. He did not even leer at her. What she did see in his eyes, however, made her hesitate.

It was hunger.
It was desire.

Shutting her eyes for a moment, she steeled herself. Accepting the inevitable, she stripped naked and tossed her clothes to the shore with the rest. Her heart was racing, pounding in her ears. Tears stung the edges of her eyes as she reached for the soap that floated nearby and began to scrub herself clean. Her hands trembled, and she despised how "little" she felt.

After working the tangles out of her hair, she pulled it over her shoulders in front of her, hoping it would hide her breasts as she continued to wash the soot and soil from herself. Soap was a luxury, and bathing was not a regular routine for her.

And all the while, he *stared* at her.

Finally, she couldn't take it anymore. "What?" The word left her as a half-shout.

Jolting, he seemed surprised. "What, what?"

"Why are you staring at me?"

"You cannot be *that* naïve." He tilted his head thoughtfully. "Or can you?"

"Well—stop it."

"Stop what? Enjoying the beautiful sight before me? A maiden, bathing in the starlight? Would you have me stop appreciating you? What would you rather I do?" He sat up, bending a knee to prop his elbow on it, and his head in his hand. He studied her like she was a puzzle. "Call you a hideous cow?"

"It's not right to sit there make me do this for your amusement." She felt the tears sting harder, even as her cheeks heated. No. She would not cry!

"It isn't? Says who?" He huffed. "Besides, I'm merely forcing you to do something for your own good. You needed to bathe. And you, who are an exceptionally stubborn thing, I've discovered, would refuse to do it simply to spite me. You are acting like a child who refuses to eat because they want their dessert first. This is corrective action."

"Corrective action?" It was her turn to laugh, astonished at his ego. Although she shouldn't be surprised. "You arrogant—"

"Careful, Abigail." His tone shifted immediately, turning dark and sharp. "Remember with whom you speak."

Shutting her mouth, she looked away, taking a moment to calm down. Taking a few deep breaths, she did her best to settle her nerves and went back to scrubbing herself with the soap. "Master of the Maze. What does that mean?"

"This place you find yourself within is my kingdom within a kingdom. You are in my Maze, and you will not leave it unless I grant it."

"This is a forest."

"Mazes need not have walls. You'll learn that soon enough."

"Why did you bring me here?" She jolted in surprise as a fish brushed up against her leg. She squealed, slipped on the rock again, and nearly went under.

"Because I control this place," he replied through a chuckle. "And here, you are as safe as I wish you to be."

"As you wish me to be."

"Mmhm." The sound left him in a low growl.

The subtext was painfully clear. But she needed the axe to land. She needed to hear him say it. "What do you want from me?"

"To finish bathing, to ask me for clothes, and then to eat. We can discuss the rest then."

She fell silent. Talking to him felt like walking in the woods—terrifying and circular. Bathing in silence, she finished and tossed what remained of the soap back to him, only to watch it vanish in midair as if it were never real.

Everything she saw could be a lie. She couldn't trust her

senses—or him. What else could she rely on?

Now she was faced with an even worse prospect. She had to get out of the pond. Naked. With him watching. Clenching her fists again, she turned to him. She knew by the overly pleased expression on his face, he followed her train of thought.

With a wave of a hand, clothing appeared beside him, laid out on the grass. A bodice, a short chemise, and knickers looked more like men's clothes. "Trousers?" The question left her without thinking about it.

"The terrain in the Maze can be challenging. And besides, these seem to suit you more." He flinched as one of her little glowing orbs darted near him, coming too close for his liking. With the talon of a claw, he flicked the orb, sending it shooting across the clearing. "Stupid things…"

"It's dark."

"Hm. No, it isn't. I don't think you know what dark is, sweet one. Now, come collect your clothes, and let's be on our way." Valroy was still sitting on the ground beside the pond, right beside the clothes he was giving her.

More favors. More nails in my coffin. But if I am already buried alive, what's one more piece of iron to keep me here? Swallowing the lump in her throat, she squared her shoulders. Fine. If he wanted to embarrass her like this, there was only one thing she could do.

Face it as bravely as she could.

He was right, though she was loathe to admit it. It was only nudity. It was only nature. She clung to that in desperation.

Climbing from the pond, she focused on her steps as the water ran down her back to the source. She didn't bother to obscure her body. He had seen plenty of it already. She refused to look at him, but she could feel his sapphire gaze raking over her.

She had to walk toward him to gather up the clothes. Bracing herself, she did just that. After a moment, she was standing on the shore. When she reached down to take them, his hand darted out and caught her wrist.

"You have not asked me what I want in return for these garments."

Her heart might have actually stopped beating in her chest. Forcing herself to speak, her voice was quiet and sounded far weaker than she wanted it to. "What do you want in exchange, fae prince?"

The options were limitless.

Limitless and horrifying.

The memory of his hot breath whispering in her ear, telling her of the terrible things he would do to her as a wild beast, played through her mind.

"Say 'thank you, Valroy.'"

Finally, she looked to him in disbelief. "That is all?"

He let go of her wrist and sat back. "That is all."

She hesitated again, unsure, before muttering, "Thank you, Valroy."

"You are very welcome. Now, change. My stomach is about to devour itself in protest." He stood, humming to himself as he walked toward the path from the clearing. He ducked his head as one of her lights darted close to him again. "Damnable—"

She couldn't help but laugh. "They seem to like you."

"No, they're trying to *illuminate* me, and that's irritating." He swiped at one, knocking it away. "Dismiss them, will you?"

"I like to see where I'm going." *Illuminate you?* What an odd choice of words. It was something to dwell on later. Eagerly pulling on her new clothes, she found them surprisingly soft. The cotton was well-made, and the trousers fit her perfectly. In fact, everything did.

Save for the bodice, which felt as though it were a size too small. Frowning, she tugged on the laces, grunting a little as she pulled them tight. It forced her breasts up, and the chemise was extremely low cut.

All by his design, she had no doubt.

"You will have no need of light while you are with me, little witch. I know where we're headed, and I can see just fine in the dark."

"I would doubly like to see where I'm going in your company, Prince Valroy." She tied the bodice off and turned to him. He was leaning against the tree by the exit, his arms folded across his chest. He flicked at the orbs that darted near him like they were mosquitos. "But very well." She released her will on the floating spheres, and they blinked out like fireflies.

The starlight still bathed the clearing in pale blue light, and she found she could indeed still see.

He held a hand to her. "Come, little witch. Dinner awaits."

What choice did she have? None.

Absolutely *none*.

Exhaling sharply, she walked up to him, and hesitantly—knowing what was about to happen would be miserable—she placed her hand in his. "Oh! Wait! My shoes—"

Without warning, he yanked her toward him with such violence that she fell. She would have hit the ground, if she did not collide with him first. Her other hand pressed against his bare chest, trying to find some kind of balance, as darkness surrounded her.

Darkness, and his wings.

As the world disappeared around her, somehow folding into itself, all she could see were those dimly glowing sapphire eyes.

And all she could hear was his laugh.

CHAPTER EIGHT

Valroy unfurled his wings as they reappeared. He had taken them to a place far, far deeper in the maze. Abigail shoved against him, desperate to be free. With a faint smile, he let her go, and watched as she turned from him, staggered a few steps, wavered…and collapsed to the ground in a heap, a hand pressed to her stomach.

Huffing a laugh, he folded his wings at his back, his claws clasping his shoulders. He stepped around her as he made his way to the banquet table. "You get used to it."

All she did was groan.

Reaching the table, he looked over what had been laid out for them. For *him*, really, but there was always enough food for a guest or ten. A large roasted goose dominated the center of the surface. Picking up a silver decanter filled with red wine, he poured her a glass and took the goblet over to where she was still half-sitting, half-kneeling on the floor.

He held it down to her silently.

Amber eyes watched him in fear, as though he were a river monster who had just opened his mouth to reveal a shining jewel resting on his tongue. *Come. Reach in. I won't hurt you. I promise.*

He grinned. He knew it didn't help. "Come now, little witch…you've already lost. Might as well celebrate." He meant the words to be comforting, but it seemed they had the opposite effect. Her eyes shone with tears—*again*—and she glanced away from him.

It was a strange position he found himself in, as he suddenly came to the realization that he did not wish to see her cry. A strange position, and one he wasn't sure he liked. "No, enough of that. I have not brought you here to kill you, mutilate you, or rape you. I have brought you here to eat and talk. Come, now, little witch. Dinner awaits. Unless you prefer to eat on the floor? Is this some strange new custom that has caught me unawares?"

Her tears disappeared with a wipe of a sleeve across her face. She looked far more fetching in the clothes he had summoned for her. He did *very* much enjoy the way the bodice accentuated her…eh…assets. Now, in lieu of despair, she was looking up at him in anger.

Good.

Much more fun than grief.

She pushed up to her feet, brushed herself off, and then hesitantly took the glass of wine from his still-outstretched hand. The way she looked down at it, he wondered if he had not summoned boiling acid instead. "Is this cursed like last time?"

"Cursed!" He threw up his hands and turned from her to go to the table. "And still, despite all my warnings and best efforts, she insults me." He collapsed dramatically into the chair at the head of the table and slung a leg over the arm of it. "What am I to do with you?" Tipping his head back, he looked up at the stars overhead and finally answered her in

THE UNSEELIE PRINCE

an exacerbated sigh. "It is not cursed, little witch. It is just wine."

She fidgeted, shifting nervously on her feet, and ran her finger over the lip of the wine glass. She walked to the table, set the goblet down, and absentmindedly picked at the sleeve of her shirt as she thought. Honestly, he hadn't wanted to give her an undershirt for her bodice, but he knew she'd probably protest if he didn't. "I don't want to be compelled to —to speak, like before."

"And why not? Why should we start this path we walk on lies?"

"Because it isn't *fair*."

That made him lift his head and cock an eyebrow at her. "Twice now you've bemoaned my so-called lack of 'fairness.' Is that really the problem?" He sat forward, grinning fiendishly. "I propose we make a deal, then. I will answer your questions and you will answer mine."

"No! No more deals. No more of this—this whatever it is you're doing." She gestured at the table. "Tricking me into…I don't even know what *this* is."

Chuckling, he poured himself a glass of wine and sat back, swirling the red liquid around in the goblet. "Then go ahead, little witch. All you have to do is ask."

With a deep breath in, she shut her eyes and clearly resolved herself to hear an answer that she dreaded. "What do you want from me?"

Valroy laughed.

ABIGAIL FELT as though she were hanging from the very end of a rope over the edge of a cliff. All she had to keep from falling into the abyss was her fingernails, dug deep into the fibers, holding on for dear life.

Everything in her life was gone. She had been a fool. She had thought it had all been gone *before* the Unseelie fae arrived to prove to her how very wrong she was. And now, she found herself alone, lost, with nothing to her name save the necklace she wore. She gripped the little wooden talisman and ran her fingers over the familiar carved grooves. Her aunt would have known what to do. *Margery never would have wound up in this situation to begin with.*

"Just ask," he had said.

And she had.

And he had simply laughed. He drank the contents of his wine glass in one gulp and poured himself another. She had never seen crystal so fine. It was so thin and delicate, she worried she might snap it in her palm if she were not careful. She was glad she had been given the silver goblet instead.

"Sit. Eat." He gestured at the table with one of the talons of his wings. He had unfurled them when he sat—she imagined so that he didn't sit on them—and now they draped over the chair like the rest of him. Casually. "Then I'll answer your question."

"And if I don't?"

"I won't let my new toy starve to death. That'd ruin the fun. I've never force-fed a mortal before, but I imagine it would be rather hysterical."

Picking up the only other chair sat at the table, she moved it farther away from Valroy. Taking a seat, she yelped as he hooked the leg of her chair with his foot and dragged her back to where it had been.

"Are you going to stab me, little witch?"

Looking down, she hadn't even realized she had plucked up a steak knife from the table and was now clutching it in her hand. "Maybe."

He laughed again, watching her as if she were an adorable

child. His wine glass was now held between the sharp tips of the claw of one of his wings, the points so sharp they were nearly invisible.

"Where's the sword I was given?" She put down the knife slowly.

"At the end of the table."

"And my shoes?"

"Not needed." He shrugged. "You're fine without them."

"I'd prefer to have a pair, if it's all the same to you."

"What are you willing to trade for them?" He smirked. "A kiss, perhaps?" When she made a face, he howled in laugher. "Oh, we have a lot of work to do, you and I." He finished his second glass of wine in a flourish and scooped up the silver decanter to refill it for a third time. He put it down on the table in front of her.

For the first time, she had a moment to examine where she was. The table was enormous, overflowing with every kind of food she could imagine, she figured it could easily sit fifty people. There were only two, however. One armchair that sat at the head that could have easily been a throne, with how elaborately the wood was carved, and a smaller, far less decorative chair directly to the left.

The throne was currently occupied by the fae, who was still watching her with a fiendish, hungry expression. She wondered if it wouldn't be long before she was in place of the goose, roasted and plopped on the white lace tablecloth.

The table was set down on a marble floor, in alternating patterns of black and white. The floor transitioned back to the forest, and she wasn't sure which was trying to overgrow which—was the grass trying to overtake the marble, or the marble overtake the grass?

There were no walls around her, save for one. It looked like the ruins of an old castle or church, the stones overgrown with moss and vines. Trees surrounded them on all sides, and she couldn't see a path leading to, or from, the strange place she found herself. She could hear crickets chirping in the distance, and occasionally the louder shrill call of a summer beetle.

The stars were bright overhead, and now the moon had come to join it. It was huge—much larger than it should have been. The shadows the moon cast were sharp and crisp. It seemed the strange smoky haze that overtook the sky during the daylight hours was not there at night.

Her stomach growled loudly. She wanted to ignore the feast before her, but her empty stomach had other plans. It all smelled *amazing.*

She furrowed her brow.

There, stamped on the side of the intricate silver decanter in front of her, was a cross and several rows of Latin scripture. "Is that…?" She glanced down at her plate. It matched. Glancing down the table, she saw it was all the same. Bowls and plates, silver goblets, small trays…it all looked intricately marked and oddly made for a specific use that was *not* sitting on a banquet table. "Is this…is all this communion silver?"

"Hm? Oh. Probably." He shrugged. "I thought they were interesting."

"How did you get them?"

"Same way I get everything I want from the human world." His voice dipped low, turning into a purr. "I stole it."

The way he said it made her break out in bumps, a shiver running down her spine. Damn him. Damn him to the pits. Her face went warm, and she found herself eagerly reaching for the wine. The wine that would likely lure her into telling him precisely everything he wanted to know, either by magical or conventional means, it did not matter.

What was the use in fighting him?

He could easily overpower her—let alone the charms she knew he could place on her. She sighed. "But why steal communion silver? I doubt you have any use for its value."

"None. I have enough gold and silver and jewels to entertain me for as long as I wish. And they don't—entertain me, that is. I find them quite dull, all things considered. No, I enjoy the artistry of them. The careful hand that was required to make something so lovely."

"You enjoy human art?"

"Mmhm. I have quite the collection. I'll show it to you someday soon." He gestured lazily at the goose and the trays of food before her. "Stop stalling, mortal. Eat."

There was no point in being stubborn. Refusing to eat would just harm her, not him. And whatever magic he'd put in the food was magic he could cast on her anyway. With a beleaguered, tired grunt, she began to serve herself dinner. Mashed potatoes, carrots, bread, cheese, and a large slice of goose. It felt so strange to place them on holy silver. She wasn't Christian—not by any stretch—but it still felt odd.

Looking down at her food, she picked up the silver knife and fork and began to eat. The noise she made as it touched her tongue was not one she intended to make, but there was no helping it. The food was incredible, and she was starving.

He smiled. At least he didn't mock her for it. He reached out the talon of one of his wings, and she watched in matched horror and fascination as he ripped a leg off the goose with a *crunch* and brought it back to him. Taking it in his hand, he bit off a portion of it, eating it straight off the bone.

They ate in silence for a while, before she could take it no longer. "You haven't answered my question."

"Ah. Yes. Right. What do I want from you. That was it, yes?"

"Yes."

He grinned. "What will you give me for the answer?"

"You told me to just ask you."

"I did. And you did. It doesn't mean I'll answer. I simply said, 'ask me.' I never said, 'ask me and I'll tell you.'"

He was going to give her a headache. She pinched the bridge of her nose and struggled with the urge to scream at him, leap over the table, and attempt to stab him with her dinner fork. "Whatever you want from me, you can steal it, just like the communion silver."

"I could, yes."

"Then, why not?"

"Are you asking me to ravage you, sweet one?"

"No! I—"

He laughed. "I never would have guessed you to be such a deviant. What a wonderful surprise." He hummed thoughtfully. "Should I have served wild boar tonight?"

"No!" Her cheeks felt like they were on fire. She felt as if she had burst into flames. "That is not what I meant."

"Then say what you *mean,* dear. Words have power everywhere, but nowhere more so than here in Tir n'Aill. You must learn to be more careful." He stretched out in the chair, leg still draped over the arm of it, chewing away on his goose leg. The chair itself was a depiction of a hunt, animals and creatures running in fear from wolves with sharp teeth poised and ready to rip the prey to shreds. And behind them, human hunters on horseback, ready to do the same to the wolves. Another stolen artifact, she assumed.

She measured her thoughts for a moment, carefully choosing her words. "If you can simply take what you want from me—whatever it is—I don't understand why it is you've restrained yourself. You certainly seem to be a creature of excess."

"Better." He tilted his head and studied her for a moment,

dark blue hair falling in tendrils over his sharp features. "It's true. I am. And I could." He took a gulp of his wine, passing it back to the claw. "I am feeling generous tonight. Very well. What do I want with you, my prickly little witch? My games with you are twofold. The first I hope I have made *painfully* clear to you by now. Even you cannot be that dense."

Her cheeks went hot again. "Yes. That much I've gathered."

"Good."

"And the second?"

"I think I'll keep that a secret for now."

"You just said—"

"I told you half."

"But I already knew half!"

"That's not my fault."

Growling in rage, she shut her eyes and put her hand over them. She prayed to the old gods for patience. Or to strike her dead. Either would be preferable at the moment. And still, the fiend sat there, chuckling in enjoyment, watching her like a far-too-pleased-with-itself tomcat.

"That *look*," he hissed in mock pain. "I think I love it. Will you glare at me like that when I rut you, I wonder? Or will you make those savory little noises like you did before?" He sipped his wine. "I do hope it's both."

She wanted to crawl under the table. Hearing him talk like that made her more uncomfortable than him watching her bathe. No. Not uncomfortable. Anxious.

And it was a strange, unwelcome kind of nervousness that twisted in her stomach.

She shifted in her chair, covering it by reaching for the bread to fetch herself another piece. "You are a cur."

"Like father, like son, I suppose."

"You said your mother was the Morrigan." *I'm not sure I believe it, but very well.* "Who is your father?"

"A demon. A fallen archangel, in fact. I am bred from royalty and gods." He gestured idly at his wings. "We fae are not all so gifted." His gesture trailed south along his body. She looked away before he finished his path. "In more ways than one."

"The Unseelie do not have wings?"

"Oh, many do. But I, in all ways, am uniquely superior among us."

"Including your ego."

He laughed, seemingly unoffended by her jab. "She finally bites back. Good!"

"I thought you hated being insulted." She ate more of the food as they talked. By the old gods, it was glorious. She had to pace herself, lest she devour half the table in her hunger.

"I am only offended when it means I can get something out of it." He picked up a piece of bread as well and began pulling it apart, eating it in small chunks. "But I still haven't answered your question, have I?"

"No. I have given up hope."

That made him chuckle again. "Why don't I force you over this table and take you? I could pin you down easily—you're no match for me. Why don't I force those slender legs apart, and plow you like you humans do to the fields? Why don't I place you under my spell, and make you love me? Make you fall to your knees right here before me, and worship me with your tongue? Is that what you're asking?"

He was trying to kill her now, she was certain. Her face must be the color of the strawberries she saw on a tray nearby. She stared dead ahead at the communion silver. "Why must you speak like that?"

"Because I think you might burst if I continue. My goodness, it's fun to watch you struggle. Are you picturing my words in your head, wondering what it might be like? I think you are. I bet you are imagining yourself spread out upon my table like the feast that you are, the sensation of my tongue delv—"

"Stop it! Please, Prince Valroy. Please, stop it."

He let out a sigh. "Fine. Because you asked nicely." A wry expression came over him again. "Even if you did not deny it."

I am beginning to dislike him deeply.

He continued, thankfully oblivious to her thoughts. "Why do I not take what I wish, though? The joy of the hunt. While I'll enjoy devouring my meal, I want you to run. I want you to run, so that I might catch you."

Gods, help me, please—"I asked you to stop!"

Laughing, his sapphire eyes twinkled in amusement as he watched her. "I did! That one is entirely your own fault. What are you dreaming of?"

"Nothing."

"Mmhmm." It was clear he didn't believe it.

The reality of her situation was becoming clear, and it filled her with dread and that strange anxiety once more. Luckily for her, the dread readily won. "You have put me in this enchanted Maze of yours, so that you might hunt me, both for your first goal and for the second, which is still a mystery. You wish me to wander about like a lost lamb so that you can play the wolf."

"I won't need to *play* the wolf, trust me." He lowered his voice to a murmur. "Or the boar."

She fastidiously ignored him. "And what if I said—very well, get it over with. What if I said I did not wish to play your game? I understand I am your prisoner, and there is nothing I can do to free myself, and this whole 'granting my wish' lie was merely that, and—"

"Ah, ah!" He waved his hand to stop her. "Slow down. First of all, if you are offering to bend over the table or crawl beneath it to sit between my legs, by all means. Do so. I will *not* complain, but it is not the same. I seek your surrender. And second, your wish was granted. This is the cost of your wish."

"I asked for a home. And now I am to be hunted."

"Yes."

"Until I—what do you mean, you seek my surrender?"

He smirked. "My hunt is complete the moment you *want* me to catch you…"

She wondered if her cheeks would ever cool again. "If—"

"When."

"If—" she reiterated firmly. He grinned into his wine glass. "I surrender, then what?"

"Mmh, good question." His voice was that dusky, rumbling purr again. *"When* you surrender your throat to the wolf, and beg him to devour you…" He grinned. "I will give you a gift." He dipped a finger into his wine. With a slow, sinful, and incredibly inappropriate slide of his tongue, licked the liquid from it. "And it will be far grander than a pair of clothes. I will take good care of you, Abigail Moore."

There it was. "No. I do not accept this. You did not grant my wish. You willfully misinterpreted my words. When I made that wish, I did not mean that I wanted to have a home here as your pet."

"Hardly my fault you did not specify the 'where,' 'what,' and 'how' of your new residence." He gestured a hand aimlessly. "Humans. You really do need to make your wishes more carefully."

"I will not—I do not accept this!" She slammed her palm down on the table, rattling the silver and glassware. "You are not dealing in good faith, Prince Valroy. You are a con."

That darkened his expression. The mirth left him, leaving only coldness and danger. "Am I?"

She didn't allow herself to hesitate, even if it meant he'd rip her throat out. It was likely to happen sooner rather than later, anyway. "You have manipulated and twisted my words, my intentions, and my actions. You understood the meaning behind my wish, and you choose to ignore it. Claiming I did not pick my words more carefully is just the crutch of a man who does not wish to deal fairly. I wish to renounce my wish."

"It is far too late for that. A wish granted is a deal struck." He tilted his head back, watching her intently from lidded, sapphire eyes. "But you want a new arrangement, hm?"

"Yes."

Silence. He stared at her, and she played out every possible ending in her head. One where he ripped her clothes off and brutalized her. One where he placed her under a spell, and she was helpless to watch as she worshipped him like he threatened. And a third where he ripped her to shreds and drank her blood.

But what he did surprised her. He smiled. "Very well."

She learned to breathe again.

"Consider your debt canceled. But…in exchange for a wager. Our new arrangement is thus, little witch. You will attempt to solve my Maze. If you do, you will be free to return to the human world. I will send you with as much gold and silver as you could ever possibly need. You will find it's easy for a human to find a place to live when they are rich."

She had no doubt about that. "And if I don't? If I fail?"

"Then you're mine…for all eternity."

This is still a trick. He still has the upper hand. I'm trapped in a world of magic I can barely even grasp. The odds of my survival, let alone my success, are slim to none.

But I have no other choice, do I?

She reached her hand over the table to him. "Deal."

He took her hand in his and sat forward to lean his head down and kiss the back of her knuckles. The gesture was slow, and far too sensual for her comfort. When he parted, those dimly glowing eyes flicked to hers, and there was nothing but sin within them. With three words, the board was set.

"Let us begin."

CHAPTER NINE

Valroy stood from the table. All things considered, he was feeling quite pleased with himself. Abigail was certainly proving to be entertaining. It was clear that she was terrified of him—as she should be—but there was a defiance in her eyes that was utterly wonderful.

There was a small, tiny, insignificant, but blossoming bud of *respect* for her that had infested him already. Or perhaps respect was the wrong word. Appreciation, perhaps? Amusement, most definitely.

There was someone hiding behind that fear, begging to lash out at him. He could see it in the way she held her head up high as he watched her step naked from the pond. He saw it again when she declared that there was to be a new arrangement. He could have said *no*, of course...he was Master of the Maze, and she was his prisoner. But what was life without a little entertainment?

What could she become, he wondered? If he tore away her humanity and made her a fae like them, what would she become? *No. That is not my goal. That is not her purpose. There is but one thing I need from her, and that is not it.*

Two. Two things I need.

He caught himself staring at her cleavage again.

He wanted to see her fire. He wanted to see what she could do when she was angry. Already the wheels were clicking around in his head, like the bizarre, notched copper disks of the human "clock" he had stolen.

There were several paths before him, and many ways he could play this game with her. Each one led to a different end. Most ended in her death. Either she would die by his hand, by those of a stranger, or by time itself.

Death at his hands was the most likely, to be fair.

Little witch. Little doe. You don't belong here. You fit into my clockwork in exactly one way. He chuckled, and she raised an eyebrow at him, unsure as to why he was just standing there, staring at her in silence. He didn't care. Let her wonder.

Pretty thing, she was. He had wanted her since the moment he saw her. Now having seen her fully, he was even more intrigued. A pity she could not breed—her hips were begging to be grabbed and squeezed. As were the rest of her ample curves. She had more than enough for him to play with—more than enough for him to dig his claws into and drag her where he wanted. She was half his size in frame, and miniscule in comparison when it came to strength.

He wanted to have her.

He wanted to *destroy* her.

He wanted to make her realize that the boar would have been the gentler night.

There was nothing in his way. She was his, after all. She even said it herself—he could place her under a spell or simply use brute force to have what he wanted.

Yet he was never able to resist a good game, was he? He did ever so much love to see what would happen *if.* If he did this, if he did that, if he let this happen—how would it play out?

Besides, pleasure was so much more meaningful when it was denied before finally being...released.

Abigail did not like the way Valroy was staring at her. Drinking the rest of her wine, she picked up a butter roll from the table and stood. She walked away from him, down the length of the table to where she saw the rusted, always-damp sword lying on the lace surface.

It was then that she realized her predicament. She had no way of carrying the sword that wasn't in her hand. Looking down the table, she saw Valroy still sitting there, *staring* at her.

"Might I have a belt?"

The unexpected question clearly jarred him out of his thoughts. He furrowed his brow. "Pardon me?"

Picking up the sword, she mimed sheathing it at her side. "A belt."

He opened his mouth for a moment, paused, shut it, and then grinned. "What do I get in exchange?"

"Never mind." Letting out a long sigh, she put the sword back down and began searching for something she could use instead. The linen napkins were too short—though she could tie them together, she supposed.

Shoving the roll between her teeth, she picked up a steak knife and began to cut a strip off the bottom edge of the tablecloth. The fabric tore easily.

"What do you think you're doing?"

All she gave him was a glare, roll still between her teeth. She kept cutting the lace until she had a long enough strip, and then put the knife back on the table. Twisting the lace between her hands, she kept going until it was tightly wound.

"You've ruined my tablecloth. More insults, I see." He

huffed. "Such disrespect. I should have you lashed for this." But the tone in his voice didn't match his words, so she felt no need to stop.

Wrapping the twisted lace around her waist, she tied it off in a bow. Picking up the rusted, dripping sword, she slipped it into her makeshift belt, careful not to slice the delicate fabric with the edge of the very sharp blade.

Plucking the roll from her teeth, she took a bite out of it, chewed, and, smiling at him, shrugged.

The fae stood and walked to her slowly, his movements painfully graceful. It was a perfect reminder of his predatory constitution. His voice was a low rumble as he stalked up to her. "You should apologize."

It took every ounce of her strength not to shrink away from him. "No."

An arch to a thin eyebrow. By all the gods, he was *beautiful*. She quickly pushed those thoughts away as he stepped closer to her, forcing her to take another back. "Apologize."

"No."

The word left her far quieter than she had intended. She squared her shoulders and vowed silently to stand her ground. He stepped forward.

She stepped back. *Damn it!*

A step to the side, another one forward, and she found herself backed up against the edge of the table. She hit it with such force that it rattled the glasses and silverware. She moved to duck around him.

A large wing snapped open, blocking her path. She tried to go left instead. Another wing blocked her. "Stop it. Let me go."

"No," he replied with a smirk, mocking her previous answers. Slowly, smoothly, taking his sweet time, he stepped into her.

Oh, gods. Oh, gods, help me. She gripped the edge of the

tabletop, leaning back, trying to keep as much distance as possible between them. But it was useless. The long length of his thigh pressed against hers. The claws of his wings gripped the table, so close she could feel the warmth from them against her skin.

She could feel all of his warmth against her.

All of it.

Her cheeks went hot as he leaned in closer, forcing her to arch backward. He smelled like the night itself. Like the breeze that would come through the cottage window as the sunlight faded. Of dewy grass and deep woods. He continued to tilt nearer, and soon she couldn't arch backward any farther without falling onto the table.

"Apologize." He lowered his head to hers, his hot breath washing over her cheek. Gods, she could feel the reverberation of his deep voice.

She turned her head away from him. "No." It was a whisper. She was trembling.

A hand took hold of her throat, thumb against her jawline, and forced her to look at him. Her eyes went wide, feeling the points of his sharp nails digging into her skin. He did not squeeze, but if he meant to kill her, he could do so effortlessly. She knew he was strong enough to snap her neck without trying.

When his lips grazed over her skin, wandering slowly to her ear, thoughts and images of death were not what spun through her mind.

"Apologize," he murmured, "and I will forgive you for everything."

"I will not apologize to you. Not now, not ever, not for anything…" Damn her for her quivering! She hated it. She hated how little she felt, how powerless she was. All she had was her will against his, and she clung to it like a blanket in a storm. *Until he uses his magic to take that away from me, too.*

Tendrils of dark blue hair brushed against her cheek. She could feel his lips moving against her skin. "Is that a promise? Is that a vow?"

Her breath caught, and she said the word more as an exhale than anything else. "Yes."

Lips pressed to her cheek then, just at the hollow of her ear, and it felt like something crawled over her, sharp and intense. For a moment, she thought it was his magic. But as it settled in her, low and smoldering, she knew he wasn't to blame. She was. When he pulled back just far enough to watch her, forcing her head to turn to him, she knew her face must be crimson.

All she could see was *him*. All she could feel was *him*. He was so total in her presence, she found herself lost staring into those bright blue eyes that flickered with so many dark emotions, she didn't even know how to name them all.

Then he smiled. "Good." His gaze flicked to her lips, slightly parted as they were, as she desperately tried to fill her lungs with air.

She waited for him to kiss her. *Gods below, please don't make me do this! Don't make me want—*He was suddenly gone. The presence that had been so overwhelming was missing in the blink of an eye.

Laughter filled the air, coming from everywhere and nowhere. "Look at you! I think you were just about to kiss me, insolent witch."

"I've moved up the ranks, have I?" She ran a hand over her face, muttering obscenities to herself, all entirely directed at him. "Charming."

More laughter. When the sound of stones, sliding and rumbling, filled the air, she jumped and whirled. The wall behind her that resembled the overgrown ruins of some ancient church began to shift. She watched in awe as the stones moved and rearranged themselves, fitting back together to form…a door.

A door to a place that didn't match where she stood. Turning about, she took in the forest around her. Dark trees, arching high into the night sky, stood as silhouettes against the glowing stars and overly large crescent moon. The grass that surrounded the two-tone marble floor was dark green, nearly blue-black in appearance.

But through that doorway?

Nothing matched.

The grass was yellowed from chilly weather. The moonlight was twice as bright, lighting up the world enough that she could see the leaves were amber, red, and brown. Some branches were bare, and a covering of fallen leaves coated the wide path.

"Go on." His voice came from behind her. She whirled, but he was nowhere to be seen. "Go," he repeated, "and let's begin our game. Solve my Maze, insolent witch, and you'll be free. Fail…and you're mine."

Stepping around the table, she picked up another roll. They were good. Besides, who knew when she would get a chance to eat again? She heard him chuckle as she did, but she ignored it. Clearly, her desperate attempts to survive were deeply amusing.

It was just another reason she hated him.

Yes. She hated him. It was decided.

But he's right. I was about to—

No, she hated him.

Standing in front of the doorway, she peered into the strange new forest. A full moon hung in the sky, easily twice the size it should be. It was amber, a harvest moon. But what —or who—was the harvest? *It's me, isn't it?*

A hand fell on her shoulder from behind, causing her to nearly jump out of her skin. "Oh. One more thing to note."

He was at her back, his other hand on her hip, gripping it tight. She couldn't turn to face him. "You are no longer under my protection. Any creature in my Maze who sees fit to make a meal out of you…may do so. But call my name, and I will be there to save you as you *surrender* to me. We'll see how far your defiance takes you."

He shoved her. Hard. She staggered forward, barely able to keep her feet under herself. The momentum took her through the doorway into the strange other forest. The feeling of marble beneath her bare feet gave way to cool leaves. The moment she was no longer in risk of falling over, she whipped around to face the door.

But it was gone.

Only the same wider, far clearer path, stretching as far as she could see into the darkness.

Swallowing the lump in her throat, she turned slowly in a circle, taking in her new surroundings. She was trapped, wandering around a world in which everything wanted to kill her…or worse.

With a long exhale, she shook her head and began to walk down the path, her hand resting on the hilt of her rusted sword.

Solve the Maze.

That was what she had to do.

Too bad she didn't stand a chance. Too bad she had to try anyway.

What other choice did she have?

CHAPTER TEN

More walking.
Great.

With a sigh, Abigail continued to bemoan the ache in her feet. Having been able to sit for a small time had been nice—even if her company had been less so. Her stomach was no longer growling, begging for food, but now she had a new problem to replace it.

She was exhausted.

She wasn't sure how long it had been since she had slept. The travel of the "sun" and the "moon" seemed to be arbitrary, sometimes moving faster or slower than before. The full moon in the sky in this strange autumn forest raced up to the center, and then stayed there for what must have been hours, before slowly starting its trek back to the horizon.

In the same direction it had come from.

This place is strange, and I do not think I like it.

It was beautiful, even if it was bizarre and dangerous. The world around her was simply that—gorgeous. Amber leaves fell from the trees, drifting down in delicate paths like snow.

It didn't even seem like the leaves were collecting on the ground or that the number of leaves in the trees were decreasing. It was simply snowing leaves, because that was what it wanted to do.

It.

She shivered.

Stunning as her surroundings were, she was starting to feel what it really was—a dangerous thing, ready to eat her. Filled with things that were ready to eat her. And packed with trees that *watched* her. There was always a soul to a forest. She believed deeply in the power of the natural world. But this was different. She had never been stared at by trees before.

As she walked down the dirt path, she began to pick up pebbles and rocks as she walked. She needed seven of them, each one around the same size. It took her a few hours, but she finally had what she needed. She began searching for a place to make "camp."

With no fire. Or bedroll. Or anything besides what she was carrying. She glanced down at the sword that hung at her side. It had left a wet mark on her trousers that was the exact shape of the blade.

Why was it always somehow *soggy?* She wouldn't bemoan it too much, though, as it was a sword and her only defense. She wasn't going to look down on it, even if it meant her leg was wet. *Don't look a gift horse in the mouth, and don't be annoyed at a gift sword for being damp.*

But there was one thing she had no problem complaining about, if only in her head and in her quiet grumblings. *I don't even have shoes thanks to that bastard.* Yes, sure, fine, he gave her new clothes and gave her dinner. But it was because of him that she was trapped here.

It was because of him that she was either going to die or

become his *pet*. She honestly didn't know which was worse. With a sigh, she rubbed her hand over her face. "I could've just let him rut me as a boar, and I wouldn't be in this mess."

Something laughed from behind her. She whirled but saw no one there. "Hello?" It didn't sound like before—like a sea of giggles. This one was singular, louder, and close. "Who's there?"

"Yes."

The voice belonged to a creature that stepped from the shadows of the moonlit trees. No—not a creature. A *monster*. Terror caught in Abigail's throat as she staggered back from the thing that walked toward her on four legs.

On four very long, painfully thin legs. Or arms, perhaps. The distinction wasn't terribly important at the moment. She would think it was a man walking on stilts, like she had seen once at a carnival, if not for the fact that it was entirely made out of bone.

Bones that looked human…but were combined together in nonsensical ways. It was as though someone else had taken up pieces of human remains and put them together to create it. She saw jawbones in its shoulders, ribs along its long and terrible limbs, and a skull served as part of its hip.

Its head was one single skull, at least. It stared at her from eyeless sockets as it moved along the path toward her, both graceful and stilted like a spider.

Dropping the pebbles she carried in her palm, she pulled the sword from her lace belt and held it aloft. "Don't come any closer!"

The monster stopped. It tilted its head to the side slowly, the sound of bone rubbing on bone, as it studied her. "I mean you no harm."

I don't believe you. "What are you?"

"I have no name…" It lowered its head, its voice mournful. "I want to have a name." Again came the terrible sound of bone sliding upon bone. She could hear it better and better as the thing took more steps toward her, unafraid of her sword.

She swung the blade at it. "No! Don't come near me." She didn't know how to fight. She had no idea what she was doing. But she had a sword, and there was a monster, and by the gods she was going to stab it if she needed to. Or she was going to try. Whichever.

It leaned back on its hind legs. "I do not want to hurt you. I do not eat mortal flesh. I have no use for it." It picked up one of its front arms, the hands made of bits of bone that she couldn't identify, but she knew they had no business being where they were. It gestured at its stomach—or where one would be. There was only an empty cavity made of ribs that were not ribs at all but thigh bones. How they were strung together, she didn't know.

"Then what do you want?" She did her best to sound firm.

"To see the newest human Valroy has brought us. To see if you are kind. I am in such need of kindness." It hung its head again. "Look at me...look at what they have done to me. I was a mortal once, just like you."

"Or several, by the looks of things." She tightened her grip on the sword. It dripped dewy water to the ground beneath it.

"Maybe." It chuckled. "Most certainly." Was it a man? She couldn't tell by the voice. It was both high and low pitched in unison, as if it had more than one voice.

"I—I am sorry for your suffering." She took a step away from it, and it took another step forward. Why was everything here always *stalking* her?

"Thank you. You are the first to say that to me. You are the first to show me kindness. Maybe we can be friends." Its tone became singsong and strange, lilting a bit, as it stepped toward her again. It was taller than she was, looming up over her. "Can we? Can we, please? Let us be friends."

Fear crawled up her spine as she backed up again, refusing to let the thing come too close to her. "I—" She didn't know what to say. Refusing its offer of friendship would mean insulting it, and that could be potentially dangerous. But accepting its offer could be equally so. "What constitutes friendship to you?"

"You will name me. I will be your friend. We can be together. The Maze is a dangerous place, and once you name me, all will be well."

That last phrase sent a chill up her spine again. "Once I name you, all will be well."

"Yes! Name us. Name us, *please.*" It fidgeted, shifting its weight from leg to leg, as if in giddy anticipation. "Will you? Please, please say you will. Name us now!"

"I—no—" She took a step back and glanced behind her to see if she had a clean method of escape. She would run like a fool if she needed to.

"Name us. Name us and we can be friends."

"And what happens if I name you?" She gripped her sword tighter. "What will happen to me if I name you?"

"We will be friends!" It jumped forward at her, as if to attack her, and that was enough for her.

It wasn't dignified. It certainly wasn't brave. But she turned on her heel and ran as fast as she could down the path.

"Come back! Come back! Name us! Name us!" The creature was screaming behind her, its voice now a chorus of dozens. "Friend, come back!"

Something heavy hit her from behind, and she impacted the dirt at full speed. She grunted in pain, feeling the rocks and pebbles rip and scrape at her. She managed to not land on her sword, nor smash her head into the dirt. That was the reason she was able to roll on her back just as the thing pinned her down with a large, bony hand made of teeth and ribs pressed against her shoulder.

"Name us! Your troubles will be over. No more running. No more fear. The Maze is a dangerous place, and this is the kindest fate. Name us…name us *now.*" The skull peered down at her, sightless as it was. Its grip on her shoulder tightened, digging in until it hurt. And then it said what she had suspected had been true. "Name us. Join us. You will be safe."

She thrust upward with the sword with all her strength. She went for the creature's head, shoving the sword up through its jaw and into the empty skull. She didn't know if stabbing a creature made of bones would do any good, but what else was she to do?

It shrieked. The sound that came from it made her ears ring. She dug the sword in deeper, ramming the deceptively sharp blade through the brittle bones of its skull.

The sound abruptly stopped. And then…the creature collapsed. It fell around her in a thousand human bones and teeth. She covered her face as best she could, but it still pelted her. Frantically scrambling out of the pile, she staggered a few steps away before her legs gave out on her, and she collapsed once more to the ground.

There, in the middle of the path, was a pile of human bones. But at least it wasn't moving…at least it wasn't chasing her. *Did I kill it?* She still clenched her sword tightly in her hand, not trusting her victory. Her heart was pounding in her ears, drowning out the sound of the crickets around her.

But not the sound of slow clapping.

Shooting back up to her feet, she tried to ignore all the pain in her body. The cuts on her arms and her knees from falling. The bruises. The pain in the soles of her feet. Her exhaustion. She turned toward the sound of the noise, gripping the sword once more in both hands.

She expected Valroy.

That was not who was standing there, leaning against the tree beside her. Standing there was a man dressed in rags. He matched her height, perhaps slightly shorter than average for a man. He was painfully thin. She could count his ribs from beneath the tattered and ragged remains of clothing that he wore. But as she studied him closer, she realized it wasn't just rags. There was fishing net and seaweed mixed in. He wore clothing and flotsam.

And the man was soaking wet. His hair was unevenly cut, as if he sheared it himself with a dull blade, and dark green. The eyes that watched her were black from rim to rim. His skin was sallow and pale, and his lips were stained a dark blue, as if in death. Despite his rail-thin appearance, she knew he could easily overpower her.

Another Unseelie.

Shite.

He eyed her for a moment, before smiling. It was an altogether unfriendly expression. "I see you're making good use of my sword."

"O—oh." She lowered it a few inches, and then realizing how pointless it was to threaten a man with his own sword—especially since she couldn't stand up to an Unseelie in a fight—she dropped her hand to her side. She wouldn't put it back in her lace belt just yet, however. "Forgive me."

"Hm. I startled you. It's fine." His teeth looked razor sharp, like those of a dogfish. They were distinctly inhuman. He glanced at the pile of bones. "You killed a Nameless."

"It…picked the fight with me. I wanted nothing to do with it." She would not apologize for defending herself.

The Unseelie laughed, revealing more rows of those

sharp teeth of his. "It wasn't an accusation. Just a statement. I'm mildly impressed."

Mildly. She took a step away from the Unseelie and winced as her foot touched a sharp rock. She picked up her foot and glanced down at it. She had a pretty decent cut. She'd need to find a way to clean the wound. "Thank you."

"Poor human. You're lucky. The Nameless are insidious, but weak." The Unseelie pushed away from the tree to walk to the pile of bones. He reached down and plucked up what remained of its skull. She had split it in two. "What did you think would happen if you gave it a name?"

"It would have consumed me. Made me part of itself." She winced. "That's why it has so many parts, isn't it?"

"Good. You're correct. You aren't an idiot like I thought." He dropped the skull back into the pile and wiped his hands together. "Trust your instincts, girl, and you might survive a week."

Now she was the one who felt insulted. She kept it to herself. "Thank you?"

He chuckled again, and then let out a long sigh, his humor fading. "My name is Anfar."

"Abigail."

"I know."

She tried not to roll her eyes. *I think I dislike the fae.* "Thank you for the sword. I have a feeling I will need it again."

"I hope you don't, because you are useless with it. Anything with any will to live could destroy you. If you are a witch as the Bloody Prince says, then I suggest you protect yourself a different way."

Why was she even more insulted than she was before? He was right. She *was* useless with a blade, and the sword *was* going to do her no good if she faced off with a creature who knew how to fight. She just didn't like having her face rubbed in it. Speaking of her face, she touched her fingers to her cheek and watched as it came away stained with blood. It wasn't bad, but it was definitely a good scrape.

Fantastic. Just fantastic.

"I doubt making trinkets and charms will do me any good. I was going to sleep in a protection circle, but I was interrupted by that…thing."

"Try. You may be surprised. Or perhaps you will not be. We shall see." He sniffed dismissively as he stared down at the pile of bones. "If another one happens upon you, heed my warning—do not call them anything at all. Not even 'it' or 'they' or 'the Nameless.' Anything will suit them." He nudged the pile with his foot. He was wearing boots, but they—like the rest of him—looked as though they had come from the bottom of the ocean.

She had heard tales of stranded sailors washing ashore on shattered masts, starved and half-crazed from the sun and saltwater. That was what Anfar resembled. She stayed silent, not knowing what to say to him.

He reached down and plucked something from the mass of bones. It was a black stone, about the size of her fist. He turned it over in his hand thoughtfully. "They were once human, like it said. The Maze stripped everything from them —their humanity, their mortality, their individuality. It could happen to you. You might lie down one night to sleep, and waken as a fleshless, empty corpse." He pocketed the stone. "I recommend you try very hard not to let that happen."

"I will do my best." She grimaced at the idea of being like that poor thing. She loathed to take any life, but perhaps its death had been a mercy.

"And we shall see what your 'best' is. I hope it improves from here." Those unnerving black eyes fixed on her.

"I—" She stopped talking as he began to walk away from her. He went ten paces before a strange black inky pool of water appeared before him. It shone in the moonlight, iridescent and swirling like spilled oil.

He dove into it headfirst and disappeared beneath the surface of the "water." A moment after he was gone, the pool shrank until it was simply gone.

I do not think I like the Unseelie at all.

CHAPTER ELEVEN

Abigail was growing very sick of walking.

Yet she knew that was going to be her new lot in life. At least for as long as it lasted. With a long sigh, she looked up at the sun overhead. The too-large moon had finally set, budging from where it seemed to hang in one spot for far too long. The haze had returned to the sky, as if the world itself had deemed that the sun should not shine on the Maze.

Or perhaps the Maze itself was responsible.

The sallow and pale sunlight that made its way through the leaves was barely useful in lighting her way as she walked down the path, rusted-and-damp sword tucked back into her makeshift silk belt.

Now that she had met the creature responsible for the blade, she understood why it was constantly sodden. Anfar wasn't nearly as infuriating as Valroy, although he was just as unnerving.

And likely just as murderous.

Marcus. She shook her head. Poor Marcus. Even though

he had abandoned her, even though he had sold the house out from under her and condemned her to a future of living upon the streets, she hadn't hated him. She understood why he was unhappy and why he had left for more *fertile* fields.

She mourned him.

But perhaps she mourned him in the way she mourned all lost life.

She could only hope that Valroy had lied—that his magic couldn't reach as far as the Americas, and that her estranged husband had escaped safely. They were the wishes of a child, holding on to a flower in a field, praying the petals might appease the gods.

Marcus was dead. She had felt it as it happened, as Valroy destroyed the candle of life that she had made.

Marcus was dead, and she was to blame. It had been her magic that had given Valroy a link to the man, and it was her foolishness that had allowed the Unseelie access to such a thing. This was her fault. All of it was *her fault.*

Tears stung her eyes, and she bit them back. No. She would not cry. She was simply exhausted, scared, and trapped in the *gods-damned Otherworld,* stuck equally within a game with a bloodthirsty Unseelie prince.

Oddly enough, it made her laugh. There was something truly ludicrous about the whole situation. "I need to sleep," she muttered to herself as her laughter faded. She hadn't been able to find any more suitable rocks since she left the pile of bones that had once been the Nameless creature who had wished to hurt her.

She stopped abruptly as movement on the path ahead caught her eye. She froze, terrified that it might be another awful monster come to eat her. If it were some manner of terrible beast who wished her dead…at least it didn't look nearly so revolting as the Nameless thing. She let out a breath that was equal parts relief and awe.

It was a stag.

He was enormous, his shoulders easily as high as she was, and far larger than she would think a deer could grow. Horns arched up from his head in jagged, sharpened points. They almost resembled thorns. *So much for harmless.*

The creature's fur was also jet black, shining in the pale sunlight. His white tail, the only thing about him that did not look carved from shadow, flicked from side to side as the creature watched her.

"H—hello," she said to him. This was a spirit of the woods, without a doubt. And a spirit of the woods that was alive and watching her. It was best to be polite. "I'm very sorry to interrupt your breakfast."

The deer didn't move, and simply watched her.

"I mean you no harm. I highly doubt I could catch you, even if I wanted." She chuckled, tucking a strand of her long hair behind her ear. "Although you are quite beautiful, you look like you could crush me easily."

The stag turned on his back legs and bounded twenty paces away, before stopping and looking at her over his shoulder. When she didn't move, or do anything, he snorted and pawed the ground, before bounding another ten paces and turning to look at her.

"Do you want me to follow you?" She blinked. That seemed to be what he was trying to signify. With a shrug, she began to follow the creature. He might be leading her into a trap, yes. But all of the Maze was a trap, and what was one set of metal teeth snapping around her ankle versus another?

At least this one was far less horrifying than the cobbled-together pile of bones. She followed the stag as it bounded along the path, but when it took a right and went into the woods, she found herself hesitating.

She hadn't yet stepped into the woods themselves, only staying on the path ahead of her. There was a smaller, thinner groove in the dense undergrowth that had clearly been made by wildlife. Chewing her lip, she gripped the hilt of her sword and sighed. Walking on the path for hours had successfully led her nowhere. She couldn't even find proper rocks.

Perhaps that was by design.

Staring up at the trees, she narrowed her eyes at them, suddenly suspicious that the forest—the Maze—was scheming against her.

The stag reappeared through the trees, black and jagged, thorn-like horns a stark silhouette against the greenery. It snorted loudly, clearly annoyed at her.

"Yes! Sorry! Yes, fine." She threw up her hands. "If I'm to die, might as well be sooner rather than later." And with that, she marched into the woods after the black stag, sticks digging into the bottoms of her bare feet. She followed the creature, all the while muttering under her breath about how very much she hated Valroy.

She decided she hated him very much indeed.

Valroy snuffed in surprise as a rock pelted him in the back of the head. It hadn't been thrown very hard, but it was still quite startling. Jerking awake, he lifted his head and turned to squint at the direction from which the rock had come.

Anfar.

With a beleaguered grunt, he put his head back down on his pillow. He slept on a nest of textiles he had stolen from the human world. He enjoyed how very silly and garish they were. But, that said, they were also exceedingly comfortable. Far more so than the branches of trees or a nest of straw. "Go away, sea-beast. You're dripping on my carpets."

"Stupid things you own. Simply because humans put fabric on the floor doesn't mean you should. I don't care."

"I know you don't care, and I don't care that you don't care. You're still dripping on them. Go away and let me sleep." Valroy rolled onto his stomach, nudging the rock away from him.

"She was attacked by a Nameless."

"Good for her." He yawned sleepily. "I suppose the silly girl gave it a name and now she's wandering around as part of a shambling pile of bones." A shame to let the game end so quickly, but that was fine. If his prize was that weak, then perhaps she was no prize at all.

"She killed it."

That woke him up. He sat up quickly, finally paying attention to the rock that had been thrown at him. It was a small, black piece of something that nearly resembled charcoal, but much harder. Frowning, he picked it up and turned it over in his palm. It was the heart of a Nameless. Laughing, he collapsed onto his back on the bed, holding the stone in the air above him and turning it over in his fingers. "Little witch, you surprise me. You stole her kill? How unlike you."

"She should not have the stone."

"She's harmless."

"She killed a Nameless."

"With what?"

"My sword."

"With your sword! And only because she was provoked." He chuckled. Anfar could be so easy to annoy. He yawned again. He did hate having his sleep interrupted. "Are you scared of her?"

"No." Anfar grimaced. "Hardly."

"Good. Then I fail to see the problem. When you're afraid of my little witch, I'll pay more attention." He tossed the rock to the side of the platform on which he kept his collection of textiles and pillows and rolled back onto his side. "Have a lovely day, Anfar."

"But—"

"Have a *lovely day*, Anfar." The second time was not nearly so friendly as the first.

He heard the sea-beast snarl in annoyance, but his second-in-command, nearest-thing-he-had-to-a-friend, finally gave up. Valroy felt him leave. He smiled and, pulling in a breath, let it out as a long, sleepy groan, and snuggled into the pillows around him.

He wondered how long it would take before she'd be there beside him.

Opening his eyes, he sat up once more and frowned. That was a stupid thought. This was *his* bed.

Flopping back down on his other side, he cursed Anfar under his breath for having woken him up. Shoving all other thoughts from his mind, he let sleep come for him again.

ABIGAIL CURSED Valroy louder the longer she walked through the woods with bare feet. Damn him for tricking her. Damn him for burning her home down. Damn him for killing Marcus. Damn him for stealing her. Damn him for taking her clothes and refusing to give her shoes. Damn him for putting her inside this Maze.

Damn him for everything.

Absolutely everything.

She'd throw a few things in there that she knew he had nothing to do with for good measure, if she could. Damn him for there being so many twigs and pointy things to jab at her.

But still, she followed the stag through the woods. She followed the impatient animal for what might have been an hour before the forest relented. It gave way to a clearing covered in soft, silky, green grass. Twenty paces ahead of her was a clear stream, and she almost wept in relief. The sound of running water joined the songs of birds and insects in the air around her.

"Oh, thank the gods." She stepped onto the grass and picked up her feet one at a time to brush the detritus off. She picked a pebble from her skin and winced at how red and raw they were. Wondering how long she could go without shoes, she also pondered how closely that aligned with how long she was going to survive.

Which happens first—my feet give out, or they get eaten? Place your bets...

The stag was downstream from her, standing in the shallow water, his head lowered to drink.

Walking up to the shore, she knelt and cupped her hands in the clear liquid. It smelled normal. The stag was drinking it. *The stag is magic. I'm not. This could still kill me.*

Everything could kill her.

Including *not* drinking water. She gave up the constant debate of "will this be the end of my life" and drank. The water was cool and crisp, and tasted perfectly normal. After she had her fill, she walked to a stone and sat on it, setting her feet in the water. She hissed as it stung the cuts, but oh, it felt so much better.

The stag lifted his head at her sound of pain, dark eyes fixed on her.

"Sorry." She smiled. "I'm not used to hiking in bare feet. Thank you for bringing me here."

The deer lowered his head again. It was not a conversationalist.

Reaching down, she began to pick up a few smooth rocks from the water. They would be perfect for her spell. She needed seven, and they were quickly in her palm. Each one was oval, worn by the passage of the water over the years.

Now that she was no longer moving, exhaustion hit her like heavy stones, weighing her down. It was growing difficult to keep her eyes open. The sound of the stream was so peaceful, even if it was a lie.

Sleep. That was what she needed now more than anything, and here seemed as good a place as any. It was certainly less conspicuous than sleeping in the middle of a path that seemed to be used by no one except her.

Stepping back onto the grass, she held the stones and cupped them between her hands. *Protect.* One word. One goal. One will.

Placing each stone down as she walked in a large circle, she repeated the word again in her head and willed it into the rock. *Protect.*

Soon, each of the seven stones was around her. There was no telling if it worked. There was no telling if the creatures here couldn't simply barge past her spell without wincing. But she had the distinct suspicion she was going to find out. Sitting down in the center of her circle, she began to unlace the bodice that Valroy had given her.

The damn thing made it rather hard to breathe, anyway.

Folding it and setting it down, she stared at her sad excuse for a pillow. It would have to do. Placing her sword down next to her, she ensured it would be within easy reach if she needed it unexpectedly.

The stag was watching her again, and she wondered if it had been doing so all through her spell. She smiled at it. "It isn't for you. But this world scares me, and I do honestly believe it intends to eat me."

All she received in exchange was the swish of a white tail.

Lying down on her side on the grass, she rested her head on her folded-up bodice. "Thank you, Mr. Stag, for bringing me here. I hope I can repay the favor someday." Her concerns about being unable to sleep on the ground with no cot or blanket were quickly dashed. She was exhausted, and her body cared nothing for her surroundings.

Sleep hit her hard and fast, and her last thoughts were of wondering whether or not she would ever wake again.

CHAPTER TWELVE

Abigail *did* wake up.
To the smell of blood and burning.
And the sound of shrieking.

With a jolt, she was instantly awake. She grabbed the sword from where it lay beside her without even thinking. Sitting up, her heart was instantly pounding in her ears, fear ridding her of every ounce of sleep with the snap of fingers.

The sun had set, whether because she had been asleep for a long time or because it simply moved fast, she didn't know. But the moon cast more light than its daytime predecessor, and it was more than enough for her to see what was in front of her.

She screamed.

Surrounding her were small, winged figures that she could only think of as a swarm. The buzz of large, beetle-like wings joined the sounds of their inhuman screams and shrieks. Their bodies were small and deformed, and vaguely could be compared to human. There were hundreds of them, maybe more.

And they were throwing themselves at her. She recoiled

in fear as one of the tiny, shrieking monsters flew at her, only to hit an invisible *something* that stood in its way. Its animalistic shriek turned into a high-pitched, pained scream as it burst into flames where it touched the barrier.

Her barrier.

One of the things flew over her. It dove, and she ducked reflexively as it smashed into the edge of her spell. It was as though the circle she had drawn rose up and around her in a dome. She dared not stand. The monster that smashed into the spell over her met the same fate as the other one. It combusted, just like its companion.

But to her increasing horror, it didn't relent. It kept pushing itself at the barrier, its flesh dissolving into ash before her eyes. Only after its fingers, hands, wrists, and arms were all but gone did it retreat.

More correctly, it tried.

Another one of its kin grabbed it and began to use it as a weapon, smashing the injured monster against the spell. The first one screamed, thrashing desperately, but it was no use. Soon, it was gone.

All the while, Abigail screamed.

They seemed to rejoice in her fear—no, they seemed inspired by it. As if they hungered for the noise she made. The swarm of them moved at her again, a dozen of the creatures bashing into the spell, burning into nothing.

She covered her mouth with her hand, sword clenched tightly in the other, trying to stifle the sound she made.

Finally, she cried.

Her shock slowly began to wear off, even if her fear did not. Biting back all her screams, she desperately tried to take stock of her situation.

The creatures quieted, although they still filled the grass around her. She could see them flocking in the trees like morbid birds. Now that they had stopped moving, she could finally see what was attacking her.

They looked like skinny, tiny, malnourished humans. Their hands and feet were barely anything more than claws. Wings, like those of roaches, buzzed at their backs. And their heads…their faces were smooth, round like a ball, and had no features. No features, save a large, wide, animalistic mouth filled with rows and rows of needle-like teeth.

"Ever hear the tale of the 'tooth fairy?'"

She jerked in shock and turned her head toward the voice. There, leaning against a tree, cleaning his nails with the end of a dagger, was Valroy. One of the tiny monsters dove for him, shrieking its high-pitched battle cry.

Without flinching—without even looking at the creature—he snatched the thing from midair in the talon of one of his wings and, with a sickening *crunch*, crushed it in his fist. He tossed it aside, the limp corpse landing in the grass. It hadn't been there for the blink of an eye before its kin were atop it, ripping it to pieces and eating its flesh, and bone, and everything else.

"Y—yes—" she whispered. She was shaking so hard her teeth chattered. She wiped at the tears that streaked down her cheeks. She didn't want to cry in front of Valroy, no matter the horror that surrounded her. "I've heard the tale."

Despite her making sounds, the monsters didn't move. They tilted their heads this way and that, occasionally inching toward her, only to hit the circle drawn by her stones and hiss, recoiling as they smoldered or caught flame.

"A tooth fairy hunts any bone left exposed to the air. They can make work of whole battlefields"—he snapped his fingers—"just like that. Vicious creatures. These are similar, except they hunt *fear*. And you, my dear little witch, are a feast." He chuckled. "Quite the mess you're in, might I say."

"I—" She paused and tried not to scream as another one

of the faeries threw themselves at her, clawing and scratching at the barrier. More joined it, spurred on by its screams of pain and agony and hunger. "Make them stop!"

"I could." He smirked at her, those glowing sapphire eyes glinting from the shadows. "But I won't."

"I *hate* you."

"I know." He went back to examining his nails, cleaning under the black and pointed things with his dagger. "You're not unique in that."

She squeaked and ducked her head as more dove down at her from above. She covered her head with her arms as soot rained down around her.

"Clever spell. I wonder how long it'll hold."

She wanted to throw something at him. His smug, mocking tone was going to drive her insane. That was, if she lived long enough, and these "fear faeries" didn't get their wish first. "Are all your kind so very ugly?"

He laughed hard at that. "Many are. Many aren't. It's the ones that *aren't* that you need to worry about."

She glared at him in silence for a moment. He didn't even notice, as he was still focused on his fingernails, occasionally turning them over to examine them. He was still shirtless, and his black leather pants were decidedly one size too small for him. She couldn't imagine they were comfortable. "Are you going to help me?"

"Hm? I thought you hated me."

"I do. It's still a question."

"What will you trade?" He grinned but still didn't look at her.

"I have nothing to give that you've not already taken from me."

"That isn't true in the slightest, and you know it." He pointed at her with the end of his dagger. "And don't you dare act like a petulant child."

"Don't you dare lecture me."

"One of us is thousands of years old, and the other one isn't."

"One of us is also an arse."

He laughed again, flicking his wrist. The dagger disappeared into thin air as he did. He strolled forward, kicking a few of the creatures out of the way as he moved closer to her. "Sharp-tongued witch."

"Fae bastard."

"I am the product of royalty, thank you very much." He huffed in mock insult, his amusement still written across his features. "But I get your meaning. Tell me, how do you plan to defend yourself? Do you plan to cower here within your spell until it cracks, and they descend upon you?" He tilted his head to the side as he eyed the rusted blade she clutched. "Or do you mean to stab them all one at a time?"

"If I must…" No, that was a foolish idea. Besides, she had no idea what would happen if she broke through the dome with her sword. Would it break the spell? She'd be doomed if it did. Rubbing her face, she tried to think it through.

"Surrender, little witch, and I'll send them away."

"No."

"You already tire of our game. You're already losing. You've walked for a night and a day, and you've made it nowhere. You're surrounded on all sides by creatures that will delight in tearing you apart." He crouched at the edge of her spell, sneering at her with every ounce of superiority available to him, of which there was plenty. He reached out a finger and ran a single nail along the edge of the dome. It sizzled and crackled, but he was unharmed. "Surrender, and I'll take you away from here."

"No." *Not yet.* She shoved the last bit out of her mind. He was right. Every word he said was right. But she wouldn't—*couldn't*—give in so soon.

"I take very good care of my pets, witch. You would live like a queen." He chuckled.

"No," she reiterated through clenched teeth.

"Then I look forward to seeing what you do next." He stood and walked back toward the forest. "Scream for help, call my name, and pray that I can get to you in time." He disappeared into the shadows.

"I hate you!"

Laughter came from all around her. "I know."

Letting out a long breath, she stared at the evil, ugly little creatures that surrounded her. What was she going to do? How on Earth was she going to get out of this mess?

Every now and then one of them jarred her out of her thoughts as it jumped forward. She held her breath, waiting to see if *just one more* was the answer to how long the power of her spell might hold. And then she had to look away in disgust as it began to sizzle and burn, only to be eaten or used as a weapon by the others.

She didn't know which was worse.

What did she have to use? A lace belt—hah—a sword that was more risky than not, the clothes on her back, her aching feet…

And one other thing.

She had access to one other thing.

It was going to be stupid to try. But she had no other options—well, that didn't involve surrendering to Valroy. Kneeling, she placed her hands down into the grass, threading her fingers between the blades.

She had the world around her.

The living world.

Monstrous as it was…it was still part of nature.

"Help me," she whispered. *"Please."* For a second, she held her breath.

The blades of grass twisted and tangled around her

fingers. She opened her eyes and watched in wide-eyed awe as they cinched around her.

Was the grass going to eat her now, too?

A scream from in front her caught her attention. She expected to see one of the monsters burning to cinders, but she blinked in surprise. Blades of grass had snatched it as well. They were dragging it down *into* the ground. And soon it was joined by another and another.

Some took to the skies to escape, but it seemed the grass was not deterred. It grew and stretched, reaching up to them in the blink of an eye, snapping like whips, wrapping around their ankles, their wrists, their necks, and dragging them back down to the hungry Earth.

Screaming was joined by more screaming. And then more, and more, and more.

She dropped her head, shutting her eyes tight, feeling tears run down her cheeks again. For a moment, she thought the sound would make her deaf. Or perhaps that it might make her mad. Or that it might go on forever.

Until abruptly...the screaming stopped. Looking up, she saw she was alone. Every last one of the creatures was *gone*. But they weren't, were they? They were beneath the ground that was just as grassy and lush as it had been a second prior. If she dug with her hands, would she find their wriggling bodies? Their bones? Or nothing at all?

The grass released her.

"T—thank—thank you—" she stammered out between chattering teeth. Sitting, she held her knees to her chin. The monsters were gone. They were dead. She had killed them, just as she had the Nameless thing. It had been to defend herself—she had not wished to do it.

She lowered her head to her knees. She would need to keep moving very soon, but in that exact moment she found herself unable to stand. Unable to do much, really. Because while the screaming had stopped, her weeping had not.

So much death...

She had caused so much death.

They were monsters. They wished to hurt her. They wished to eat her.

Pressing her hand into the dirt, she gripped her necklace and prayed to the old gods that their suffering had been brief.

And she prayed that they returned to nature.

And hoped her tears were penance enough.

VALROY WATCHED as the little witch clutched her knees to her chest and cried. What for? He furrowed his brow. She had defeated the pragglings who had smelled her sleeping fear and had come to devour her.

She was victorious. She should be celebrating. She should be standing there and shouting at him, shaking her fist in the sky and cursing him. But she was sitting there alone...weeping. What could possibly be wrong?

He didn't like puzzles, which was ironic, considering how much he loved to put them in front of others. Frowning, he watched the young thing, trying to understand the issue. When she shifted to fold her legs beside her as she wiped at her eyes, he saw the cuts on the bottom of her feet.

Oh!

Now he knew what it was.

He smiled. The puzzle was solved.

Silly mortals.

When she finally had the strength of will to move again, she put her bodice on and laced it up—damn thing was still too tight. Standing, she slipped the sword into her improvised lace belt, turned, and walked to the stream.

And promptly tripped.

Yelping, she fell flat on her face with a groan. She had only barely managed to break her fall. She heard laughing from around her. Many smaller voices, underscored by one deeper one that she recognized.

Rolling onto her side, she looked down to see what she had tripped on.

It was a pair of shoes.

Boots, in fact. Sturdy, burly things that looked as though they were made for a man, but small enough she knew they would fit her. A pair of stockings were shoved into the neck of them.

A gift from Valroy.

But why?

It must be because I defeated those terrible creatures.

"Thank you," she grumbled as she began pulling on the stockings and then slipping on the boots. They were made of soft leather, and she had to admire their craftmanship. There was no reply, and she was fine by that.

Wiping her eyes again with her arm, she stood and brushed the bits of twigs and leaves from her clothes. "I still hate you, however."

That time, she heard him laugh again.

And she barely resisted the urge to throw rocks into the darkness.

CHAPTER THIRTEEN

Titania watched as the sun dipped lower toward the horizon. Soon, shadows would begin to stretch long over the world of Tir n'Aill, and the Unseelie would waken. Her jaw ticked. "He has done *what?*"

"The Bloody Prince has taken a mortal girl and stashed her away in the Maze." The answer came from the corner of the room, from a figure that stayed hunched to remain within the safety of the one shadow that had already formed within the throne room. It was a room, perhaps only by use, if not by design. It only had two "walls," and they were little more than rubble.

She narrowed her eyes, walking to one of those ruined structures, watching as the sun crept lower and lower to the horizon. The golden throne was perched high upon a hill, and she could see the vast forests and lakes that stretched out before her. And wherever the sun touched, the Seelie ruled.

And wherever it did not…

She hated meeting with the scum that hunkered within the darkness created by a great oak and a ruined wall. She despised it. She also hated being outside the safety of her home so close to when the dark things came to take their place. But it was also deeply necessary.

"If the prince has decided to take himself a toy to torture, why is this of import to me?" She wrinkled her nose. "His proclivities aren't unknown to us."

The figure in the shadows shuffled, lowering its head, pulling the ragged blanket higher up over their head, protecting itself from the glare of the sun. "This time, it is not a toy he seeks."

She placed her hand atop the remainder of the wall, letting her fingers trail over the crags of the limestone. "You think he seeks to wed her?" She shook her head. "He would not take a mortal bride. That is beneath his *impressive* ego." She huffed a laugh and made a rude gesture with her hand. "She would die in their wedding bed."

"I believe that is his intention."

Titania paused and turned to look at the creature hiding underneath a blanket like he was an old hag at the market. "He plans to wed her, then kill her?"

"It would get him his throne. The letter of the Morrigan's law is that he must marry...not that he must *stay* married." The figure sighed. "She would not need to survive their wedding night for him to take the throne."

Titania knew the Unseelie prince was a cruel, sadistic, *evil* thing. And she was not one to look down her nose at toying with mortals for personal amusement and fulfillment. The sun above knew that she did the same when it suited her.

But to take a mortal, wed her, and then kill her the moment the deed was done? She sighed and turned to watch the sunset once more. "Why must the dark throne always be occupied by some half-demon, half-blood, fully-rotten bastard?"

"It is by the Morrigan's design. She bred the demon. She

spawned the bastard. And she paved the road to his ascension."

"It was a hyperbolic question, cur. I know all that." She rolled her eyes. Unseelie. There really was no suffering them. "Never mind. Well. Then tell me. If this is the bloody prince's scheme, then why has he not done it yet? Why have I not received a wedding invitation?" She smirked. "Quite an insult."

"No. He bides his time with her. I do not know why. She may be dangerous. She has killed a Nameless. She has killed a swarm of pragglings. She is a witch."

That made Titania laugh. "Did he know before he took her?"

"Yes."

Putting her hand over her eyes, she sighed. Valroy was unpredictable in all ways but one—if a situation could be made more challenging, he would seek to do so at every turn. But it didn't matter. "They cannot be allowed to wed. Does she know his plot?"

"No."

"Good. I hope it stays that way. Mortals have a greed for power that transcends all else." She took a step back from the wall as the shadows grew long and began to stretch toward her. She watched as the warm green grass where she had once stood turned silver and cold. The fallen leaves were no longer lush tones of yellow and olive, but pale blues and whites.

The sun would set, the moon would rise, and the Seelie would trade places with their kin. Such was the way of it all. Such was the balance that was required.

And such was the law of the world that Valroy sought to upend.

With a shake of her head, she retreated to the last portions of the warm sun and prepared to leave for the safety of her home, where the rays of the moon could not touch her. "I believe we only have one course of action ahead of us, if we do not wish to see him take the throne."

The figure no longer crouched in the shadows, standing upright as the darkness grew. But they still kept the blanket around them like a shroud. They didn't speak. That was fine by her—she paid for their information and actions, not their opinion.

Summoning a bag of coins to her hand, she threw it at the figure, who caught it easily. And now she would pay them for something else. She would pay them for murder. "The witch dies."

The figure bowed their head and, taking a step back, disappeared as though they were never there.

A shame, what she had to do. Titania hated spilling blood and taking life, even when it was necessary. But if the witch did not die—and soon, she feared—then there would be even more crimson to soak the ground.

And if Valroy had his way? All of the Seelie would fall beneath his boot.

The sun would never rise again.

What was one mortal life, compared to the end of Tir n'Aill? Compared to her people? Nothing. Nothing at all. But still, she regretted that the choice had been forced upon her all the same.

Shutting her eyes, she let herself pass through the barrier of the world, disappearing into the rays of the sun just as her dark visitor had passed through the shadows. It was time for her to rest.

The witch would die.

The witch *must* die.

THE UNSEELIE PRINCE

ABIGAIL DECIDED she very deeply despised Valroy.

But the boots made her life *considerably* less miserable, she had to admit. She decided to walk along the stream, heading in the direction of the flow. Perhaps she'd find—she didn't honestly know what she was hoping for. A town?

Did the fae *have* towns?

Did they live in the trees?

Did they have a society? She assumed so. If they could have a prince, she figured they probably had other things. She had heard all the stories of the fair folk from her aunt—although the lessons had clearly not sunk in enough for her not to accidentally invite one into her home. But even with all the fables and lore of boggarts and goblins, elves and pixies, she realized…she knew nothing of where she was, or what she might find.

Nothing except that it was filled with terrible, horrific monsters. Ones that wished to feed on her individuality, her fear, and more. But the stag that had led her to the river had seemed harmless—and, in fact, benign. Were there others like that in the woods? Creatures that if she found them, might help her?

"Good evening, little witch."

She yelped in surprise as the voice came from right beside her, whispering in her ear. She whirled, staggered over her own feet, and landed in the grass with an *umf*.

Valroy laughed. He loomed over her, although she supposed that wasn't too hard to do with his considerable height and broad shoulders. She saw those sharp eyeteeth again as he watched her with a playful smirk. He held up a basket. "I was going to ask if you would like to picnic here by the river, and you've already taken a seat. How lovely."

She shot back up to her feet and took a step back. "Get away from me!"

He arched an eyebrow. "What have I done *now?*"

"It isn't about what you've done in this moment, it's about what you've done to me to date." She put her hand on the hilt of her sword.

That made him laugh again. "Oh, you want to fight me, do you? Do you think you'd win?" He took a slow, pointed step forward. She took a stilted one back. Damn him and his constant stalking! "Let's play."

"N—ah!" She didn't even get the word "no" out of her mouth. He leapt at her. Her head reeled with the sudden movement, and stars filled her vision for a second as it hit something hard.

When she could think again, she found herself pinned against a tree. The bark dug into her shoulders as he pressed her there. One of his hands was around her throat.

"I—" She squeaked as his grip tightened. Not enough to hurt, but enough to restrict her air.

"Shush." The word left him in a noise that reminded her of a cat. Somewhere between a growl and a purr—and distinctly inhuman. He leaned in close to her, the tendrils of his dark blue hair brushing against her skin as he hovered his lips by her ear. "Do not threaten me with a weapon unless you know you'll win…or if you want to lose."

Her heart was pounding like a drum. He was so much bigger than she was, and with the wings that curled around them, caging her in, it felt as though he were the only thing that existed in the world.

It wasn't until he chuckled that she realized her hands were pressed against his bare chest, desperately trying to push him away. Her right one rested on the azure-colored tattoo of a labyrinth. "Wait—"

"You can't win. You can't beat me. I am this place—I am the master of all around you. The only path before you is one of defeat. You must understand that this game you play is futile."

She could only whimper.

He pressed his hips against her, and she squeezed her eyes tight. "Which are you, I wonder? Tell me, little witch, are you the kind who wants to surrender or the kind who wants to be defeated?" His hand tightened around her throat, ever so slightly. "Either way, you're my spoil of war. Now or later, it matters not. You're mine, little witch. This game is just a diversion. Remember that."

"Stop—" The word left her as a breathy whisper.

And in an instant, he was gone. He paced away from her, humming a tune, as if nothing had ever happened. It left her standing against the tree, panting for air, gripping the bark in a desperate attempt to hold on to something.

Valroy plucked the basket up from where he had dropped it, replaced a few of its contents that had fallen out, and smiled at her once more. "Dinner? You must be starving."

She was. But…

This game is just a diversion.

He thought she was harmless. Helpless. Hopeless. And she probably was.

He sat down at the edge of the stream and plopped the basket down beside him. He patted the grass on the other side of it. "Don't be stubborn. Mortals need food, and I don't want to end our game so soon. I am having a great deal of fun."

"I hate you." She pressed a hand to her throat where he had been gripping her. She could still feel the warm, rough palm against her.

One of the talons of his claws waved at her dismissively. "Yes, yes, learn something new to say. I already own two parrots—I don't need a third."

She could see a collection of meat, cheese, bread, and wine in the basket. Her stomach growled, reminding her she hadn't eaten in at least a day. Perhaps two. She honestly had no idea how time passed in this place.

Hesitantly, she stepped forward. After a long moment, she sat. There was no point in being stubborn, even if he *was* threatening to do terrible things to her. "Am I getting closer to solving your Maze?"

With a snicker, he leaned back on an elbow and began tearing up a piece of bread and eating it. That was all the answer she needed, and all the answer he was willing to give.

Dismay settled over her like a blanket. A cold, unwelcome, clammy blanket. Taking the sword out of her makeshift belt, she put it down in the grass beside her.

"You could give up, you know." He handed her a piece of bread. "You needn't suffer."

"I know." She took it, paired it with a chunk of cheese, and began to eat. "But I won't."

"It's only a matter of time."

She nodded. She knew it might be inevitable, but she had to try. "Who was the stag? I owe them a thank you."

Silence.

She looked over at him. He had an odd, unreadable expression on his face. He was sitting up now, a sense of urgency in his broad form. *I really wish he would put on a shirt. It's distracting how his muscles move.* And it made her cheeks go warm.

He's very attractive. Why wouldn't he be? He's a fae prince. Of course, he's a work of art. She shoved all those thoughts into a barrel in her head and pushed it over a cliff into the abyss where it belonged.

"What stag?" He brought her back to the conversation. "Describe it to me." There was a threat in his voice. "In great detail." *Or else.*

"I—It—I don't want them to get in trouble. They were only—"

"Tell me what you saw, Abigail Moore." He bared his teeth as he grimaced at her. His sharp, dark nails dug into the dirt beside him, raking trenches in the turf. "Tell me *now.*"

She blinked, stammered uselessly a few times, coughed to clear her throat, and decided she might need more wine. Even sitting, even an arm's length away from her, he was suddenly terrifying. Her blood ran cold. "It was all black, with antlers like thorns, and—"

He stood so quickly she fell back in shock, landing hard on her own elbow. Spreading his wings wide, she believed she was about to die. He snarled down at her. Yes. This was the moment she was going to die.

But he turned and, with a powerful beat of immense wings, took to the sky. She covered her head with her arm, flattening herself as low as possible. When she felt brave enough to look for him, he was gone.

"I sincerely hope I didn't get them in trouble…" With a hum, she looked down at the grass. Valroy was gone, but the food wasn't. "Waste not, want not, I suppose."

Alone, she began to eat.

And wondered if she didn't just make a terrible mistake.

Seems like those are the only kinds I'm capable of.

CHAPTER FOURTEEN

"Mother!"

Valroy stormed into circle of stones. *"Mother!"* He dug his pointed nails so deep into his palms that they began to bleed. The pain calmed him, grounded him. If only by a measure. "Answer me!"

A crow landed atop one of the monolithic slabs beside him. It was covered in etchings and carvings that were ancient when he was born, and that was a thousand years ago or more by this point. The crow eyed him, cawed, and then flew off once more.

The message was clear.

No.

"You cannot meddle in this! She is *mine*. This is by your doing—your rules—your *stupid* law that you put into place! Now you want to stick your fingers in my scheme?" He laughed, snapping his wings wide out at his sides. There was no intimidating the Morrigan, he knew that. But he couldn't help it.

Blood dripped to the grass at his feet, and he glared up at the night sky and the crows that circled there, black silhouettes against the starry sky. "The throne shall be mine, Mother."

He held his palms up before him, watching the blood pool and slowly ooze over the sides. "And the trees shall be fed from the corpses of your Seelie children! All of Tir n'Aill will fall before me." He sneered. "And you know what will follow."

The crows cawed above him, and he could only grin and laugh again at the sound. "Meddle all you like. Not even you can stop me, Mother Morrigan. Not even you."

ABIGAIL HAD WALKED for another few hours along the stream with the basket of food in her hand. She sang to herself as she often did when she walked through the woods. For a little while—even just a moment—she could almost trick herself that this was Earth, and everything was *fine,* and she had merely gotten turned around and lost on the way home.

Never mind the gigantic moon overhead, and the darting shapes she would see in the shadows out of the corner of her eye. Shapes that were too big, and too silent, to be any normal forest creature.

She had found herself in a strange moral conundrum as she sat on the shore of the river, still stunned after Valroy's sudden departure. The arse had clearly wanted them to eat together, judging by the two wine glasses clinking around in the basket she was carrying. It felt rude to leave.

But…Valroy.

She had debated the pros and cons of it for minute or two, before finally realizing that she owed him nothing, and she had a Maze to solve. A Maze that, for all she could tell, had no walls or corridors to speak of.

How am I to find my way through a labyrinth with no walls or direction? How am I to solve something that doesn't even seem to be a puzzle?

"What're you singing?"

She screamed.

Whirling, she expected Valroy. But the man who prowled out of the darkness of a tree was not nearly so tall, nor did he have wings. Well, that wasn't true. The man had a pair of gossamer wings folded at his back that looked like those of a dragonfly.

The fae wore a black silk shirt that draped loosely from his shoulders, tucked into a pair of white linen pants. Bright and shining silver markings ran from the corner of his eye down his cheek, his neck, and under the collar of the shirt. His lips were painted an identical color. He was—and she suspected most fae were—almost painfully beautiful to behold.

He moved smoothly as he strolled up to her, an easy and friendly smile on his face. "Sorry to startle you, good lady. I didn't mean any offense." He reached out to take her hand. "I am Lord Na'len, at your service."

"I—ah—um." She shook her head, took a breath, and started again. "Abigail. A pleasure to meet you." Nervously, she watched his hand for a moment, before deciding it would probably be best not to offend him. She placed her hand in his, hoping he didn't tear it from her wrist and leave her with nothing but a bloody stump.

But Na'len bowed, kissed her knuckles with a smile, and straightened, releasing her. She took a step back from him when he was done, all the same. He frowned. "Prince Valroy has frightened you terribly. And no wonder, leaving you to wander about in his Maze on your own." He clicked his tongue. "That cretin knows no shame."

"Isn't he—I'm sorry, I assume that you are Unseelie, but—"

"He is my prince, yes, if that's what you're asking." He chuckled. "That doesn't mean I agree with him or find him agreeable at all. Do you agree with the workings of your lords? Or that of your king?"

"I can't say that I know much about them." She chewed her lip as she regarded Na'len thoughtfully. He made her nervous. *Never trust the fae.* Valroy had even warned her that the pretty ones were the ones to worry about. "I lived too far away from cities for them to much matter to me."

"A peasant girl! How sweet." Na'len smiled broadly as he stepped toward her. She froze as he circled her—literally stepped around her, taking her in. He plucked at the hem of her bodice, and she jerked in surprise. "And our prince has dressed you accordingly. Pah. Not even a coat or a cloak to protect you." He flicked the hilt of her sword. "I see at least Anfar took pity upon you."

"Y—yes. Alarming creature, but…I appreciate the gift."

Na'len laughed again. "'Alarming creature.' I don't think our dear sea monster has ever been so well described."

She frowned. "Sea monster?"

"Oh, indeed! Be wary of deep lakes and wide oceans, lovely girl." He shrugged. "But I doubt he'd eat you. He may disagree with the Bloody Prince's ways, but they are still allies. Neither here nor there."

Sea monster. The fae she had met was a *sea monster*. She put her hand over her eyes and sighed. "I want to go home."

"I hear whispers that it is what got you into this mess." He tutted. "Valroy granted your wish, didn't he? Just not in the way you had hoped."

"How do you know that?" She dropped her hand to return her focus to the silvery fae.

"Spies." He smiled sweetly, as if that were the most normal thing in the world to say. "We do so very much like to pry and peek. It's in our nature, and here, nature whispers." He motioned at the trees. "Word travels fast in Tir n'Aill."

"I suppose so." She glanced at the river. "I'm sure I won't be entertaining to you lot for much longer. This 'game' he plays with me will likely mean my death before long."

"Oh, most certainly."

She winced. She had walked into that. She couldn't be angry at him for agreeing with her. "It was a pleasure to meet you, Na'len. But I think I should be going." She began to walk away from the silver fae. Under her breath, she added, "Not that I know where I'm headed."

It seemed he heard her all the same. "That is why I'm here, in fact. This path you're on will get you nowhere. No one moves forward in the Maze without his permission."

"Wait. What?" She turned to face Na'len again. "What do you mean?"

"Precisely what I said." He smiled piteously. "This place is shifting and alive. Constantly remaking itself to his design. You'll never go a step farther unless he lets you, or if you have a guide." He hummed. "And I doubt he would let either happen. He hasn't told you why he took you, has he?"

"As a toy…a plaything. He wants me to be his—" She cringed, hating to say the word out loud. "Pet."

"Typical Prince Valroy," Na'len said through a heavy sigh. "Never the truth, never the lie." He swept his arm wide at his side. Abigail jumped back in shock as two enormous, silver spiders came from the trees. They were as big as her head. For a moment, she was terrified they meant to eat her, but they came nowhere near her.

They spun a web between two trees, working in unison to build a shining, intricate shape. When it was done, she watched in fascination as the web began to glow, and then shift.

It formed a doorway. Like the one Valroy had made from

his dining room to the forest she was now wandering in. But this time, on the other side, she didn't see trees—but a bustling marketplace.

Even if it was unlike any marketplace she'd ever seen before. Monsters and creatures walked among people who looked at first blush to be human, even if she did know better. Colorful banners and swaths of fabric hung from beams or flew from posts.

"Come, Abigail. Let me show you the City of Dusk." Na'len held out his arm to her with a gentle smile. "Let me buy you some proper clothes, a proper meal, and I will tell you all that Valroy truly wants from you."

"I—" *Never trust the fae. Never trust the fae. Never trust the fae!* She couldn't help but stare at the market, fascinated. She wanted to know what Valroy plotted. "How do I know I can trust you?"

"You can't. You don't. And you shouldn't." He shrugged again, a lithe lift to thin shoulders. His wings buzzed briefly at his back. "All the legends you've heard of us are true, and more. And no one is more treacherous than the Bloody Prince."

"Why do you call him that?"

"Come with me, and I'll tell you. This is our deal—our exchange. Place your trust in me, and I will take care of you." He held out his arm to her again, as though he were a gentleman, and she were a lady.

"Mark your words. Define 'take care of me.'" She narrowed an eye at him. "There are many ways that could be interpreted."

He laughed hard. "Very true! All right, clever witch." He turned to face her. "Here is our deal. Come with me to the City of Dusk, and I will ensure that you will live as long as you desire to do so."

"I suspect Valroy will be hideously angry with you."

"His power in the Maze is absolute. But once we leave its borders, he is strong, yes—but not omniscient." He wrinkled a nose. "Not yet. That's why I'm so eager to take you from here."

"What do you mean, 'not yet'?"

The silver fae's expression fell. "Oh, mortal child…you don't understand any of this at all, do you?" He sighed. "I'll tell you this much. Valroy is poised to take the Silvered Throne and become king. And once he does…all of Tir n'Aill will be turned to nothing but bone, and blood, and ash. And his carnage will not stop there." He reached out a hand to her.

"That has nothing to do with me."

"Why, of course it does." He smiled. "Because he means to make you his queen."

Gone.

Gone!

Valroy ripped a limb off a tree in his rage and hurled it into the distance with a crash. The girl was *gone* from his Maze! With a howl of fury, more of the world around him met his wrath. But the trees did not bleed and scream like flesh, and he wanted to feel a ribcage collapse beneath him. He wanted to rip the face from their skull and force them to eat it before he put them out of their misery.

Because he did not know *where* she had gone. But he knew how.

Someone had taken her.

Someone had come into his Maze, found her, and stolen her. She was his! First Mother Morrigan and her meddling, and now this?

They are working together. This was a concerted effort. Mother

Morrigan played the distraction while someone else wormed their way inside without my notice and took her. Damn her, damn them, don't they understand?

"She is *mine!*" he hollered, knowing no one was listening. Spreading his wings wide, he hissed in his impotent anger. But it would not be useless for long. Someone was going to die for this.

Someone was going to die *slowly*.

There were only so many places they could take the girl that would keep her hidden from him. Only so many places where someone could hide a mortal from the High Lord of the Unseelie Court.

And only one place where her death might go unnoticed.

Folding his wings around himself, he stormed into the shadows and let them take him where he wished to go. The City of Dusk would bleed this night.

It would just remain to be seen if Abigail would join the dead.

Or if he could find her in time.

CHAPTER FIFTEEN

Abigail had been to a fair once.
Perhaps the City of Dusk would be something like that?

No.

It was nothing like that.

She clung to Na'len, not because she trusted him, but because she was afraid that if she let go, she'd be swept away. He chuckled to her, a warm smile creasing his utterly perfect face. The silver paint on his lips was strange, but it suited him, she decided. He wasn't human—why look like one?

The flashing swirl of colors around her, the shouts of sellers, the sea of creatures that she could barely recognize as living things emerging from the movement before they were gone again, were all too much for her to behold. It nearly left her dizzy and reeling as they walked.

Two humans—or at least resembling them—wearing the finest garb she had ever seen, strolled by her, arm in arm, like gentleman and lady. It took her a moment to realize they weren't two people at all—but one. They were not linking arms, they were joined.

THE UNSEELIE PRINCE

Another figure went by a moment later whose constitution seemed to be made entirely out of swarming *bees.*

Then, a giant cat whose legs were like sticks, and who had far too many of them for her to count. Upon its back perched a bird made only of bone.

They had to stand back to let an enormous slug go past, its width taking up the entirety of the market path. She stared at it, agog.

Na'len patted her hand where she still gripped his arm like a vise. "Violence is banned in the market. You're safe here, believe it or not."

"It wouldn't take much for one of them to carry me off," she muttered. "Rather like how you did."

He laughed, a flash of white teeth. He didn't have fangs like Valroy. That was nice, but she suspected he had no need of fangs to kill her. "I think you need a drink, eh? Come. My friends are nearby, and we can sit and tell you all that the dread prince has planned for you."

Once the slug had passed, he took her from between the colorful stalls and stepped over the path of slime the creature had left behind. She had to jump over it, glad for her trousers and boots. When she missed, and still got some on her shoes, she was *very* glad for them. She wiped it off on the stones as best as possible.

"Pretty girl, oh, pretty girl! Might I interest you in a wonderous piece of technology from the human world?" the seller working the stall beside her called out to her. "My, oh my, a *mortal?*" Someone touched her arm, and she jerked in surprise, whirling to look at who had come near her.

She had to cover her mouth to repress a scream.

The man—the thing—in front of her had no head!

But that didn't mean he wasn't looking at her. His shoulders led to a bloody, ragged stump of a neck covered in a swath of white lace. It did nothing to hide the gore underneath. Jutting up from where the spine should have continued to a skull were a series of brass metal rods. Several of them held up a magnifying glass. It was wider from edge to edge than her handspan twice over. And on the other side of that magnifying glass—the image distorted, warped, and several times the size it should have been—was an eye.

An eye.

A single, disembodied eye.

On a stick.

And it moved.

She could see it focus on her, dart around as it looked at her.

She wanted to be sick. She wanted to scream. She wanted to faint. But all she could do was stand there, locked solid, staring at the thing that was staring back at her.

"I'm terribly sorry, my lady," he said. The thing was definitely a man. He was wearing exceptionally fine clothing for a creature who had no head. She could not imagine a lord or duke wearing anything nicer. She could see the chain for a pocket watch dangled against expensive fabric. He bowed at the waist with a flourish. The buckles on his shoes were shined and immaculate.

He would look like the perfect gentleman.

Except for the simple fact he had only an eyeball for a head.

"I know my visage is quite alarming. Those around here, I suppose, are quite accustomed to those of us in the market who are…ah…less than human." The man straightened and extended a hand to her. "My name is Lord Gregory Wilson, at your service."

For several beats, seconds that stretched on for what seemed like ever, she found herself unable to move. Unable to do anything, except stare at that disembodied eyeball that was staring back at her.

Na'len nudged her.

With a jolt, she stammered every possible syllable she could without forming an actual word, and then with a small, exhausted whine, she put her hand into his. "Abigail."

He mimed kissing her hand, an act that was patently impossible considering his entire lack of a face, before releasing her. "Charmed! Perfectly charmed. Forgive me if my visage gives you nightmares. Is what it is, I suppose. Such I was made by my mistress, and such I shall forever be."

"Y—y…" She coughed. "Forgive me. I don't mean to insult you, but this is all too much. I—I am—I am not meant to be here."

"Oh, but you are! Don't you see?" He motioned for her to come over to his stall. "Come, look. You must be the one the wheels spoke of!"

"We must be going, Wilson." Na'len wrapped a hand around her upper arm, preventing her from stepping forward. "The prince will be along shortly, and we must away before he arrives."

Lord Gregory Wilson let out a long, exaggerated sigh. "Your efforts are valiant, Na'len, but pointless. You know how this will play out."

"No. I don't. And neither do you. Your little clockwork trinkets tell you nothing but lies."

Wilson's shoulders stiffened, and his tone grew defensive and harsh. He pointed at Na'len accusatorially. "They divine the movement of the stars themselves. They aren't—"

"Enough." Na'len tugged her along. "Let's go. It isn't safe to be out in the open. Goodbye, tinker! I will come read your charts and watch your copper bits and bobs spin about another time."

"Wait—" she squeaked. But it was too late. He had already pulled her around a corner, and she didn't know if she was relieved or dismayed.

"Don't mind the tinker. If we stopped to talk to him, we'd

have been trapped there listening to him blather on about cogs and bolts and whirly-things until the sun rose." The silvery fae rolled his eyes. "I know more about 'soldering' than I ever cared to."

"I—I see."

He wrinkled his nose. "Disgusting things of his. We'd have run him out of town, or ripped him to shreds, but Valroy entertains his presence due to his own personal perversion. And sometimes there are some edicts from the High Lord that we can't avoid." When she made a face of her own, Na'len howled in laughter. "No, no! Not *that* kind of perversion. He's obsessed with the *things* you humans make. Things that have no business being in the world."

"Oh." She didn't know what else to say. She glanced back over her shoulder. He had led them down an alleyway between tents and ramshackle buildings that looked as though they were set up in a hurry. She wondered if this whole market didn't travel and do so abruptly. But at least it was quieter here, and the stone path gave way to packed dirt, and then dirt to grass. "Where are we going?"

"To see some friends, and to get you a mug of beer. Something tells me you need it."

Her nerves were rather shot, but she knew she shouldn't drink a damn thing they gave her. "I want to know what you meant. About Valroy making me a queen."

"Yes, yes. We'll get there soon enough. Let us sit where it's safe, out from where Valroy might see us." He pointed up at the sky.

It took her a second. Right. Yes. Valroy had wings.

She glanced back over her shoulder again. "If you all hate human things, and Lord Wilson is a tinker, how did he come to be here in the first place?"

"Easy." He huffed. "Valroy. Again. Lord Wilson was made by Lady Astasha as a gift. It was supposed to be a wedding present. A sign of her 'devotion and her love.'" He snorted. It was clear how much he thought of it. "He refused her. Because he wants the throne, but he doesn't want it *that* badly." He cackled.

There was a great deal going on about which she had literally not even the smallest scrap of a clue how to decipher. Feeling like a lamb led to slaughter and knowing that was quite possibly exactly what was happening, she fell silent as the fae guided her through the corridors between the tents. Finally, after taking her through what might have been a second labyrinth for all its twists and turns, he pulled back the flap of a tent and ushered her inside.

She staggered in, blinking at the sudden darkness. The moon outside was bright, but in here, there were only a few sparce candles around the edges.

"Hello, hello!" came the chorus of three female voices. Thin, pale hands grabbed hers and tugged her farther into the tent. Before she could even see where she was or who they were, she was sitting on the ground.

And being petted.

I really am a lamb.

She ducked her head away from the hands that stroked over her hair, already playing with the long red strands. "Please, st—"

They weren't listening to her. Three women—three astonishingly beautiful women, who were so pale that they seemed to glisten—surrounded her. And they were talking to each other and to Na'len in a flurry of conversation.

"She's beautiful!"

"Her hair, can I braid it?" She already was.

"No wonder Valroy took her." A pair of hands brushed over her waist, and she jolted at the contact.

"What color are her eyes?" A hand caught her chin and turned her to look up at one of the women beside her. Her hair was a rich purple, like the shade of an aubergine. Her eyes matched, and so did her lipstick. She smiled, a dazzling expression. "Amber—oh, like the leaves in the fall. Oh, but she is not an Autumn child. She is of the Spring. She should have green eyes."

"And she is a witch." Hands stroked over her shoulders, pulling off her bodice. "Can't you feel it?"

Wait—wait! When had they unlaced her clothes? "Stop, please stop—" She pushed at them, trying to clutch her clothing back to her, but it was too late.

The fairy—that one was red—had already pulled it out of her reach. When she stretched out her arm to grab it back, the third fairy, this one colored a shade of forest green, leaned forward and kissed her.

Abigail froze.

The woman kissed her.

She smelled like grass, recently cut low by a scythe. Of hay and straw. She tasted like sweet corn.

When she parted from her, the woman looked at Abigail's stunned expression and giggled. A soft, pale hand stroked over her cheek, soft and tender. "So beautiful…and you taste like apricots."

"Let me!" Hands turned her to face the one with the crimson hair, and before Abigail could stop her, still stunned from the last one, lips pressed to hers again. Strawberries.

The third kissed her next. She tasted like blackberries. Three sets of hands stroked over her, touching her, comforting her. When had they laid her back against them? Her shoulders were against the chest of the red woman, whose legs were parted around her. The fae woman was nude, and Abigail felt the woman's breasts pillow at her back, soft and supple and warm.

Wait—

Lips touched hers. Kissed her with such passion, such

pleasure, that she whimpered. She was turned to meet another embrace. And another. And another. Kiss, after kiss. Hands combed through her hair, soothing and sweet.

This isn't—

Hands stroked her body, lithe and soft and gentle. She arched, trying to press into those hands, wishing they would squeeze, or grip, or press. But they never did. She moaned quietly, furtive, and unsure.

Hands slid beneath her clothes, teasing her. Not giving her enough of what she wanted. Not lingering long enough.

Something is wr—

Her legs were parted. Careful hands bent her knees, and someone moved to settle between them. Someone different. A tender press of fingers to her cheek turned her from the kisses of the fae women. Her mind was reeling, thoughts swimming, everything felt strange and warm…but wonderful.

Until something sharp pierced her throat.

She cried out in pain as the haze that had been put over her mind snapped like a twig. But the sound was swallowed by lips pressed once more to hers, as the figure lowered themselves down to her body.

He pressed against her like a lover; the only thing separating them was the clothes they wore. He kissed her, and his lips tasted like ice. Na'len.

She couldn't think. She jerked beneath him, feeling the stabbing pain in her throat increase as she moved. She instantly froze.

He pulled away from her and shushed her. Dark eyes creased as he smiled sadly. "It's all right, Abigail…don't move. Don't fight it. It's already done. It's already too late. Struggling will only make it hurt more." He kissed at the corner of her mouth.

"I—" she whispered. "What—what's happening—?"

He kissed the edge of her lips again, then her chin, then her cheek. "You're dying, Abigail. And it's all right."

"N...no, you said—you said—" She could feel it, then. Something being pushed into her body from the point in her throat. She gasped.

It was thick. It was warm.

There it was again, surging into her. She tried to resist it, but it was no use. Her muscles went slack. She whimpered and struggled, but the women around her wouldn't have it. Their grip on her finally tightened. Not like they had to try hard. Her limbs felt like lead. Heavy and unusable. "You said…"

"That you would live as long as you wanted to. And I'm afraid you won't want to live for very long." He hummed. "I'm so very sorry, Abigail. We could have had such fun together. I didn't want to do this."

His hand was resting on her throat. It was as though one of his nails had gone into her skin. But how? She gasped as she felt something push into her body again. Too hot, and too thick. It was doing something to her. Something awful. She arched, her eyes going wide. It was poison. He was poisoning her! "But—but why?"

"You have to die to save us all. Valroy needs a queen to take the crown, you see…and we have to do everything in our power to make sure he *never* ascends to the Silvered Throne." He kissed her cheek, his long dark hair brushing against her. "It isn't personal."

Another surge of that awful liquid into her body, and she whined. It was not quite pain. It was not quite pleasure. But suddenly, something settled low in her body like a raging inferno. She could feel sweat break out over her body. It should have been agonizing, but instead she found herself overcome with *need*. It was overwhelming. She writhed, needing contact. Needing someone to touch her. *Needing.*

Na'len hummed. "Good. It's working quickly." He kissed her slowly, deeply, but it wasn't enough. She ached. Everything ached.

Never once had she ever experienced anything like it. She moaned as he touched her, slipping his hand under her cotton shirt to squeeze her left breast in his hand. *Yes, yes!* But it still wasn't enough!

He broke his kiss and whispered to her. "One dose of my poison brings warmth and calm. Two feeds the fire within. Three sets it alight…and four consumes it."

Another surge of that terrible substance, and her moan turned into a scream. Her need turned to agony. Every part of her felt as though it had been seared with a hot iron brand. Or as though a thousand little needles were impaling her everywhere.

She screamed again, wailing in torment. A pale hand snapped over her lips, stifling her cry.

The pain in her throat ended. Na'len knelt between her legs and held up his hand. It was then that she saw what had been inside her throat. Extending from underneath one of his nails was a long, thin, black needle, like the stinger of a bee. It dripped with a viscous, pale substance.

He smiled piteously.

Pain blinded her. White-hot and terrible, it felt like she was being ripped to pieces. She thrashed and struggled, flailing uselessly. Hands kept her pinned.

"This won't kill you, sadly." Na'len sighed. "You could stay like this, poisoned by my gift, for all eternity. And that's what will happen. We have a coffin ready for you. We'll chain you and bind you and toss you into a deep, dark hole. You'll starve to death before this pain kills you."

She could barely hear his words through the agony.

"Why?" She tore away from the hand covering her mouth to demand an answer. "If you do not wish to hurt me, why—"

The pain surged. When she went to scream, the hand over her mouth returned.

"Well…if you have to die, why not make it enjoyable for the rest of us?" He smiled. "And to spite the Bloody Prince, of course. I want to make sure he knows you suffered for his greed."

Pain.

Torment.

I am on fire.

Her aunt had warned her of what some countries did to witches and warlocks. Of German witches being tied to stakes and lit aflame. And that was what it felt as though she suffered now. Her body burned with no fire to touch it. She could almost imagine the skin turning dark and black and flaking away as she turned to ash.

Please, make it stop.

Please.

"This is a kinder fate, sweet one," one of the women whispered into her ear.

Another one of the women continued, gently stroking Abigail's hair that was now matted in sweat. "Valroy would marry you, and you would be the first to die in the slaughter he would unleash upon us. He wants to take all of Tir n'Aill as his own. And then your world would fall next. You have to die."

"Your death saves millions of lives. Not just the Seelie, but your kind as well," the third urged. "This is a noble sacrifice."

Please, the pain. Make it stop!

"He would have tricked you into being his wife." Na'len reached down to stroke her cheek. Every touch on her body felt like a thousand insects biting and stinging her. She flinched and wailed against the hand still covering her mouth. "If he hasn't raped you yet, he would soon. He'd do terrible, awful, miserable things to you. He would desecrate your body, your soul…everything you are. This is a kinder death. I promise. And you can make it end."

End.

Make it end.

Make it all end.

The Maze. The fae. The monsters. The pain.

Tears rolled from her cheeks, and the women around her stroked them away. It didn't matter. They were replaced with more.

Na'len lowered himself to her again, that long, dark stinger hovering close to her throat. "Tell me you wish it to stop, and I will end your suffering."

Yes.

Please.

Make it stop.

Gods forgive me, please, take me away from this.

The hand over her mouth moved, and she pulled in a gasp of air.

And she begged for death.

But her words were swallowed by the sound of screams.

A shadow fell over them.

Na'len's eyes went wide.

There was blood.

And then there was darkness.

Please,

Make it stop.

CHAPTER SIXTEEN

Valroy removed the stinger from beneath his victim's fingernail first.

Then he removed the man's fingernails.

One, by one, by one, he ripped them from Na'len's digits. He listened to the little lord scream and cry and beg for mercy.

There would be none.

The three pathetic fae Na'len had cajoled into joining him in betrayal and treason were already dead. The lot of them made for easy prey, and far too boring to warrant his time. He would impale their bodies on the tent poles and leave them as decorations for the next market night.

But first.

"Please, my lord—my Master, please—" Na'len screamed as Valroy ripped another nail from his flesh. "Mercy—"

The high-pitched sound made him grin wide. It sounded so very wonderful. It fed an itch in his soul. "Mercy? Ah. Yes. I know that word. I don't tend to pay it much favor, in case you haven't noticed." He threw Na'len to the ground, face down, bloody fingers digging into the grass as the pathetic little *shit* tried to crawl away from him.

Valroy put a foot in the middle of the man's spine. Reaching down, he grabbed the wings of the little lord by the base with the talons of his own and *pulled.*

Cutting them off would be too easy. Too quick.

The sound of tearing flesh and more beautiful, delicious screams filled the air. It took a minute, maybe more, and all of his strength to rend the wings from the man's back. He tossed them aside, the dead flesh hitting the grass with thumps.

He licked the blood from one of the talons of his wings as he looked down at the weeping, sobbing, broken thing beneath him. "Tell me I am your prince."

"Y—yes—yes, you are my—my prince."

"Tell me I am your High Lord. Tell me you worship me."

"I worship you, m—my—my High Lord, p—please, mercy!"

He sneered. Pathetic, sniveling, treacherous, worthless trash. He crouched down, grabbed Na'len by the hair, and yanked his head back. The man gasped in pain. He dug his fingers into the man's mouth, and grasping the squirming, writhing muscle inside, digging his sharp nails into the soft flesh, he once more *pulled.*

The little lord screamed, and screamed, and screamed… and then his screams grew wet, and wetter, and then there was blood pouring from his jaw.

Valroy smiled and tossed the severed tongue aside with the rest. "You are a liar, and now you can do so no longer." He glanced over to Abigail. She was lying on the grass, in naught but her shirt and trousers. She was covered in sweat, and her chest was heaving. He could see the perfect swell of her body beneath the now-translucent cotton.

If he did not know better, he would say that was a well-ridden woman he saw before him. But even unconscious, her brow was knit in pain.

He sighed. He knew the poison at work.

She might die. Her heart might explode from the strain.

With a shrug of a shoulder, he looked back down to the weeping, bloody thing beneath him. "Do you think I care if she dies? Do you think I cannot simply steal another?" He chuckled, baring his teeth. "You have merely paid me an inconvenience. And that is all you have been—your whole life—an *irritation.* That is how you have lived, and that is how you shall die, little lord."

Standing, he stepped off Na'len and headed toward Abigail, ensuring to put all his weight on the dying man's back as he did. He would leave the broken cretin to bleed out. He wouldn't give him a quick death. There was no one around who would help him—no healer who would dare challenge the wrath of the "Bloody Prince" when he was in a mood.

Valroy licked the blood from his hand.

He was in a mood, indeed.

Moving to stand beside Abigail, he looked down at the tormented girl. Unconscious, panting for air, he could see the dark veins of poison beneath her skin, stemming from the small pinprick on her throat.

Tilting his head to the side, he debated his options.

Option one would be to put the girl out of her misery. He would take her to the Gle'Golun and feed her to the hungry flowers that wanted nothing more than to devour her mortality and return her to the nature she worshipped. It would be a fitting death for her. He could then find a new mortal girl to steal and start over.

But this one was fun, and he wasn't done with her yet. Finding a new girl would set him back some time, and it was so…difficult to find one that he felt had potential. Yes, his queen only needed to last until the following morning, but he wasn't going to wed just *anyone*.

He had his dignity to keep, after all.

He was a prince.

Option two was to let the poison do its work. Either she would die, or she would survive on her own. A test of her strength. But she was mortal—a witch, yes, but poison was poison, and she was unable to work her talent in such a state—and she was unlikely to survive.

Or he could help her.

There was no cure for the poison. And even if one could be made, the source of such a potion was bleeding out behind him in the grass, gagging and drowning on his own blood. He could take her to a healer, but the sun was already starting to inch toward the horizon. When it broke, the Seelie would reign over Tir n'Aill, and all the Unseelie would be hiding away in their little homes and shadowy nooks. He did not have time.

Only in his Maze were the Unseelie safe from Seelie wrath during the day. Currently, no one in the Maze was safe from *his* wrath. The healers would hide from him. He was not sure he could fault them for it.

Licking a long trail of blood from his fingers, he let out another beleaguered sigh. He knew what he needed to do.

Option three was to help the girl himself, and perhaps save her life.

Maybe if I save her, she might find me more palatable. Perhaps she'll be so grateful, she'll agree to be my queen. That was how it was supposed to work, wasn't it? Weren't there human tales of women saved by men in shining armor, so grateful that they were immediately wed?

It was worth a try. He would play the valiant savior and receive kindness in return. Smirking, he made up his mind. Yes. He would take this turn of events as an opportunity.

Crouching, he scooped up the girl into his arms. "Come, Abigail. You and I are going to have a very interesting day." He sneered. "A very interesting day, indeed."

ABIGAIL DREAMED OF BLOOD. It was beneath her, pulsing with the beat of a heart. *Tha-thump. Tha-thump.* With each beat, her head throbbed in pain.

Pushing up onto her hands, she felt the ground beneath her squish and give, like raw steak. It was warm, and the veins that crawled over the surface were black as pitch. Lifting her head, she saw that each of the veins ran ahead of her, growing thicker, before slowly they became the roots of a tree.

Some fifteen paces ahead of her, growing from a raised stone dais, an enormous and ancient oak stretched up high overhead, its bare and gnarled branches twisting and cutting sharp silhouettes against the starry sky behind it.

Buried in the tree were weapons.

Thousands of weapons.

As if an army had come and attempted to tear it down with whatever they had, she saw spears and knives, swords and arrows, axes and spiked clubs. Each one embedded in the tree, which had begun to grow and heal around it.

Standing, eager to be off the warm, wet ground, she took a step toward the tree. The surface depressed beneath her, like sinking into moss. And around her shoes, the space filled with crimson blood.

As she drew closer to the tree, she realized it wasn't one army that had tried to kill this tree—it was several. Some of the blades and weapons looked new, but some looked ancient, rusted and crude.

Climbing onto the stone platform the roots had overtaken, she furrowed her brow. There were carvings in the stone, deep trenches and marks that had weathered over time. This place was ancient before the tree had claimed it.

"Where am I...? Am I dead?"

A caw of a crow overhead made her duck her head, startled. Turning, she looked up at the animal who eyed her. Somehow, she knew—just *knew*—that the crow was disappointed with her. Planting her hands on her hips, she glared at the creature. "Pray tell, bird, what have I done to annoy you?"

"Mind yourself."

The voice came from everywhere around her. She turned but couldn't see anyone. Frowning, she gripped the wooden necklace around her throat, the one her aunt had given her. She knew who she was speaking to. "Forgive me, Morrigan." She bowed her head in reverence. "I meant no disrespect."

Silence. Then a touch on her shoulder.

Everything happened all at once.

Turning to face the source, her eyes flew wide at what she saw before her. But the image of the woman who towered over her, face adorned in blue paint, black eyes glaring at her in disdain, was second to the fact that the woman had suddenly buried a dagger into Abigail's heart.

Tha-thump.

Tha-thump.

Abigail could only watch in shock, the pain barely even registering in her mind, as her blood flowed from the wound and began to pool at her feet. It oozed into the carved groove surface. There was more of it than should have been possible. She fell to her knees onto the stone, her limbs weak and heavy. The blood joined the substance that surrounded the tree.

As her blood joined the rest, the pounding sang in time

with hers. All sound was gone, save for that ever-present drum of the heart.

"Surrender."

A heart that hers now matched.

A hand grabbed the blade from her heart and wrenched it from her.

Abigail screamed, and the vision shattered.

Or perhaps, she assumed it did. She was no longer kneeling on a stone surface, bleeding to death. She was lying in a clearing. And she felt as though she were aflame.

A figure knelt over her, straddling her body, his huge frame nearly blocking out the sun. The light behind him was dull and faded, and she knew they must be back in the Maze. His wings were unfurled. A clawed hand traced over her cheek, and a deep voice tutted quietly. "Poor little witch. What have you done?"

"I have—" She gagged in pain, writhing beneath him. She needed—she did not even know what she needed. She only knew she was in agony, and if it went on any longer, she would go mad. "This is not my fault."

"Isn't it, though?" He lowered himself to her, pressing a knee between hers, propping himself up with one elbow next to her head. His handsome, smirking face was next to hers, those sapphire eyes glinting even in the dull sunlight. "You left the safety of the Maze. You followed that traitor out of here. This is the price you pay for your foolishness."

"Please…" She felt tears sting her eyes, and she let them be free. They rolled from the corners of her eyes along her temple and into her hair.

He hummed. "Is this your surrender?"

With a frustrated whine, she turned her head away from him, gasping and whimpering in pain as another flash of the red-hot agony seared through her like coals. Now she knew the true price of her surrender. "Tell me they—" She cringed. "Tell me they were lying."

"Hm? Ah. I suppose that little pile of rat turds told you why I took you, didn't he?" At her silence, he sighed. "I need a queen, little witch. Whatever else they said to you was probably only *mostly* true." The chuckle that left him was a deep, dark rumble that resonated through her.

"You're going to destroy the world." She could barely breathe. Her words left her as stilted whispers. "Both of them."

"You think there are only two? Pah." He smiled, a thin twist to his lips, as he lowered himself farther, until she could feel him touching her. His lips grazed over hers. "I shall have what is rightfully mine. No more, no less."

"And what…what do you believe is rightfully yours?"

He grinned. She could feel his hot breath wash against her cheek. "Everything under the sun and moon, on Earth and Tir n'Aill, little witch. Everything. Including you."

With that, he kissed her.

Valroy felt her go tense beneath him. He hadn't hypnotized her. Hadn't lured her into a daze like the others had done. *Where is the fun in that? Too easy. Too simple. A pauper's game, seducing by magic.* He needed no such crutch.

Her body twitched and writhed in pain. Her hands pressed weakly against his bare chest, trying to push him away. But she was still in the throes of the poison, and her attempts were nothing more than touches. To be truthful, there was little she could do to resist him, even if she were not dying of poison.

He kissed her slowly, tenderly, just hard enough that she couldn't resist him, but soft enough that it wouldn't feel forceful. He would take her in time, but today…today was about his *kindness.*

Her lips were soft and perfect, supple and yielding beneath him. She tasted of sweet spring fruit—of apricots and cherries.

When he broke away, he was treated with another one of her withering glares. He loved the way she glowered at him, and it made him smile. "I am a covetous thing, sweet one. And the lips of another took yours before me. I had to right the wrong."

"Wh…" Her cheeks were red, and he knew it was not from the pain. She was blushing, even as she glared at him.

Delicious.

When he ran his tongue along the line of her lower lip, she gasped. Truly delicious.

She turned her head away from him, pressing her cheek to the grass, and he let her hide her enjoyment of the gesture. It was plain to see. He kissed her cheek.

"Wh—what happened to them?"

"Dead. Painfully dead. The girls, sadly, went too fast for my liking. They're decorating the fairgrounds as…we'll call it *art.* As for Na'len? I am not sure if the Seelie got to him before death paid him the mercy he so hopelessly sought to win from me. I don't rightly care."

She shut her eyes, and he watched tears streak from them once more. "You killed them."

"They were going to murder you, little witch. Life is life, and death is death."

"There is too much death here."

"Mmh…and I will bring it just a little bit more." He licked up one of the tears, enjoying the taste of the salt on his tongue.

She shivered beneath him and quietly asked him to stop. "If you're to kill me, do it now."

"I have no desire to kill you, little witch. I have something I need from you first."

"I will not marry you."

"We shall see."

"I *will not* marry you." That time, those amber eyes fixed to his and tried to level him with a glare. But it lasted precisely a second before she cried out in pain and writhed once more beneath him. He enjoyed the feeling of her wonderful body squirming against his, but sadly, the context was wrong.

Perhaps he could change that.

"A discussion for another time." He stood before crouching and lifting her into his arms. The poor thing was too weak to even struggle. He stepped into the pond—the same one as before. He wondered if she would be dismayed to discover she was right back where she started.

He hoped so.

Tasty, wonderful, foolish Abigail.

Sitting on a boulder below the surface of the water, he lowered her into the pond. She jolted as the cold water touched her. At first, she thrashed against the liquid, but she quickly went still and let him sit her down between his knees. The crease between her brows lessened.

For the first time since he had found her in that tent, she pulled in a breath that was deeper than a gasp. He smiled. "There we go…that's better, isn't it?" He cupped water in his hands and poured it over her left shoulder, then her right, then down her back.

Her eyes slipped shut, and he felt her go lax against him. Twirling her long hair, he tucked it over her shoulder and poured water over the back of her neck. "The poison won't kill you, little witch. Not on its own. Not at the dose you've been given. But it will make you very much wish you were dead. And I can help you."

"What will it cost me?" The words were muttered under her breath.

He laughed. "Finally! She *can* be taught."

"I would hit you if I could lift my arms."

"I know." He leaned down to her and pressed a slow kiss to her shoulder. That made her go rigid once more, arching her back. She tried to squirm away from him, but he banded an arm around her waist and pulled her flush against him.

She was so *tiny*. Well, no. She wasn't. She was of perfectly normal height, if perhaps a little bit more than average. He, however, was just ridiculously tall. And while it made many things convenient—such as being terribly intimidating—it also made some things remarkably inconvenient.

He picked her up and sat her on his lap.

She yelped at the movement. "What're you doing?"

"Saving your life."

"You just said it—"

"Shush. I know what I said, you contrarian little thing." He stroked her hair away from her throat once more. "Now, try not to squirm too much. Hm? I would rather like to do this without the aid of a healer."

"What're you—"

Finding the spot where the pissant Na'len had injected her, he ran his tongue slowly over the small, circular wound. Circling it once, twice, he smiled as she shifted in his lap.

He sank his sharp teeth into her throat.

CHAPTER SEVENTEEN

There was a burst of sharp, terrible pain.
And then immediately…there was not.
Abigail once more couldn't breathe. The relief of the cold water against her burning skin had lasted only a few moments before Valroy ruined it. Or had he?

He had kissed her. *Kissed her!* And oh, how he had tasted of the night sky. Of deep forests and rushing rivers and stone. Of the breeze that would move her curtains and drift through her home, carrying with it all of the wild world around her.

All the wild world that she held sacred.

It had been like nothing she had ever experienced. Though she would wish to deny it, would be so easy to lose herself in his embrace. She thought her day could not possibly get any more intense.

He proved her wrong.

Again.

Something washed over her. Something that was not fire. It was not ice. It was both. It thrummed in her. Pulsed in her. She pressed against him, her body moving of its own accord.

The noise that left her was embarrassing and damning all in the same moment. Gods forgive her, gods help her, gods guide her—

She moaned.

It was pleasure. Raw, unstoppable, undeniable. He had sunk his teeth into her throat, puncturing her, drinking her, and she wanted *more.*

He broke away, and she shuddered. She was suddenly glad for his arm around her, for she might have collapsed into the pond face-first and drowned if he weren't securing her in place. She expected him to laugh. Expected him to mock her for her reaction. To chide her, and relish in her weakness.

Instead, the sound that left him was some kind of deep, primal growl. "The poison is deep, witch. This may take…time."

Time.

And blood.

She would have nodded, but she was afraid to move her throat. Her words left her in a small whisper. "I understand."

"You will not die." He ran his tongue over the wound, and she shivered. "I promise."

Oddly enough, she trusted his word. When his teeth sank into her throat a second time, there was no pain. Only the strange, heated bliss as he drank, pulling from her in time with her heartbeat. He growled again at her back, pulling her tightly to him.

Predator and prey.

She whimpered.

Gods…

She felt him there, pressing against her—all of him. *All* of him. If she had the strength to move, she wasn't sure what she would have done. Perhaps turned in his lap, wrapped her hand around the impressive thing she felt against her backside, and demanded he make good on his threats.

Need roared in her.

No, no, no!

But her thoughts were reeling, spinning from one point to another, growing hazy like her dreams. She couldn't spare any energy on morals or righteousness. There was only him. Him, and his teeth, and the touch of his hands. The strong arm around her, holding her in place. The wolf, consuming his prey.

He drank.

She whimpered in ecstasy.

A wing wrapped around them, pushing through the water, the talon gripping her opposite shoulder as he caged her in even more.

She leaned her head back against him, exposing her throat. Her body throbbed. Everything ached. The burning had stopped, but it had been replaced with something far more frightening to her. She remembered Na'len's words about his poison. A single dose would warm and ease. A second would "feed the fire within."

She was no prude.

She knew what that meant.

When she thought perhaps darkness might take her and spare her the shame, Valroy once more proved to be beyond cruel, even in his kindness. He broke away, his chest heaving at her back, and ran his tongue slowly over the wound.

"Little witch…" The words were a dusky growl in her ear. "I needn't take more. The poison will fade on its own now." She could feel him shudder. "For us both."

He drank her blood. He drank the poison.

That meant… "Oh, no."

He laughed quietly, tightening his arm around her in an embrace. "I will be fine. Thank you for your concern."

"That—" The feeling of his arm around her, the wing against her shoulder—the hot breath against her cheek. She squirmed. She wanted to feel more of him against her. She wanted to feel all of him. "Wasn't my concern."

"I know." He grinned against her skin. "I am stronger than you. It is easier for me to resist the pull." A thoughtful hum left him, rumbling in his chest. "If I want to."

His arm shifted, and she felt him press a hand against her stomach, fingers spread wide. The wing around her moved away, causing ripples in the water. She was too weak to go anywhere. Gods, if she tried to move, she'd likely just drown.

Drowning might be better.

Drowning might be preferable to what I feel.

"I should have chosen the boar."

He laughed behind her but said nothing.

She wanted him. Gods help her, it was worse than that. She needed him—she needed him or else it felt like she might die. The throbbing might drive her insane if it were not sated soon. "Valroy..." She didn't know what she was trying to say as she whispered his name.

Please make this stop.

Please don't mock me.

Please, please touch me.

"This is not surrender, I understand." He shushed her gently. "This is not your doing." His hands slid down her thighs slowly, first the outside, before dipping into the center. He pulled her legs apart until they rested on the outside of his. "The poison is to blame."

Yes. It was the poison. Of course, it was. She nodded and leaned her head back against his shoulder.

"Only enough to quell the thirst, hm?" Where the other fae had caressed and paid her whispering touches, he did not. She could feel every press of his fingers as they dragged slowly up her body, one spreading over her stomach as the other slipped under her cotton shirt to grab roughly at her breast.

She cried out as he sank his fingers into her skin, groping and kneading her. His touch was *nothing* like the other fae. They were kind and sweet, luring her into a state of confusion.

They were cajoling. He was a conquering force. They were gentle. He was a warlord.

And he was incredible.

Claws tangled in her hair. But his hands were—

His wings.

The talon of one of his wings fisted in her hair and pulled it back sharply, causing her to arch into his grasp. The sting in her scalp lit a very different fire in her, and the noise she made was profane. She pressed her body into his grasp, needing more of his rough touch.

"It's just the poison." Still, he whispered into her ear. "Good, little witch…don't fight it. Don't fight me."

His other wing was beneath the water, shifting like some great monster, and she felt the claws grasp her knee, urging her to part her legs. She did, and as she split her legs wide, his followed, keeping her there. But she led, even as he prodded her along.

This is just the poison. This is treatment, the same as his bite. This is not— "I do not surrender."

"Of course not." The claw tangled in her hair moved her head so she could watch him. He wasn't smiling. She had expected him to look smug and terrible as he ravished her. But there was none of that. His sapphire eyes smoldered in lust, half-lidded as they were. There was darkness in his expression—darkness, and a need that matched her own.

When his hand undid the tie of her trousers, she held her breath. When his hand slid beneath them to cup her body, she shut her eyes and moaned.

His other hand still worked her breast. When he pinched her nipple, she expected to feel agony. But what she felt was anything but. There was nothing she could do. She might not have surrendered to Valroy, but she surrendered to what he made her feel. "Please, Valroy—"

Fingers stroked her, thumb finding the sensitive bud of nerves at her core that screamed for attention. She jolted against him, her body finding strength enough to writhe as pleasure crashed over her like the cool waves of the pond.

"Say it again," he growled at her, voice ragged and dark. His expression matched his tone. His teeth were bared, his lips still stained red with her blood. "Say it *again*."

"Please, Valroy…"

The sound he made was one of the most beautiful things she had ever heard. It was his turn to undulate beneath her, his muscles rippling as he gripped her tightly and leaned back against the shoreline. She was lying atop him. But she couldn't find the will to be ashamed of what she must look like in the crystal-clear waters.

His hips pressed up into her, instinctual and primal. He hissed, angry and frustrated, as if his body were betraying him.

Gods, it made her want him more.

The mighty prince can come unhinged. And I am to blame. "Valroy—kiss me." The words came from nowhere, but they left her before she could stop them.

And he obliged. The claws of his wings cradled her head in his grasp as his lips devoured hers in a mad passion. It was not the tender, gentle embrace of before. This was a stallion let loose from his pen to wreak havoc upon the mares.

His tongue was in her mouth an instant later, demanding and unstoppable. This was the Bloody Prince she expected. Bruising and needy, his sharp eyeteeth pricking her lower lip.

To her utter shock, to her utter surprise, and to her utter shame...she was kissing him back.

The claw on her knee tightened as he played her body like an instrument. He was deft and sure, even as he was wild and overwrought. His fingers never entered her. *This is not surrender. Of course not.*

This was pleasure.

And oh, what pleasure it was.

When her white-hot release hit her, he parted from their kiss, as if he wished to watch her as she arched. Her hand sought the one that tormented her breast. She tore it from her body and wove her fingers through his, squeezing his hand tightly in hers. Her other arm wrapped around behind his neck.

She cried out his name.

What she received was an order she didn't know how to resist. *"Again,"* he snarled in her ear.

And she did. Ecstasy replaced everything she knew—pain, fear, uncertainty, shame. It was all pushed away by the crashing tide.

And again.

And again.

And again.

Until darkness finally took her.

HE LAID her down upon a bedroll atop the soft grass. He knew how humans did so very much hate to sleep on the raw earth. He kissed her unmoving lips and allowed himself one more press of his hand against the soft, tender flesh of her body.

Abigail, Abigail, Abigail.

What am I to do with you?

He lay down beside her, resting on his side, and nuzzled into her hair. He had undressed her and clothed her instead in garb that wasn't soaked through. He had done the same for himself. No reason to drip on the poor girl while she slept.

There was a dark, blue-black mark on her throat in the shape of his teeth. His bite had erased the wound paid to her by Na'len. Good. *She is mine. Mine!*

The need roared in him painfully, but he tamped it down. No. He would not ravage her. He would not rut her this night, no matter how badly he wished to do so. And oh, how the organ stuffed painfully in his pants throbbed and begged to find a home deep inside her lush, warm, wet flesh.

She had begged for him. *Begged.* She had cried his name in release and whispered it in shameful need. And how he had granted her wish. Over, and over, and over again, he fed the poison that worked through her veins until it was too much for her to bear.

And she had sought his hand to hold as he did.

Stupid, silly, foolish, naïve, childish, precious, delicious, *wonderful* little witch.

His little witch.

Soon to be his queen.

He kissed her cheek, cradled her head against the crook of his arm, and watched in awe as she murmured and tucked herself even closer.

His needs could wait.

There was painful pleasure in denying the beast to be fed.

Especially when he knew the meal would come soon enough.

She would be furious when she awoke, he was certain. When the poison had finally run its course, and she was once more entirely her own, she would despise him for what he had done. But that was all right. For now, he had her. For now, she was his. And "for now" would have to do.

He kissed the top of her head and draped a wing over them both to keep them warm.

Little witch.

Precious little witch.

CHAPTER EIGHTEEN

Abigail sat up.

More accurately, she tried.

Something was over her, warm and soft. And moving. She thrashed, shoved at whatever it was, and rolled away from…wherever it was she had been. She got tangled up in fabric and wound up making it worse as she tried to free herself.

Someone laughed. It was deep, dark, and resonant.

It made her cheeks instantly feel as though they were on fire. Sitting up, she swept her hair out of her face and found herself sitting in the grass by a pond.

A pond she recognized.

She groaned in dismay.

Valroy, who was lying on a bedroll over the grass, laughed louder, revealing those sharp eyeteeth. "I knew it! Oh, how beautiful."

Her hand flew to her throat, and she winced in pain. It was a deep bruise, but…no wound. She should have gashes from where he had buried those teeth into her neck, but she felt none. More magic, she assumed.

"I told you, you would live." He stretched out like a great cat, reaching his arms up over his head. He folded his arms beneath his head and smiled at her once more, precisely like a cat that was far too pleased with himself. "Did you not believe me?"

"I—" She wasn't wearing the same clothes as before. Trousers, yes. But they were a dark gray that was nearly black. Her cotton shirt was a deep scarlet. *My face likely matches it.* "You undressed me."

"I've seen you—wait. That is what you're upset with me about?" He quirked an eyebrow. "That after you fainted from the poison that I *saved you from,* you're annoyed that I took you out of your soaked clothing and gave you something new to wear?" He shook his head and looked up at the stars overhead. "Humans."

"I'm angry at you for a great deal of things. It needn't start and end with your cavalier approach to personal privacy." Searching around on the grass beside her, she found a bodice tangled up in the fabric of the blanket she had tripped over. The fabric matched her trousers. She quickly put it on and began lacing it up.

"Do you even remember what happened this morning?" Another arched eyebrow.

"Yes. Yes, I do." Her face felt like the poison was at work again, making her feel on fire. "And I would like not to speak of it. You needn't remind me."

"Why not?" He rolled onto his side to face her. Gods, he was so *long.* So perfect. The way the muscles of his abdomen disappeared into the pants that were entirely too tight made her want to—

No, no, no!

"You're mad at me, aren't you?"

"No." She searched for her shoes. She found them—well, a pair anyway, they weren't the same—sitting nearby. "Well, yes. I'm furious with you about a great many things. But not —not about that." She paused. "About what we did."

"We?"

After a pause and a cringe, she answered. "We." She focused on tying the laces of the boots. "The poison was at work, yes, but…I was hardly an unwilling participant. I was inebriated, but you—" She bit back her shame and her embarrassment. "You were shockingly restrained, given the situation. You could have gone farther, and you did not. For that, I am grateful. I understand you showed restraint, and you were saving my life. It would be bad manners to be angry with you over what you did."

I wanted it. I can be angry at myself for that, but not at you.

"Hmm…perhaps there's hope for you yet."

She squeaked as she suddenly found herself on her back. She had no clue how he moved so quickly. But in the blink of an eye, she was in the cool grass once more. He straddled her, his silhouette now blotting out the moon that shone brightly overhead. "Valroy—"

He kissed her. Lips devoured hers with a passion that left her stunned. The poison had fed her hunger, but it had done nothing to amplify his touch. That, apparently, had been entirely Valroy's doing.

Gods help me.

She shoved his chest, trying to get him off her. He growled loudly, lowering his weight a little more onto her thighs to pin her there. She shoved a second time. He didn't budge.

It was too good.

The lure was too strong.

If he didn't stop…

She bit his lip. Hard.

He reeled back, touching his lower lip where she had done the deed. There was a spot of red, and she could taste the coppery substance on her tongue. Freezing, she waited for his wrath. Waited for him to haul back and slap her.

Instead…he laughed.

He laughed hard. Sitting back on his heels, still keeping her trapped beneath him, he wiped the blood off onto the back of his hand, and then licked it clean. "You are too much fun."

"This morning was not surrender, and this—you can't just—" She sat up and shoved him. "Get off me!"

The claw of a wing gripped her shoulder and pressed her back to the grass. Resting his hands in the grass on either side of her, he loomed over her. "Make me."

"I—What?"

"Summon your little balls of light. Call upon the grass to destroy me. Make. Me." He lowered himself just a little more.

"This is your Maze. I don't think—even if I could—that it would hurt you."

"Smart. You're correct." A white flash of a wicked grin was all she could see in the shadows cast by his dark hair. That, and his ever-glowing blue eyes. "Your power cannot harm me."

"I can't fight you. You are four times my size. And if I cannot summon my magic to help me, then this is a game I cannot win." She glared up at him. "You are a cheat and a scoundrel."

"Correct on both counts." He lifted one of his hands from the grass to place it against her cheek. His palm was rough, but not unpleasant. He rested his thumb on the valley of her chin, the sharp nail pressing just lightly against her lower lip. "What will you do, then?"

"Curse your name until the day you end my life."

"End your life? Oh, little witch. What did those fools tell you?"

"That you need a queen to take the throne. And that once you have it, your queen is no longer needed."

"Needed? No. Wanted?" He hummed. "We shall see." He slid his hand to the back of her neck, cradling her head in his palm. "Kiss me, little witch, and I'll let you up."

"Or?"

"Or I'll tear these clothes off you and make you realize the boar was the gentler option." He grinned. "Your pleasure last night was unrequited." He pressed his hips against her, and she held back a choked gasp at what she felt. "I feel rather *neglected.*"

"That is—entirely—your own fault." She swallowed the rock in her throat. "You have hands. Four, by my count."

Valroy turned his head to laugh loudly. When he turned back, he devoured her lips again with his, pulling her head up to meet him. She let out a startled cry against him that was immediately swallowed by his greed.

It was like kissing the sky. There was so much power in him, so much surety in his embrace. It was so easy to get lost in the feel of him, in the way he demanded and took what he wanted. *It would be so easy to surrender. And it would feel so good. But I can't.*

Especially now that I know my life isn't the only one at stake.

When he parted, her chest was heaving. When had she shut her eyes? She blinked them open. There was no smugness in his expression. No gloating. She saw reflected in him only what she felt herself.

"Marry me," he whispered. "Marry me and let us dance."

"No." She was glad for how quickly the answer came to her. "You'll destroy whole worlds if I do."

"Some things are worth destroying, if it means something new and beautiful rises in its place. I will not burn all of creation into ashes. I will simply fix it." He ran his thumb slowly over her cheek, back and forth. "This is my destiny. And this is yours."

"No."

"Tir n'Aill is filled with treacherous creatures who want nothing more than to sow distrust and murder. There are more like that bastard Na'len than not. Every single soul that belongs to our damnable, cursed race would rather stab you in the back than to pay you the barest bit of pity. Why do you want to protect them?"

"Death is never the answer. Your way of solving the problem is wrong."

"We shall see how long you adhere to that answer." He smirked. "This will not be the first attempt on your life. I can only hope that the rest are equally as …enjoyable."

Her face went hot again at the innuendo.

"Now, to our more immediate game. You're trapped, and the price to be released from this particular situation is a kiss. If you do not, I will flip you onto your stomach and f—"

She was sick of hearing him talk. Very sick of it. Reaching up, she fisted his dark hair in both her hands and yanked his head down to hers. She kissed him, matching his tempo and his depth. The growl that left him was low and pleasured, and the way it rumbled through her made her wonder if the other outcome would really be so bad after all.

When his muscles relaxed, she couldn't help it. She bit his lip again. He jolted in surprise, parting from her. He smiled down at her, chuckling in astonishment. His expression darkened quickly, however. "She enjoys giving pain. Good. I wonder if she likes taking it as well. You seemed to like it earlier…"

"I paid your fare, bridge troll." She shoved on his chest. "Off."

"Bridge troll!" He rolled off her obediently and stood, ever graceful. "You haven't ever even met one. How would you know? Or are you saying I'm hung like one, perhaps? Would you like to find out?" He went to untie his trousers.

"Stop!" She picked up a rock from the grass nearby and lobbed it at him. It bounced off his shoulder.

He laughed, lifting his hands in mock surrender. "As you wish."

"You are *terrible*."

"No. I'm quite wonderful, actually. What you're complaining about is that you are a prudish little creature, and I am neither of those things." He folded his wings at his back like a cape, the claws resting on his shoulders, one on each side.

"I am not—" There was no point in arguing. Where was her sword? She had a distinct need to stab him with it. "Compared to you, perhaps. But compared to you, everything is prudish."

"That's fair." He sat down on a boulder by the pond and watched her, pointing a finger. She followed the line until she saw the rusted blade sitting in the grass. "It tends to... puddle. I dislike waking up in water."

"I'm hardly going to complain." She picked up the blade and—oh. Her belt.

He chuckled.

She glared at him.

It only made him laugh harder.

"I despise you."

"And lo, it is as if we are already wed." He put his elbow on his knee and his chin in his palm. "I could create a belt for you. A proper one of real leather. Imagine that."

"You could, but it would be at a price. Like all things with you."

"I aided you with the poison free of charge. And I didn't even get a thank you." He frowned in mock hurt, the sarcasm laid on thick. "I'm very insulted."

THE UNSEELIE PRINCE

"Somehow I feel as though the treatment was part of the payment." She struggled not to keep her face from heating again. She failed miserably. "But as you wish. Thank you, Prince Valroy. I would be dead if you did not help me. But as you are to blame for putting me in this entire terrible situation in the first place, I rescind my 'thank you' immediately and replace it with this." She made a rude gesture at him.

He howled in laughter. It wasn't cruel, it wasn't harsh, it wasn't mean. It was pure amusement. As though she were really quite funny to him. She couldn't help but smile just a little bit at his joy.

"Come here, Abigail." He gestured a hand, a rare and tender smile on his face.

"Why?"

"Just—" He rolled his eyes with a sigh. "Just come here, will you?"

With a shake of her head, she put the sword down on the ground and crossed the spot of grass to stand in front of him. She made sure to keep out of his reach.

Wings.

She forgot about his damnable wings again.

One of them reached out, and one of the long, dangerous claws tucked down the laces of her bodice, and yanked her forward. She staggered and nearly fell. The only reason she didn't land squarely atop him was due to her hands that were now on his shoulders.

He smiled.

His other wing wrapped around behind her, keeping her there, standing between his knees. "Tell me something, little witch, and I'll fashion you a belt. Just a few answers to my questions, and you can go back to wandering about my Maze in pointless, indignant anger."

She pulled her hands from his shoulders, but almost

immediately had to put them back. His wings were pulling her into him, and if she didn't push, she'd be in his lap.

Again.

Her face went hot.

"Do you want me?"

Her face roared like her hearth with fresh firewood. "I—this—this isn't—"

"I am not asking if you plan to act on it, silly thing." He smirked. "Just a question. Do you want me?"

He knew the answer. She wasn't that good of a liar, and she had been…rather compromised as of late. "Yes. Who wouldn't?"

A flash of white teeth in a wide, amused grin. "A very good answer. And very few people, if you're truly curious. And they usually have extenuating circumstances."

"I wasn't. But thank you. Now the state of your ego makes more sense, I suppose."

"One day of poison and suddenly you've found some bite." He snickered. "Literally and figuratively." His hands wandered up her thighs and rested against her waist. For the moment, he seemed to be content to just leave them there. "If you want me, why not have me?"

"I'm not sure I would be the one doing the 'having,' Valroy."

"You assume we would stop after one go. Sure, I plan on ravaging you like a wild animal, but who says you couldn't take the next turn?"

She resisted the urge to slap him. Barely. She shut her eyes, sighed, and decided she very much did not like the fae in general. "Having sex with you would be wrong."

"How so?"

"You're my enemy."

"Am I? Are we?" He huffed. "I missed whatever broadside was posted to that regard."

"You abducted me, trapped me here, are tormenting me, threatening to ravage me, wish to marry me so you can take the throne and unleash a blood war upon two worlds, only to kill me—"

"That last bit has not been established as fact."

"But it's a possibility."

"Yes." He smiled. "Everything's a possibility."

That time, she couldn't resist any longer. She wanted to wipe that smug expression off his face. She rounded back to slap him.

And then was instantly airborne.

She hit the water and was instantly beneath it. Thrashing, she pushed up and gasped for air.

He threw her. The bastard threw her!

Wiping the hair out of her face, she glowered at the laughing cretin where he still sat on the rock, smacking his leg in pure amusement. "I hate you!"

"I know." He laughed and stood, folding his wings behind him once more. "You deserved that."

She climbed from the pond, water pooling around her. She was, once again, soaked to the bone. She took off her boots to pour the water out of them.

"This time, you can dry out on your own. But here." He motioned his hand, and in it appeared a brown leather belt with a brass buckle. He tossed it to her. "Oh. And Abigail?"

"What?" she snapped at him, wringing the water out of her stockings.

"When you realize we are not enemies, then you will be my wife. And when you realize desire is not surrender…then I'll be waiting." He smirked. "Enjoy your night."

"I—"

He was gone. Just disappeared in a blink.

Howling in useless rage, she sighed and sat down to finish wringing out her sodden clothes. It was all too much. It was all too overwhelming. She wanted to lie down and cry. She wanted to go home. She wanted to scream and throw things at him, to punch him until her knuckles bled.

But she couldn't do a single damn thing about any of it. Well, all right, except for the lying down and crying bit.

If I solve his Maze, he'll set me free.

It was the only way out. The only way out that she had that didn't wind up with her being dead, or a pet. Or both, possibly in that order.

I have to keep going. I have to keep trying.

Slinging her belt on, she picked up her shoes and stockings—she was not going to put them back on while they were that wet—and did the only thing she figured she could do.

She began to walk.

CHAPTER NINETEEN

"Anfar!"

Valroy threw a rock into the lake. "Anfar, get out here and talk to me!"

Silence. He snarled. Picking up a boulder, he hurled it into the air and watched it sail out over the water a hundred or so feet before crashing into the surface with a loud *sploosh.*

Folding his arms, he waited. When a huge shape began to move beneath the level of the waves, he knew he had guessed correctly precisely where the sea beast had been sleeping. The water crested and broke as the monster rose from the depths.

A huge, reptilian head at the end of a long neck reached up from the crashing water and stretched high overhead. He let out a loud, deafening screech.

Valroy rolled his eyes. "Yes, yes. You wake me up all the time. Now get *down* here, so we can talk." He stepped back as the waves reached the shore. When the monster lowered his head close to him and opened his maw to reveal rows of razor-sharp teeth, he smirked. "No need to be dramatic."

The creature let out a loud, heavy sigh that shook the

surface of the water, and shifted. He watched as it shrank down and warped, bones snapping and popping, as the creature painfully turned itself into a man.

"Easier to talk like this, don't you think?" Valroy folded his hands behind his back.

Anfar stood up, cracking his neck loudly. "I suppose. What is it, prince?"

"Someone tried to murder my witch. They were very nearly successful."

"That sounds like your problem, not mine. Moreover, you should have expected this." Anfar snapped his neck in the other direction, quite loudly, and groaned. Valroy knew the shift from such a very large monster to such a very small one was painful. He mostly didn't care. His friend fixed him with a black-eyed stare. "Why should this trouble me?"

"Because I want to know who was behind it. Na'len was a fool, but he wasn't *that* much of a fool. Someone was paying him, and I want to know who."

"And…you cannot do this yourself…because?"

"I forgot how irritable you are when you've just woken up."

It was Anfar's turn to roll his eyes.

He grinned at his friend. "I cannot do it myself because I have to protect her. Your future queen would be most grateful for your services, I promise you."

"Mmhm." He sighed. "Does she know?"

"Yes. The little shit told her everything." Valroy grimaced and paced away, a new wave of anger rolling over him. "I had hoped I could trick her into marrying me. But now I have to devise a new plan."

"Oh? You cannot seduce her?"

"I could, and I am making great progress, but now she has to weigh the fate of millions against it." He grimaced. "She is a noble thing. It will be a difficult and slow process to convince her I'm right. In the meanwhile, she is under siege."

"You could simply convince her to love you as the mortals do—with kindness." Anfar's expression remained flat. "If you tell the courts you plan to woo her and win her heart, they'll stop the assassination attempts immediately."

"Why is that?" He shot Anfar a dubious look.

"Because they would know the marriage would never come to pass." Anfar sniffed dismissively. "No one would marry you of their own right mind."

"Har-har, very funny." Valroy frowned and went back to pacing. "Astasha says she loves me. Proof to the contrary."

"I said 'right mind.' Besides, Astasha loves herself. You two are wed only in your mutual narcissism." Anfar turned to head back into the lake. "She sees in you only something her enormous ego can aspire to."

"Are you going to help me, friend?" He threw up his hands. "Or simply insult me?"

"Hm. I do not think the two are mutually exclusive." Anfar stopped when he was up to his knees. With a sigh, he nodded. "Yes. I'll help you. I'll find out who conspired to kill 'your' witch. You didn't happen to leave Na'len alive, did you?"

He scoffed. "Of course not."

The sea-beast sighed again, and once more the whole of the lake rumbled with it. "We have been through this. It is impossible to question the accused if *they're dead.*"

"Impossible? No. Inconvenient? Yes." Valroy waved a hand dismissively. "Go talk to the Bonesmith if you have to. I care not."

Anfar grumbled to himself, something very likely rude, and dove into the water without another word. Valroy smirked and unfurled his wings, ready to take to the skies. The sea monster was not the most graceful negotiator, but he made for a wonderful enforcer. He would know who, and whose court, was responsible for the near death of his witch.

But he knew who else to blame.

Glaring up at the skies, he bared his teeth at the crows he saw circling and hissed at them. They were watching him closely. Every time he left the Maze, there they were. Mother Morrigan had blessed the attempt on Abigail's life, he was certain of it.

He clenched his fists. "She *will* be my queen. The throne *will* be mine." He glared at the lake, the words of his friends troubling him. *No one would marry you of their own right mind.*

Lies. Insults. His mood was as dark as the skies as he took wing.

I'll show them all.

ABIGAIL SANG to herself to stave off the loneliness. She sang to herself to stave off the hopelessness that clawed at her heart. She pressed her hand to her throat, feeling the bruise there. *What have I ever been, but a pawn? A toy for others to play with and discard?* Marcus had filled the role of the lovely husband, but in the end, his kindness had run dry.

Valroy would have his crown from her, tire of her, and murder her. She would only be one in a sea of the bodies he would leave in his wake.

Perhaps I should have let the assassins do their work.

Perhaps they weren't wrong.

But her vision troubled her. Why had the Morrigan shown her that tree? Why had she embedded a knife in her heart, and shown her blood mixing with the rest? There was a parallel to be seen—the blade stuck in her the same as they were in the wood of the great old oak.

Surrender.

That was what the Morrigan wanted. That was what Valroy wanted. There was no question in her mind that the goddess wished her to marry the prince. She wanted war, and with him on the throne, she would have it.

But she had to resist.

"I hate visions," she muttered. Her shoes and stockings were still soaked, so she carried them. The squishing would have driven her insane otherwise. And the constantly dripping sword wasn't aiding in her desire to be dry. But at least she had that much, as Valroy could have left her with nothing at all.

Taking in a deep breath, she held it, and let it out in a rush. Solving the Maze was turning out to be the impossible task she had figured it would be. She had walked for hours along the path and seen no marks of progress.

And it was making her damn feet hurt.

Sitting down on a rock beside the path, she ran a hand through her hair, combing the strands. Walking was not helping. It had not gotten her anywhere to date. But how else was she supposed to travel? The stag had shown her a way through the thick underbrush, but she didn't dare strike off into the darkness. At least on the path, she could see.

She could summon her orbs to light her way, but they didn't last forever. There was *one* thing she could try, even though it made her feel like an abject moron. "What else is new? I've been threatened, nearly eaten, poisoned, dunked in a pond several times over…*handled…*" She shivered, and promptly blamed her damp clothes. "All the while, I'm made to be an idiot. Perhaps I am."

Aunt Margery smiled and kissed her temple, helping guide her hand to draw the right symbol in the dirt beside the stream.

"How will this help me catch fish?" She blinked up at the older woman.

"Because it never hurts to ask." Margery tapped a finger on the end of her nose, making her giggle. *"And it never hurts to ask nicely."*

SHE STOOD and picked the largest tree that stood guard on the side of the path.

She had always been able to listen to the trees.

It was for them that she sang as she walked through the woods. She sang to them, because she could hear them singing back.

Her love of the forest was one of the first reasons that her aunt had suspected that she also had a gift. As an adult, she understood that her mother had been eager to pass her off onto her "crazy" aunt. As a child, she hadn't quite grasped why she had gone to live with Aunt Margery. But she had quickly not minded, when it became clear she wouldn't get hit with the switch when she placed rocks in strange circles or talked to people others couldn't see.

Placing her palm against the tree, she shut her eyes. The Maze was alive. The sensation of the trees staring at her made her skin crawl. They were not like the ones she was used to, and she knew they likely meant her harm.

But it was worth a try.

"Please help me find my way," she whispered. "I am lost, and your world is so new to me. Please." She fought the tears that stung her eyes. "I am alone, and I am afraid. I know not what else to do. I do not want to die. I do not want to lie down and surrender to him, or to the grave. I want to find another way." Anger surged unexpectedly in her. Frustration at all that had been levied on her. "And I am *sick* and *tired* of walking!"

There was the sound of creaking and movement, of rustling branches and leaves. She opened her eyes and took a step back and watched in awe as a new path opened up before her. The trees simply…stepped back. The ground wasn't even disturbed where their roots moved and shifted.

She blinked. "Oh! Th—thank you."

She wasn't sure where it was leading her, but at least it was somewhere.

She hoped.

Anfar stepped into the Moonlit Court, uncaring for the footprint-shaped puddles he left in his wake as he approached the gathering of fae lords and ladies. There were a dozen or so of them, standing about whispering to each other. They were gossiping—which might actually be, in his mind, the most revolting thing a person could spend their time doing.

Besides, he knew what they were speaking of.

Because the subject never changed.

Valroy.

Oh, yes, the specifics changed as time went on. But it always revolved around one thing—what has the Bloody Prince done now, and what are we to do about it?

"He murdered nearly fifty fae. Two of them lords!" Duke Hanlen rubbed a hand over his broad face. "All for *what*? Because of the mortal girl?"

"He means to—" Lady Yuna glanced over her shoulder to where Lady Astasha was standing, and then immediately lowered her voice to a whisper. "He means to make her his queen."

"I know that, you insipid child," Lady Astasha said loudly without looking over. "And I can *hear you*."

Anfar hated coming to the Moonlit Court.

He hated it so very, very much.

"The fact remains," he said loudly, demanding the attention of the room. He was a court member himself, after all, though he never willingly chose to attend any single one of these gatherings. "That someone attempted to murder Valroy's new plaything, and regardless of his intentions with the woman, that stands as an act of aggression. Do we have any idea who ordered the deed be done?"

Silence.

"Do we know if it was one of our own, or one of the Sunlit Court?"

Silence.

"Good. Good." He shook his head. This was going to get him nowhere. Turning, he began to walk away. A hand grabbed his arm, and he hissed at its owner. Lady Astasha.

The beautiful woman frowned at him, her long, pure silver hair barely a shade lighter than her pale skin and eyes. Only her lips, which were painted a stark crimson, brought any color to her features. Anfar felt his jaw tick at the sight of her. Not because he did not find her ghostly appearance appealing—but because he *did.*

He very much did.

And that was a matter of much dismay for many reasons.

"Does he mean to do it?" She frowned. "Does he truly mean to marry a *mortal?*"

"Yes." Anfar gently pulled his arm from her grasp. He rubbed his arm where he touched her. "And you know why."

Astasha looked away and let out a long, sad sigh. "He plans to kill her. She'll join the rest of the corpses he'll leave in his wake once he takes the crown."

"Yes. A loophole in the law the Morrigan set."

She shook her head. "The poor little thing…swept up in all our drama."

You should be one to talk. He bit his tongue. Astasha meant well. She honestly did. But she was, above all else, a courtier. And a courtier with designs at being the queen. "He could do the same to you, if you were successful in convincing him."

"I suppose." She shrugged a shoulder. "He could not kill me without legal recourse in the Court. But there is no law against killing mortals." She chuckled. "If there were, we would all be caged." She paused. "One thing troubles me, though. This seems too simple. Why do you think the Morrigan did not predict this, and set forward a clause?"

"Perhaps she did not think he would sully himself with a human, I do not know. I do not dare pretend to think I can fathom the mind of a goddess." Anfar's shoulders slumped. "But you are right. I feel for the girl. She has no part in this save for that which was forced upon her."

"May I meet her?" Silver eyes glinted in hope. "Perhaps I can help her."

"I…" He hesitated. "I do not think it is wise right now. Valroy is furious, and likely to lash out at anyone who gets too close to her."

"Posh." She gestured her hand dismissively. "It is only me. He and I have been friends since childhood. He knows I will mean no harm."

"Step carefully, Lady Astasha. That is my only advice to you." Anfar took a step away from the blindingly beautiful woman. "He is protective of the human."

"Hum." She chuckled. "You don't think he's become smitten with her, do you?"

They both laughed at the absurdity of it.

No. Valroy would never give his heart to anyone, because it firmly belonged to his own reflection. With a shake of his head, he turned to leave. "I must go. Coming here will not lead me to who ordered her death."

"I fear you will have many suspects in your search, dear

Anfar." Astasha clicked her tongue. "For no one wishes to see him take the throne."

He paused and turned to face her. "Not even you?"

"He is to wear the crown someday, no matter what we do. I can only hope to fix him and his temper well enough that some of us may survive his wrath." She looked off toward the throne. It was made of branches and bones in equal measure, and all cast in silver. It shone in the moonlight, beautiful and terrible. Life and death. That was the balance the fae represented. And Valroy wished to destroy it all.

Killing the girl made sense.

Until one considered the alternatives.

"We shall see." Anfar turned on his heel.

"Send him my love, will you?" Astasha chuckled, a sound like bells in the night air. "If I do not see him first."

"He is in the mood to spill blood. I would like it not to be yours."

"Oh, Anfar. I didn't know you cared."

Grimacing, his teeth clenched tight, he lowered his head and departed the Court. Her teasing made him wish to tear apart the court by the very rocks that made its ruined walls and dash the silver throne to pieces. Damn her. Damn Valroy. Damn the courtiers.

And damn himself.

I love her. And she shall never know.

But such was a tale that was as old as Tir n'Aill. For what were the rivers, oceans, lakes, and streams, if not a mirror to shine back the beauty of the stars above? And yet the distance would never be closed.

She can never know.

He loved her. And it did not matter. Her eyes were on another.

And he had a job to do.

Perhaps I'm in the mood for a little murder as well.

CHAPTER TWENTY

The sound of song filled the forest once more, but this time it was not Abigail's doing. She froze as she listened to them. A dozen voices, perhaps, lifted in a chorus that flowed through the air around her like a stream. It pulled her along the path, her feet moving of their own accord.

The sound was one of the most beautiful things she had ever heard.

When she reached the edge of the forest, the trees gave way to flowers and grass. It stretched ahead of her a few paces before turning to rocks and going down an embankment to…the ocean. It wasn't grass beneath her bare feet; it was sand.

It wasn't possible.

She furrowed her brow and looked behind her, hoping to see the path stretch behind her. The trees were gone, replaced with a field of long grass that blew in waves before her, matching the crash of the sea now at her back. The smell of saltwater and the ocean filled the air as much as the beautiful singing.

The forest was gone. She shook her head. Someday she'd stop being so surprised by the magic around her. *I probably won't live long enough for that.* With a sigh, she turned back to the voices that filled the air.

There was a cove, cut in the cliffs, where the water grew shallow. Rocks jutted from the pool, and she could see figures sprawled leisurely around. Figures that were not quite human. She saw the shine of silvery scales as something large moved along the shore. It was a creature whose lower half looked like that of an enormous fish, but from the waist up, was a beautiful woman. She wasn't alone.

A man was sitting on a rock near the stone wall—if he could be described to be sitting at all, as his lower body was a mass of tentacles that were coiled around him or draped in the water of the cove.

Merfolk.

It was risky to approach them. Everyone in Tir n'Aill was likely her enemy until proven otherwise. She knew this, and she knew she should simply walk away—but the Maze had brought her here. Why?

Her toes touched the cold water, and she jolted, dropping her boots. They splashed beside her, getting wet *again.* It was enough to jar her out of her thoughts. She hadn't even realized she had been walking toward the singing until she had stepped into the sea.

"Oh! Hello." A figure moved, half submerged in the water.

The song stopped.

She scrambled to pick up her now-salty-and-wet shoes and staggered back out of the water. "I—Forgive me, I didn't mean to intrude—"

"Of course, you didn't." A young man chuckled. He was beautiful, with broad shoulders, a narrow waist, and the lower body of a snake that had a fin that ran down its back.

No, not a snake—an eel. He smiled at her. It was a shockingly kind expression. "Siren songs are hard to resist."

The woman with the lower half of a fish that shone like liquid silver slid through the shallow water until she could climb up onto the rock closest to Abigail. She had gills along her sides, and her skin color was as pale as the moon itself. She smiled. Her hair was a rich shade of dark teal. She was also naked. "You must be the mortal girl!"

"What gave it away, Talla?" The octopus man laughed.

"I—um—yes, my name is Abigail," she shyly introduced herself. Giving her real name to the fae was dangerous, but that was under normal circumstances. Besides, the "Bloody Prince" had laid claim to her already. She doubted anyone would fight him for it.

"Abigail." Talla smiled dreamily and propped her chin on her arms. "You're very pretty."

"Thank you. And you are, too." She bowed her head and took another step back. "I should go."

"Why?" another merfolk—siren—asked her. She jerked in surprise to see how close the woman was, and then how many friends had come with her. She had heard a dozen voices, and now she could see a dozen sirens around her.

"Because you're all scaring her, you lousy nits." Someone walked up at her side. She looked up at the face of a young man. The pelt of a seal was wrapped around his otherwise bare shoulders. He gestured at them. "Take a swish in the other direction, will you all?"

The sirens all complained, but did so, giving them both more distance. She looked up at the man in the pelt and nervously smiled at him. "Thank you."

"Not a problem." His eyes were the strangest shade of green she had ever seen in her life. He extended his hand to her. "Perin."

She shook his hand. He walked toward the ocean and

took a seat on a large rock that sat in about two feet of water. Turning to her, he patted the spot next to him. "We won't hurt you."

"Forgive me if I'm dubious. I've already been betrayed."

Perin nodded. "That you have. But if you live your life wary of the kindness of strangers, I fear you won't live very long at all. Especially not in Tir n'Aill."

"Especially not in the Maze," Talla chimed in.

They had good points. With a sigh, she rolled up her trousers and waded into the water. She had asked the Maze for help, and it had led her here. If it was leading her astray, so be it. "If you do plan on killing me, please just make it quick."

That earned a laugh from several of the sirens, even if it wasn't meant to be funny. She climbed up onto the rock next to Perin. He nudged her shoulder with his. When she startled from the touch, he let out a puff of air. "Oh, boy. You're in a state, aren't you?"

"I have been—I have had a terrible few days. Or weeks. I honestly don't even know." She cringed.

"It's just a spate of bad luck," one of the fishmen said. He was lying on his back on a rock, stretched out and watching her upside down. "It'll pass."

"Honestly, my bad luck goes back farther than this nonsense." She chuckled sadly. "Maybe the villagers were right. Maybe I *am* cursed. But I appreciate the sentiment."

"Witches can't be cursed. That's silly!" Talla jumped from her rock into the water, and in one powerful swish of her tail, popped back up near Abigail's feet. She swept her wet hair out of her face and smiled up at her. "You are a witch, yes? We heard the rumors. We heard you singing."

"I—you did? How?"

"The trees. They sang with you. The ground, the grass, the flowers—they sang, too. They love you." The woman picked up one of Abigail's feet. It was such an odd action Abigail wasn't sure what to do and just let it happen. The beautiful mermaid poked at her big toe, and then pulled on it. She giggled. "Feet are so weird looking!"

"They really are, now that you mention it." Abigail's brief smile faded into a frown. "I didn't hear them singing with me...usually, I can."

"They sing a different song than human trees." Talla let go of her foot and swished onto her back. Her nudity didn't bother Abigail. It made sense with how utterly stunning she was. "And I bet you've been too scared to pay closer attention, haven't you?"

"I'm not certain how anyone can fault me for that." She pulled a knee up to her chest and hugged it. The moon was low over the water, hovering there with its unnatural size. It reflected off the pitch-black waves in pure white. The sight took her breath away. "This place is so beautiful, and yet…"

"We are the venomous spiders that weave webs of shining silk. We are the graceful hunter in the shadows, perfect in our ability to kill." The man with the lower half of an eel slithered closer to her. "That is what Unseelie are. We are the beauty that kills."

"And the Seelie?"

"The beauty that lies." Talla huffed in disgust. "That *cretin* who attacked you always wanted to garner favor with the Din'Lae."

"Din'Lae?" She blinked.

"It means 'Sunlit Court.'" Perin sat back, resting on his hands. "The Court of the Seelie. And we are the Din'Glai. The Moonlit Court."

"The one that Valroy is attempting to rule. Are you all part of the court?"

"Mmhm. All fae are members of their respective courts,

even a lowly little selkie like Perin." Talla laughed teasingly and splashed water at the man sitting next to her.

He laughed and kicked his foot into the water, splashing her back. "We are all in the court. But most of us do not even warrant a rank, like myself." Perin shrugged. "It troubles me not."

"Will you sing with us, human witch?" The octopus man smiled. He was, like the others, perfect. There was something graceful and beguiling about them all, even in their inhuman shapes. *They are sirens. That is what they do.*

"I fear you are all better singers than I. My voice is nothing compared to yours."

"That isn't your fault. You're human." Talla swished her tail, draping it in the air over her. Water dripped from the spines of her body, shining like rain in the moonlight. "Sing with us anyway. We would love it. The world sings with you, and we want to revel in it."

"I…" She frowned. "I don't know your music." Suddenly, she felt so very shy. She never cared who heard her sing before, but in front of the sirens, she felt her cheeks go warm.

"Then sing us something *you* know, and we will join you." Another siren she hadn't heard speak before folded her arms on the stone near her. Her tail was that of a catfish, broad and flat. The woman's skin was dark, and her hair was long and thick, and as dark as the deepest shadows. She was, like all the others, breathtaking.

After a long moment, Abigail nodded and swallowed the lump in her throat. Dipping her feet into the sea, she looked down and watched the reflections on the surface of the water. Shutting her eyes, she listened.

She truly listened.

And she heard the sea.

. . .

"Oh, my love, I say goodbye
 For what the sea did do.
 She tipped the bow, and split the stern
 And ran me through and through.

Hate her not for what she does,
 For she's a jealous lot.
 The sea has taken what is hers
 And only what she ought.

A sailor's doom is waiting
 A'deep beneath the waves
 Where man and ship become as one
 And share their final graves.

Do not weep for me, oh sweet,
 I rest where I belong.
 But in the whispers of the sea,
 My love, you'll hear my song."

Music came out of her as if by possession. And perhaps it was. For she had never heard the tune before, and never once whistled the melody. But it came from her, borne from the ocean itself. She heard the waves. She heard the creak of ships and the screams of men as they were dragged down below.

She felt the sailors drowning. She felt the cold and merciless ocean. It was in her words, her song—no. *Their* song. For joining her voice was that of the sirens. Even Perin repeated the chorus in his rich baritone.

When she finished, she was shaking. It felt as though something had used her—like lightning striking a tree, it had come to ground. But it was the other way around. The ocean had come *up.*

She pulled her feet from the water.

"That was so beautiful," Talla breathed and shut her eyes. "The ocean gives you her blessing, mortal. And her thanks."

"But I didn't—" Her throat felt parched and dry. "I didn't do anything."

"Oh, but you did!" Perin smiled and wrapped an arm around her, hugging her close. "You listened. And sometimes that is what's required."

"I suppose." She felt so tired, suddenly. "I should be on my way."

"Where are you going?" the octopus asked, quite sincerely.

She turned to look back at the fields behind her where the forest should have been. "I was trying to get to the center of the Maze."

"Hm?" Perin blinked. "Oh, that's easy. But why?"

"I—Wait! Can you take me there?" She straightened, suddenly babbling. "I need to get to the center of the Maze. It's important! Please?"

Perin laughed and waved his hand at her excitement. "Calm! Be calm. Slow down, lovely. You haven't answered me why." There was such quizzical confusion on his face that she was suddenly concerned she was missing something. But it didn't matter. She had a chance!

"Valroy told me that if I went to the center of the Maze, he would let me go home. Please, it's my only way out of here." She took Perin's hand in hers and squeezed. "Please."

He blinked. And then shrugged. "All right. Makes no sense to me, but sure." He slid from the rock, splashing into the water, and began to walk to shore. "Come along, lovely."

THE UNSEELIE PRINCE

She followed him eagerly, nearly missing the calls of goodbyes from the sirens. Shyly, she returned their waves and said goodbye, almost forgetting her soggy boots on the rock before running after Perin.

"They like you." He smiled at her. He had moppish brown hair that fell around his face in wild curls. He was perhaps a bit more plain than the others, but that meant little. He was still almost alarmingly handsome. "The sirens rarely take to humans. Unless they're taking them in a very different way."

"Why is everyone here constantly so *sexual?*" She wrapped her arms around herself, as the cold air on her still damp clothes sent a chill through her. "It makes me nervous."

He laughed. "I didn't mean like that, but I see your point. And why shouldn't we be?"

"I mean..." She paused. No, there was no reason at all that she could see. Sex was shamed by the church, and there was no church here. There was nothing shy about nature. She let out a sigh. "Never mind."

"There you go. Tell me. Has the Bloody Prince had you yet?" Perin winced. "If so, I'm shocked, and I'm sorry."

"No, and—" She blinked. "Why would you be shocked and sorry?"

Perin looked away, his neck growing a little red. "No reason."

"Tell me." Anxiety suddenly rose in her. She knew there was nothing stopping Valroy from simply taking what he wanted. And when he finally grew frustrated with her and did so, she very much wanted to know what was going to happen. "Why would you be sorry?"

"It's nothing, I promise."

"Liar." She snatched the pelt from his shoulders and clutched it to her chest.

"No!" Perin yelped in surprise and reached to grab it

back, but his hands hovered an inch away. He wasn't able to take it back. "No, no, no—"

"I won't keep it." She hugged it tighter to her. "I know what it does to a selkie. But I need your promise, Perin. I need your vow. I'll give you back your pelt if you swear to never lie to me."

He paused. His shoulders slumped. "Fine."

She handed him back his pelt, and he quickly wrapped it around his shoulders again. He eyed her narrowly. "That was mean. I'm already helping you."

"I'm sorry." She chewed her lip. "I know. And I—I really wouldn't have kept it. But everyone here has lied to me. *Everyone.* I can't take any more falsehoods."

He sighed. "I understand." His gaze went down to his feet as they walked. "The bite on your neck. I thought…" He hesitated. "Valroy is violent. If you had slept with him, I was shocked because you're…in one piece. I was worried you had other bruises. That's why I was sorry."

"Oh."

They walked in silence for a long time. She knew Valroy could be violent, but he hadn't ever struck her. Or forced her. Or hypnotized her. She kept her arms wrapped around herself now for a very different reason. *He'll tear me apart soon enough.*

With a wavering breath, she murmured, "I want to go home."

It was a silly sentiment. She didn't even have a home to return to. Valroy had burned it to the ground, but even then, Marcus had legally sold it. She had nowhere to go, just the word of the Unseelie Prince. Just the hope that when she got to the center of the Maze and solved it, he'd let her go with enough money that she could fend for herself.

But he was a liar.

A violent liar.

THE UNSEELIE PRINCE

Desperately, she missed her aunt, and she clutched the small carved wooden talisman she wore around her neck. "I just want to go home."

Perin put a hand on her shoulder and squeezed. She walked a little closer to him, and he wrapped his arm around her.

"I shouldn't have taken your pelt. I'm very sorry."

He kissed the top of her head. "Forgiven, lovely. You could have done far worse than ask me to be a friend."

The sand beneath her feet turned back to dirt, and rising out of the shadows came the forest once more. But this time, the trees were made of pure white bark. It came off in sheets like birch. A scent filled the air that she didn't recognize, cloying and sweet, but not overwhelming. It was coming from the trees. "What are these?"

"They only grow here." He smiled. "Aren't they beautiful?"

Nodding, she kept walking. "What are they called?"

"They don't have a name. No need." He shrugged. "Come, we're almost there." He took her hand and led her through the rows of white trees. "We should hurry, if we're to make it before the sun rises."

"What happens when the sun rises?"

"Hm? Oh, don't you know? The courts trade places." He smiled helpfully, as if he were truly enjoying teaching her something. "During the sunlight hours, the Din'Lae rule the land of Tir n'Aill. We Unseelie must hide, lest they capture us. During the moonlight hours, we take their place. And if we find a Seelie, well…" He shrugged. "They don't stay Seelie for long."

She shivered and hoped she never had to learn the details. "You rule the same places? What about the market I saw?"

"You visited the City of Dusk. As soon as the sun rose, it became the City of Dawn." He had the tone of someone explaining letters to a child. And to be fair, she was in dire need of tutelage at the moment.

"But the sun here doesn't ever seem quite right, though."

"Oh, the sun in the Maze never shines bright enough that we're in danger. The Seelie can't come here. It's the only place their magic can't touch. That's why a lot of us hide here, where it's safe."

How odd. "Huh." Best not to insult the entire fae way of life. "It must be terribly inconvenient, trading places like that all the time."

Laughing, he pulled her into another hug against his side. "It is our way. You are adorable, do you know that?" He glanced down her cotton shirt rather pointedly. "And I can see why Valroy took you. If we weren't in a rush…" His hand draped down to her waist, and then his hand grabbed the globe of her ass and squeezed.

"Stop that, you dog." She shoved him aside, her face exploding in heat, and she shoved him a second time for good measure.

He staggered, laughing loudly. "I am no dog—I am a seal. Close, but not quite." With a shrug, he kept walking. "I can truly see why Valroy picked you. That blush alone is worth a sonnet."

For a moment, she wondered why they had to race the sun to reach the center of the Maze. But she had seen the transformation in the world, even through the haze that protected it from the sunlight. Whatever rested at the center of the Maze, it would change once the sun rose.

A moment later, and she saw firelight from up ahead. It cut the trees in sharp, flickering silhouettes. She could see ruins, as well—like great old walls and archways that once had made up some huge, towering structure. Now, it was left to be grown over and consumed back to the Earth from which it came.

THE UNSEELIE PRINCE

But she was beginning to suspect that the ruins were just as much a part of the world around her as the grass, and flowers, and trees.

She also heard laughter. And voices. A *lot* of voices.

"Uh—oh, no. No, I was mistaken, this isn't the way." He grabbed her arm and stopped her. "We should go. Immediately. I'll take you there tomorr—"

"What is it?" She studied his face. He was afraid. There was real terror in his eyes. Whatever was up ahead, he wanted no part of it. "What is going on?"

"I—uh—*damn you—*" He muttered in a language she didn't understand, but fully gleaned the meaning from his tone. The words were unkind. "I cannot lie to you, so I will say nothing at all. Nothing save for that you do not wish to see what is happening. We should leave. Now."

Tugging on her arm, she yanked it out of his grasp.

Just as she heard the sound of a scream. Turning toward the firelight, she heard it again. Whoever it was, whatever it was, they sounded young. She began to run toward the fire.

"Abigail! Come back! Don't—" Perin was half-shouting, half-whispering at her.

When the scream came again, she had just reached the edge of the ruins. Just past the wall was a crowd of…of monsters. She froze. Goblins stood about in a circle that descended into the ground, rows and rows of pews until it stopped some twenty feet below. A great cauldron burned there, the fire licking up the sides. The walls and benches were stone, but she couldn't see much of them through the horde of misshapen and malformed *things* that seemed to fill every available space.

One of the things next to her turned to peer at her through the single eye it had, shoved in the place where its nose should have been. It cackled and placed a heavy, bulbous hand on her shoulder, and shoved her closer to the center. "Front row seat! Front row seat!" it cried.

A sea of hands. They grabbed at her. She heard them laughing, tugging at her hair. She cried out, swatting at them. "Stop it, let me go!" But she was moving. They were dragging her down the rows of seats. The world tipped around her, this way and that, before she finally came to a stop.

She found herself seated right in the front row. The roar of the cauldron fire was so hot, she wondered if it might burn her. When she tried to squirm away, more of the creatures held her in place. Her arms were behind her back, gripped tight, and somehow, something was even holding her ankles.

"Oh. Hello, Abigail! What a wonderful surprise." A voice chuckled. "And fantastic timing." She looked up to see Valroy standing before her. She wasn't surprised. He gestured over to another figure that was similarly restrained. "We have another guest tonight."

He was a young boy, perhaps ten or twelve years of age. He was sobbing, tears flooding his cheeks, his small frame trembling in terror.

The boy looked to her, and in his face, she saw pure desperation. "Help—me—" he choked out between broken sobs.

A sharp black nail, as long and thin as the sharpest knife, touched her chin. With the talon of his claw, he tilted her head back to look up at him. He smiled wickedly. "What are you doing here, little witch?"

"You said if I solved your Maze, you'd set me free. Keep your word, Unseelie prince."

"Solved?" He furrowed his brow. "Whatever do you mean?"

"This is the center of the Maze, is it not? Keep your word!"

"Oh!" He barked out a laugh. The claw slipped into her hair and fisted it. He yanked her up to her feet, tearing her from the grasp of the goblins. She could only hiss a breath of pain through her nose as he pulled her flush against his chest. "I have kept my word."

"Have I not reached the center of your Maze?"

"Indeed, you have."

"Then set me free."

The sight of his sharp-toothed grin made her neck ache. "I said to solve it. Do you think I meant reach the middle?" This time, his laugh was cruel. "Silly mortal girl...they are not the same thing. You have not even *begun* to solve my Maze." He threw her back into the stands. The goblins snatched her eagerly, yanking her to the bench. "I think..." Turning slowly, he stretched out his arms and unfurled his wings. "I think that tonight we shall have a trade!"

I should have listened to Perin.

The crowd roared. Valroy smirked down at her. "Yes. A trade it shall be." He crooked a single claw beneath her chin. "Marry me, little witch...or the boy dies."

CHAPTER TWENTY-ONE

"No!"

Valroy watched as the little witch struggled against the grasp of his grobles and goblins. But she was easily overpowered. The strength of one of them outmatched her, let alone the hundreds that surrounded her.

By the stars, she looked good, surrounded by creatures, pinned in place, fear and desperation painted on her face... clothes rumpled. He savored the sight. It nearly broke his train of thought.

"No?" He chuckled and took a step away from her. This was so wonderfully delicious. "Very well. The boy dies, then." Summoning a sharp blade to his hand, he stalked toward the human whelpling.

"Wait! Don't!"

The crowd laughed. He couldn't help but grin. "Hm?" He turned to her and feigned confusion. "You tell me no, then you demand I wait. What will you have me do?"

"This is no trade—this is piracy. Unseelie prince, your deals are cheap! You are a cheat, and a liar!"

The grobles gasped, and he heard murmurs amongst

them. Valroy sneered and met the witch's fiery amber gaze with a glare of his own. "I will warn you once, Abigail…I tolerate your insults in our private moments. And only there."

She paled, perhaps. But her glower remained firm. Good. He loved it when she was angry. "Then give me a trade worth making."

Another murmur from the crowd spurred him to action. "Very well! A trade worth playing, eh? Let's see…" He paced around the cauldron thoughtfully, dragging one of his claws through the tar-like, viscous substance. It did not burn him. It never would.

"Ah!" He paused and faced her again, folding his wings about him dramatically. "Here is my revised offer, witch. A ticking clock—an addendum to our previous game. A change of the stakes, if you will." Stepping up to her, he realized she was at just the perfect height if he were to unlace his trousers. Oh, how he wanted to see her *snarl* and *glare* at him as he plugged those pink lips and muffled her furious sounds.

Soon.

"Spare the boy," she begged him through her anger. Desperate and furious both in the same expression. *Oh, stars, have mercy on me. I might take her here.*

Forcing himself to focus, he sneered. "You have until the moon wanes and goes dark to solve my Maze." He pointed at the orb in the sky, which was just slipping out of full as it dipped down low on the horizon. "If you do not, you will agree to be my queen."

She hesitated. "And if I agree to this…you will spare the life of the boy?"

"Yes."

More hesitation. The roar of the fire beneath the cauldron and the murmured and eager whispers of the gremlins and grelocks filled the air.

Finally, her shoulders slumped. "Deal."

The crowd erupted in cheers.

"Good." He unfurled his wings once more. "Now, we can continue. Bring me the boy." He flicked the sharp dagger over his fingers, rolling it deftly around his palm and back. "Let us begin."

Abigail screamed. "Wait! You said you would spare him!"

"Ah-ah!" He lifted a finger to her. "I said I would spare his *life*. The boy shall live." He grinned viciously. "You need to learn to mind your words more carefully, sweet one."

One of the goblins thrust the sobbing, wailing boy into his grasp. He took the child by the throat and yanked him closer. "This boy stands accused of wishing his sister to death!"

The crowd cheered.

"N—no—no—" the boy wailed. "I didn't—I didn't mean it!"

"Stop this, stop this, you insufferable *arse!*" Abigail was screaming at him, struggling and kicking, but he didn't care. It was drowned out in the eager shouts from his horde.

"You found one of our circles, you stepped between the mushrooms, you looked up at the mother moon and you said *'Make her die. Make my sister go away. I wish she would die.'*" He picked the boy up off his feet and wrinkled his nose in disgust. "For shame! Your baby sister, no less. An infant. A defenseless little thing."

"Please, plea—"

He tightened his claw around the throat of the boy. The boy gagged in pain and grabbed at his talon in a desperate and futile attempt to free himself.

Valroy bared his teeth. "The baby girl breathes no more. Your mother wails and weeps. And she shall not know that the *fiend* who did the deed no longer sleeps in her house. For someone with such a black and vile heart as yours…belongs with us." He threw the boy to the ground, face down. The goblins nearby rushed forward and pinned him there, limbs spread wide. "Your wish was granted, and this is the cost."

The boy screamed.

"You can do better than that." Valroy stepped over the boy and twirled the knife once more.

With a laugh, he went to work.

And the boy did better.

Her screams were drowned out by the cheers of the goblins around her. Their bulbous hands still kept her pinned in place. When Valroy stuck the tip of the knife into the back of the young boy's neck, Abigail had to look away.

She had to squeeze her eyes tight.

But she did not need to see to know what kind of horror the Unseelie prince was unleashing. She could hear it just fine. Even through the cheers of the crowd, the sound was unmistakable.

The sound of skin being removed from muscle.

When Marcus had gone out hunting and come back with a deer, she had helped him clean the animal. Even as she had thanked the mother Earth for her gifts and thanked the spirit of the deer for its gifts, she had run the knife between the membrane and helped pull the hide from the corpse.

It was a wet, thick, ripping sound.

Abigail doubled over and retched, glad for the first time that she had an empty stomach.

At some point, the boy had stopped screaming. She knew why. *Please, let him be dead. Please, at the very least let darkness have taken him.*

A hand tangled in her hair. One that was too deft to be the heavy fists of the monsters around her. Her head was yanked back sharply, and she found herself looking up at the demon himself. And if Satan did not grin like the creature who loomed over her, spattered in blood, then perhaps the scorn was misplaced.

His hands dripped in blood. But something else was in his hand with the knife. It was…

She felt ill again. "But—but why?"

"Why?" He chuckled. "Humans. So naïve." He held up the item in his hand, bloody and raw, draping like fabric. "Allow me to demonstrate." He released her, and she could smell the coppery tang of the blood that he left staining her hair.

She tried not to look at the body of the boy.

She tried very hard.

But there was nothing she could do. Her mind forced her to see—forced her to imprint that image into her mind where it would linger for the rest of her days.

In two easy strides, he crossed to the burning cauldron. From where she sat, she couldn't see what simmered within. He reached in a hand and, cupping the liquid, raised it and let it pour from his fingers. It was thick and black, like tar.

The goblins and gremlins laughed and cheered.

With one of the talons of his wings, he thrust the raw, bloody skin of the boy into the liquid. He held it submerged for a time. When he pulled his hand back, the skin was mottled purple and green, and unlike any pelt she had ever seen before. It hung in weird ways, and seemed far larger than what had gone in.

Returning to the body of the boy, he nudged it with his foot, turning it over with a wet plop. Blood pooled on the ground, dark in the moonlight.

With a flourish, he placed the boiled leather over the boy like a blanket. Returning to his remains that which he had taken.

The boy screamed.

His body arched and thrashed.

The purple-green leather snapped to his body, far too large for his small frame, and seemed to consume it. The scream was joined by the sound of snapping bones and crunching tendons. The boy convulsed.

The boy turned over to crawl away with arms and legs that no longer resembled what they had been before. But he collapsed, and then went still.

Valroy watched, an eager and cruel grin on his sharp features.

The boy laughed. Thick and coarse, and unlike any sound she could imagine a boy of ten might make. It was not a boy any longer. The creature stood and, pound for pound, was three times her size and a foot taller than she was. Its features were distended and swollen, bruised and sallow. The creature cackled.

That is how goblins are made.

Valroy turned to smile at her and bowed elegantly at the waist, his wings furling about him.

It was not precisely dignified, but Abigail was not certain what other choice she had.

She fainted.

"Well, I'm certain that set me back. Think she'll want me now?"

Anfar rolled his eyes as he watched Valroy place his human on a pile of pillows and blankets that the Unseelie prince used as a bed. Anfar leaned back against the tree behind him and rolled his eyes. "You have an odd form of courtship."

"You said it yourself." Valroy reached out and stroked the girl's hair back from her face, before flopping down beside her, smirking fiendishly. "No one will love me. No one 'in their right mind' will marry me. So why bother trying? Hm?"

"You are the definition of a self-fulfilling prophecy."

The prince scoffed. "There are enough prophecies about me. I needn't add another. No, you're simply complaining because I embrace the role you lot have set before me." He propped his head up on his hand, his elbow on a large pillow, and began to toy with some of Abigail's long, red hair.

Hair that was just a little bit redder due to the blood that streaked it. "You should not have made her watch." Anfar shook his head. "You are cruel to her."

"I want her to know what we are. Who we are. More importantly, who *I* am. I will not apologize for my nature. Especially not to my future queen. She shall know all of what I am capable of before the end."

"You truly intend on wedding her, don't you?" Anfar had clung to the hope that he would change his mind. That he would get bored with the girl and quickly be rid of her. But now, he was not so certain.

"Oh, very much so!" The prince stroked his hand through her hair once more, carding it through his fingers. "Did you see how she looked at me? How she *glared* at me while I boiled that boy's pelt? She was terrified—horrified—but oh, she was furious. By the stars, how I want her when she's angry. I think if I had let her, she would have attacked me." He hummed. "What a tasty thought that is. I expect she is a terrible fighter, however."

Anfar put his hand over his face. "You are impossible, and I am done with this mad game of yours."

"Yes, yes, I've heard it all before." Valroy paused for a moment. "Wait. You *will* still help me find who tried to kill her, yes?"

With a long, deep sigh, he fixed his own glare at the prince. He hoped it didn't have a similarly arousing effect.

Valroy frowned. "What? What did I do to offend you now?"

"These games of yours. You play with her too much. Take pity on her. No more."

"The deals I've brokered with her are fair and willing. She has known each time the truth of what she has chosen." Valroy bared his teeth in annoyance before rolling onto his back, staring up at the trees overhead. "She agreed to marry me by the new moon." After a long pause, he finished. "I am not a cheat, nor a pirate. She'll understand in time."

Anfar furrowed his brow. "In time?" He tilted his head. "You do not intend to keep her, do you?"

"I have not yet decided. She's mortal, besides." He shrugged a shoulder. In his claw, he dangled a necklace. At the end of it dangled a wooden talisman, carved loosely in the shape of an owl. He toyed with it idly. Anfar thought that he had seen it on the girl. "I would have to work some mighty magic to keep her here as one of us, and I doubt she would approve of living forever at my side."

"You intend to wed a woman who despises you and keep her as your queen." Anfar had to repeat it just to make sure he had the insanity perfectly clear.

"She doesn't hate me as much as she claims. She wouldn't let me touch her if she did. Nor would she agree to kiss me." He smirked, tangling the thin leather cord of the necklace he had stolen from her around the long claws of his wing. "And oh, how she *wants* me. Isn't that fun?"

Anfar wanted to punch the tree until it splintered, fell, and crushed the Unseelie prince to death. Instead, he swallowed his annoyance and went to leave before he caused more violence.

"Wait."

He paused.

"Have you made any progress?"

Anfar shook his head.

"Then why are you even here?" Valroy snorted. "Besides to insult me."

"To warn you." Anfar sneered. Oh, this was going to be fun. "Lady Astasha has requested to meet your witch. And you know there is no stopping her."

Anfar laughed as he left, hearing the angry shouts of rage behind him.

CHAPTER TWENTY-TWO

Abigail woke up and let out a contented sigh. She was so very comfortable. Whatever she was lying on was thick, and soft, and perfect. She was warm. She snuggled into the surface beneath her.

Wherever she had been before was terrible, and awful, and smelled of blood.

This was far more preferable.

Clinging to sleep for as long as she could, she tried to will herself not to wake. But like the dawn, it was inevitable. She blinked her eyes. It was daytime—if such a thing really existed in the Maze. She heard birds chirping, and they darted about in the sky above her.

Trees with silvery-white bark and leaves that were nearly purple surrounded her. Drawing a line around the space she was lying in were white marble walls that were long since fallen into ruins, like the rest of the places she had seen.

She was on a platform that was absolutely covered in cushions, blankets, and lush bedrolls. It was the most eclectic collection she had ever seen. Some looked worn and old, some looked new and shone in brightly colored silks, velvet, and more. Draping from the branches overhead, long swaths of dark blue silk were tied to each edge of the platform.

Something firm and warm was draped over her.

It was an arm.

She rolled onto her back. Sleeping beside her, his face smooth and devoid of all the monstrous inhumanity she *knew* he was capable of—was Valroy.

She couldn't find it in her to be surprised.

But she could find it in her to punch him.

In the nose.

As hard as she could.

He howled, grabbing his face and rolling onto his back, hollering and shouting. "What in the *blazes—*"

Jumping out of the bed, she was glad to see she was still clothed. Barefoot, but fully clothed. She glowered at the fae prince. "Get *away* from me! How dare you?"

He was touching his nose and then inspecting his fingers, checking for blood. "Why, precisely, did you punch me?" He frowned. "That was uncalled for. I didn't even grope you." Climbing out of bed, he rubbed his face. "Please refrain from doing that again. That actually smarts."

She was shaking in fury. Searching around for something, she saw a large dagger sitting on the table nearby. It was the size of her forearm, but she didn't care. She picked it up and flew at him in a rage. "You *beast!*"

A rage that was made far worse by his laughter. He defended himself easily, avoiding her wild swipes with his dagger. He was impossibly fast, his movements lithe like a cat. It was almost as though he could predict her actions.

"Your stance is too wide. Narrow it, lest this happens." He sidestepped another stab with the knife. His foot nudged the back of her knee hard enough to make it buckle, sending her down hard to the carpeted floor.

"Damn you to the pits, you revolting monster!" Scrambling back to her feet, she went at him again, not caring for the sting in her knee.

"That's better!" He laughed, smiling broadly, clearly enjoying every single second of her pathetic attempts to stab him. "Now, next piece of advice. Don't start your swings so early. Also, it's a dagger, not an axe." He snickered. "Stab, don't swipe."

With each word, she tried to gut him, to no avail. "Shut *up* you vile, disgusting, contemptible, perverted, depraved—"

His hand caught her wrist, and with a smirk, he whirled her around and shoved her forward. She hadn't even noticed that he had managed to back her straight toward the platform where they had been sleeping. Her thighs hit the edge of the platform, and she tipped forward with the momentum. The dagger flew into the pile of pillows.

She scrambled for it, but a sudden weight pinned her down. Valroy was pressing against her back. A talon pinned her wrist to the bed in front of her, halting her progress. A hand pressed down upon her lower back, pushing her into the soft cushions.

And something very hard was digging into her rear.

She froze.

"This is better…" he purred. "Isn't it?" He pressed his hips forward, grinding himself into her.

She squeaked in surprise. "W—wait—"

The pressure relented, only to begin again, and he groaned quietly. "You better start minding your temper around me…I don't think I've ever wanted anyone quite as badly as I want you when you are so very furious." One of his arms wrapped beneath her hips, holding her against him, ensuring she couldn't escape.

Her breath caught in her throat. The presence of him was total once more. Total, demanding, and unstoppable. "Get off me, Valroy!"

"Oh?" He dug himself into her again, miming the act he clearly wished to perform. "Do you not enjoy this? I think you do..."

"No!"

"Liar." His teeth dug into the bruise on her throat.

She gasped, her eyes slipping shut against her will. It sent a thrill through her, sharp and unstoppable, and she felt her muscles loosen beneath him. When his tongue rolled over the spot where he had bitten her, she had to grit her teeth. "Get. Off. Me. *Now!*"

His voice was a whisper in her ear. "It's all right. I understand. I'm a disgusting"—he ground his hips to hers—"contemptable"—and again—"perverted"—the pressure relented and returned—"depraved..." The pattern was going to drive her mad. "Did I forget anything?"

She could barely breathe. What kind of power did he have over her? What kind of spell did he cast on her? But anger and disgust rushed up in equal parts to match her other more confused emotions. She elbowed him hard with her free arm, trying to push him off her. "Stop this—right now—you treacherous demon!"

"Treacherous?"

Suddenly, the world moved around her. He flipped her onto her back. Damn him for being so much stronger than she was! "Get—" Her words choked off. He was standing between her legs, his body pressed tightly to hers, his face barely a hand's span away.

He smiled and tilted his head thoughtfully as he looked down at her. "Not bad. I like the other way better. But not bad." He sank his hips to hers, and she watched his face smooth in bliss. He groaned. "Not bad at all."

"Stop—stop—get *off me*—" She shoved on him desperately. This was wrong. This was very, very wrong.

"Not until you explain how I'm treacherous. What did I do?"

"You l—" She gasped. The way he rolled his hips—the way he pressed into her—*No!* She punched his shoulder. "You lied to me!"

He caught her wrists in the claw of his wing and snapped them over her head, gripping them tight. He straightened a few inches but didn't break where his lower body met hers. He looked honestly confused. "I did? Recently? When?"

"You said you would spare the boy…"

"I did exactly that." He smiled again and tutted quietly. "Oh, silly witch. Don't you understand? There was nothing you could have said to change what was going to happen. His fate was sealed the moment he wished his baby sister would die."

"You played me."

"I—" He paused, let out a hum, and then shrugged. "Fine. I played you. But I didn't *lie.*" Hips rolled and dug against hers with that last word.

It was all too much. Overwhelmed, overwrought, she yanked her hands free of him and shoved, hard, against his chest. "Stop."

"Why?"

"I—I need you to stop. Please."

With a disgruntled sigh, he straightened, releasing her. "Fine. Because you asked."

Scrambling out from underneath him, she nearly fell off the platform on the other side. She definitely took a few pillows with her. Her face felt as if it were on fire.

Shutting her eyes, she tried to calm herself. But all she could see was the image of that boy lying there in his own blood. All she could hear was the sound of Valroy's sadistic laughter. The sound of a body twisting into a grotesque goblin. Anger rose in her, and she was now standing there shaking for several reasons. "What you did to him…it is unspeakable. You are a beast, a fiend, and a demon."

"Half-demon. I am a predator, little witch. We all are. This is who the Unseelie are. I suggest you adapt." She opened her eyes in time to see him drop himself back onto the bed as if this were the most casual situation in the world. He let out a small sound of surprise and dug underneath him. Plucking the dagger out from between two pillows, he turned to inspect a small bleeding cut on his side. He laughed. "You stabbed me after all." He swiped up a trail of blood and licked it off his finger.

"What you did to him was disgusting. It was cruel. It was—it was horrific."

"I agree with you. And?"

"What you did was wrong!"

"Ah." He lifted a finger. "That's where you miss the mark. What I did was tradition. Do you think I'm the first High Lord to make a goblin, gragnal, or gremlin from the flesh of a foolish mortal? Do you think I *invented* this cruelty? I'm simply the prince waiting in a long line of cruel kings. I was merely acting as all High Lords have before me." He snorted. "You're adorably naïve, but come, now. Have some sense."

"Stop insulting me!" She couldn't take it anymore. She was at her wits' end. "I cannot—" All her anger shattered like the fragile glass that it was. And with it, she cried. She turned to hide her face and paced away from him. Fisting her hair in both her hands, she hoped the pain might stop the tears.

"Abigail? What's wrong?" He was close to her again, the sound of his deep voice rumbling at her back. She jolted—she hadn't heard him approach. Arms wrapped around her, pulling her back to his chest, and they were followed shortly by wings. His touch was shockingly tender, as was his voice. "Why are you crying?"

"The fact that you cannot comprehend why I might cry

right now is both perfectly telling and hideously *astonishing*." She shoved at his arms, but he refused to let her go.

"Now you sound like Anfar."

"Perhaps he is the one here with some sense to him!"

"You really do sound like Anfar. Has he been coaching you?"

It was meant to be a joke, but it was a bad one. She tried to pull out of his arms, and that time, shockingly, he let her go. She wiped at her face and moved to one of the marble walls, leaning on it for support. "Leave me alone, Valroy."

"You know I can't. You know I won't. You will soon be my queen."

"No, I *won't be*." She glared at him, blurry through her tears as he was. "I will not marry you. I will *never* marry you."

The gentleness in his expression was gone. "You made a deal. A deal that was witnessed. When the moon has waned and is dark in the sky, when the shadows are their deepest, you and I will be wed. And we will be one."

"I will solve this damnable Maze of yours. I will do so, and I will be free."

"I know you will try. And I cannot wait to see what happens. It's been so wonderfully exciting so far." He folded his wings at his back. "Oh—how did you manage to reach the Cauldron, anyway?" He chuckled. "I certainly wasn't expecting you."

"I asked the trees for help, and they led me there." *By way of a pack of sirens and one selkie who was charmingly not murderous for a change.* But she wouldn't put them in danger by listing them. She did not know how Valroy would take to her having assistance.

"Interesting…" He hummed, watching her thoughtfully. "You are lying to me again. But that's fine." He shrugged. "I have my secrets, and you might as well have yours." His expression suddenly fell. "Please stop crying, Abigail."

"I witnessed you—you skinned him alive, you boiled his hide, you turned him into a monster!" She was shaking again, some perfect combination of grief and fury. "You expect me to feel nothing for what I saw? He was just a boy!"

"He wished his sister to death. He—" Valroy paused. "Oh. Oh, I see. You don't understand how it works."

"I don't know how any of this works, you bullheaded pile of cow shit!" She wanted to throw something at his head.

Ignoring her anger, he took one careful step toward her, as if she were a deer about to bolt. "Before you humans came to this world, we were all wild things." He pressed a palm to his chest. "We belonged to the Earth, and she belonged to us. But humans are not of the grass, and trees, and sea, and flame, and sky. You—witches like you—you try. Some part of you hears the song of what you should have been. You're close. But you're not the same."

When he took another step toward her, she took a quick one back and shook her head. Swiping at her tears, she looked away. He was too much. It was all too much.

Thankfully, he stayed where he was and came no closer. "We can turn humans right-side out—make you the way you were supposed to be. We can peel"—he paused at her wail of disgust—"wrong choice of words for the moment." Clearing his throat, he tried again. "We can make you part of nature again. Spirits, sprites, pixies, bogles, kelpie…we can turn you back to what you should have been. But we don't get to decide what you are."

She found the strength to look at him then, the question written plainly on her face.

"That boy only now reflects on the outside what he already was on the inside. I could not have turned him into a goblin if he was not already a murderous cretin in his soul." Valroy took a step closer to her.

"He was a boy of ten."

"And?"

"It doesn't matter, even if he was destined for evil. You enjoyed it! You stood there, laughed, reveled in his pain, and you *enjoyed it.*"

He smiled, that wickedness returning to him. "Should a man not derive pleasure from his profession?" He took another step closer.

She didn't move as he took another step, closing the distance between them. There was an inevitability about him. Something she just couldn't avoid. Each time he overtook her—each time he caught her—she felt such a thrill rush through her, like a wild twist of snakes in her stomach.

Even now.

Even after what she had seen.

And I know that is not the worst of what he has done.

It was wrong. "You are a monster. A sick, demented monster." She wanted to claw at his face. She wanted to kick him until he was nothing but pulp. But she stood there, overwhelmed, feeling her body shake from exhaustion and emotion.

"And I am much worse than that." His voice was a low, dusky growl. It sounded like thunderstorms upon the horizon. He lifted his hands to her cheeks and carefully stroked her tears away. "And in a fortnight, you will be my queen."

"I will solve your Maze in time."

"You know you won't. We both know. I don't blame you, you know, wishing to fight me. But we know you will try, and fail, and then we will be wed." He smiled gently down at her.

She pulled her face from his touch. "How long after that will I be dead, Valroy?"

"We shall see." He tilted her head up toward his and, leaning down, kissed her cheek at the corner of her eye. "No more tears, little witch. I would rather taste your fury."

"You will be in no short supply of it, I think."

"Good." He stepped away from her. "Now, I believe you have a Maze to solve, don't you? The moon will wane quickly. Or…you *could* surrender and stay here in my bed with me." He grinned. "Or don't surrender, and just let me have you for the night."

"No. No, I will not do either of those things." She turned from him, thoughts reeling.

He was cruel. A tyrant. A warlord. And a bastard. She had watched him skin a boy alive not hours before.

Yet when he touched her, it was like nothing else in the world mattered. He was a dangerous, venomous temptation.

"I hate you." She stormed off into the woods.

"We shall see how long that lasts!" he called after her, his laughter echoing through the trees. "We shall see, indeed."

VALROY WATCHED her storm off into the silver birches, as if walking would actually get her anywhere. He sighed with a faint smile on his face, shaking his head. Charming girl. But still quite ignorant to the ways of his world. He fell onto his back on the pillows of his bed and stretched out wide.

She wanted him.

She wanted him very badly.

It was not affection, and it certainly was not anything approaching love. "Most human marriages are built on far less than lust," he muttered to himself. *It is all any marriage with me could ever involve. Lust and hatred.*

We're off to a great start.

He toyed with the necklace he wore. He had stolen her talisman while she slept and donned it. And in her furious rage, followed by her crushing anguish, she hadn't noticed he wore it. He frowned. It was meant to be a silly prank, just an idle game with her. But now, he was not so certain she would take kindly to his harmless pilfering.

Disappearing from his bed, he reappeared directly in front of her. She screamed in fright and staggered back. She reached for a sword that wasn't there.

Right.

That stupid thing.

"I forgot one thing." He smirked. "You dropped this." Lifting the talisman from around his neck, he held it out to her, dangled from the end of his finger. "I was keeping it safe." Yes, very well, it was a bold-faced lie. But a harmless one.

She snatched it from him and clutched it to her like it was the only thing in the world that mattered to her. Perhaps that was true. She hastily put it back around her neck and kissed the little wooden owl with the symbol carved onto its back.

Her eyes were watering again.

"What now? What have I done? I am being nice!" He threw up his hands in frustration.

"Please, never take it again." Perhaps she wasn't so foolish, after all. Her voice was quiet as she spoke. "My aunt raised me. Taught me everything I know, and…and this is all I have left of her. She made it for me. Thank you for giving it back." She still clutched it in her hand. "I know you didn't need to return it for free."

That was right, he didn't. He could have kept it or made her do terrible things. He smiled. Perhaps he was more of a gentleman than people gave him credit for. He bowed at the waist and disappeared into thin air once more, but not before he dropped a soggy, sodden, rusted, stupid short sword onto the ground with a dull thump.

"Remember," he crooned, enjoying how it made her skin explode into gooseflesh and her cheeks go pink every time he did. "Time is wasting."

He watched her scramble to pick up the sword and with a harried shake of her head, rush down the path away from where he slept. She likely wouldn't find it again if she tried. Nor would she find the Cauldron, unless he willed it. Nothing in the Maze was ever in the same place twice. It was filled with beautiful and terrible sights. To date, she had merely walked about the edge of it.

But perhaps that should change.

If she was to be his queen…she should see it all. Then perhaps a single boy's skin would not trouble her so deeply. Returning to his bed, he shut his eyes, finally intending to sleep.

And he dreamed of where he would send her next.

CHAPTER TWENTY-THREE

Abigail felt just as hopeless and despondent as she had before. Yes, it had felt nice to sit and talk to the sirens and Perin the selkie, but...after what she had seen, and her bizarre interaction with Valroy afterward, she still hovered on the edge of tears.

I have to solve this Maze.
I have to.
Or else...

The thoughts that followed made her sick. Wrapping her arms around herself, she glared down at the dirt of the forest floor. She had a fortnight to solve the maze before she was forced to marry him. She didn't want to know the consequences if she tried to resist.

Brutal, cold-blooded, tyrannical pig.
Or boar, as the case may be.

She groaned and shook her head. Clutching the necklace she wore, she worried her lip between her teeth. He didn't need to give it back. Why had he? So she wouldn't cry again? Or because he wanted to pretend he could be kind?

"There you are!"

She jolted in surprise as someone ran out of the woods next to her. She went for her sword before she hesitated. "Perin?" She blinked at his smiling face. "How did you find me?"

"Not so hard, when you know how to look." He shrugged, and then his expression fell. "I…You shouldn't have gone to the Cauldron. I'm sorry you saw that."

Shaking her head, she began walking down the path once more. He fell in step beside her. "I'm glad I did. I should know precisely who he is." *As I am soon to be wed to him.* She grimaced. "What he did to that boy was wrong, and he—he derived pleasure from it. From the torture."

"I can see why you think he takes too much joy in it, perhaps, but so have all the kings before him." He puffed out a hard breath in a sudden sigh. "That is who we are, you know, the Unseelie."

"I know."

"There are worse than him in this place."

"That is not a consolation, Perin."

Rubbing the back of his neck, he smiled sheepishly. "I suppose not. Oh! I came to ask you—I brought you to the center of the Maze, but you're still here. Did Valroy not keep his promise?"

"First of all, how did you *know* I was still here?"

He gestured at the trees. "They whisper. I am better at listening to the sea, of course, but…they told me. And they led me to you."

"Oh." She frowned. "Does everything in the Maze know where I am?"

"Probably."

"Fantastic." She shut her eyes for a moment, feeling that wave of hopelessness come over her again. "I was mistaken about my wager with the prince. I thought that to solve the Maze, I had to reach its center. But that isn't true. And now, I do not even know what I'm even attempting to accomplish. How else can one solve a Maze?"

"I—" Perin blinked. "I don't rightly know. Perhaps you could ask him?" When she shot him a withering glare, he smiled nervously again. "Or not. I take it you and he are not on friendly terms?"

She began to count out on her hands the offences of the prince. "He tricked me. Killed my estranged husband. Threatened to rape me as a boar in public if I didn't make a wish that he said he would grant, only to place an insurmountable task in front of me as part of the price." She had to stop to breathe. "Then, I learn he has taken me only to make me some temporary bride so he can take the throne. And now, he tells me that if I cannot 'solve the Maze,' a task we have *already* established is esoteric and likely impossible, in a fortnight, he will force my hand in marriage. And then, I will be partially responsible for the brutal war waged upon two worlds."

With a growl, she clenched her fist. She wished she had something to punch. "And he is a crude, perverted, arrogant, irritating, *tyrant* of a man!"

Perin blinked, and then chuckled. "I've heard him called worse."

"Then I lack the proper language."

"What did you wish for, Abigail?"

"Hum?" She glanced at him briefly before looking away. "It doesn't matter."

"But I'm curious."

"I asked him for a home. But that hope is gone to me now."

"How so?"

"Even if I knew the nature of the task before me, I do not for one second believe I have the strength to achieve it. I am...painfully aware of my own fragile state, compared to those around me." She could feel the pebbles once more digging into her feet. "If I am not gobbled up by some terrible beast, the tyrant himself will devour me instead." She cringed. *If entirely in a different way.* "But I will not surrender. I will not accept death."

"For what it's worth, I think it's a lovely wish." Perin reached out and put a hand on her shoulder. The selkie was a gentle creature. Perhaps it was because she was so desperate for a friend, or for some sense of solace, but she stepped into his side and let him wrap an arm around her in a brief hug as they walked. "So many humans wish for riches and gold, for revenge, for power…you merely wanted to have a home."

"I would have wished for a child if my husband Marcus had not already abandoned me over it." She snorted. "I'm not so noble, Perin."

"I think you are."

They walked in silence for a moment, his arm releasing her. Abigail took in a deep breath, held it, and let it out. It did feel nice to have someone to talk to who was not glowering at her like Anfar or leering at her like the prince. "Besides… what guarantee do I have that Valroy would not twist the deal if I succeeded? How do I know he would not instead turn me into a flower so that I might grow amongst my peers, and call that a home? I asked for somewhere to belong. I was an idiot to not be more specific."

"It's more likely that he would do something awful than keep his word. But he would more likely turn you into a cat and keep you as a pet, or as a bird and release you to the flock." When she wailed in dismay, he grunted. "What? I can't lie to you now." He chuckled. "Even if I wanted to."

"I suppose that is my own fault."

"Entirely."

She smiled faintly, even as she bit back tears. "Thank you, Perin."

"For what?"

"For talking to me. For walking beside me. For trying to help me. It means more to me than you can imagine."

"I know what it's like to be lost and alone in this place." His tone darkened. When she looked to him, she saw his expression overcome with the shadow of a haunting memory. "I sympathize."

"You were taken here, too?"

He nodded. "I was a sailor, once. Like the one in your song. My ship was torn apart in a squall, and it drove us onto the rocks. I was so close to shore that I could see it. But the ocean takes what she wants, and it wanted me. A seal saved my life—or so I thought. But as I grabbed on to it, hoping it would take me to the land I could see just outside my reach, it brought me here instead."

"I am so sorry." Reaching out, she took his hand, weaving her fingers into his.

He blinked in astonishment then smiled at her, before squeezing back. "Thank you."

"What happened after?"

"I wandered, terrified and alone. I walked in circles, just like you. Finally, after two weeks of nearly dying of thirst, with no food in my stomach, completely alone save for the monsters who nearly killed me many times, I found myself right back at the shore where I had crawled from the waves." His voice wavered. She watched as he fought his own tears. "I—I surrendered. I knew then, that was my only choice. It was inevitable."

Stopping, she turned Perin to her. She hugged him then in earnest, wrapping her arms around behind his neck and pulling him close. A tear slipped down her cheek, but this time it was for him. "I am so sorry, Perin. I am so very, very sorry."

He hugged her back, burying his head into the crook of

her neck for a moment. When he parted, he kissed her forehead. "Thank you, Abigail." He brushed the tear from her cheek. "But it's all right. That was a long time ago. I have made friends here."

"If it were not for Valroy, I might not be so frightened." She began to walk again, not knowing what else to do. Standing about and talking in the middle of a forest path felt wrong.

"Oh?" He easily kept up with her.

"Well, that's not entirely true." She made a face. "I firmly believe pragglings are awful no matter the context."

Laughing hard, he nodded. "That they are."

When he fell silent, she continued. "I want somewhere to belong. Somewhere I feel connected. When I was born, my parents were not keen on having a witch for a daughter. My father would take the switch to my back each time he found me doing something he said was 'against God.' My mother…I was the middle child. I wasn't wanted for anything more than helping with the chores. She was more than happy to give me up when my Aunt Margery asked to take me."

Grasping her necklace, she toyed with the wooden talisman as she continued to talk. "I was eighteen when she died. It happened silently in the night—I didn't know, save for the bay of the wolves outside. I was on my own. When I met Marcus in town, he was the only one who smiled at me. Everyone knew what I was. They didn't *hate* me, they just… didn't like me, either. They thought my aunt was cursed, and figured I shared in it." She chuckled. "I think they were probably right."

"Might be. You do have terrible luck."

She smirked halfheartedly. "We were married a few months later. We moved into the cottage his father built, and…life was good. For a time. Until it turned out that I—" She hesitated, and then shook her head. What did her pride matter now? What good was it? "I am barren. I cannot have children. When he left for the Americas, and he told me that he would send for me—I didn't believe him."

Perin stayed silent, but his hand found hers again.

"When one of my neighbors appeared at my door with a letter from Marcus, selling our home and all our land, with no mention of me? I cannot honestly say I was shocked. It was a week after that when Valroy appeared."

"O…oh."

"I have had an awful few weeks."

"That you have. That you truly have."

Something clicked together in her mind. "Do you know what it is, Perin? I have only ever been a means to an end. For Marcus, it was to breed. For Valroy, it is his crown." She grimaced. "If I could find a way to spite him—if I could find a way to ruin this for him, I would do it in a heartbeat."

He pulled his hand from hers. "Be careful, Abigail."

Confused, she looked to him, only to see his expression had turned to a wary one. "What is it?"

"This place can hear you. If that's truly what you seek—if that's what you *want*—it might act on it." He walked a step farther away from her, as if he were suddenly frightened she might explode like a bottle of warm beer. Perhaps she might. "Spiting the prince is a dangerous thing to seek."

"I find myself surrounded by things that wish to kill me, fuck me, and if I am being honest with myself, in most cases, *both*." Anger boiled in her. "Tell me how my situation is to become more dangerous?"

Suddenly, the forest around them shifted. Like the wave of an ocean, the world itself simply changed. Without warning, the path beneath her was long, blue-green grass. The trees were pushed back, allowing a circle of huge boulders to surround them instead.

Sitting atop one of the boulders was the single most beautiful woman Abigail had ever seen. Each time she saw a fae, she thought perhaps she had seen what they were capable of. But there was proof to the contrary. She wore a sheer dress of translucent gossamer fabric that did nothing to hide her full, round breasts.

Long hair that shone and glinted like silver in the moonlight flowed down her shoulders and long past her waist, draping down the rocks beside legs that were crossed one over the other. "Hello, little mortal!" The woman's crimson lips parted into a dazzling smile. "How wonderful to meet you! I am Lady Astasha. Welcome to Tir n'Aill."

"Think your situation could not get more perilous?" Perin stepped behind her, as if using her like a shield. "It just did."

Shite.

CHAPTER TWENTY-FOUR

Abigail froze. She didn't know what to say. All her words failed her.

The astonishingly beautiful fae just sat there and smiled patiently, as if she were fully accustomed to leaving people stunned. She kicked one of her delicate, bare feet and simply waited.

"I—ah—um." Abigail put her hand on the hilt of her sword, as if it would do her any lick of good. "My name is Abigail. It's…it's a pleasure to meet you."

"And you." The woman smiled, her snow-white eyes flicking to Abigail's sword and back. "I mean you no harm. You needn't worry."

I have a hard time believing that. She took her hand off the hilt all the same. Why bother? She'd be trounced in a second. "Truth be told, I don't know why I bother carrying this thing…"

Astasha laughed, a sound like tinkling bells. "I heard you killed a Nameless Thing. They aren't so easy to slay, you know. It takes both a blade, *and* the magic to wield it properly. I wouldn't give up your sword so soon."

She blinked in astonishment. "Oh."

"You did not know?" Astasha frowned and hummed. "You poor thing. Has no one told you anything at all? Come here, darling. Sit by me, and I will tell you all you need to hear." She patted the boulder beside her.

"The only one in Tir n'Aill to tell me anything was also attempting to murder me by poison at the time. Forgive me, but I have quickly learned that all the warnings ever given to me not to trust your kind were very likely accurate."

"She wishes to wed Valroy. Be wary," Perin whispered to her.

The fae woman rolled her eyes. "Be quiet, selkie, lest I stitch your lips shut for a season for slander." She flicked a strand of her hair over her shoulder. "I mean the girl no harm, as I have said. My word is my bond, and I—unlike our dear Bloody Prince—am not one to enjoy toying with mortals…not with such games, at any rate." The woman's gaze raked down Abigail's body and back up. "He dresses you like a pauper. For shame. Such a figure…" She made a noise like someone enjoying fine wine.

She felt her cheeks go warm, and she glanced away.

Astasha chuckled. "I can see why he likes you."

"I—I did not mean to get in your way. I have no desire to wed him, or be here, or—"

"Stop, stop." The other woman laughed. When Abigail looked back to the fae, she was surprised to see something that might have been true sympathy on her face. "I am not jealous of you. Oh, well, perhaps I am. I have been trying to bed the prince for *years.* He spurns me to spite me." She shrugged a slender shoulder. "But perhaps it is for the best. I do not like being ripped apart by a rabid animal. Come closer, Abigail. I give you my solemn word, as a Lady of the Din'Glai, that I shall not harm you."

"I—I should go—" Perin turned to leave.

"Stay, selkie." Astasha's tone was suddenly hard and commanding.

Perin whined but obeyed.

Abigail turned over Astasha's words in her mind, searching for the loophole. For the flaw in the words that would allow her to break the implied spirit of the pact yet keep to the precise letter of it. But she could find none.

"Come closer, dear one." Lady Astasha patted the stone once more. "I wish to meet our new, if brief, Unseelie princess."

With a cringe, she stepped forward, thinking it best not to insult or anger the other woman. As she approached the stone, Astasha shifted aside, making room for her. What was she to do? She climbed atop the stone and sat.

Perin fidgeted, obviously frightened, and likely feeling very out of place.

"Let him go," she asked the fae. "He only means to help me."

"I know! And such is the reason I bade him stay. You have had so little companionship here, I hate to rid you of it. But if you insist." She waved a hand dismissively at Perin. "Go on. You may find her later if you wish."

Perin left as quickly as he could without running. He was clearly terrified of Lady Astasha. And so, therefore, was she. Abigail watched the selkie leave and wished she could join him. "I…once more, profess that I am sorry. I did not mean to come here."

"No one ever does." The woman wrinkled her nose, a brief imperfection to a flawless face. "The Maze is awful, even to us Unseelie. We seek it for shelter, yes, but only the truly depraved and monstrous call this place their home. Or its Master a friend."

It was not the first insult she had paid Valroy in the

moments they had shared. "It sounds as though you are not fond of the prince."

"No. Not in the slightest. No one is, dear girl." Astasha reached up and combed a long nail along Abigail's hair, slowly stroking it back. "Sometimes, I suspect, not even he, despite his bluster. The sodden fool of a sea monster only tolerates him out of some strange sense of kinship, as they are both half-bred demons."

"Oh." She pondered over the woman's words as best as she could. "Then why do you seek to marry him? Power?"

The woman huffed. "That is what the others think. No, I already have as much power as I could seek to wield. I am the highest-ranking member of the court, besides the prince himself, and being queen would make me no less his second and grant me no more than I am now."

"Then why?"

"To save Tir n'Aill." Silver eyes met hers, serious…and forlorn. "I do not wish to see all of our kind bent beneath the sword and shield. Not even the Seelie." She straightened and held her hand out to Abigail. "Come. Let me show you something."

"The last time someone took me from the Maze, it did not go well."

Astasha chuckled. "I am no lowly fae lord. And besides, we are not leaving the Maze. Our dear prince is sleeping, and I would *hate* to rouse him into a bad mood when he senses your departure." She rolled her eyes dramatically. "Selfish lout. Now, now, don't be silly—I've already given you my word."

That was true. And from what she could tell of the fae, their word—when specific and careful—was true. With a long, beleaguered sigh, she put her hand in the fae's.

And tried not to scream as her world collapsed around her.

When it righted, she fell to the ground in a heap. Her head was spinning, and she groaned and tried desperately not to be sick.

"Oh! Goodness, forgive me! I forget how jarring that can be to the unprepared." Delicate hands pressed to her shoulders. "That was not my intention." She chuckled. "You poor, overburdened thing, you."

"I'm all right." She shut her eyes and took a deep breath. She instantly regretted it. She knew the smell of blood, and it was thick in the air around her. Opening her eyes, she looked up before her…to a field of blood.

Of blood, and bodies, and weapons.

Her hand flew to her mouth, only to find it covered in crimson. Flying up to her feet, staggering and nearly falling over again, she looked down. Her knees were soaked from where she had landed in the muck. And muck it was. She was not sure what portion of it was mud and what was blood. It all joined together to form a deep, reddish-brown slurry.

Bones and bits of body parts jutted up from the mess like branches covered in a thick snow. Spears and swords, all of them ancient, joined their owners in the gory scene.

She was barefoot. She wailed, picking up a foot, realizing she was now covered up to her ankles in it.

"It will wash off." Lady Astasha smiled as she…hovered four inches off the ground. She was floating there, the silk of her long, translucent dress swirling in some unknown power.

Abigail couldn't help but glare at her.

The beautiful woman chuckled. "Oh. Yes. I suppose this is rude of me." She stepped down as if from a ledge. She made a face as her own feet sank into the mire. "Ugh. It's quite cold and…it squishes between my toes."

"That it does." Abigail laughed quietly at the woman's discomfort. Not in a cruel way, but because for all the woman's unreachable beauty, there was a strange charm about her.

Astasha smiled at her, and it was a remarkably warm expression. But as she turned her attention back to the scene before her, she sighed, her features falling into one of sadness and disgust. "This is where he was born. This is what he is. This is what he will do."

Turning to the battlefield, Abigail shook her head. "I know he wants to wage war on the Seelie, but—"

"No, dear girl." Astasha sighed. "Not just the Seelie. But *Earth* as well. And every world and scrap of space after that, he will not rest until it's fallen to blade and claw." She lifted a hand and gestured at the field. Abigail watched in awe as ghastly, translucent figures began to appear before her. They were the corpses at her feet, playing out their last moments.

It had not been a war of man versus man. Nor was it fae versus fae.

It was all of the bodies before her…against Valroy.

"Behold," Astasha murmured. "The Bloody Prince."

Standing in the fray, wearing nothing but blood, teeth bared, and face contorted in fury—was the Unseelie prince. In one hand he carried an axe, the blade as dark as obsidian. In the other was a sword that matched it, shining in the dim sunlight like black glass.

He was slaughtering *everyone.*

And as he did, he laughed.

Arrows dug deep into his flesh. Swords bit and bled him. But nothing slowed him. She watched as he ripped an arrow from his chest and flung it aside as though nothing happened, only to turn around and dig his claws into the skull of the bowman, sundering it in his grasp with a sickening and wet *crunch.*

Abigail had to turn to keep from being ill.

"You humans take more than you give. Our forests and

fields shrink and shrink. The Morrigan was—is—furious about this. She never wished to surrender the Isle to humans and take to the under-hills of Tir n'Aill. So, she sought to take it all back. But Bres was weak and now is dead, and Oberon, the Seelie King, wants nothing of such total war."

A gentle hand on her shoulder urged her to watch the terrible scene of slaughter before her. She obeyed, feeling some kind of obligation to witness it all.

"The Morrigan wanted a creature who could retake all that we had lost. Someone who could destroy all of humanity for her," Astasha continued. "She sought out a creature who could give her what she wanted. Asmodeus, the fallen archangel…and then, when she had the demon's child within her, she birthed him in blood." She pointed at the specter of Valroy, who continued his dance of murder and carnage. "Behold his first breath."

"Fully grown?"

"We are not humans." She chuckled. "We are not born in the way you think of it."

"Oh." It felt like such a stupid question, now that she had asked it.

"This was meant to be a battle between two opposing warlords. But as Valroy appeared, they discarded their differences to slay the beast before them. They failed."

The last shadowy figure lay dead, leaving only Valroy standing in the field of mutilated corpses. His body was nearly blackened with the blood and muck. He spread his terrible wings wide in celebration…and laughed.

"This is what he will do to all the world, if he takes the throne."

"I understand." Shutting her eyes, she let the tears run down her cheeks. Not just for the bodies she saw around her, but for the fact she knew she had to join them. "If—when—I die, he'll find another."

"Yes. He will, in time." Another thin hand landed on her shoulder, and she felt Astasha step in close. "His rise to power is inevitable. It is foretold. But all we can do is attempt to…stall him. To temper him. To cage him."

"And if you were to wed him, you would do so how?"

"I honestly do not rightly know." She chuckled once. "But I would try. The Seelie are our enemies, but they are our brothers and sisters. The humans…you lot have every right to exist, just as we."

"Balance."

"Exactly." Astasha kissed her cheek. "I will not hurt you, dear girl. I will not. I gave you my word, and I will keep it. But if you cannot defeat this impossible game he's set before you…"

"I cannot marry him." She clenched her fists at her sides, and looking up at the hazy sun overhead, she accepted what she knew had to happen. "I have a fortnight."

"You do." The fae nudged Abigail's hand with hers and placed something in her palm. It was a small glass vial. "Should the time come."

"Will—will it hurt?" She grimaced at the memory of the poison Na'len had injected her with.

"No. It will feel like sleeping. Only that." Astasha kissed her temple. "I am sorry, my sweet, wonderful girl, but—"

"Traitor!"

Astasha screamed and was ripped away from Abigail.

Valroy had come.

And this time, the bloodlust in his eyes was no phantasm.

Abigail turned to see not the apparition of rage, but the creature instead in his full glory. Valroy had Astasha by the hair, fisted in the talons of one of his wings, and now had her down on her knees before him. His sapphire eyes flashed in dangerous fury. "Insipid *traitor!*"

"Please—my Lord—I—I would have not hurt her, I—ah!" Astasha cried out as Valroy twisted her hair harder in his fist.

Throwing her down to the muck at his feet, he snapped his wings wide around him. The translucent skin did little to curtain off the battlefield behind him. "You steal her. You bring her *here*. You show her this—and then give her a vial of poison!"

"Tir n'Aill is a cruel place. And nowhere does a place exist any darker than your Maze." Astasha pushed up onto her knees but stayed there at Valroy's feet, her head bowed. Her silver hair was streaked and tipped in crimson from the mud. "I gave her only what she needed to protect herself from a terrible fate."

"We all know what 'terrible fate' you wished to spare her. For that, you die, Astasha. I name you traitor to the throne, and you will lie here in this forgotten place of death. Your body shall never rot. Your soul shall never find peace."

"Wait—please—don't—" Abigail stepped forward but found herself shoved violently aside by one of his enormous wings. It took all her strength not to fall into the mud.

"This does not concern you, little witch." Valroy did not even spare her a glance. "Stay silent."

Astasha looked up at the prince, unflinching and unafraid. She squared her shoulders. "I am no traitor to the throne. I am now, and forever shall be, loyal to the Unseelie."

"Jealous *bitch*," he snarled. "You sought to kill the girl because you wish to be Queen."

"I wish to lead our people. To be—" Astasha fell into the muck once more as the prince rounded on her, backhanding her hard across the face.

"You spin a pretty lie. I am sure you tricked her into believing you are only trying to *save the world.*" He snorted in laughter. "Did you tell her how you have killed before, to ensure the seat at my side remained empty for you? Hm? How many maidens lay dead for that I doted upon them?"

"What?" Abigail blinked.

"Oh! She didn't tell you, then." Valroy looked to her, sneering in cruelty and sick pleasure. "There was another, long ago, who I sought to wed. And this covetous, pathetic quim had the poor thing put on trial and executed for crimes that did not exist. She was not the last."

Astasha once more straightened, kneeling before the prince. Fear was written on her face for the first time. "She—she was a true traitor, Valroy. Please, I did not put her to the blade. I had nothing to do with—"

"Lies! More lies. They end here, Astasha. As I should have ended them long ago." The talons of his wings flexed, and she heard him crack the knuckles as he prepared to drive the long, dangerous claws down into her.

He struck.

And for a moment, everything seemed to freeze.

Abigail held her breath. She had not known she could move that fast. She had not known that she was that brave. But there she was, standing in front of Astasha.

The needle-like point of one of Valroy's claws stuck deep into her chest.

CHAPTER TWENTY-FIVE

Valroy stared down at the little witch in confusion. He pulled his claw from where it had stuck into her chest. It would have been a fatal blow for Astasha. Instead…it nearly had pierced Abigail's heart.

What had she done?

Why?

He found himself muttering the question to her, again and again. "Why, Abigail? Why?"

She did not answer him. She merely looked down at the wound on her chest. She touched it with her fingers, watching the crimson ooze and stain her blouse. The injury was small, but it was deep. "Huh…"

"She was going to kill you," he said to the mortal as she slumped against him. He caught her in his arms. "She was going to kill you, you *stupid* girl."

Her knees went out from under her as she slumped against him. "I'm not meant to be here," she murmured. He stretched out his wing and laid her down on the ground atop it, using it as a barrier between her and the muddy gore beneath her. *I will not let her die here like this. I will not let her rot in the mud with the rest.*

Grabbing her blouse, he ripped the fabric open, uncaring for once about her nudity. All he cared about was that she looked up at him with an odd, glassy expression. There was no anger in her eyes. No indignant flame. And that…scared him.

I do not want her to die. Snarling in fury, he ripped another portion of her cotton blouse and pressed it to the wound. He needed a healer. *I do not want her to die!*

That made him nearly as angry at himself as he was at the girl for getting in the way. "You stupid thing. You stupid, foolish thing! Why did you do this? She was plotting your death. Can't you see? She would have twisted you, warped you into taking that vile poison—"

"No more death…" She reached up to him, pressing a palm against his bare chest. Those amber eyes searched his, as if begging him. "Please, no more."

"You will not die." He grimaced, fear starting to send his heart pounding. "You will *not* die."

"Not me." She smiled weakly, looking at him as though he were the fool. "Her. Anyone. Everyone." Her eyes fluttered, and then slid shut. "No more death, Valroy…"

"No, no, no—" Now he was in a panic. She was unconscious, bleeding faster than he could stop it. He could not heal. That was not his place in the world. And with the sun high in the sky, there were no Unseelie he could reach who could—

"Let me help." Someone knelt in the mud at his side.

Astasha.

He hissed at her, clutching Abigail closer to him.

The Lady fae held up her hands in supplication. "I can heal her, Valroy…you know I can. And you have few other options. The sea would make her a siren, if you asked. It is very fond of her."

"No." He snarled, curling his lip in disgust. "I will not have her be one of Anfar's minions."

"Then you have no other options." Astasha smirked. When he growled, panic and desperate fear rising in him as he watched the blood pour from the innocently small wound, she sighed. "Let me heal her. We do not have much time."

"You wish her dead! How do I know what kind of curse you will put upon her?"

"If you are not careful, I'll soon be cursing a corpse." She rolled her eyes. "You are a spoiled child. She saved my life, Valroy. Let me save hers in return. I will not owe a favor, even to a dead mortal."

He glared at her, seething in rage. He wanted to tear the woman's face from her skull with his fingernails. He wanted to drink the blood from her severed tongue. He was shaking with the need to kill something. "You gave her poison."

"To do what must need be done, should the time arise! By the *gods,* you get worse with every season. I do not know what you need to fuck, prince, but I suggest you do it soon and get whatever this is out of your system."

"You undermine my rise to the throne. You wished her to kill herself in lieu of marrying me." But he knew it was pointless to argue with Astasha. The woman was right. If he wanted his little witch to stay as she was, this was the only way forward.

"I did, and I do. And no one wishes you to take the throne, for we know what will follow."

"It is my birthright, and this is my destiny!" Teeth bared, he spat a series of obscenities at her in the ancient tongue, all through the inhuman growl that rose in his chest.

His head rocked to the side.

The whore had *slapped* him.

It was as jarring as it was infuriating. But it had succeeded in turning his rage from white-hot into a cold, deadly chill. When he turned his face back to her, he wondered if she might die from his thoughts alone.

"This is between us, prince." She shifted closer, reaching for Abigail. "Let me heal her. Then you can kill me, and her, as you intend."

He let Astasha place her hands on his witch, even as he clutched her dying body close to his. There was no other path forward. He could not ask the Seelie—they wished her dead for the same reason it seemed everyone else did.

He watched as a white light bloomed from Astasha's hands. Abigail gasped, filling her lungs with air. He watched the wound begin to shut, healing from within. He paid careful attention to see if there was any other magic Astasha wove into Abigail's body at the same time.

I am surrounded by traitors.

"I will not kill you here." He kept his voice low. He let the bubbling lava of his anger cool and begin to temper. It would turn to steel. "You will stand trial for your crime."

Astasha smiled, even as she worked her magic. "You want a public display of my death. Of course. How charming." She pulled her hands from Abigail, the work finished. There was blood, but no wound. The little witch was now merely sleeping. She would live.

Relief, unbidden and strange, filled him. He was left to study his panic and wonder why he troubled so deeply at her death. *Because it was not at my hands. Because it was not by my design. If she dies—when she dies—it will because I have allowed it to happen, and not a moment sooner.*

"You care for her, don't you?" Astasha laughed, a cruel and unkind sound. "Oh, what a poor, sad, pathetic thing you are."

"Dig your grave no deeper, wench." He cradled Abigail closer to his chest, scooping her up in his arms, and stood. Hands—some disembodied, some belonging to the corpses around him—rose at his command and took hold of Astasha. The bitch would stand trial. The bitch would be stuffed and mounted like a human's trophy kill by the time he allowed her suffering to end. "For it is well and truly finished."

"She will never love you." Astasha grinned, even still, triumphant in her destruction. "Remember my words, *my prince*. She will never love you—because no one can."

The swing of one of his claws, bound into a fist, was enough to shut the woman up, sending her slumping to the mud, unconscious. There would be a trial. A very public, very brutal trial.

But first he had other matters to attend.

Folding his wings around himself, he took his witch to where she would be safe. *I do not seek to be loved. I seek to wear the crown.*

"Weak."

Abigail found herself standing in the center of a circular row of stones. They looked like a series of gateways—of doors. Two, enormous plinths were capped by a third. Ancient peoples had made them. Or ancient fae, perhaps.

Pressing a hand to the spot where Valroy had pierced her, she pulled her hand back to find it clean of blood. There was no wound. She frowned. The voice had come from nowhere and everywhere. "I am weak. I know this. You needn't remind me. Twice now I have nearly died, and twice—"

Something knocked her to the ground. She fell face-first to the grass, grunting at the impact. Rolling onto her back, she stared up at a woman dressed only in a great feathered cloak that shone like oil in the moonlight. Her face was streaked with battle paint and blood.

The Morrigan.

Shifting, she knelt and bowed her head to the goddess.

"Weak. You avoid your fate. Coward." The woman's lips didn't move as she spoke. The voice continued to come from the world around them.

Abigail cringed. "My fate? To be his wife? And to end thousands if not millions of lives? I am not so significant. If my death saves their souls, so be it. I—"

Something struck her across the chin, and she fell to the dirt again. Wincing, she stayed there, as she didn't want to be put back there by violence a third time. "Will you tell me my fate, Goddess?"

"No."

Abigail shut her eyes. "Guide me, then. What must I do?"

"You are prey."

Something grabbed her. Something thin, and cordlike, and *everywhere.* She looked down as the ground reached up for her, the grass taking hold of her just as she had commanded it to do to those poor pragglings. She screamed, but they bound her mouth as the strands dragged her to the dirt.

She could only watch in horror as they began to drag her down beneath the soil. She was helpless. She was powerless. She was prey. She could only watch as the Morrigan stood over her, eyes as black as those of a raven.

"You will become his prey."

Darkness closed around her.

She struggled and thrashed, but there was nothing she could do. The cords still held her tight as they buried her alive. This was the fate she had paid the pixies who had wanted to eat her.

It was right she suffered it in turn.

"Surrender."

What other choice did she have?

ABIGAIL WOKE up once more shrouded in comfort and warmth. She was shocked to wake at all. Something beneath her was firm, but soft, like velvet over rocks. It smelled like the night sky. She shifted, and whatever was around her tightened.

With a jolt, she realized where she was. And what was happening.

Sitting up, she slapped at the thing below her. Her blow landed smack in the center of Valroy's chest, which was precisely where she had been resting.

The talons of a claw caught her wrist before she could go for a second strike. His expression as he looked up at her was not what she was expecting. She would have predicted a smug sneer, something devilish and scheming. Something that delighted in the fact that she was once more in his bed.

But his expression was flat. Not cold, but…too muddy to discern. He watched her, sapphire eyes flicking between hers.

It was then that she realized she was not in her previous clothes. Looking down at herself, she blinked. She was wearing a silk top that had no sleeves, only straps where they should have been, much like a bodice. And on her lower half—she squeaked and grabbed a blanket to cover herself. While she was not naked, the small triangle of fabric that was tied onto her lower body was certainly not proper.

"I have seen you nude." He sighed. "Your clothes were ruined. I thought you might sleep better with less on, but I knew how you would react if I left you in nothing at all." He paused and added. "And if I wore nothing at all." He looked down at himself, and at the trousers he was wearing. "This is not how I normally sleep."

He sounded so very morose, it caught her off guard. She was used to his leering and his cruelty. Not…this. Tugging her wrist out of his grasp, she sat there and regarded him as he laid his wing back down at his side. "Thank you."

He shut his eyes and said nothing.

"How…?"

"Astasha. Your debts are now squared. Her life for your life."

Pressing a hand to the spot where the wound should have been, she found she couldn't even remember the injury having hurt at all. It was just…a sting, and then nothing, so thin and deadly were his talons. "Is she dead?"

"She is imprisoned. She will stand trial, and her death will be spectacular." He smirked for the first time, but it did not last long.

Silence.

She knew little of the Bloody Prince, but she knew silence was not the norm. It gave her a moment to study him—his long blue hair that pooled around him. His wings—enormous, monstrous, and beautiful. The markings on his chest, including the circular and cryptic labyrinth over his heart.

The muscles.

She held back a laugh at her own stupid mind.

An impulse struck her, and she couldn't help herself. Reaching out, she touched the marking on his chest. That prompted him to open his eyes, if only halfway, watching her as she traced the lines. "This is your Maze."

"It is what gives me power over it. And no, before you ask"—he shut his eyes again—"it is not a map." He sneered. "However, it *is* the center."

"What?" She furrowed her brow.

"You asked that little selkie to bring you to the center of the Maze."

"And he did. To that awful Cauldron."

"No, little witch. He brought you to me. I am the center of the Maze." He put his hand over hers, trapping her palm against his chest over the inked marking on his pectoral. *"This* is the center."

It shifts and moves at will. At his *will. I only go where he allows. I only see what he wishes.*

This is utterly hopeless.

It felt like the grass was pulling her down once more, deep into the dirt, burying her alive. The words of the Morrigan echoed in her head. *"You will become his prey."* Was that her fate? Was this what she was meant to do? Surrender to him, become his bride, and die in the dirt with all the rest? If even the gods worked against her, what hope did she have?

None.

But there was still fight in her. She would not bow her head to him so soon.

"You put before me an impossible task." She pulled her hand out from under his. Not because his touch disturbed her, but because it didn't. "You asked me to solve a Maze that has no solution."

"You thought you could walk to the center of a labyrinth with no walls." He laid his head back and watched her. "That you are thinking about it incorrectly is not my fault." His amusement faded again, unable to take purchase.

"What is it?"

"The solution? I can't very well give it to you, can I? That would ruin all the—"

"No. I mean, what is wrong?"

That inspired him to look at her, eyes open fully, brow creased in confusion. He blinked then looked away from her. "I am tired. That is all. I have not slept this day."

"You are lying to me. But that is all you do." She sighed. She, too, was exhausted. Every part of her ached as if she had been thrown down a hill, and her head felt stuffed with cotton.

"So it seems." A claw gently wrapped around her upper arm. They were so much like hands, and yet so foreign and strange at the same time. "Sleep, Abigail. Rest here, with me, where you are safe. You may continue your angry rampage against me soon enough."

"I shouldn't."

"Why?"

"You are my enemy."

"And so soon you have made up your mind."

"What else could we be?" She furrowed her brow. "You have taken me, tormented me—"

"I have saved your life twice. Thrice, if you count the fact that what I took you from was no life at all."

She glared at him for that cheap punch. "For your own ends. And Astasha was not killing me, she was just trying to help me."

"Help you kill yourself." The claw tightened slightly. It wasn't a harsh act. It seemed more desperate than anything else. "Stay."

It wasn't an edict. For once, he wasn't barking an order at her. It was something else, but she could not put her finger on it.

The look on his face was so…forlorn. Something had happened, and she did not know what. Empathy would be her downfall. *My downfall has already happened, and it was loneliness that undid me. Not empathy.*

"You are my enemy," she repeated quietly. For whose sake, she did not know.

"I do not wish to be."

That shocked her. "But…"

"I am who I am." He shut his eyes. "My world is one of torment, torture, and violence. What you have seen me do is a fraction of what goes on every second in this place. And I am its prince. And I am very tired. Please, little witch. Stay with me, just for a little. I cannot sleep if I think others will come to harm you."

Confused, overwrought, and also exhausted, she nodded. *There is no point in trouncing around the Maze in these sad excuses for undergarments and nothing else. I do not want to sleep here at his side.*

But was that true?

With a breath, she lay back down, facing away from him. *I will sleep here, but I do not have to like it.* When he shifted to press his chest to her back, she went rigid.

He draped his arm over her, and then his wing, holding her.

She waited for his hand to snake into her pathetic excuse for undergarments. Or grasp at her breasts. Or for the prod of his manhood against her backside. But nothing happened. After a long moment, she let the tension out of her shoulders and her body. For the moment, he seemed uninterested in molesting her.

Perhaps he is telling the truth, and he is simply tired as well.

He pulled her tight to him, squeezing her in a hug for a moment, before releasing her. "Rest, little witch."

She found that in that, she also had little say. Sleep came for her quickly, and there was nothing she could do to fight it.

Especially when she was so very comfortable.

CHAPTER TWENTY-SIX

Abigail awoke. Alone. Which was…unexpected. Not unwelcome, but unexpected. Sitting up, she looked around for the first time without feeling under siege. It was the same stone platform built up with pillows and blankets, many in styles she had never witnessed before. The blanket over her was a thick fur pelt. *He must have pulled it over me when he climbed out.*

She could see how it would be easy to get cold sleeping nearly naked as she was. The swaths of fabric that ran up to the trees overhead were two shades darker than his hair, but were remarkably similar. *Egotist.*

But she knew that.

There were not many pieces of furniture laid out on the marble floor that stretched out to one side of the platform bed. A few tables, a single chair. There were books and trinkets, random bits and pieces of things she couldn't identify. There were several broken-bladed swords shoved into a glass vase like a morbid bouquet.

A low and irregular stone wall, crumbled into ruins like all the rest she had seen, surrounded three sides of the area that she did not know if she could truly classify as a *room*. It was a defined space, she supposed. Several columns, large and intricately carved white marble things, rose up at various heights and angles, broken off and shattered by time. The trees around her were all those odd birches with their flaking paper that seemed to reveal the wood itself beneath, both bright white in the moonlight.

It was looking up at the full moon when she finally found Valroy. One of the columns stretched high enough that she hadn't noticed him at first, perched atop it like he was. He was crouching, arms resting on his knees. His wings were unfolded. He was staring off into the woods and seemed not to have noticed she had woken.

By the gods...he is astonishing. And despite all the horror she had seen him perform—more of which she was certain would come if she did not die first—despite all the cruelty... he took her breath away.

Perhaps it would be better to think of him like a force of nature. Just like the lightning that burned the forest, or the storm that threw rocks into rivers and rerouted the path, killing the fish and the life within.

But those things did not *cackle in glee* while they did it.

Or maybe they did. To be fair, she had never spoken to either storm or lightning, so she could not rightly be sure.

She was captured by the sight of his deep blue hair that stretched past his waist, blowing in tendrils in the breeze. At how, like that, he was just as much a part of the moonlit sky behind him as the stars themselves.

Swallowing, needing her thoughts to end and remind her of why precisely she should hate him, she shifted to sit on the edge of the platform, wrapping the blanket around herself. "You make a rather good gargoyle."

His shoulders shook in a single laugh, but it was too quiet

for her to hear. He still didn't look at her. That was more troubling to her than it had any right to be.

"Have you slept?"

"No." His answer was curt. Short. And very unlike him.

Why did she feel as though it were somehow her fault? More importantly, why did it sting? She frowned and ran her fingers through the fur of the pelt where it draped over her lap. "What is wrong, Valroy?"

"You cried out in your sleep."

"It…it must have been a nightmare. I'm sorry if it disturbed you, but it was you who insisted I sleep in your bed, and—"

"You begged me to stop." He cut her off. She was getting terribly sick of that. But she had no time to correct him on his bad manners, as he sneered and continued, mocking her tone. "'No, Valroy. Please, don't—please, stop—don't hurt me.'" An inhuman noise left him, like the growl of some great beast. "I have never once harmed you!"

Oh.

"You have taken me from my home, and—"

"Those are not crimes!" His hands clenched into fists, along with the claws of his wings. "I am *fae,* Abigail. I am Valroy. All that I have done to you is what is expected of me." His teeth flashed white in the moonlight as he grimaced while he spoke. "I have been made to be this, and that is what I am, yet I am hated for it. All I have ever done is what is expected of me!"

Silence.

Oh.

She paused. "You needn't enjoy it so much."

That got him to laugh. It was a tired, overwhelmed laugh. He dropped his head, veiling his features behind his dark blue hair. After a long moment of silence, he spoke again, his voice calmer. "Death. Cruelty. Ruination. Slaughter. These are my birthrights. I am to be feared. I am to be hated. I am the Unseelie prince."

He stood and jumped from the column, landing gracefully on one of the carpets that spanned over the marble floor. When he straightened, he looked to her for the first time. "I delight in the suffering of others, for it is why I was made. But I find…I do not delight in yours." After a pause, he shrugged and corrected himself. "Perhaps only a little."

"You enjoy it plenty when it is at your hands, that is the distinction. You do not like other people touching your toys."

"Hm. Accurate." He moved to stand in front of her, tilting her head up to look at him with the crook of a finger under her chin. It lingered there. "Marry me, Abigail. Become my Queen. No one could touch you then."

"Save you."

There was the wry fiendish smile. "Precisely."

"I will not marry you, Valroy." She pulled her head away from his hand. "And you have already set a date for this, regardless."

"You have lost two days, I fear." He pointed up at the moon that was indeed beginning to wane.

"Two days?" Her eyes went wide. "What?"

"Astasha's magic is strong, but healing a fatal wound for a mortal is no laughing matter." He didn't seem to care that she had pulled from his grasp. He cupped her cheek in his palm. "Why did you save her? Are you so eager for death?"

"No. Precisely the opposite." She wanted to walk away, to put some distance between them. She was not quite comfortable with how he made her feel when he stood so close. "This place is filled with death. That terrible field of destruction, all those bodies…I cannot let you add to it."

He let out a breath. "But you would rather die than marry me."

"I would rather spare the lives of entire races than marry

you. And as I have established, I do not wish to die. And that is the fate that awaits me if I accept." The Morrigan's words echoed in her mind, twisting her stomach in dread. *You will become his prey.*

"Ah, yes. My great war. You have heard it all from others. Yet you have not asked me what I plan to do when I take the throne."

"Tell me that all their concerns are false, Valroy—but do not lie to me." She took his hand from her cheek.

He dropped it back to his side and shrugged. "There will be a war. I will conquer and rule Tir n'Aill. But I will not kill all the Seelie."

"Oh?"

"Some will become slaves."

With a cringe, she looked away. That was no better. "And what of the mortal world?"

"Well. That is more complicated." He pushed her onto her back, and she gasped in surprise as he was suddenly over her, a knee between hers, caging her in. When she went to protest, he placed a finger against her lips, silencing her. "Humans have their uses, don't they? Art…inventions…music…and this."

"I—"

"Shush."

Resting his weight on an elbow by her head, he slipped his hand into her hair at the back of her neck.

"Valroy, w—"

He never did let her finish a sentence.

He kissed her, swallowing her words with his lips. She could feel his sharp eyeteeth prick against her lower lip. He devoured her breath as though he wished to consume her soul. She pressed her palms to his chest and pushed against him, but he did not budge. He tilted his head to deepen the embrace.

A quiet mewling sound left her, unbidden and unwelcome, as he flicked his tongue against her lips. When she refused his entry, his hand in her hair pulled, and she gasped once more. The parting was all he needed, and he was there, conquering her as if she were that terrible battlefield.

Slapping her hands against his chest, she tried once more to push him off. She needed air. She needed him to stop. Not because she did not want him to continue.

But because she very much did.

When he only growled in response, his claws grasping her knees and, bending them so he might push her farther back onto the bed, lowering himself down to her, she did the only thing she could think of.

She bit his tongue.

He reeled back, laughing, his sapphire eyes dark with lust and hunger. His lower lip was tinged red, and she tasted blood in her mouth. "You pretend as if I do not enjoy that, little witch."

"This is wrong."

"You are to be my queen. I beg to differ." He snaked his injured tongue from his mouth to lick the blood from his lip. She could not help but stare.

Whatever wound she paid him seemed to already have closed. She had seen how quickly he healed from the phantasm of the battlefield—pulling arrows from his chest as if they were only pricks from thorns.

"Valroy—I—I cannot. You mean to murder millions."

"So?" Pushing himself up onto his hands, one of his claws reached between them to snatch her blanket away, leaving her only in the scandalous excuse of nightclothes he had dressed her in. "Perhaps you can change my mind. *Temper* me as Astasha wished to do."

"I highly doubt such a thing is possible."

"Marry me and find out. Or perhaps lying with me will

do the trick." He laughed. "Perhaps your flesh will be what finally sates me of my warlike ways, hm? That all I ever needed to calm the rage within my heart is to bury myself in your heat. Perhaps your heat is *enchanted.* Come, witch, cure me of my darkness with your magical cu—"

She slapped him. His head rocked to the side, but she knew she hadn't hurt him. A claw snatched her wrist and pressed it to the pillows beside her head.

"I enjoy that, too, little witch."

"I have heard tell you are a violent lover. I did not figure you enjoyed being on the receiving end of—" She shrieked as her world whirled around her. In one movement and using far too many hands—damn his wings—he had her on her stomach. When he yanked her up onto her knees and pressed his hips into her body, she could only whimper.

The scrap of fabric that shrouded her lower body did nothing.

Nothing at all.

She felt him there, thankfully still trapped in his trousers, pressing to her. And by the gods, she did not know if she would survive it if she relented to him. *If my willingness even matters.* She tried to push up onto her hands, hoping she might be able to escape him. "Valroy, p—"

"Shush, witch." He pushed her back down, pinning her there with a hand between her shoulder blades. "I will not rape you." He slid his body against hers, pressing, *grinding,* miming the dance.

She desperately tried to breathe.

"I will not have to, in the end." His voice had turned dark and dusky, thickened with need like the rest of him. With each slow movement, each slow press, it seemed a little of her sanity left her.

Because she did not want him to stop.

"In the end, you will fight—you will struggle—you will

claw at me, and strike at me, and bite me. You will resist, and I will *take* you. I will show you precisely the kind of violent lover I am." A harder movement dragged a moan from her lips. He chuckled from above her. "Because you will ask me to do it."

Suddenly, all at once, he was gone. The weight on her, the pressure of his body against her, was missing. It left her stunned for a moment, before she quickly scrambled to turn herself right-side up and cover what she knew must have been clear sight of her shame.

Her cheeks were on fire, and she lowered her head to hide her embarrassment. But it was too late. He must have seen all. Damn the pathetic undergarments!

He stood at the side of the bed, watching her, eyes still ablaze with desire. She couldn't help but stare, even with her head ducked, at what was outlined in far too much detail against his trousers. *Dear gods, yes, that might actually kill me.*

"If you want me, you can have me, little witch. I will try to be gentle." He smiled. "As much as I am capable."

"I will not surrender. I will not be your queen." *I must defy the gods. I will not be your prey. I cannot be.*

"Surrender comes in many forms. This is not the same as admitting defeat."

But it will be. Because you are a temptation, and once tasted, I do not know if I would be able to stop. She glanced at his body again. *Shite. If I lived.* She kept those words internal. "You are a tyrant and a fiend."

"Yes. And?"

She sighed, shutting her eyes, wrapping the fur tighter around her. Shutting her eyes rid her of the visual reminder of what she could have—what was waiting for her—if she allowed it. But she could still taste him on her lips, both the sweetness of the cool night air and the tang of his blood.

"As you wish." He walked away, and she felt both relief

and disappointment wash over her in equal measure. "There are clothes for you at the end of the bed. That rusted letter opener of yours is over there." She looked at him to see him point to a blade resting in the dirt by the tree line. "I believe the saltwater will kill my grass. Damnable, foolish sea monster."

"Are you and Anfar friends or enemies? I cannot tell."

"Sometimes, neither can I." He jumped, and in one graceful leap followed by the powerful beat of enormous wings, he landed atop the column where he had been perched before. He sat that time. "Take your things and go, Abigail. Only seven nights remain."

"What? No! I have twelve."

He chuckled. "Not by my math." Lifting a hand, he held it out toward the moon as if he were grasping it. Twisting his wrist, she watched in horror as the moon began to wane before her eyes. He stopped when it was about halfway. "Seven nights, little witch. Best make haste, if you wish to solve my Maze."

"What does that even mean, precisely? How am I meant to 'solve' a Maze whose center is not the solution?"

"That is for you to discover. In *seven* nights."

"This is not fair!"

"I am a tyrant and a fiend, am I not?" He cackled. "Take your sword and go, little witch. Best prepare yourself for our wedding night, however. One I find I am very eager for."

Jumping up, uncaring for her mostly nude state, she quickly found the clothes he spoke of. Trousers, and nothing else. He meant her to wear the sleeveless thing he had given her. At least it was silk and hid her breasts from view, if they did nothing to support or secure her otherwise. *Fine. I have larger concerns.*

Including the memory of one very large, very eager concern that still burned away at the back of her mind. She shook it away. "I will find a way to stop you, Valroy. I do not know how, but I will not let you wreak destruction upon the world." She picked up the sword from the dirt and was glad to see he had left her leather belt beside it. "May I have shoes?"

"No."

She looked up to him, and at the devilish expression he wore. Narrowing her eyes, she sighed. She knew it was pointless, but she had to try. "Please?"

"Hmm…" He scratched his chin in mimed thoughtfulness. "I will give you shoes in exchange for a gift. You have left me in quite a state." He trailed his hand down his body, and she looked away before it reached his obvious destination. "But do not fear. You would only need to part those pretty lips of yours to give me relief. I'll do the rest."

"No."

"I will spare your aching feet if you spare my aching—"

"No!" It was her turn to cut him off for once. She did not know if her face could burn any hotter. "I will be fine!" She turned and walked away to the sound of his laughter.

It was a cruel trick, but he was so very, very impatient. And what good was being able to control the phases of the moon if he did not use it from time to time? It was so delicious, changing the game on her. Each time he pulled the rug out from under her feet and left her staggering, the way she composed herself with such indignant fire made him smile.

And it made him want her more.

Besides, keeping her off-kilter was key to his plan. Let the doe believe she was about to be cornered, inspire panic in her, and she would tire faster.

Especially a doe that wished to feel the teeth of the wolf.

The desire was mutual. She wanted him very, very badly. Of that, Valroy had never been more certain. But her mind fought what her body desired. He could force the matter, but then there would only be losers once the battlefield was cleared away. Neither of them would win the war in the end if he did not wait for the deer to tire and submit to the inevitable end.

But he was *impatient.* And by the stars, he was needy. He lay in the pillows that smelled of her and let his hand wander down his naked body—he did prefer to sleep naked. However, he knew she would be terrified upon waking up with him unclothed.

Better to leave some mystery for their wedding night.

She would become his queen.

She would surrender.

She had to.

I might go mad if she doesn't.

CHAPTER TWENTY-SEVEN

Anfar paced the throne room. Back and forth, back and forth, uncaring for the trail of water he left in his wake. He was seething in anger.

He was also terrified.

"Forgive my tardiness, friend." Valroy appeared, stepping from the shadows by the silver throne of bone, unfurling his wings as he did. He ran his fingers over the surface of the chair, smirking in some private amusement. "I was…busy."

"Playing with the mortal."

"Playing with myself, if you must know." He laughed at Anfar's eyeroll. "Oh, come, now. That was funny, and you know it."

"Astasha is your prisoner."

"She attempted to murder my future queen. Yes. She is my prisoner. She should be glad she is alive. What of it, Anfar?" Valroy folded his wings around him like a cloak and leaned against the throne. He wasn't allowed to sit in it…yet.

Stars help us the day that he does.

And that was the crime Astasha had committed—to openly practice the mutiny and insurrection they all whispered and enacted in secret. Even if it was not *that* secret. Anfar clenched his fist and then released it. "Release her. Grant her clemency."

Valroy laughed. "Why? She has been a thorn in my side for centuries. All *you* do is complain about how much of a treacherous quim she is. I thought you would be happy to see her dead." When the prince turned to look at him finally, he frowned. "Are you well, sea monster?"

Anfar shut his eyes. "Spare her life." Mortified, he lowered his head. He could not look at the prince while he debased himself in such a way. "If you value our friendship, spare her life." After a pause, he put the nail in his own coffin. "Please."

Silence. When he finally dared look to the prince, Valroy was sitting on the stairs that led to the silvered throne. His head was resting on his hand. For the first time in what seemed like centuries, the fae lord looked…exhausted.

Anfar did not know what to say.

And for a long time, it seemed Valroy did not know either. He let out a breath, finally, and spoke without lifting his head. "Are we friends?"

Fear crawled up Anfar's spine. Was he now to be considered a traitor as well? Party to some manner of whatever foolish scheme Astasha had attempted? "Yes?" He could not help but keep the hesitancy out of his voice.

"Then why do you keep secrets from me?" Glowing blue eyes finally met his, and they were now darkened in anger. "Why do you hide such truths from me?"

Anfar shifted. "I have never done so. I have told you, from the moment you and I met, that I did not wish you to take the throne."

"That is not what I am speaking of. *No one* wants me to sit upon that chair. I understand that. I don't care, but I understand that." The prince grimaced. "What I am speaking of, dear friend, is that not once—not once in all our years—did you ever tell me you *love her.*"

Silence. The words seemed to echo off the walls around them, but he knew that was only in his mind. He dug his sharp nails into his palms and enjoyed the pain and the feeling of the blood welling and dripping from his fingers.

He would not lie and deny it.

Nor would crawl upon the floor and kiss the high lord's feet in supplication because of it.

Valroy put a hand over his eyes and let out a long, beleaguered sigh. "For as much as everyone levies the insult of 'child' at me, you truly are a piece of work, Anfar." He stood and brushed himself off before walking toward one of the shadow exits.

"Wait. What is your decision?"

"That I am going to go to sleep." Valroy's jaw twitched. "She will stand trial when the moon rises tomorrow, as she must. Then we shall see." He resumed walking. "I am going to bed." Just before stepping into the darkness, he paused and glanced over his shoulder. "For what it's worth, I think you two would be abjectly terrible together, and you should let your heart find another."

With that, he was gone.

Anfar picked up a table and shattered it against the wall.

ABIGAIL MARCHED THROUGH THE WOODS. She didn't know it was possible, but she was somehow furious, terrified, and about to collapse from grief, all at the same time. She thought the three emotions were all rather juxtaposed, and yet, they made a wonderful pit of misery for her to wallow in.

It was pointless. All of it was pointless. Where was she meant to go? What was she meant to do? *I am just waiting to die.* She knew the Maze was only leading her in circles, twisting her around through the white-barked trees in meaningless ways.

She needed to solve the labyrinth. She needed to go *home.* Living on the streets or in the woods as a hermit was a fine enough life for her. Anything that was not trapped in this place, hunted and pursued, with only death ahead of her.

You will become his prey.

No. She refused. She would not wed him. She would not! But what other option did she have? Death seemed to be so very close to her and yet so very far away. Everywhere she looked in the shadows, she could see dark shapes shifting in the distance, watching her. *I would be dead in an instant if he had not commanded the monsters to leave me be.*

She thought of the Nameless and the pragglings who had attacked her those first two days. A monster had not attacked her in a long time. Why? *Perhaps he was not certain he wanted me to be his queen. Now that he does, I'm protected.*

A trout in a bucket. That's all she was. Protected only to be consumed later.

"I will solve the Maze." She murmured the words to herself in a desperate attempt to make them real. But there were no whispered words of power that she could summon. That was not within her capabilities.

But how was she to do it? There was no solution to be had—not one she could possibly understand. If it was not a destination, what *was* it? What could it possibly be?

Walking to the line of trees beside her, she placed her hand upon the white wood that had been revealed by the flaking bark strips that peeled off like paper. "Would you kindly take me to the cove where the sirens are once more? I need to speak to a friendly face."

To her astonishment, the trees parted before her again. Valroy might command the Maze and work it to his will, but it was polite enough to listen to her desperation. She smiled at the new path they made, even if it was far thinner than the main path. She strode down it without hesitation. "Thank you. Thank you so very much."

She walked for what seemed like another hour or two, if the trek of the moon through the sky was any indication—the moon that was half the brightness of what it *should* have been.

Seven days.

She wrapped her arms around herself and fought the urge to cry. She almost wished she had the vial of poison Astasha had tried to give her. Where it had gone, she did not know—taken by Valroy, she assumed.

Damn him! Damn that bastard.

Seven days was much to lose, but it was nearly double what she had. Each second she had to do this impossible task, she would take.

Because the other options…

Either she would die soon, or she would die slightly sooner.

Those were the choices before her. And truth be told, she had no agency in the decision. *You will become his prey.* She winced at the words of the Morrigan. How could she fight Valroy, a creature who was as strong as a god to her? How could she fight the Morrigan, whose will was absolute?

"I am just Abigail Moore." She shut her eyes, a single tear escaping. She let it roll down her cheek and hit the dirt path. It didn't matter. It would have friends soon. The Morrigan was right—she was weak. Even with what might have been middling magic amongst fellow humans, she was nothing here. *Nothing.*

The trees parted before her, and she found herself standing upon the shore of not some great ocean, but a lake. It stretched wide before her, hills rising up steep from all sides. The shore was dotted by jagged rocks, edges softened only slightly by time and water and grown over with moss.

She stepped toward the lake, wondering why the Maze had brought her there. She could not see anyone nearby. "Hello? Perin? Talla?" No one answered.

Touching her toes to the cool water, she idly wondered if there were fish in the lake. Then she wondered if they were monsters. She took her toes back out of the lake. Sighing, she turned to leave. The Maze was toying with her, and there was no one here.

There was a rumble behind her. Turning…she screamed.

Rising from the waves was a creature unlike any she had ever seen. It looked like—she did not even know—a giant lizard? A giant snake, crossed with a lizard? Its maw was enormous, with teeth stabbing up and down from its jaw, sticking through its own flesh and bone. Water poured from it like a waterfall.

The thing towered taller than the trees as it stretched its long neck upward. Fins ran down its spine, just as sharp and deadly as the rest of it.

A dragon.

When she had fallen in shock, she did not know. But her hands were pressing to the damp shore beneath her, and she could only stare up at the creature in awe and terror. *I am going to die being eaten by a dragon.*

Huh.

A claw that was bigger than the stones around her, bigger than she by a count of ten, rose from the water, sending waves crashing against the rocks and the shore. For a terrified second, she believed it meant to crush her. But it stepped down beside her, the ground shaking with the impact.

It stared down at her, black eyes like those of a fish, turning its head to one side to better peer at her. Seaweed dangled from its teeth, and she thought perhaps she could see shards of wood tangled up with fishing nets as well.

This is how I die.

Not what I would have expected.

"If—if you are to eat me—" How she managed to find her voice, she did not know. *I asked for a friendly face. Perhaps this is the only friendship that can be paid to me now.* "Please, make it quick."

A sigh left the thing, something deep and rumbling that shook the water and the ground in equal measure. And then —it changed.

How something so big could turn into something so small, she did not know. But yet it happened before her eyes, and it nearly made her sick again with the terrible *crunching* of bone and the sound of snapping tendons. But piece by piece, bit by bit, the monster that was larger than any building she had ever seen turned into…Anfar.

The fae stood at her feet, staring at her with a muddled expression of annoyance and beleaguered amusement. "I am not going to eat you. Valroy would be quite angry with me. Hello, Abigail."

"I—oh. I—I am sorry, I didn't—" She cleared her throat and tried again. "You make quite the impressive sight."

With a faint smile, he offered her a hand up. "That is my true form. I take this one only when I must."

Putting her hand in his after a moment's hesitation, he pulled her up to her feet. His touch was wet. Then again, everything else about Anfar always seemed to be dripping water. "Thank you."

"'Tis nothing." He walked away from her to sit on a log that had fallen by the shore. She joined him, not knowing what else to do. "Why are you here?"

"I asked the Maze to bring me to a friendly face. I suppose it thought you were as close as I could find."

He tilted his head at her curiously. "You are sad. Why?"

"Do I not have a right to be?"

"Hm. Yes. But you have not been *sad* before." He let out a hum and gazed out at the moonlit lake. "What has Valroy done now?"

"Besides that he has taken seven days from me?" She gestured up at the glowing orb in the sky. Anfar squinted at it then grunted in response but said nothing. "I—I do not know how I can escape my fate." She pulled a knee up to her chest and hugged it to her. She felt naked, wearing only the silk and lace top with no sleeves that Valroy had given her, but considering that most fae seemed to walk about *actually* naked, it was likely not a problem for anyone but her.

"You do not wish to marry him." It was a statement.

"And cause the death of unknown thousands? To start the slavery of entire races, only to die when he tires of me?" *Or when he splits me in twain on our wedding night?* Her cheeks went warm at the thought, and she looked away to hide it. "No. And besides, he is an egotistical, violent, tyrannical louse. He is manipulative, fiendish, unapologetically cruel, and delights in the suffering of others."

Anfar smirked. "He is not so uncommon for the Unseelie. Perhaps simply just the best at all those things you listed. Indeed, he is not so rare for the fae as a whole."

"You do not seem so bad."

"I eat whole ships."

The way he said it made her laugh. It wasn't appropriate. It wasn't the right response in the slightest. And yet, she found herself almost doubled over with it. The quizzical look on his face only made it worse. When she could breathe again, she wiped away at the tears that were in her eyes for a different reason.

"I fail to understand the joke," he muttered.

"There wasn't one. I don't know." Sighing, she hugged her

leg tighter to her chest. Her humor dissolved like mist in the dawn. "I do not want to die, Anfar. But that is all I am meant to do. Either to spare the world or to ruin it. Even the Morrigan…" She shook her head.

"You spoke to the Morrigan?" Anfar turned to her then, brow creased in confusion and surprise. His eyes were unnerving—jet black as they were, lid to lid—but he was slowly becoming less horrifying of a sight. Even if she could not help but stare at his sharp teeth when he spoke. "Visions are private. If you do not wish to tell me what she said, I understand, but it may be important."

"She has told me nothing of use. Only that I am to become his prey. And that she wishes for me to surrender." She cringed. "I think that is her way of telling me I am meant to wed her son. It makes sense—she wants these wars to happen."

Anfar let out a heavy breath. It was just as deep and rumbling as it was when he was a sea beast. It was unsettling, to say the least. "I find it difficult to believe she would wish the extinction and subjugation of half her children."

"That may be the sacrifice she is willing to make to see my kind treated the same. But I do not pretend to guess the motives of gods. I am an ant to them, and a lamb to you. Who am I to have any will of my own at all?" Damn her tears. Damn them for choosing now to fall. She wiped at them. "Forgive me. My troubles are not yours."

A hand fell on her shoulder.

When her emotions had calmed enough that she could look out again at the water without crying, he slowly removed his hand. She smiled at him gently. "Thank you again for your kindness."

"It is nothing." After a pause, he furrowed his brow and began to speak again before stopping. It took him a moment to gather his thoughts. "Tell me of what happened with Lady Astasha."

"I was walking with Perin—"

"The selkie?" He blinked.

She nodded. "I met him at the cove of the sirens."

"Ah. Hum. Continue."

"He has also been kind to me. He sympathizes with my plight, having shared a similar fate—if perhaps with not so spectacular of an end. We were talking when Lady Astasha appeared. She wished to show me something and took me to the battlefield where Valroy was born."

Anfar grunted but said nothing. He wasn't a terribly talkative creature.

With a shrug, she continued. "She told me the war I saw before me would pale in comparison to the one Valroy would wreak upon both our worlds. She gave me a vial of poison and told me that if I could not win my game with the prince, then for the good of all, I should die."

He slapped a hand over his eyes. "Astasha, you *fool*."

"Valroy arrived and, as you can expect, didn't take kindly to her actions. He went to kill her. I—I couldn't allow it." She touched the spot on her chest where a wound should be. "I believe I would have died from the wound, but—"

"Wait." Anfar put a hand on her elbow. "You took the blow for her?"

"I was tired of the death and the slaughter. I have been responsible for the deaths of many since I have been here, and I'll be responsible for many more before I join them. I couldn't—I couldn't let someone else die because of me."

He was watching her, eyes wide for a moment. Then tiredness overcame him—the weariness of a creature far older than he appeared. He shook his head and dropped his hand from her elbow. "Humans. You never cease to amaze me, even in your futility. You saved her life, and in return, she saved yours."

"I suppose it wouldn't be proper for an Unseelie to owe a human a favor, let alone a high-ranking member of the court."

"High-ranking for how long, we shall see. She stands trial tomorrow night. She will be found guilty by the tribunal."

"Couldn't you all just…vote her innocent?"

He shook his head. "Not with the evidence against her. We cannot impinge the honor of the Court simply because we wish for a different outcome."

"What happens when she is found guilty?"

"The wronged party chooses her fate. In this case, the prince."

"And I have no say in this matter?"

"None." He curled his lip in something that was half a sneer and half disgust. "You are a lamb, as you said. And a farmer attempted to kill their neighbor's livestock."

The words were true. But oh, how they stung. But it was hypocrisy, pure and simple. *How many chickens have I killed? How many lambs have I slaughtered to feed my husband and me? How many lives have I returned to the dirt so I might avoid it for another day?*

But it did not stop her from crying again, all the same.

He wrapped an arm around her and pulled her close, and she let herself lean into his embrace. He turned to hold her. He smelled of the ocean and bogs—of that scent of sea life at low tide. Shutting her eyes, she accepted the comfort offered.

When the moment passed, she straightened and wiped again at her face. "Forgive me."

"Salt and water bother me none."

That struck her as funny again, but she only chuckled. "Thank you, Anfar. For a creature that eats whole ships, I am grateful for your kindness. I hope I live long enough to return the favor."

"We shall see."

They sat in silence for a long moment, before she had no choice but to ask. "I know he is your friend…"

"Mostly."

She smirked. "He has told me to 'solve the Maze.' But he does not mean to find its center—I know now that is the marking tattooed on his chest. I still do not understand how that is possible."

"He was given the Maze upon his birth. It answers to him, and him alone. And he is perpetually at the center, no matter how he moves about within it. When he leaves this place, his power is greatly diminished."

"It responds to my call, when I ask it kindly to bring me somewhere."

"It allows this because its Master wishes it. He has likely willed it to be as gentle to you as it can be. It seems he no longer wishes to test your mettle."

"I've noticed. I have not been plagued with monsters of late." She paused then smiled. "Present company excluded."

That made him chuckle.

"Why do you all stay within the Maze?"

"It is safe for us when the sun rises. This place is a world of darkness, and we are made of the same cloth. While we may disagree with the actions of its owner, it is still home." Anfar shut his eyes, and sorrow played across his features.

It was her turn to put a hand atop his arm. "Anfar?"

"It is my turn to beg forgiveness. For the problems of the farmer are not those of the lamb."

"I talk to my livestock all the time." She smiled sadly. "I do hope James is all right. I hope he escaped the fire and is living in someone else's field."

"James?"

"My goat."

"Ah."

Silence. She laughed at the absurdity of it once more. "I am talking to a dragon about my goat."

"I am not a dragon. A wyrm, perhaps."

"You looked well enough like one to me."

"Have you met a dragon before?"

"No."

"Then how do you know?"

Opening her mouth to reply, she realized she had none, and chuckled. "I concede."

Silence stretched long before them again before he broke it. "I concede your point as well. I—" He hesitated and winced as if in great pain before his shoulders caved in as if under some great weight. "I love her, and now she is to die. And I—I am helpless to stop it."

This time, she held her arms out to him. And for a great long time, she held a sea monster while he wept in her arms.

CHAPTER TWENTY-EIGHT

Titania paced the throne room, looking at the sun overhead. It was setting slowly, but it was not setting fast enough. It was uncommon for her to desire nightfall, as she had to retreat with the others to safety.

But the night would bring news.

The shadows began to creep longer, shrouding the corners of the space and changing the softly worn and mossy granite to the cold, white limestone of the Unseelie. Tonight there would be a trial here. And if Titania could stay to voice her opinion, she would.

But it had been thousands of years since a court held the other's queen as prisoner, and Titania was not keen on changing that fact. Nor was she keen to have Valroy put her head on a platter. A shape appeared in the shadows, hidden by a cloak pulled tightly over them. The sun was beginning its descent, but it was still the time of the Seelie.

"You have failed." She was going to wear a rut in the rich woven carpet, a mixture of all the colors of summer and spring. "She was to die, and you have failed."

"Attempts were made."

"Attempts that were not successful! The mortal witch must be dealt with. And now there is to be a trial, I hear?"

"The witch is rarely out of the prince's reach. And the few times she wandered away, we were quick to work. She will die. She will not wed the prince. The balance *will* be maintained, Queen Titania. This, I swear." The figure tightened the cloak over their head, ducking farther into the darkness. "She does not wish to wed the prince."

She laughed with a roll of her eyes. "Oh, good. That is such a consolation. Seeing as I'm sure he has no plans to let her opinion weigh on the matter." With a sigh, she looked at the white clouds that dotted the sky overhead as it turned from its perfect blue to ambers and reds. "What is his latest ploy?"

"He has given her seven nights to 'solve the Maze.' Only six remain."

How many thousands of years would she live before she was too tired to continue? The antics of the Unseelie prince were sure enough to take many years off her life from exhaustion alone. "Six nights until total war. No. He is impatient. He will trick her again. Listen carefully, Unseelie." She turned to the creature lurking in the darkness. Clenching her fists at her sides, she narrowed her eyes as she spoke. "She dies. And she dies *tonight.*"

ABIGAIL HAD FOUND SOMEWHERE with enough stones that she could create for herself somewhere to sleep, safely tucked inside her protection spell. This time, no swarm of terrible, flesh-eating pragglings were there to greet her when she woke.

In fact, no one was there. Sitting up, she yawned and stretched, arching her back and hearing it crack. Sleeping in the grass of a clearing by the edge of the trees was not exactly the most comfortable thing in the world, but it was a world less confusing than waking up next to Valroy.

The moon had risen, and she glared at it like it was the enemy. It was not the moon's fault that it had been turned into an hourglass, its sand quickly running out to the bottom. Six nights remained. Six nights to do an impossible task. Gathering up her things—which was only her sword and belt, so it did not take long at all—she released the spell that protected her.

Instantly, something snatched her.

A hand went around her mouth, yanking her back against a wall of muscle. She screamed against it and struck at whoever had grabbed her. The ground rushed up to meet her as she was pinned down. She went for her sword, but sharp and rough fingers wrapped around her wrists and forced them to the grass over her head.

"Good evening, little witch. Sleep well?"

She growled against the hand still over her mouth. She knew the smug voice instantly.

She bit his palm.

A second later, and she was once more beneath him, flipped onto her back, staring up at the smiling, pleased expression of the Unseelie prince. His long, dark blue hair fell around his face in tendrils that brushed against her. He was straddling her thighs, her wrists caught in the grasp of one of his wings.

He eyed his palm and wiped it down his trousers. "That was uncalled for."

"Why did you attack me?" She kicked, but he was thrice her size, and now she was pinned beneath him. "Get off me!"

"You let your guard down." He shrugged a shoulder. "I like to hunt."

"Off." She glowered.

His smile broadened. "Make me."

Shutting her eyes, she let out a breath and reached out her fingers to touch the grass around her. Silently, she called for help. She felt the power surge to answer her, the Earth rising to her aid.

But something quickly quelled it, as though it had never been there. "Ah-ah." Valroy leaned down closer. "This is *my* world. Remember? Your magic is nothing more than that of a child."

Hopelessness clutched at her heart again, sinking her attempt at defense like a paper boat in the rapids. She turned her head away. "It's worked before."

"Only because I allow it." Fingers touched her cheek, turning her back to him. She could feel the points of his nails against her skin. He watched her, a lazy smile still across his features. "I did ask you a question, though. Did you sleep well?"

"Yes." There was no point in lying. "Mostly."

"You could share my bed, you know…so much more comfortable than the ground." His fingers drifted slowly down her cheek, trailing along her throat, his pointed nails scratching against her skin. She couldn't help it. Her face burned in heat, and her skin broke out in gooseflesh. She was too warm and too cold all at once—and all it took was one look and one touch from the bastard.

"Get off me, Valroy. Please."

"Hm—no. Not yet." His voice lowered to a deep purr. "I am having too much fun right now."

"Doing what?" She squirmed beneath him, trying to wriggle away, even though it was useless. The hunger in his eyes, the pressure of his touch—it was all too much.

"Watching you struggle with your own desire." His fingers lingered at her pulse. Her heart was pounding beneath the soft pressure of his hand. "Watching you try to lie to yourself about how much you enjoy this."

"I don't!"

"See?" He chuckled. "Denial."

She kicked her feet, trying to buck him off. But he might as well have been a house, with how heavy he was atop her. "Off!"

"Oh, very well. Spoilsport." He climbed off her, laughing as she scrambled away from him.

Climbing to her feet, she put a good twelve paces between them, straightening her clothes. "Stop attacking me."

"Hm. No. It's fun." With a grin as her only warning, he jumped at her, shouting as he did. *"Grah!"*

Shrieking in surprise, she jumped back, tripped over a rock, and fell to the ground with a hard thump. Groaning in pain, she held the back of her head where it had whacked into the dirt.

Hands were on her then, scooping her up. "Foolish thing, are you all right?" He touched the back of her head tentatively, as if checking for a wound. When she looked up at him, he was frowning, his brows knit in concern. "Why did you fall?"

"I fell because you scared me. This is your fault, you ninny." She rubbed the back of her head. It was a bump, and she would likely have a little bruise, but she would be fine.

One of his wings was wrapped around her, as if he were trying to protect her from the world. Even though *he* was to blame. He stroked her hair, frown still etched onto his sharp features. "I was only playing."

I was only playing.

The words resonated through her. She found herself studying him. He combed his fingers through her hair, untangling a snarl in her red waves as he inspected her for more damage. His cruelty was, for the moment, missing.

I was only playing.

"This is all a game to you." The words left her as a whisper. "All of it. Isn't it?"

He blinked, blue, faintly glowing eyes meeting her gaze. A faint twist to his lips was all she received in return. At least in words. Because a second later, and those lips were against hers.

To her own shock and dismay, she didn't struggle. She didn't pull away. She didn't slap him. She didn't want to. The sensation of his lips against hers, one of his hands cradling the back of her head, his wing wrapped around her—gods help her, it felt so good.

No one has ever kissed me like this.

It was slow, tender, and passionate. It was not gentle, but it wasn't harsh or conquering as he had kissed her before. It was sexual—everything about him was—but it wasn't *hungry*. He was not devouring her.

This was something else.

And she wanted more of it.

For the first time, she found herself willingly kissing him back. Before she could stop herself, she ran her fingers into his hair. She had wanted to touch it since she had first seen him. It felt like the softest silk, and she was not disappointed.

Marcus never kissed me this way.

He never kissed me like he truly wanted me.

To Marcus, she was always a means to an end. A presence to perform chores, and a womb to plant his seed. He cared for her in his own way, and she had felt a measure of affection for him in return. But it had not been like this.

Means to an end.

She pulled away from Valroy and turned her head. She retreated from him as far as she could. "No."

"Forget about my war...let it just be about us." Teeth

grazed her earlobe, causing her skin to break out in gooseflesh once more.

She shivered but still pushed him away. Shockingly, he let her go. "No. This isn't about—this isn't about your stupid plans to destroy Tir n'Aill and Earth." Standing, she walked away from him, wrapping her arms around herself.

"What is it, little witch? What is wrong?"

"I am a means to an end for you. That is all. I am only desired by you insomuch as I am *useful.*"

Silence.

He did not deny it.

Hurt twisted in her heart like a blade. She did not know why she cared what Valroy thought, or wanted, or didn't want of her. "Once you have your crown and your war, and you have either killed me with that *thing* between your legs—"

He snickered.

"—or grown bored of me, you will discard me."

"You speak for me now, do you? Hm? Have you become a mind-reader with all your infant magic?" Hands fell on her bare shoulders. They began to run slowly down her arms, wandering, tracing back and forth until they reached their destination—to circle his own arms around her. He was so muscular—so strong. It was easy to sink into his embrace and let it all go away.

If she just surrendered...

No.

She couldn't.

He nuzzled into her hair, tilting her head to the side as he grazed his lips over her ear. His hot breath washed over her as his arms tightened around her, holding her to his chest. "I will tell you this...I do not think I will end your life until I have counted every single freckle on your body. *Everywhere.*"

She shuddered, biting her lip to keep herself from making a noise.

One of his hands left her arm to wander lower, spreading wide over her abdomen, pressing her against him. "You may not be able to spawn, my beautiful little witch…but I plan to enjoy breeding you regardless."

Her knees almost went out from under her. She would have fallen if he were not holding her up. "I—I won't—"

"Sssh…relax. I will not hurt you." He growled, a deep and inhuman sound. His lips pressed against her throat, where she still had a bruise from before. "Not any more than you will enjoy. And I look forward to finding out how much that is." The memory of his hand touching her, finishing her, even as he drank from her—

Surrender would be so easy. It would be bliss. She wanted to feel him again. Even if it was just for a moment, even just for a night.

She pushed him away, and for the third time, he let her go. "Leave me be, Valroy."

"Would that I could, but I can't. I didn't come here to seduce you, believe it or not." He chuckled. "Although I was having a great deal of fun."

She shot him a vicious glance.

He hissed in mock injury and clutched his heart. Darkness filled his eyes as he grinned at her like he was the devil himself. "I want to see that glare when you finally spread your legs, little witch. I want to rut you into the dust like a beast and watch you *hate* me for every thrust. I want you to curse my name even as I make you cry it in ecstasy."

She had to turn around. She had to hide her expression. Because she knew the mix of horror and disgust she wore was marred by how red her cheeks must be. "Enough of your foul tongue."

"You will not think it so foul when it's buried in your sweet body."

"Stop it!" She wailed in dismay and covered her face with her hands. "By the gods, have you no shame?"

"None." He laughed. "But as I said, I did not come here to seduce you. I came here to fetch you."

"Fetch me for what?" She was so very, very glad for a change of subject.

"The trial of Lady Astasha. I thought you should see how we carry out justice in Tir n'Aill. Especially as you will soon preside over the court as its queen."

Turning to study him again—and ignoring the sizable bulge in his trousers—she furrowed her brow. "Excuse me?"

"In six nights, you will be my wife. You will become Queen of the Unseelie fae. You will have great power over the court and its lords and ladies." He rolled his eyes. "What did you think was going to happen when I married you, you silly thing? Keep you on a leash and make you lick my feet?"

"Possibly, yes."

"Hm. The first half of that would be quite lovely. Exquisite, now that I think of it. The second"—he made a *mleh* noise—"I find I don't terribly enjoy it."

"Stop, stop, stop." She waved her hands and turned her back on him again to hide her embarrassment. "You are saying all this simply to make me uncomfortable."

"Partially? Yes. You are adorable when you wriggle on the end of a hook." He chuckled. "But no, dear girl. You are to be the Queen of all those you seem to disdain so very much. I thought perhaps it was best for you to meet a few of those poor souls you are about to rule."

"I hold no disdain for the Unseelie. Astasha was quite kind to me. Talla and the sirens were the same. Perin is a charming young man. And indeed, even Anfar seems like a lovely…uh…lizard? Or is he a fish?" She blinked, turning back to Valroy. "Is he warm-blooded? I suppose it doesn't matter. He is quite lovely for a sea monster."

The prince laughed hard, nearly doubling over. He stepped up to her, a warm affection in his eyes. "You are adorable. Come, or we shall be late. Unless you do not wish to attend." He held his hand out to her. The silver rings he wore shone in the moonlight. She was caught once more by the sight of him.

If I go, perhaps I can stop him from murdering her. Again. Although I may wish to rethink my methods this time. Sighing, she put her hand in his and braced herself for his abrupt and sickening mode of travel.

It was no less terrible when she was prepared. The world folded around her, collapsing and swirling. For a moment, everything went dark. Her head reeled, and she almost felt outside her own body. When she came back to awareness of where she was, she was no longer surrounded by grass, but crumbling limestone walls.

And creatures.

She froze, going rigid and wide-eyed, as she found herself staring at twenty or thirty Unseelie fae, standing in a crowd.

And they were staring right back at her. Some with fewer eyes than two and some with far more. Many of them had wings. Some had tails—some had lower bodies of snakes or beasts. Some had the heads of monsters.

But they were all *staring* at her.

She took a step back, right into Valroy. His hands caught her shoulders again, and he chuckled at her obvious fear. She could hear the grin in his voice.

"Welcome to the Moonlit Court, little witch…welcome to the Din'Glai."

CHAPTER TWENTY-NINE

Abigail had never felt so tiny and insignificant in her life.

And there had been some damn good moments of that as of late.

Staring at the crowd of creatures before her, she did not know what to say or do. They were beautiful and terrible each in their own right. Monstrous and gorgeous like Valroy with his enormous, batlike wings. But no two seemed alike. Even the ones who were human in appearance varied in coloration, markings, or…unnatural appendages.

The only one she recognized was Anfar, looking forever like the drowned sailor draped in the flotsam of his wreckage.

There was a woman beside him who was…transparent. She was a ghost, with nothing for her eyes but black voids.

A man whose lower half was a snake, curled around him, was ignoring her and idly cleaning his nails. Next was a man whose arms were the wings of a vulture, and his teeth—oh, why did they all have to have such sharp teeth?

Another man stood taller than the rest. His legs were the

hooves of a great beast, and horns arched away from his head. His face was broad and bold, and something about him made her think of an ox, though his face was human.

Then again, so is Anfar's. They appear like this now. Who knows who and what they truly are?

What of Valroy? Could he change shape? The thought barely had time to take purchase as two of the fae stepped forward.

The first was a man who looked for all the world like the devil himself. Long, jet black hair was pulled back in a simple queue. It was hard to tell where it began and ended, as his greatcoat was just as dark. But the coat was split, and she could see that his lower body was that of a goat. Oh. Goodness. *He is not wearing pants.* The fur seemed to cover him, and his anatomy—she had raised enough animals to know how it worked. She quickly turned her attention elsewhere. Namely, to the two sharp, dark horns that spiraled up and away from his head.

He was gorgeous like all the rest, though his features were sharper cut and harsher in their angles. Handsome was the word for him, perhaps. But what made her uncomfortable was *not* the fact that he was not wearing pants and that his anatomy greatly resembled the goat whose lower body he shared. It was the way he was watching her with eyes that glinted in crimson.

Next to him stood a creature who seemed to be made entirely from shards of glass. Each piece shifted and twisted, spinning and switching places, but always forming the same shape of a beautiful woman. She watched as the creature changed its shape to resemble a man instead, and the shards smoothed and grew to resemble human skin. Before her very eyes, a woman made of glass turned into a perfect human man. She—now a he—smiled at her. It was filled with a hunger that made her cheeks warm.

She quickly looked away.

She heard Valroy's wings snap wide, and his grasp on her shoulder tightened. "Step no closer, Lord Bayodan, Cruinn."

The man with the legs of a goat bowed low, dropping his horned head. She saw he owned a long tail of an animal she did not recognize. It was smooth and furry until it turned into a larger tuft of fur at the end, also black like the rest of him.

The fae who was made of glass curtsied, though it bore the face and voice of a man. "Forgive us, High Lord. We merely wished to be the first to welcome our future queen."

"I fear you are not the first to 'welcome' her, though perhaps you are the first not to *openly* wish her death." Valroy pulled her beside him, keeping her within the span of his left wing that now curled around her. He kept a firm grasp on her wrist. "And that is why we gather here tonight. It is time to see who is loyal to the throne, and who is not."

A murmur went through the crowd.

"We are here for the trial of Lady Astasha," the ghostly woman said, tilting her head back slightly. The voids that were her eyes seemed to shift and curl like the blackest smoke. It made her shiver to watch her for too long.

Valroy sneered. "Her, and who else? Who else is here to make an attempt on her life?"

That time, there was only silence.

"I am the Crown Prince of the Unseelie Throne. I am the High Lord of the Moonlit Court! I am Champion of the Blood Ring. I am the Master of the Maze, and I shall be King of all Tir n'Aill!" Valroy shouted as once more his wings snapped wide around him. She cowered at his side, wishing she could shrink away from his rage. But he held her fast. "I am the son of the Morrigan—I am Valroy—and no one shall stand in my way! *Kneel!*"

Twenty or so inhuman and beautiful faces twisted in fear

as the Moonlight Court recoiled and stepped away from the prince's rage. The first two to kneel were the goat man and the false human. They both quickly dropped, bowing their heads low. The goat man wrapped his tail about his legs.

Behind them—slowly, reluctantly—each figure knelt to the Unseelie prince. Those who could not, due to not having knees, lowered themselves down to the ground in supplication all the same.

Valroy tilted his head back slightly, his voice dropping low and dangerous. "I present to you Lady Abigail Moore. A human of the mortal realm. I have taken her, and she shall be my queen. She is under my protection, and any who harm her shall meet my wrath. Death shall come slowly to any who wish to defy me."

All the figures stood slowly, save for the two before her.

"High Lord Valroy," the goat man said from where he knelt, "we have heard tale of the foul attempts on our future queen's life. Our hearts break for it. And now, as I see her beauty, I am raptured." He placed a hand over his heart, over his bare chest. Dark hair patterned the back of his knuckles. Red eyes met hers, and his smile grew into a grin. "My name is Bayodan, my beautiful future queen. And I vow to you this night my fealty and my protection." He once more bowed his head low. A strand of his dark hair slipped from the red silk tie she saw at the base of his neck. "I am your servant. *Ain h'ouree, aelist i'liaid.* I am your Guardian."

"And we, Cruinn, vow the same." The human man smiled. She realized why they were so very eerie. Their human male shape seemed to be painted on—or like they had been modeled entirely out of wax. "I am your servant. *Ain h'ouree, aelist i'liaid.* I am your Guardian."

Abigail felt naked. She did not know if it was because of the terrible excuse for clothing that Valroy had given her to wear, or if it was merely that it seemed as though every layer of her skin had been peeled away.

Everyone was *staring* at her, and she felt as though she were meant to do something. What was she to do, besides tremble in wide-eyed fear? "I—ah—"

"Do you accept their pledges, little witch?" His sapphire eyes twinkled in amusement as he smirked down at her. "It is a mark of dishonor not to."

"I do not know what it means to accept," she whispered harshly at him, glaring.

He snickered. "It means there are two members of my court who are loyal to me. Who wish to see me wear my crown. Now." He yanked her forward, releasing her wrist, only to hold her by the back of the neck. The warmth of his hand sent a shiver down her spine. "My darling thing, do you accept their pledges, or do you mark them forever in dishonor?"

A goat man and a creature of glass and illusion.

"Y—yes?"

The two fae lifted themselves from the ground. "We shall not fail you."

"I am still not quite sure I know what has just happened." She swallowed. "But I thank you. I think."

Bayodan chuckled, his eyes creasing in the corners. Now that he stood closer, she could see a few stray gray hairs in his goatee and at his temples. There were laugh lines etched lightly into his features. "In short, our fealty is now only to you, and above all else, Lady Moore."

Their fealty is to me? She twisted to glance up at Valroy, who was watching the scene with a deeply pleased grin. She still did not know what that truly meant. But whatever it was, it seemed to be a wonderful development for the prince. "I am not a lady."

"You are now. Because I said so." Valroy yanked her back to his side.

Staggering, she glared up at him again. "Will you stop jerking me about?"

"Why? You are so very little." He rocked her from side to side. "And you are quite stunning when you're angry."

How could he go from one extreme to another so quickly? From boiling, terrifying rage, to sarcastically amused with the world around him? She sighed and said nothing in reply, crossing her arms. She was being both physically and metaphorically tugged around behind him, and there was nothing she could do about it.

One of his wings curled to rest its long taloned claws over her left shoulder, keeping her close to his side. "Now. Let the trial begin. Bring in the accused."

The group parted as two other fae bearing silver painted markings dragged Lady Astasha forward. She was hanging limp in their arms, her bare feet dragging along the floor. Her body was covered in bruises and cuts. Her naked body was stained in blood that was clearly her own. Her long white hair, stained crimson, covered her lowered face. They threw her to the floor at Valroy's feet. And hers.

Abigail gasped, her hand covering her mouth. Tears instantly stung her eyes in sympathetic pain for what Astasha had clearly suffered. She rounded on Valroy. "How dare you put on this farce!"

"Hm?" He arched an eyebrow.

"What manner of trial is this, if she has already been found guilty?" She pointed down at Astasha, who was just barely moving.

"Ah." Valroy chuckled. "You misunderstand." A slow, sly twist to his lips revealed just the tips of his sharp eyeteeth. "This is how we treat all our prisoners."

That sent her blood running cold. She shrank away from him as far as she could, with his wing still holding onto her shoulder. He let her hide in his shadow as he turned back to the fae gathered before them. "Astasha, former lady of the court. You stand accused of the following crimes—interfering with the games of a higher-ranking lord, treason against the crown, and attempted murder. How do you plead?"

The broken, battered woman chuckled from the floor. "Guilty on the count of interference. On all other counts, I am innocent."

"We shall see. Let us present the facts of the case. I awoke from my slumber to find my future queen missing. When I searched for Abigail, I found her in the Broken Fields with you. Do you deny this?"

"No." Astasha did not bother to lift her head, silvery hair obscuring her features.

"Abigail had been given a vial of poison. Where did she get this poison, Astasha?"

"From me." There was blood slowly pooling on the limestone beneath the poor battered fae. It was dripping from her face.

"Why did you give her the poison, Astasha?"

"To allow her an escape from the impossible game you placed her within. It was an act of mercy to a human trapped and afraid. To this, I plead guilty in interfering with your game." Astasha's voice was strained and tight, as if every word was a struggle to say.

"That is the lie you told me when I arrived. Abigail, why did Astasha say that she was giving you the poison?"

After stammering like an idiot for a moment, she cleared her throat and tried again. She twisted the lace edge of her silk undergarment between her fingers. "To—to take, should I—" She broke off, her face going warm for another reason.

"Should you what, my little witch?" His claw on her

shoulder tightened just slightly. If it was meant to be a threat or a reassurance, she wasn't sure. "Tell the truth, and only that."

She muttered it, but she knew it was plenty loud in the end. "She gave me the poison to take should I be forced to wed you." The court of the fae murmured. She winced at the sound, knowing that she had just damned Astasha. "She was only trying to help me! She wasn't trying to kill me like Na'len. She…it was kindness. Not assassination."

"She acted to prevent you becoming my queen. I, the crown prince, had already made it known that you are my intended. Therefore, you are the crown princess. And she sought to kill you before you ascended to the throne." Valroy looked back to the gathered crowd and gestured wide with his hand before him. "Is that not true, Astasha?"

Silence. The woman said nothing. There were more drops of red beneath her lowered head.

Valroy smiled. Gods, she wanted to smack that smug expression off his face. "As per the rules of our court, no denial of guilt is considered admission by default. But we shall note that you did not wish to incriminate yourself with a guilty plea to the charge of treason against the crown."

She knew he was explaining it for her sake, not theirs. He wanted her to understand what was happening and why. *This is happening because you will not marry me. Her suffering is because you fight me.*

Now she deeply wished to stab him with her rusty sword.

"I have proven thus the charge of treason and attempted murder."

"It is not attempted murder." Abigail hugged herself tight, trying to give herself the confidence to speak. "She did not act against my life. She merely gave me the method should I wish to kill myself. Those are not one and the same."

The twist of Valroy's lips was one that was so deeply

amused she instantly realized she had taken a dangerous path. "Explain your argument."

Suddenly, the foolishness of what she was doing snapped into focus. She was arguing in a court whose laws were entirely unknown to her. "I—ah—" She coughed. "I could have used the gift of the poison on anyone, yes? It was not designed specifically to only poison *me*."

Valroy tilted his head to the side slightly, regarding her with a new level of thoughtfulness. "Correct."

"Then I could have wielded against anyone. Her, you, another fae who sought my death. It was a gift of a weapon, and a suggestion that I use it upon myself should I have no other recourse." Her hand grazed the hilt of the rusted sword she wore, and she hung onto the wooden handle as if it were the rope of a raft. Like a flash of lightning, a thought hit her. "Anfar! He gifted me this sword. If he had suggested that I slit my own throat with it, or drive it into my stomach, if I could not take the Maze any longer—would he also be here before you?"

Valroy was silent, staring at her. She could not tell if he was angry or not. He did not move. No one moved. They were waiting for her.

Abigail swallowed again. Her throat was dry. She was beyond terrified. But this was all his fault—Valroy was to blame for every second of suffering since this all began. She clung to her own anger even as she clung to the sword at her side. "If I were to hand you this sword and tell you to go pleasure yourself with it, would that be attempted murder?"

Shock finally cracked his frozen expression. His eyes went wide at her words, and then the moment the surprise faded, he cackled in laughter. He pulled her against his side in an embrace, his wing tightening on her. The crowd of Unseelie laughed with him. She could even see Cruinn applauding.

"Well said, little witch. Well said." He kissed the top of her head. When she looked up at him, he was smiling down at her. "Very well. I shall rescind the charge of attempted murder." He looked back to the crowd. "With a guilty plea of interference, and the released charge of attempted murder, that still leaves treason against the crown. Moonlit Court—consider the charge carefully."

The crowd murmured, talking to each other.

Valroy lowered his head to whisper to her. "That was a masterful show." For a brief moment, she felt a little proud of something she had done. "Too bad it will not matter." And like that, her pride crumbled like damp sand.

"Why?"

"The price for interfering in the games of a higher-ranking lord or lady is already steep. The price for treason is even higher."

"What is the price?"

"You shall see." He smirked.

He kissed her temple, and she tried not to flinch. She didn't imagine it would be good to insult him in front of Moonlit Court. Well—not more than she already had, anyway.

Someone at the center of the group took a step forward. For once, they appeared vaguely normal, for a fae. That was to mean they had the proper number of eyeballs, legs, and arms. And had no extras of anything else. "A verdict has been reached."

"What was the count?" Valroy reached an arm around her waist, a thumb threading through the belt loop of her trousers.

"Unanimous, High Lord." The fae squared their shoulders, as if knowing the price of the word he was about to speak. "We find her guilty of treason against the crown."

Her heart fell into her stomach. "No, Valroy—"

"Shush." He lowered his head and whispered, "All will be well. Wait your turn."

Wait my turn?

He straightened, and for the first time walked away from her. Small and alone, and finally able to see around him and his wings, she found herself standing beside a throne. And for the longest moment, she wasn't quite sure what she was staring at.

The throne was carved of wood, each surface an illustration or a relief of some great battle or running animals. But that was not all. Mixed into the intricately carved of winding wood and vines…were bones. And they were carved to match the rest. Depictions of slaughter and death, of humans and monsters alike being overtaken by their hunters. It had been dipped or poured in silver, the thick coating of shining metal turning it all into one. It was beautiful, morbid, and terrible, all at once.

It was a throne of death.

It was *his* throne.

"Astasha, former lady of the court, you have been found guilty of interference and treason against the crown." Valroy stepped up to the woman who still lay upon the floor. He reached down and, grasping her by the hair, yanked her up to her knees.

Abigail covered her mouth with both hands.

Iron nails had been driven into her face. Across both her eyes, and deep into her cheeks, the pointed metal jutted from her at different angles. She was blind, her eyes destroyed. But the fae woman sat back on her ankles and did her best to compose herself.

What kind of strength did it require to seek some manner of pride while in such agony? Abigail was trembling once more, staring in horror at the scene before her. *This is how we treat all our prisoners.*

The Unseelie were monsters.

She had known that before, but she had forgotten it in the wake of brief kindness from Anfar and Perin. She had chosen to forget their malice. How quickly she had discarded the cruelty that Valroy had paid that boy at the cauldron, in the wake of his warm touch and passionate kiss. It churned her stomach.

Disgust—pointed at herself, just as much as it was at Valroy—made her turn away from the scene. She ducked her head, her tears falling to the limestone. They were a poor tribute to Astasha's blood.

"Astasha, you are guilty. As High Lord of this court and as your accuser, I get to choose the price you shall pay." Valroy's voice was a low, amused purr. "And I choose death."

"No." She barely kept herself from shouting. She turned to glare at Valroy, even through the haze of her tears. "No more death, Valroy. No more suffering." She moved to go to Astasha, to provide what little comfort she could to someone who had suffered so much.

"My future queen demands mercy, does she?" Valroy hummed and stepped between them. "Mercy comes with a price in this court, my dear."

"Oh, no." She sighed.

He grinned. And then came the words she knew he was going to say. "What shall you give me in return?"

All her cleverness seemed to have vanished. Defeated, she opened her mouth to answer—

When a knife was rammed deep into her chest.

CHAPTER THIRTY

Abigail looked up at the face of a sneering creature that had shimmered from nothingness. It had appeared before her at the same moment it rammed a dagger into her heart. She jolted from the impact, her hands flying reflexively to grasp the hilt.

But it did not hurt.

Was it poisoned?

She blinked at the fae in astonishment. She barely heard the chaos around her. She barely even registered as Valroy ripped the assassin from her and promptly tore his arm from his chest.

There was shouting. Running. She looked down at herself.

Glass.

The knife had pierced glass. She watched as the piece it had broken through shattered and broke, twisting into new shapes. Her body began to change and shift.

And then it was not her body anymore.

She collapsed to the ground. But she did so not beside the throne of silvered wood and bone. She fell into the arms of a creature who smelled like Earth, or like a cave. She was lowered to the ground, placed into the lap of whoever had her. He was whispering calming words to her in a deep voice that resonated in his chest.

Looking up, she found herself gazing at the smiling, handsome, inhumanly sharp features of Bayodan. His two crimson eyes…were now joined by others. Opening from where they had been invisibly hidden, he now had seven eyes upon his face. Two upon his cheekbones where they should not be, two where they ought, and three arranged on his forehead, slotted vertically.

His abnormal eyes were pure red, with only black dots in the center.

"Oh…oh, my."

He smiled. His extra eyes all closed and vanished into his skin. Dazed, she reached up and touched his cheek. There was nothing there. But she had *seen* it. And…wait. Where was she? What—Lord Bayodan had caught her. But where was she? How had she crossed the room? She touched a hand weakly to her chest and found no wound—no blade.

"It is all right to be confused. But you are safe, my lady. This, I swear."

"How…?" She was so dizzy it made her stomach churn. "I…I'm dying. Again."

"Ssh." He stroked a piece of her long hair behind her ear. "No, you are not. Cruinn took the wound, not you."

"Cruinn?"

"Forgive me for my magic. But Master Valroy rightly predicted the need for the illusion. You have been Cruinn, and they you, since the moment you arrived."

"You switched us?"

"A powerful glamor, but nothing more. A very useful gift, all the same." He helped her sit up, and she couldn't tell if it made her head spin more or less. "And it takes far more than a simple dagger to hurt my mate. Come. Let's get our future queen back on her feet, eh?"

Strong arms lifted her, and she jolted in surprise as she looked into the face of *herself*. Standing in front of her was another Abigail. The only difference between them was that the duplicate had a dagger protruding from her chest. Her smile broadened into one that she knew she had never worn, and the not-Abigail ripped the dagger from her chest. Glass shards fitted back into shape. "Ouch."

"Drop the mask, love. You are frightening her."

"Oh!" Abigail watched the other version of herself shift once more before her eyes. Shards of broken glass, a hundred million strong, rolled over each other and removed the illusion. Now that she was close enough, she could hear the sound of it. Like glass sliding on glass, high pitched and shrill. It set her teeth on edge.

It was not long before they were once more that beautiful, handsome man she had seen before, if this time made of glass and not flesh. "Forgive us, my lady. We forget." They chuckled. "We are not so spectacular amongst our kind."

"It's…it's all right." She was trembling all the same. She wanted a stiff drink and a long rest. "If you have—have acted to save my life, I thank you."

Cruinn reached down and picked up her hand. She expected to be cut by them and their million shifting shards. But beneath her touch the glass was smooth and perfect, and shifted beneath her touch like liquid. They were slightly chill to the touch, like she would expect glass to be. They bent their head, and the broken pieces of their lips went smooth and pliable as they kissed her hand.

Perhaps a little slower than they should have.

They stepped into her, protecting her from the chaos and shouting that still surrounded them, and pressed her hand to their chest. Wherever she touched them, or they touched her, the shards fitted together.

If she weren't so afraid, she would be fascinated.

"Enough!"

Silence rang in her ears just as much as the shouting did. She found herself stepping into Bayodan, recoiling from all that she saw painted before her. And painted was perhaps the right word, for blood was splashed along the floor, and all along the creature who she knew had acted both as artist and executioner.

The markings of blue along Valroy's chest were marred with crimson splashes and splatters. Three bodies lay at his feet—and she was relieved to see that Astasha was not among them.

"Liars! Insipid, dissembling fools!" He snapped his wings wide, his voice somehow that which she recognized and mixed equally with the growl of a beast. "Who here has done this? Who here has schemed to take her life? Astasha is not to blame, for all her treason, for she has been *preoccupied.* That means it is one of you! Step forward, and face your crimes with pride, and I will make your death quick."

Silence.

Nobody moved.

Reaching down the claws of one of his wings, he picked up one of the bodies by the head and held it off the ground as though it weighed nothing. With a howl of anger, he drove the claws of his other wing into the corpse's chest cavity.

A cry escaped her at the sound of the bones snapping. He tore the body in two, ripping the ribs from the spinal column. Gore splashed to his feet as he shredded what remained of the fae into two parts.

He threw both halves at the crowd.

"Cowards!" He bared his teeth. "If no one steps forward, I

must assume you work in unison. And if that is the case, then all of you shall die this night."

Gasps and murmurs, but nothing else. The crowd, all save Bayodan and Cruinn, shifted farther away in fear.

"Very well…" Valroy licked some of the spattered blood from his lips. "Death it is."

"No!" Before she even knew what she was doing, the word had left her. She nudged away from Bayodan and Cruinn, stepping toward Valroy. "No, please." She was shaking like a leaf, but she tried her best to hold strong.

There was so much blood.

Save the few to damn the many.

Spare these lives now only to kill a hundred thousand more tomorrow.

Make a deal with a fae to avoid being fucked by a boar. That last thought almost made her laugh as she shut her eyes, bracing herself for what she had to do. Tomorrow's problems were meant for tomorrow.

He would have his throne someday. He was a force of nature. If it was not she who gave it to him, it would be someone—anyone—else. Perhaps even the broken form of Astasha who still knelt in the mess, her blood mixing with that of the dead assassins.

Opening her eyes, she took in the creature before her. Truly saw him for all that he was. As if sensing it, he spread his wings and held his arms to his sides, dropping the bit of shattered skull he had in his grasp. A warlord, covered in the blood of his enemies.

"I ask you for mercy, High Lord Valroy." She held her head high. It was a terrible lie, and she knew everyone saw it for the sham that it was. But she was doing her best. "I ask you for mercy for the Court, and for Astasha."

"And in exchange?" He had won. Everything in his posture, in his voice, declared him the victor.

"I will give you anything you want." Tears ran from the corners of her eyes. She did not bother to wipe them away.

"I accept your offer. Mercy is granted." He extended a hand to her. "Come here, little witch."

Stepping forward, doing her best to avoid the puddles of blood and pieces of carnage, she made her way to him. Reaching out a hand, she hesitated, wavered, and then placed it in his. He pulled her close, drawing her against his side, wrapping a wing around her. With a hum, he bent his head to hers, whispering so no one else could hear. *"Anything I want, you say?"*

A hand grabbed her ass. She would have not minded so much if she did not remember his wings were almost entirely translucent. She jumped, but the movement only allowed him to pull her tighter to him.

He sank his fingers into her flesh and growled in her ear. "There are many things I want. I only get to choose one, hm?" He tilted her head to look up at him, cradling her cheek in his hand. With the pad of his thumb, he wiped her tears away. His voice was still a whisper as he spoke to her. The words were for her and no one else. "Then here is my price. This is what I ask for in exchange—stop crying."

"What?" She blinked.

"I dislike your tears." He lifted his hand to run a knuckle over her other cheek. "Stop crying, and mercy will be yours."

Like pieces of a puzzle, it all snapped into place. "You wanted this to happen." She kept her voice low.

He smiled. "Will you join me for dinner? I assume yes."

"You *knew* this was going to happen!" She hissed at him through her teeth. "You vile, monstrous—"

He kissed her, swallowing her protests before they grew too loud. His other wing curled around them, and she felt the world dissolve out from around her once more.

When Valroy released her lips, he knew what was going to happen. He braced himself for it. And sure enough, as unpredictable as Abigail was, he was at least correct in this regard. He turned his head with the strike of her palm against his cheek.

It stung, but only for a moment.

The pain went right to a part of him that had been eager for her for a long time now. He fought the urge to groan. Desperately—so desperately—he wanted to throw her over the dinner table and break the furniture with the force of his thrusts.

But he did not.

Because she might cry.

What is wrong with me?

He let Abigail go and watched as she put some distance between them to try to gather herself. She pulled out a chair from the table and collapsed into it. A wise choice, as she looked as though she were about to faint.

"I *hate* traveling like that."

"It can be unsettling." He licked more of the blood from his lips. "I'll give you that." He lifted his hand to lick another line of blood off the back of it. He would need a bath. *I wonder if she will let me have her like this. Oh, to taste her after a battle—yes. I think I would like that.* The image of her tied to a post in his war tent, angry and frightened as he stormed in, naked and eager for her, danced in his mind. He imagined taking her while she gasped beneath him, trying to keep her dignity and fight him off until she grew supple and surrendered to what they both wanted.

That time, he did grunt.

She didn't hear it. Good.

That was for the best.

"You—you did that all on purpose. All of it."

"I knew Astasha would make an attempt on your life. But I knew she wouldn't kill you outright. She is too much of a clever *sh'nil* for that." Looking down at himself, he decided it was probably rude to eat dinner whilst splattered in blood. Pouring water from a pitcher onto a table napkin, he began to clean the gore off.

Abigail watched him, angry and horrified. "The trial. It was a sham."

"Not at all. The trial was very valid. You were astonishing, by the way." He grinned. "Proving my attempted murder charge false! How brilliant." He laughed at the memory of her choice of words. "I think I like you with a bit of a tongue on you. Although, I think I'll like your tongue even more soon enough."

Her horror flickered into indignance and bashfulness as it always did when he teased her. He wondered if she would blush and look away as he lavished her body with his own tongue. It was beautiful, matched evenly with her anger. "I could have asked for that, you know."

"You could have demanded I marry you on the spot. Why didn't you?"

"We already have a deal in place for that. One you are losing at an incredible pace." He grinned. "I'm immortal. I can wait six days."

She glowered. "Can you?"

Perfect.

"Never mind." She shut her eyes and sighed, leaning back in the chair. The poor thing was exhausted. "I am glad you did not ask me to get on my knees and play your whore in front of the court. That is about what I was expecting."

"Hm. I am not in the business of killing the cow because I want for milk." He began to clean the blood from his other arm. "If I force you to do anything of the sort, even if I know that is what you secretly wish I would do, you will hate me for it. And we are to be wed. While I know many human pairings despise each other, I do not wish to start off that way at the very least."

Now she was studying him in confusion and revulsion in equal measure.

He blinked. "What did I say?"

"Did you just call me a cow?"

"I—" He paused. "I called your s—" He broke off. No, that wasn't going to get him to higher ground. "I didn't mean it that way." He folded the wet cloth over to clean his chest. It was already stained crimson. "My *point* is—"

"I get your point!" She turned in her chair to pour herself a glass of water into a copper goblet, and quickly downed it. Her hands were trembling. The poor thing was on the edge. He frowned as she refilled her glass.

The decanter slipped from her fingers. He moved fast enough to catch it with the claw of his wing, keeping it from tipping over and spilling its contents.

That seemed to be the last straw. He watched as all her fire failed her, and she began to sob. He knew there was nothing he could say. He knew that pointing out that she was defying their deal for mercy would only make it worse.

For once, he decided not to pull that rope and unfurl that particular sail. When he gathered her into his arms, she didn't resist him. That worried him just as much as he enjoyed the result. She draped against his chest, and he held her to him, cradling her and humming to her quietly as he tried to soothe her tears.

He had caused every single one of them. He knew that. He wasn't a fool.

But he was who he was.

Tipping her head, he began to do the only thing he could think of to fix the moment. He kissed her. Slow and tender, wanting for nothing more than the embrace. Stroking away her tears once more, he kept his lips against hers in a gentle dance until she stopped crying.

When he parted from her, her eyes were shut, her lips parted and swollen. Her breaths hitched a little as she tried to deepen them, but she was no longer weeping.

"There we are." He smiled and stroked her cheek with the back of his knuckles. "Now, may we eat dinner? I'm st—"

His head rocked to the side with a slap.

That time he had not seen it coming.

CHAPTER THIRTY-ONE

Abigail found herself once more sitting at the banquet table of the Unseelie prince, looking down at the stolen communion silver she was meant to eat from. She was no less confused this time than she was the last. Although perhaps she was just a bit more overwhelmed.

And now I have a new scale by which to measure the disaster that is my life. The hole has only grown deeper. After she had slapped Valroy a second time, he had only chuckled, released her from his grasp, and gestured for her to sit back at his table.

She was quietly eating bread and cheese and sticking to the water. The last time she had drunk his wine in any great quantity, she had gotten herself into this mess to begin with. He was sitting at the head of the table, studying her in silence. He had been for some time.

"What?" She finally could not take it anymore.

"When was the last time you ate?"

Now that he mentioned it, it had been a long while. As if on cue, her stomach grumbled. It wanted more of the savory offerings on the table, or at least the fruit. But it worried her.

Accepting his hospitality was a dangerous slope. The more of it to which she availed herself, the easier it was to accept it. And him. And what he had done.

He sighed. As if he could read her mind, he reached out and pushed a tray of fruits closer to her. "The food is not enchanted. Neither is the wine. Eat and drink, little witch, before you faint."

"It isn't an enchantment that worries me." She reached out and took a small bunch of grapes from the tray and some strawberries. There was concern over hospitality, and then there was starving herself out of foolish pride.

Even if the roast goose in front of her was calling her name.

"Then what does?" He chuckled, and then his expression and humor fell as he must have put it together. "Ah. Yes. You do not wish to be here, nor do you wish to spend time with me." Picking up a serrated knife from the table, he began cutting off slices of the goose. "You are angry with me."

"About a great many things, yes." When he put the slice of meat on her plate, she murmured a thank you. "I need—" She stared down at her plate and shook her head numbly. "I honestly could not tell you what I need. I want to go home to a place that does not, nor has it ever existed. I want to sleep without fear of being beset by monsters or assassins. I want a moment to breathe."

"Then agree to marry me now, Abigail. The assassins will not cause you grief when you are no longer that which prevents me from my throne. No one will dare challenge me when the crown is mine. You will be safe at my side."

"Until you decide to kill me." She picked up her fork and began to eat, though it rather tasted like ash in her mouth. "Until you tire of your mortal pet and rid yourself of me."

"Your lives are so very short to begin with." He hummed. "I've decided not to kill you, I think."

"You think."

"Mm. You conducted yourself brilliantly at court. I think I could train you to become quite the hellcat of your own right." With a grin, he waved his fork idly as he talked. "You can give Titania quite the run for her money, once you are no longer shitting your trousers in fear."

"I—" Indignant anger rose in her and she found herself once more glaring at him. "How else was I to react in front of a sea of monsters, each one who could easily tear me to pieces? I am hopelessly lost in a world of demons and beasts, against whom I only have, as you put it, 'my child's magic'! What can I do against a place like this? Throw rocks and sticks? Hope the grass might heed my call?" She scoffed. "Against things that are made of shifting glass and assassins that manifest from thin air? I have nothing with which to defend myself. I have nothing at all in this world. You have seen to that."

When she had begun gripping her knife so hard her knuckles turned white and her hand trembled, she did not know. She only noticed because he reached out and placed his own hand atop hers.

She forced herself to breathe, forced herself to calm her racing heart. Allowing herself to be lost to the panic that edged at the corners of her mind would do her no good. She reached out, grasped her goblet of wine, and took a hard swig from it.

Valroy chuckled again and, carefully weaving his fingers into hers, lifted her hand to his mouth and kissed her fingers. He did so slowly, and he did so one at a time. The gesture made her cheeks warm.

This is why I don't want to eat with him. Because when I spend too much time around him, I become so very tempted. She watched him, and he watched her in return.

When he finished his gesture, he lowered her hand back

to her knife. "Eat. Slowly. I also will not have you throwing up because you devoured your food in a nervous haste."

Her shoulders slumped as she laughed, a weak and overwhelmed sound. "You are exhausting."

"Why did you bargain for mercy for the court, Abigail?" He returned to eating his own meal. "Saving Astasha, I understand. You bond with whatever in this world shows you kindness."

"I am not a stray dog, Valroy."

"Aren't you?"

She threw a strawberry at his head. It bounced off him, and he laughed loudly at the impact. When she threw a second, he snatched it from the air. Leaning back in his chair, he watched her with equal parts amusement and hunger. Slowly, sensually, he took a bite from the strawberry.

Her cheeks felt as though they were aflame. "Why must everything be sexual with you?"

That earned her a snort and a gesture of a hand down his body. His playful smile grew wider. "Have you seen me?"

Growling, she glared down at her plate and went back to eating. She would eat as quickly as possible, then wander off into the forest to find somewhere with enough rocks that she could cast her spell again. She needed rest.

"I tease you so very much because it is a fun game. One we both enjoy, even if you haven't come to admit it to yourself yet."

"I do not!"

"See?"

She was shaking again, this time in anger. "How can you slaughter three people—rip them to *pieces*—and then sit here laughing, covered in blood, as though nothing transpired?"

"You have not much dealt with warriors, or Unseelie." His lips curled in a lopsided smirk. "Trust me, inviting you to dinner is the most polite of all the options I had running through my head. And—oh, did I miss a spot? I thought I caught it all."

"No. You did not. Not in the slightest. You just"—her stomach lurched—"smeared it about."

"Damn. Want to come over here and scrub me clean?"

There was his constant innuendo and teasing, rising right back to the forefront. She put her forehead in her palm and stared down at her food. "Please, stop."

He laughed, clearly enjoying how put out she was. "Very well. Eat your food, little witch. I will refrain from making more salacious commentary at you until after you have finished."

That meant they ate in silence.

Honestly, she was happy for it.

But the moment she put down her fork, he burst into action. "Come." He snatched her wrist and pulled her from the table, tugging her along behind him as if she were nothing but a toy. All her sputtering and protests were pointless, as he seemed set on ignoring her.

He dragged her through the woods for a hundred yards before they reached a pool. A waterfall poured into it from a cliff, and she was struck by the way the moonlight glinted from the surface. Reeds grew from between mossy, smooth rocks, swaying lightly in the breeze.

Valroy released her wrist and stepped to the edge of the water. She watched as he…undid his trousers.

She looked away quickly just as the fabric slipped from his waist.

"You expect me to bathe fully clothed? Come, now. I thought you were offended by the blood I was wearing. I fear those trousers may have been part of the problem." She heard water splash as he must have waded into the pool. "Will you join me?"

"No."

"There is blood on you, you know. Not all those dots are freckles."

There was? She glanced down at herself and grimaced as she realized he was right. She had not missed out on all the carnage. With a horrified moan, she ran to the edge of the pool and knelt, cupping the cool water and rinsing the substance from her.

He chuckled. "Poor thing. You'll adapt soon enough."

"I shall never grow accustomed to slaughter."

"You will. You've come so far already."

"I have come nowhere. I have learned nothing and achieved nothing."

"I believe *you* believe that."

Water splashed over her in a wave, and she shrieked in surprise, falling back onto her ass. She looked up to see Valroy standing there, laughing in harmless amusement. For once, he wasn't laughing *at* her. Even if he rather was.

And he was also naked.

On full display.

The water only reached his thighs where he was standing.

Her eyes went wide.

And then she squeezed them shut as fast as she could.

Now he was laughing at her. "So bashful! You were a married woman. You have seen a man naked before. I hope so, yes? Otherwise, I think I have discovered the reason Marcus had difficulty breeding you."

"That isn't the problem!"

"Then why so bashful? I thought you were a hedge witch? Don't you believe in the sanctity of nature?"

"I am. I do."

"This is what I was born with."

"I highly doubt it came with such adornments!"

He howled in laughter.

There was the reason she was truly horrified. Not

because of what she had seen—although, Valroy was far, *far* different than Marcus or any other man she had ever been intimate with. His shape looked mostly human, though she did not stare for long. But it was not the strangeness of his body that made her look away.

Nor did she look away because she was not curious. If she were honest, she supposed she was. No, she looked away because just like his ears, it seemed his lower body was pierced to match. Silver had shone in the moonlight.

She had not seen much. She did not know the details. But the idea of learning them more intimately sent a shiver down her spine. "I see the warnings were true." *Those things would rip me apart, wouldn't they?* "What kind of torturer are you, to do that to your lovers?"

"The sweetest kind, I promise you. They are there for pleasure, not pain. They will do anything but hurt you. Come here, let me show you."

"No!"

"You're frightened, I understand. Touch me. Explore me. I can be gentle. There is no reason to be afraid. Tonight, I will not a lay a hand on you until you ask. Tonight, I will be *your* plaything. Come to me, little witch. The prince wishes to kneel to you."

Raising her head, she looked at him. He had shifted backward so that the water barely reached the line of his hips. The muscles that sculpted his abdomen led her gaze downward in a V, hinting at what lay just out of sight.

He spread his wings, creating ripples in the water, a slow movement that did not belie the strength she knew he had. *I can be gentle.*

Horror stabbed through her like an assassin's knife. But it did not cut her in twain. It was not white-hot terror; it was not the sudden snap of fear. It was slow, it was methodical, and it was total. It poisoned her.

It was not horror at the beautiful monster she saw before her. It was not because she did not believe his words that he could be tender.

It was that she did not wish him to be.

All his threats of brutal, primal acts?

With sinking dread, she realized…he was right.

She wanted it.

She wanted *him.*

Being his wife, however brief, would bring me pleasure unlike any I have ever known. I might die from him, but—

Her wish to him snapped back into her mind like a crack of lightning. She had asked him for a house. A house! That was all. *I am such a fool.* She had said her deepest wish was to have a home.

It was a lie.

All of this was predicated on a *lie.*

If only she had spoken true—if only she had known it herself—what could have changed? Anything? If he granted that wish, what could have been different?

She stood from the shore, sopping wet as she was, and began to walk away. "I am sorry, Valroy." Tears were stinging her eyes again, born not from frustration and hopelessness, but from understanding. "I need a moment to think."

"I will be here waiting for you, my future queen. Do not wander far."

She walked into the woods, for how far she did not know. She wasn't exactly paying attention. Leaning against a tree, she bowed her head and let out a long, wavering breath. Hugging her arms around herself, she prayed to the gods for guidance.

"I want him," she whispered to no one, the words simply needing to be free. "I want him, but I cannot give in to him. If I do, thousands and thousands of lives will be lost. I cannot surrender." In him was the answer to her deepest wish. He could grant her what she truly wanted, if perhaps only for a time. "What he offers me, I do not think I am strong enough to resist." She shut her eyes. "Because my deepest wish is to be—" She broke off. She could not say it. "Please…help me."

The sound of a movement nearby made her lift her head. Whatever it was, it was large, having moved through the underbrush to stand before her. She froze in fear, instinctually expecting some manner of monster had come to kill her.

It was the black stag.

It peered at her through inhuman eyes, but she saw the intelligence that burned behind them. She had asked for help —for guidance—and the stag had come. He huffed, steam rising from his nostrils, breath hot in the chill night air. Turning, the stag walked away, and she knew she was meant to follow.

She hesitated, glancing back in the direction of Valroy and the pond. She did not know where the stag would lead her, but it was not to him or what he promised her.

Perhaps he could grant my deepest wish, if just for a moment, but all would pay the price.

There would be no escaping him. There would be no stopping him. And slowly but surely, she was ceasing to care. He was winning her. And she couldn't allow that to happen.

Turning, she followed the stag deeper into the woods.

And somehow, deep inside, she knew it meant the end.

CHAPTER THIRTY-TWO

The woods parted, opening wide to a field of grass and beautiful flowers. Or at least, that was what it looked like at first blush. Abigail stopped at the edge of where the flowers grew and tried to make sense of what she was seeing in the moonlight.

When she did, she took a staggering step back.

Skeletons.

Scattered amongst the flowers and vines, sticking up from the petals of the most vibrant crimson she could imagine, were the remains of…things. Of humans and humanoids, of beasts, and of monsters. Their white, sun-bleached bones stabbed up toward the sky, abandoned where the creatures fell.

But how had they died? Picked clean and left where they were? Did some mighty monster lurk beneath the dirt, waiting to snatch up anyone who came close? Was this the lair of some mighty dragon? Or was she simply looking at another of Valroy's battlefields—a pointless reminder that the fae who was so successfully seducing her was a monster?

The stag walked up beside her, emerging from the forest. She looked up at him, at the deer's towering height. Silently, he strode forward into the field of flowers.

And she learned from whence the skeletons had come.

There was no dragon, waiting to burst up from the Earth. There were no insects, waiting to devour the flesh of anything that came near.

It was the flowers themselves.

She watched in horror as they instantly attacked the stag. He screamed in pain as vines, thick as her wrist and thorned, snapped around his powerful legs and torso. The stag kicked and struggled, bucking and tossing his great horned head in agony. Hopelessly, helplessly, he bleated and cried.

The vines dragged him to the ground, and soon the pained screams of the stag became agonized whimpers. And soon the whimpers became silence. And she watched, in tear-streaked dismay, as the beautiful, delicate, crimson blooms…devoured the stag whole.

It took only a minute, maybe less, before the creature that had helped her, who had guided her here, was nothing more than bone.

They were not sun-bleached.

The flowers simply left nothing behind but bone.

She was shaking; her body felt too warm. Her heart was pounding in her ears in fear.

The stag brought me here to die.

This is my only choice.

Either I die…or Valroy takes the throne.

"He will find another," she whispered. "My death will not matter in the end."

But it would delay him. All those lives who might end in the future would live another day because of her sacrifice. How many years of life lived did that equal? How many moments of joy would be brought to those who were spared for even just a single day?

What was the value of her life, weighed against that?

Nothing.

She was now, and forever would be, *nothing*.

Prey. Food. The means to an end.

This was her fate.

Taking her sword from her sheath, she propped it against a rock beside her. Anfar would want it back. "I hope you tell Astasha how you feel," she murmured to the blade, as if it might carry the message to its owner. It was possible. This was the Otherworld, after all. "And I hope it is requited. Thank you for your kindness."

But it was time for it all to end. The fear, the terror, the running. The Maze.

Valroy.

She stepped toward the flowers. The ground was soft beneath her bare feet. *I never did get those shoes back.* She expected vines to snap around her—to devour her like they did the stag.

But nothing happened.

They parted around her, vines and blossoms forming a circle where they did not touch her. She frowned, her brow furrowed in confusion. Was this the work of the Maze? Refusing to devour her, because it obeyed the will of its Master? Was she even still inside the Maze? She did not honestly know. She couldn't tell, if the veiled sun was not overhead. But the fact remained that the flowers stayed away.

Was even her death going to be denied to her?

Soon, she was in the center of the field, passing skeleton after skeleton. Some looked fresh, like that of the stag. Others looked worn and faded by rain and weather, slowly rendering to dust.

That is what I want. To return to the Earth. That is the only place I have ever belonged.

That is only where I am wanted.

But still, the flowers parted around her, even as they reached for her, as though she were the sun, and they were starving for her light. She reached out a finger toward one, and tendrils of its vines reached back to her, but stopped short of touching.

She could close the distance. She could end it.

Then, she understood.

They are waiting for me. They want me to surrender. Like the Morrigan, like Valroy—they want me to wish to die.

It would be a painful, violent death, like that of the stag. But at least it would be fast. She wept. "I do not want to die," she whispered to them. "I do not want to die, but I do not know what else to do."

"Abigail!"

Looking up at the sound of the voice, she froze. Valroy was standing there at the edge of the flowers, his wings spread wide, face a mask of anger and terror. "Abigail—do not move. Do not *touch* them! How did you get out there?"

"I—I walked in," she stammered, numb.

"Do not touch them. Whatever you do, do not—" He was panicking. She could see it in his expression, in the way his muscles were taut. In the way he stammered. She had never seen him afraid before.

He stepped forward, but he did not make it far. The vines reached for him, moving impossibly fast. He had to rip one from his arm, and he could see the gashes left behind by its thorns. Snarling, he bared his teeth like an animal and hissed at the flowers. "She is *mine!*"

"No, Valroy. I'm not." She wiped her tears away as best she could. "I am sorry, but I am not. I have to die. They are right. They are all right."

"That—this does not have to end here. Please, come to me. Please, little witch." He reached for her. "We must leave here. I will keep you safe."

"No."

Furious, he bared his teeth again. "The Gle'Golun will devour you, Abigail. They feed on mortality. They will drink you dry of everything that you are. Your humanity, your flesh—it will be theirs. They will return you to the Earth after they have consumed you! If you are lucky, you will only know suffering the likes of which you humans could not imagine. *Do not touch them!*" He moved toward her again but had to jump back as the vines once more made an attempt to grab him.

"You will find another queen, Valroy. You will find another to replace me."

Violently, he shook his head. "But you are mine, and they shall not take you from me!" He reached for her again. "Please, Abigail—please—come to me. Forgive me for all I have done. I shall give you whatever you desire—riches, servants, the world shall be yours—*please—*"

She watched him for a moment, and then smiled sadly. "I am sorry, but no."

"We had a deal! We had an exchange. Solve my Maze, and I will give you the home you desire. I will grant your deepest wish. Do you really wish to quit so soon? You are so close to finding the secret. Don't you wish to know what it is? What about your wish?" Another, seemingly instinctual step forward was met with the snap of vines, and he had to jump back, swearing at the field in a language she didn't understand. "I promised to give you a home, and I was cruel. Let me grant it again—this time in truth. I will build you a cottage by a lake, where no monsters will trouble you, and—"

"My wish was a lie." She looked down at the flowers gathered around her, each one straining to reach her. "I lied to you, Unseelie prince, because I was lying to myself. I didn't mean to deceive you. I hope you can forgive me." She could only smile down at the flowers that she knew would soon rip her to shreds. "I understand now what my greatest wish truly is."

"Say it."

She smiled at him and saw no harm in telling him the truth. Looking at the stars and moon overhead, she made a wish in a field of deadly flowers. Her aunt would lecture her for days in the afterlife—if she ever found her. "I wish to be wanted." Shutting her eyes, she let her tears streak down her cheeks. "I wish to be wanted, Valroy, Crowned Prince of the Unseelie."

"Be my queen—let me *keep you*. Stand at my side. I have already granted your wish." She watched as he knelt, his wings drooped low beside him. He reached for her again, pleading with her to cross the flowers and take his hand. "I want you, Abigail Moore."

"I know." She smiled at him. One of the vines grew taller beside her, reaching up almost to her shoulder height. A bud of a flower bloomed a bright, burning red. "I know…and that is why I have to die. Because I want you, too."

She touched the vine.

She heard Valroy's furious, agonized scream.

But it was the least of her concerns.

She watched in fascination as a tendril of the vine, as small as the newest growth in her garden, began to weave its way along her fingers. They did not snap around her, dragging her to the dirt, ripping her flesh from her bones like the stag.

It was slow. It was delicate. Soft.

She could pull her hand away if she wished.

But this was her surrender. This was her sacrifice. When

the tendril reached her wrist, it pressed against her pulse, writhing in time with the beat of her heart. When another gentle touch brushed against her other hand, she looked down to see a slightly thicker vine begin to encircle her palm. It pulled her gently down, urging. Asking. Pleading.

Surrender.

She knelt.

"Abigail!" He sounded so far away. So unimportant.

Her breathing was slow and even. She wasn't afraid. She watched as the vines circled her arms, growing thicker, spreading over her. Their touch was warm, and when their grip on her tightened, she gasped, her eyes slipping half shut.

It felt…

Oh, it felt so wonderful.

When they pulled her down onto the soft grass and writhing tendrils of vines onto her back, she didn't resist. They were around her ankles, slipping up her calves, climbing higher. They wormed beneath her trousers, along her body, and—

She arched her back, shutting her eyes, and let out a small sound that was equal parts surprise and pleasure. They wormed around her waist, circling again and again, lacing between her breasts. She could feel the press of a soft bud against her throat, seeking her heartbeat.

Her mortality.

They would drink her dry.

She was their prey.

She tilted her head back, baring her throat to them, and shut her eyes.

With a whisper, she gave them what they were waiting for. Stretching out her arms, she said the words they wanted to hear. "I surrender."

In an instant, it began. And in that same instant, all hope

of escape was gone. It was too late. Her choice was made. Tendrils, thin and fragile, pressed into her skin.

She expected pain. She expected carnage. To be rent asunder, like the others in the field. She felt a sting, as a thousand tiny barbs embedded into her skin. But the sting did not last. And what came next…

She writhed. It was not agony. It was not pleasure. It was something else—something *more*. They pressed into her skin, and then into her body. She felt the vines under her skin, burrowing deep, wriggling farther and farther into her.

She moaned. They drank from her. Not her blood, not her pulse, but all of it. Flowers pressed to her body, and with each one that came to feed, she felt another stream join the river that rushed from her and into them.

Larger vines joined the smaller ones, pushing deep into her body, splitting organ and muscle. It did not hurt. She felt not an ounce of pain. She welcomed them in. The vines pulsed, surging with her heartbeat, and she watched in awe as the vines nearest her sprouted new buds that quickly grew and bloomed to full, beautiful flowers.

Flowers that then came to her to feed. *Yes. Take what I have. It's so little…but if you want it, it is yours.* And they wanted her. She could feel it in the press of red blooms to red wounds. Stream after stream opened, her life bleeding away.

Life from death.

A tendril wormed into her mouth, and she parted her lips to let it in. She was prey. This was her purpose. When it entered her throat, she tried to think of it as a lover, even as it pushed impossibly deep, writhing, squirming, pulsing, drinking. It joined its ilk, tangling together inside her flesh. It…it felt like bliss.

This was not her body anymore. This was not her corpse. It did not even belong to the Gle'Golun. She felt the roots beneath her, deep and running out in all directions to the forest that surrounded the field. She felt every tree, every blade of grass, every blooming flower. Every bee, every cricket, every bird and bat in the sky.

Vines pushed deeper inside her, and she knew it was time.

Release.

This was their love.

The Gle'Golun were granting her wish.

They wanted her.

And she gave to them.

She gave to them all that she was.

And all that she had been.

VALROY KNELT beside the field of flowers, screaming in his impotent rage and violent fury, for how long he did not know.

Abigail was gone.

The Gle'Golun had taken her.

No. They did not take her. She gave herself to them!

Fisting his hair in his hands, he howled. *She would rather die that awful death than to be with me! She would rather be eaten alive than be my queen. Better she surrender to suffering than to desire.*

Was he truly so vile? Was he really so terrible?

No. No, he couldn't accept that.

Finally, his screams died down. He was too tired to continue cursing a creature who did not care for his rage. The void left behind by his absent anger left him kneeling there, gazing down at his palms, unable to truly comprehend what had just happened.

The flowers had not devoured her of their will. They had waited until she submitted to them. Why? How?

But it did not matter why. Or how.

Abigail was dead.

And someone was to blame.

Someone took her. Someone led her away. Someone brought her to the field of death. He bared his teeth and clenched his fists. Someone would pay dearly for this. He did not know as he even much cared to discover who. It did not matter. Because all would suffer for what he felt.

The worlds would burn.

Because *his* Abigail was dead.

VOICES WHISPERED IN HER MIND. As many as the stars, yet as together as one. The vines pulsed with them and drove deep into the mother Earth, and out into the forests. The trees, twined together in branch and root, sang as one.

And she sang with them.

Life blazed and death cooled. One created and the other consumed. Prey began, and predator ended. Again, and again, and again.

You will become his prey.

A voice, singular above all, rose from the chorus. It pulled her from the many; it forced her from the whole. It made her remember.

Surrender.

She had already given all she had. What more could the world want from her?

Surrender.

It pulled her back. It yanked her from the whole and to the part. Surrender to flesh? But why? She would live only to die again. She turned away from the suffering and the pain, from the strife that life brought her. No, she would not go where the voice commanded her. She would not.

The memory of a touch. Of lips against hers. Of darkness—of the taste of the night sky. Of powerful wings, and wicked laughter. Of him. Of teeth, and claw. Of death. Of the promise of *more*.

Again, and again, and again.

Life blazed, and death cooled.

Surrender.

A vision came to her then, unbidden and unwanted. The sight of the forests ablaze, of slaughtered thousands, lying in the fields where they had been struck down. And there, standing amongst them, covered in their blood, was the prince.

Was this the future, or the past?

She supposed it did not matter.

Surrender.

The balance would be broken. The wheel would cease its turning. The seasons would end. The song would ring out no more. She was one, she was many, and she would die once more, and all the same would follow.

And forever.

Again, and again, and again.

If his wrath were not stopped?

Never, and never, and never.

Death from life, and life from death.

Surrender.

The voice continued to pull her from the song. It continued to rip her from the whole and make her one. It made her remember. She remembered being small, and helpless, and weak. Why? Why her? What could she do in the face of his strength?

Surrender.

It was all she could do.

And so, she did.

And somewhere, a field of crimson flowers wilted and died.

To Be Continued In
Maze of Shadows: Book Two
The Unseelie Crown

ABOUT THE AUTHOR

Kat has always been a storyteller.

With ten years in script-writing for performances on both the stage and for tourism, she has always been writing in one form or another. When she isn't penning down fiction, she works as Creative Director for a company that designs and builds large-scale interactive adventure games. There, she is the lead concept designer, handling everything from game and set design, to audio and lighting, to illustration and script writing.

Also on her list of skills are artistic direction, scenic painting and props, special effects, and electronics. A graduate of Boston University with a BFA in Theatre Design, she has a passion for unique, creative, and unconventional experiences.

Printed in Great Britain
by Amazon